Sweet Dreams, Baby Belle

Kim Carter

Published by Raven South Publishing

Atlanta, Georgia 30324, USA

Copyright by Kim Carter 2016

Cover Design by www.mariondesigns.com

Library of Congress Control Number: 2018933815

ISBN 978-1-947140-01-1 paperback

ISBN 978-1-947140-00-4 e-book

Dedication

To my dear friend, Lisa Mobley Putnam, who was with me when a small broken tombstone inspired not only a mystery novel but a deep love for a child that we would never know. Lisa–I'm so grateful you shared this journey with me. What a ride it's been. I love you.

And to the real Baby Belle who we know very little about. Her mother, Isabella, died in childbirth and although Belle's own life was very short, we are uncertain of her date of death. Mother and child are buried side by side in The Old Biloxi Cemetery.

Acknowledgments

Many thanks to the following:

- Annette Barhanovich with the Biloxi City Hall, who was the first face to meet us when we began our research. Once a stranger, now a friend.
- Jane Shambra who works so diligently with the Biloxi library and genealogy department.
- Laurie Rosetti, with Biloxi Main Street, who has such a love and excitement for Biloxi that it's contagious. Love you.
- Julius Redmond, who made a trip with his divining rod to meet us in Biloxi. May God continue to use you in his work.
- World renowned psychic, Helene Frisch, whose tireless efforts were so helpful.
- Mike McDonnell, the caretaker of the Old Biloxi Cemetery, who has such compassion and respect for his work.

- John Cross, Fulton County (Ga) Medical Examiner's Office, who came through once again to help my novel come together.
- Kelly Keylon of Atlanta Water Gardens whose generosity and kindness continues to make the world a better place.
- Julius, my far better half, who so lovingly tolerates the mind of a writer. I love you.
- Bill Metcalf, Funeral Director at Bradford-O'Keefe Funeral Home, was so helpful in sharing history with us. Many thanks for your continued efforts.
- Carol Jones, for without her, I simply wouldn't still be writing. I love you dearly.
- Eve Gray Callaway, an old friend who helped to get the rhesus monkeys from Mumbai to Charleston. Thanks for your ideas.
- Pam Carter Youngblood, last but certainly not least, thanks for being my unofficial editor and critic, even though it's often just two pages at a time.

Kim Carter's Other Works

Murder Among The Tombstones
When Dawn Never Comes
No Second Chances
Deadly Odds
And The Forecast Called For Rain

Prologue

The cool night air in Ocean Springs, Mississippi bit at Lizzie Chatsworth's ears as she made her way through the headstones of the old cemetery. What would have seemed an eerie place for some had become a place of comfort for her. The heavy fog seemed to illuminate the moss that draped down from the large, overbearing oaks, helping her to stay ahead of him as he hunted her.

Run toward the bayou. You can do it, Lizzie.

Why? Why are you telling me to run toward the water, a dead end? Surely, he'll catch up with me there and—

It's the only way. Follow my voice. He's getting closer!

Lizzie grabbed her stomach, bending over, in an attempt to catch her breath. All along, she had known this day would come; it had only been a matter of time. A great deal was at stake for him, and she was a threat—or at least that was how he would see it.

"Lizzie! You can't run forever. I'll find you."

She dared not answer, for that would simply lead him closer. The wet grass silenced her footfalls as she made her way toward the marsh.

"You can't just walk away! I gave you everything. Why wasn't it enough?"

She wanted to scream at him, to explain that there was more to life than money, but she knew he'd never understand. The baby was unhappy with her, violently kicking the inside of her belly. "Hang in there, little one. We're gonna be okay," she whispered.

The bayou, Lizzie. Concentrate. You're almost there.

But what am I supposed to do when I get there? He'll catch me, and it'll all be over.

Just follow my voice. Don't give up now.

Weaving in and out of the tombstones she had come to know so well, Lizzie could see the water coming into view. She ran down the old dock, hoping to reach the boathouse but the baby had other plans for her.

"Oh, God!" she screamed as a painful contraction radiated through her body. "Help!" she shouted. "Someone help!"

"It is too late for that," he said calmly, his figure becoming visible. "You are the last of my unfinished business, the final loose end to tie up before I can begin my new life."

"Who is she? Who's in this with you?" she demanded.

"You don't need to know that, Lizzie. You have learned far too much already. It's over now."

Lie down, Lizzie. Just lie on the dock.

"Why?" she wanted to ask but instead allowed her legs to bend into a squat. She then fell and lay back, shut her eyes tight, and wrapped her arms around her stomach and unborn child. *I never thought it would end like this,* she thought as the sound of the gunshot reverberated through her ears.

Chapter 1

Three months earlier...

The brutally hot summer had finally given way to autumn, and the leaves had begun to turn those striking hues of yellow and deep orange that everyone in the South always looked forward to after the blistering heat. Atlantans would soon be making their way to the apple houses in north Georgia to purchase and sample their wares. Bushels and pecks of red and golden delicious, gala, and granny smiths would be ready to transform into pies, cobblers, fritters, and cider.

Lizzie Chatsworth looked out the window of her opulent Buckhead estate and longed to go apple-picking, then dirty her spotless, stainless-steel kitchen with sifted flour and granulated sugar. That, however, would be inappropriate for a prominent surgeon's wife; it might give the impression she had not come from wealth and privilege, a reputation her husband was so eager to project. She allowed herself a few moments to fondly recall the many summers when she, her father, and her older sister had loaded up the old, rusty Chevy pickup and made their trips to Ellijay. Her daddy had been so patient with them, giving them both all the time they wanted to peruse the different types of apples, from tart for baking to sweet for eating. Every apple house carried the same varieties, but each had their own special baked goods or specialty ciders. The girls sampled them all until their little bellies was as full as they could get them. Her grandmother would be anxiously waiting on the front porch when they got home, wearing her perfectly pressed apron as she marveled at their selections. It was one of Lizzie's fondest memories of childhood. Years earlier, she'd suggested to her husband that they go one autumn afternoon, but he had quickly put his foot down: "There will be none of that...and cooking is to be done by the staff we pay." Lizzie had never mentioned it again.

At the ringing of the doorbell, she slipped on her espadrilles and linen jacket, then ran peach-colored lipstick over her full lips.

A light knock on her bedroom door was followed by Flossie's sweet, Southern drawl. "Miss Chatsworth, honey, it's the party planner. He's waiting in the dining room."

"Thanks, Flossie," Lizzie answered as she opened the door. "I'm on my way down now."

"Coffee or tea, dear?" Flossie asked.

"Just bring us some tea please."

"I'll do that. I made some cucumber sandwiches too. You skipped breakfast again, and you're lookin' awfully thin."

Lizzie made her way down the winding stairway and to the dining room. She tried to hide her impatience as the caterer pushed yet another list of suggested hors d'oeuvres across to her.

"Really, Lizzie," Antoine said, sighing heavily. "You could show *some* interest. I've spent a great deal of time on this menu, and Dr. Chatsworth is investing a great deal of money in this get-together."

"Get-together?" Lizzie struggled to keep her composure. "This is hardly that."

"Gathering, event, soiree…whatever you choose to call it."

"I choose to call it a ridiculous waste of money," she said smugly as she leaned back in the mahogany dining chair.

"Oh, for heaven's sake," Antoine said. "Just play the game, Lizzie. How many times have we been through this?"

"Hmm. I don't know," she snapped but instantly regretted her demeanor and tone. "Look, I'm sorry, Antoine. I'm just not… I don't feel very well. Maybe it's just the time of year. I always get nostalgic. I'm sure the menu is acceptable. You have always done a fine job and should know by now that I know very little about entertaining."

It was Antoine's turn to lean back in his chair. He studied Lizzie's face. She was an amazingly beautiful woman, and he was relieved that the five years of marriage to an arrogant, condescending husband had not done more damage than it had. "Why do you do it?" he asked, as kindly as he could. "Why have you stayed?"

Tears slowly filled her eyes as she looked away from him. It didn't surprise Lizzie at all that he had asked; she was sure Antoine wasn't the only one who wondered, for even she had questioned it many times. "I wish I knew," she stammered. Sitting up straight and leaning forward, Lizzie reached for the latest menu her friend and confidant had compiled. As always, it contained a wide assortment of delicacies that would surely impress any of her husband's colleagues. "You've really outdone yourself, Antoine," she smiled. "This will be another successful fundraiser for Grant's research."

"I worry about you, Lizzie. You've gotten so thin. Are you ill?"

"No, I'm fine. Nothing seems appetizing to me lately." She wanted to ask Antoine to stay, but Lizzie knew he was far too busy to spend time with her. "You know, you're the only friend I have here," she said, her eyes lighting up.

He chuckled and shook his head. "Girl, you really need to get out more if this flamboyant homosexual is the closest friend you have."

That drew a genuine laugh from her, something she rarely did anymore. "I've always been able to talk to you, Antoine. I'm thankful Grant hasn't noticed, or you would have been replaced."

"Go visit your sister. Maybe some time away would make you feel better. She's in Biloxi, isn't she?"

"Yes, she's still there. I miss her terribly but now is not a good time. Grant is busy with this fundraising campaign, and he needs me."

"You mean he needs a beautiful hostess."

"That isn't very kind. His work is important to him."

"His *money* is important to him. Will it ever be enough?"

"He's getting close to a breakthrough on his congestive heart failure research. This could make a big difference, Antoine. I'll visit Maggie soon. I'd love to see the twins. I bet they are growing by leaps and bounds by now."

"Go to the mall, take a class, go out to lunch. For God's sake, get out of this oversized museum and get some fresh air!" he said, flailing his arms around like a hysterical woman. "The world is passing you by, Lizzie Chatsworth."

"Grant doesn't like me to go out too much. He…worries."

"Give me a break, child. He doesn't worry. He just doesn't want another man to set eyes on you. This isn't the eighties. You

3

have a cell phone and can call if anything goes awry. Trust me, he'll live."

"Perhaps you're right," Lizzie said after some thought. "Maybe I'll take in a movie."

"Better yet, go pick some of those apples you're always talkin' about. Isn't it that time of year? It'd do you some good, all that fresh air and nature, like when you were little."

"You know, maybe I'll do that. It could be just what the doctor ordered."

Chapter 2

Dr. Grant Chatsworth was a commanding presence. It was hard to deny his good looks, but his pompous air certainly detracted from his appearance. He was tall and well-built, and he always made sure his tailored suits captured the countless hours he spent in his personal gym. He wasn't very well liked by his colleagues or his staff, but they couldn't deny him the respect he deserved in the medical field. As one of the region's most renowned cardiac surgeons, he had two upscale offices in Atlanta, operated out of two different hospitals, and still made time to oversee a Research Facility that was working diligently on a new medicine that might slow the progression of heart disease.

It was yet another busy day, not at all different from his normal routine. Nurse Clara Samples was behind the desk sorting through the daily patient files when Dr. Chatsworth came through the door.

"Good morning, Clara," he said blandly. "I assume you have the day planned for me."

"Yes, Sir," she answered. "Your office is open, and your coffee is on the desk. Your first patient is in fifteen minutes. The first three files are on the desk for your review."

He nodded his head in acknowledgment; that was the only response she ever got from him.

Clara was in her mid sixties and could have retired three years ago, but she liked her job. Her husband had died ten years prior, and her only child lived in Missouri and made little effort to keep a relationship going. Clara needed something to get up for, and she adored her patients and was quite fond of the other nurses. Besides, no one else could manage the office or Dr. Chatsworth as well as she could. He was a very demanding, thankless boss, but if nothing else, Clara appreciated his consistent demeanor.

After taking one last sip of her morning coffee, she opened the door to the waiting room and called Mr. Godfrey back. He was a kind gentleman in his early eighties, and she waited patiently as his son helped him up and stabilized him with his walker. His health was declining rapidly, and Clara couldn't help but think that Dr.

Chatsworth's new medication could benefit him. *If only the wheels moved more quickly at the FDA...*

"Good morning, Mr. Godfrey," Clara said patiently. "How are we feeling today?"

"About the same," he answered, his breathing labored. "This ol' body's about had it, Clara. I'm getting tired."

"None of that now," she teased. "You look pretty spry to me. I'll just take your vitals, Nurse Baldwin will draw blood for your Coumadin levels, and then Dr. Chatsworth will be back to see you."

He feigned a weak smile and held out his right arm for her to attach the blood pressure cuff. Clara went through the motions, just as she would several more times throughout the day, and exited quickly; there wasn't time for lengthy conversations with a waiting room full of patients.

She passed Nurse Baldwin, who had her eyes glued to a computer screen, and nodded toward Mr. Godfrey's door. "He's ready when you are," she said, then made her way toward the waiting room for her next patient.

On the way, Clara was sidetracked by Dr. Chatsworth's angry, muffled voice coming from his office. She slowed to shut his cracked door but not before hearing him say, "We are not nearly as far along as we should be. Make it happen...or I'll find someone who will!"

Chapter 3

Lizzie took one final glance at the party menu and scrawled her initials across the contract. "It will be nice, Antoine," she said, smiling. "You always ensure that everything is just exquisite."

He reached across the table and patted her pale hand. "It will be quite eloquent, and you, my dear, shall be the belle of the ball."

"I'm not so sure about that," Lizzie said, then smiled at him. Antoine was one of the most handsome men she'd ever met, but unlike her husband, his personality was equally attractive. His green eyes were in contrast to his smooth, caramel skin and finely chiseled features, and perfectly straight, pearl-white teeth completed his smile.

She was sure Grant would never have allowed the two of them to work together had Antoine not been so open about his homosexuality. Their friendship had blossomed almost instantly, and Lizzie would always be grateful for that. When she married Dr. Grant Chatsworth, she was quick to realize that she was clearly a fish out of water, but Antoine had clandestinely led her by the hand and taught her all that someone of newfound wealth should know. That had always been their little secret and would remain so. The only person who had any suspicions that Lizzie didn't come from money was dear, sweet Flossie, who ran the household. She often gave Lizzie a knowing and encouraging glance or reached for her hand and squeezed it lightly when she sensed Lizzie was unsure of herself.

"Do you have a dress to die for, or do I need to call Natalie over at Phipps to find you one?" Antoine asked.

"Oh I have several I haven't even worn yet. I'll find something in that vast closet of mine."

"Dear Lizzie," he sighed, grabbing his chest and simulating a heart attack. "You never take these things seriously."

"You can stop the theatrics. Everything will be fine. I made hair and nail appointments for early that afternoon and will be ready to accept guests, just as Grant will expect me to."

Antoine gathered up his papers and slid them neatly into an expensive leather portfolio. "I'm off to handle someone else's party of the century. If only everyone was as amenable as you. Now, do as I said. Go pick you some apples or even eat some of those godforsaken fritters, whatever the hell they are."

Lizzie laughed and stood to hug him before he made his way to the door. "I'll do that. Have a nice day, and I'll see you in a couple of weeks."

She closed the large double-doors behind him and made her way to the kitchen where she found Flossie busy with cucumbers.

"That was quick, dear," Flossie said. "I haven't even brought out the sandwiches."

"That's okay, Flossie. You know Antoine always has everything planned to perfection. There was nothing to hash out." She reached over and picked up a small finger sandwich and bit into it. "Mmm. Delicious."

"I love to see you eat, dear. You've gotten so thin."

"You're the second person to tell me that today, Flossie."

"Well, maybe that's because it's true."

"You know what I'd love to eat?" Lizzie said, her eyes sparkling at the mere thought of it.

"What is that?"

"Some of your fried chicken, with mashed potatoes and gravy."

The suggestion brought a wide grin to Flossie's old, kind face. "Oh, Lizzie, you know I only fix fried chicken when Dr. Chatsworth is away on business. He doesn't believe in fried food."

"Grant is working late tonight. He has a meeting at the Research Facility and told me to have dinner without him. You said it makes you happy to see me eat, so…"

"That's hitting below the belt," Flossie said with a laugh. "Okay, but I'll stick to frying up boneless, skinless breasts. Now, shoo, and let me get my work done. Why don't you go get some fresh air? There's a festival down at Piedmont Park. You could take one of those nice ladies from the bridge club."

"Flossie, none of those women are real friends. They simply tolerate me because Grant is a surgeon."

"They're just jealous of you, dear. Now do as I say and get out of here. You can't spend the rest of your life moping around this big ol' house."

"You sound like Antoine. I'll grab a book and sit in the sunroom, but tomorrow, I'm heading to North Georgia to pick apples. My family and I used to do that every fall."

Flossie's face wore an expression of instant shock, and she placed her hand over her bosom as if she was suddenly suffering from heart palpitations. "You can't do that, child. What are you thinking?"

"What do you mean? Why can't I? It's an hour and a half away, and the scenery would do me good. It'd be nice to see the leaves changing and breathing some unpolluted air would do me well."

"A young woman should not make such a trip alone. I don't think Dr. Chatsworth would allow it. Matter fact, I know he won't."

"*Allow* it? You act as though I'm trying to sneak off and take a vacation without him or something. It's a short day trip, and I'll bring back lots of apples for us to bake with."

Again, Flossie reached for her chest. "Dr. Chatsworth does not want you cooking. He has made that clear to both of us."

For the first time since she'd met her, Lizzie was sure she could detect fear on Flossie's face. "It'll only be a pie or two, no big deal really. I'm sure he meant he doesn't want me to prepare meals for guests. I don't see anything wrong with doing a little baking for myself. After all, this is *my* home too."

Flossie waved a dishrag in the direction of the door. "Enough of all this foolishness. Go on and find a good book, and I'll fry up this chicken." She turned away and opened the refrigerator, an indication that the conversation was over.

Lizzie made her way to the library, absentmindedly plucking a book from the shelf, then headed to the sunroom. It was a beautiful day, and the sun shone brightly into the pretty, glass-enclosed space. It was one of her favorite rooms in the house, perhaps the one where she spent most of her time. The walls were a cheerful sunflower yellow; the trim was clean white. She chose a plush chaise and stretched out her long legs. Unaware of what book she'd taken from the shelf, she placed it on the side table and watched a group of squirrels as they nibbled from one of the bird feeders. She often saw the gardener shooing them away, but she enjoyed watching them steal their share of birdseed.

As she sat, her mind drifted back to the day when she'd met Grant. At the time, Lizzie was waiting tables at a popular restaurant in town, and he had brought in a colleague for dinner. He was so handsome that night that it almost took her breath away. She remembered fumbling through the night's specials, but Grant just seemed so confident and sophisticated. He left a generous tip, followed by a large bouquet of roses the next day. It had been a whirlwind romance of expensive dinners, spontaneous shopping sprees, lavish vacations, and then a four-carat engagement ring. Before she knew it, she was closing the door of her small studio apartment for the last time and moving into a mansion in the heart of the city. Lizzie couldn't deny how wonderful it had been at first. There weren't any financial worries, she had a household staff at her disposal, and she was in love. But less than six months after the nuptials, reality set in with a vengeance, putting a harsh end to the fairy tale. Her husband was no longer just Grant; he was Dr. Grant Chatsworth, and what had seemed sophisticated was now arrogant and patronizing. He would not tolerate any talk of her childhood memories on the farm, with the goats and chickens, nor did he wish to hear about memories of baking with her sweet, now deceased grandmother. He was mortified at the thought of anyone finding out that she had not come from wealth and status. He encouraged her to shop and buy things that would suggest that she came from old money, and he demanded that she visit the internet and read books to learn all she could about etiquette. Her sister was forbidden from visiting, and Lizzie was not to make the two-hour drive to visit the gravesite of her father or grandmother. The positive side of it all was that Lizzie rarely saw him. He left first thing in the morning to perform his surgeries, then went straight to his offices to see his patients, then ended the day at the Research Facility. A year after the marriage, he had insisted on separate bedrooms so his precious-too-little sleep would not be interrupted; while most wives would have scoffed, it came as instant relief for Lizzie. Sexual encounters were limited to Saturday nights and vacations as on schedule as everything else in the busy doctor's life.

Lizzie was surprised to feel a lone tear escape her eye and roll down her cheek. She brushed it away quickly as if to deny that it had ever existed. Emotions were rare for her anymore. At first, she

10

had cried often, longing for her small apartment and the old life she'd left behind. Somewhere along the line, though, she'd resigned to it all, accepted her fate. Since then, she'd simply been going through the motions of living, pretending to be a happy queen in a castle she wanted to leave.

"Wake up, Lizzie," Flossie said, waving a newspaper back and forth in front of her face. "You've been asleep for three hours. Musta needed the rest. Anyway, that meal you requested is ready for you in the dining room."

Lizzie opened her eyes and remained in a daze; she didn't even recall drifting off. "Oh. Hi, Flossie." She sniffed as something wonderful wafted into her weary nostrils. "Mmm. That smells delicious, but let's eat in the kitchen."

"Why do you always have to rock the boat?" Flossie asked, looking tired and exasperated. "You know the rules, Lizzie. Dr. Chatsworth demands that you eat all meals in the dining room. That's the rule."

Lizzie looked at Flossie's wrinkled face and felt as sad for her as she did for herself. Grant ruled all of them with an iron fist, and the full impact of that suddenly hit her. "The *rule*? I'm an adult, for crying out loud. I can eat my fried chicken on the toilet if I want to."

Flossie shook her head in defeat and walked back into the kitchen where she placed Lizzie's meal on the table, in front of a chair that faced a window that overlooked the immaculately landscaped back yard. "Suit yourself," she said as she busied herself with cleaning the skillet.

The meal smelled wonderful but had lost its appeal due to Lizzie's stubbornness. She was almost ashamed of herself but then thought better of it. She regretted taking her frustrations out on Flossie, who'd never done anything but help her.

She was on her third bite of gravy-drenched potatoes when she saw Grant enter the kitchen. His face immediately turned crimson, and he turned his anger on Flossie, who simply shrugged her shoulders as if to say, *"I can't do anything with her!"*

"What the hell is going on here, Elizabeth?" he said, seething through his perfectly aligned teeth. "I have made it painfully clear that you are to have your meals at the dining room table like a

11

civilized person. And fried chicken and gravy? Are you deliberately trying to clog your arteries and put on unnecessary pounds?"

Lizzie felt her stomach begin to knot up, just as it always did when her husband was disgruntled. This time, though, she found the strength to fight it off. "Don't worry, Grant dear. No one is here to see your wife eating at her own kitchen table. And what worries you more, Doctor? The clogged arteries or the extra pounds? Are you afraid you'll have to buy larger sizes of all those gowns I never even have occasion to wear?"

He gasped. "You will *not* talk to me like that! Quit acting like a spoiled, rebellious teenager!"

"As a matter of fact, I can eat gravy-covered shit if I want to. I am a grown woman, Grant."

Lizzie was not sure what she heard first: Flossie's shocked gasp or Grant's palm slapping her face. Her fingers immediately went to her cheek as she felt the heat of the sting.

"Get up and go upstairs," he demanded. "I will see you in the bedroom."

Lizzie thought of getting up, but she knew she couldn't give in now. Tears stung her eyes as she picked up a biscuit and slathered it with gravy. She could see Flossie's eyes glistening from the tears springing up in them, but she wasn't going to let Grant win, as he usually did. She was sick of him getting his way in everything, just because he was the one with the money. She had just moved the biscuit to her mouth when he slapped it from her hand.

He grabbed her roughly by the forearm, dragged her across the kitchen, and pushed her up the stairs. "Get to the bedroom, you obnoxious bitch. I will not tolerate this."

She made her way up the stairs and into the room where he pushed her down on the bed.

"I will not be made a fool of. Do you understand me?"

"I was just having a meal in the kitchen, Grant. You are overreacting," she said, unable to control her sobbing.

"You were just white trash when I married you. I pulled you out of nothing, made you something. Don't make me regret it."

Lizzie sat up on the bed and looked him in the eye. "You arrogant son-of-a-bitch. Do you really think I care about any of this? I was perfectly happy with my small apartment. Do you think *this* impresses me?"

"You ungrateful little whore! I have to get back to work, but this isn't over. I'm taking your keys, and you are not to leave the premises. Trust me. You don't want to test me on this one, honey."

"I'll decide what to test you on, Grant. You are just a man, nothing more." The last thing Lizzie saw was Grant drawing back his fist, and then her world turned black.

Chapter 4

For the second time that day, Flossie stood vigil over Lizzie, fanning a magazine back and forth in front of her face. "Wake up, dear," she whispered. "It's gonna be all right." She left her only long enough to go into the master bath and wet a washcloth with cool water, then returned quickly and rubbed it across her forehead, then up and down her arms. It seemed to work because Lizzie struggled to open her eyes.

"What's going on, Flossie? Did I pass out?"

"Something like that, child. Everything's going to be all right. I'll bring you some tea. Don't get out of bed now, ya hear?"

Lizzie sat up quickly. "I remember now. It was Grant. He hit me." She reached for her face and felt her right eye; it was almost swollen shut, with sharp pain running through it.

"Stay in bed. You need to rest."

"No! I want to see it," Lizzie said defiantly as she jumped up and walked on unstable legs, making her way to her vanity. Lizzie gasped when she saw her face. It was swollen immensely and had already begun to turn a deep blue.

Flossie helped to steady her and lowered her down onto the wrought iron chair in front of the mirror. "It's not as bad as it seems, I'm sure of it," she assured her.

"Oh, my God," Lizzie said, as more tears fell. "I can't believe it's come to this. I need to go to the emergency room, Flossie. This might have damaged my eyesight."

"No," Flossie quickly responded. "You will stay here and rest. I will take good care of you. This doesn't need to get out, and nobody needs to hear about it. Matter fact, we must never speak of it again. Do you need me to help you get into a gown before I bring up something for pain, along with your tea?"

"I don't need tea, Flossie. I want to go to the hospital. If you don't help me, I'll call an ambulance."

"You will do no such thing. Dr. Chatsworth gave strict orders to me and all the staff. You are to remain in bed. The phone has been removed so you can get some proper, uninterrupted rest. Now quit acting like a child and let me help you settle down."

Lizzie opened her mouth to speak but thought better of it. Things had progressed much further than she had realized. She was a prisoner in her own home. Grant would never allow her to see a doctor with an injury resulting from spousal abuse. She prayed silently that she wasn't hurt as badly as it appeared. "Could you bring me the mint green gown from the closet?" she asked softly. "I can put it on myself, and then I'll nap for a while. Thank you, Flossie."

The words seemed to relieve her caretaker, and as she slipped out of her clothes and into the silk gown, Flossie left her alone. Lizzie lay beneath the sheets and duvet for several minutes until she was sure she was alone. In spite of the piercing pain and slight confusion, she made her way to the bathroom and shut the door behind her. In only the few minutes since her first glance at her injury, her eye had worsened. She felt the eye socket and surrounding facial bones as much as she could, in spite of the discomfort, and she was relieved to find that she could feel no fractures. She wasn't sure if there had been any damage to her eyesight because she could no longer open her eye at all; she could only hope for the best. Knowing that Flossie would be up soon with a pain pill and a hot cup of tea, she shuffled back to bed. *I'll play the game, for now,* she decided, biding her time. Her injury was a hindrance, but she would be better soon, and by the time she healed, she would have an infallible plan in place.

Chapter 5

Dr. Grant Chatsworth strode into the dimly lit bar and made his way to his usual booth near the back corner. The top two scientists at the Research Facility, Jean-Luc Phillips and Zahir Chavan, were already seated and nursing their fine aged scotch.

"You both look like hell," Grant barked, noticing that they were in dire need of rest and some clean clothes. "What's this problem I'm hearing about?"

"We need more men," Zahir answered. "We're exhausted. We do not have enough help."

"What the hell are you talking about, Zahir? I just sent you two lab technicians and a geneticist with impeccable credentials."

"They cannot be trusted, Sir. I want someone from my own country. This is very… How shall I say? Sensitive."

"And you think I can just fly a doctor here from New Delhi with no questions asked? Make the best of what you have. Time is of the essence."

"We understand that, Doctor," Jean-Luc interjected, "but there's clearly a trust issue here. They ask too many questions, and it's making me uncomfortable. I can't work like that."

"Uncomfortable? Well, by God, we wouldn't want you to feel *uncomfortable*, would we?" Grant sneered. "What progress has been made in securing the monkeys for the research trials?"

"That's one of the problems," Zahir spoke again. "There are many questions being asked about the use of nonhuman primates. They make up less than one percent of mammals used in research such as this. I expected questions, but—"

"But nothing, Zahir. You expected questions, and now you have them. Don't worry about it. We need the primates to bring more attention to our research. More attention equates to more funding by these wealthy, greedy investors. They aren't impressed or motivated by rats and mice."

"But one can't dismiss the economic wisdom in utilizing rats," Zahir continued. "The housing and maintenance costs are substantially lower, and it is easier to acquire rodents."

Grant reached across the table to take his scotch from the waitress. He nodded a greeting to her, then took a long slug before continuing, "You're concerned about expenditures when we're looking at investments of close to a billion dollars? You've got to be shitting me!"

"Rats and mice make up close to 95 percent of mammals utilized in biomedical research, and they don't throw up red flags. On the other hand, I am unsure if we have the adequate facilities to house nonhuman primates. It is a security risk, not to mention the additional funding."

Grant sipped the remainder of his drink slowly, making the two doctors wait uncomfortably for his response. "Make it happen," he demanded. "As I said, our filthy rich investors are not impressed with mice or hamsters. On the other hand, we don't want the publicity of monkeys escaping either. Make sure the staff prepares adequate quarters and enclosures for them and be prepared for their arrival within the next month."

"But, Sir—" Jean-Luc began but was immediately cut off by Dr. Grant Chatsworth.

"But nothing. I'm sure I don't need to remind you that you are both paid very well for your efforts. There will be money for us to burn when this is over. I recognize that you're tired, but you can rest with your frozen drinks on the beaches of Tahiti when the final payday arrives. For now, keep an eye on the new employees. If they become too intrusive, they will be dealt with."

Chapter 6

Just as suspected, Flossie was back in just a few minutes, carrying a cup of hot tea, a pain pill, an ice pack, and a small glass of water. "Sit up, Lizzie," she said firmly. "This pill will help with the pain and the ice with the swelling."

Lizzie accepted the cold water and took the medication, but the ice pack was simply too painful to tolerate. "I can't do it," she said, wincing when Flossie gently placed it against her injury. "It hurts too much."

"You are behaving like a spoiled brat," Flossie said flatly. "There are less than two weeks left before that fundraiser. You know how much it means to your husband. We have to get this swelling down. A black eye is not a suitable accessory to wear to such a gathering."

"Maybe Grant should have thought of that before he hit me."

Flossie sat down on the bed and leaned in close to Lizzie's face. "I'm only going to say this once. Make no mistake where my loyalties lie. I have made every effort to help you, but Dr. Chatsworth is my boss, the man who signs my checks. If you have any brains in that pretty little head of yours, you'll do as he says."

Lizzie heard herself gasp and felt her hand go up to her mouth. It was a side of Flossie she had never seen before, and it frightened her. She had always felt that Flossie was an ally, but now it was painfully clear she was alone.

"Now," Flossie said as she slid off the bed and stood, "if the ice hurts too badly I will soak a dishrag in some witch hazel, and you can lay that across your eye. My mama always used it to reduce swelling. Tomorrow, we'll put some cayenne pepper and Vaseline on it. Should be back to normal in no time." With that, she was gone, leaving Lizzie to contemplate the reality of her situation.

Lizzie let her mind drift to the employees on the estate. There was Santiago, the gardener, and Lonnie, who came by twice a week to fix anything in need of repair and to replace any blown light bulbs. There was also the young pool boy she had only seen from a distance, along with the housekeeping staff, all of whom were clearly under Flossie's close supervision. Of them all, only Santiago seemed like he might aid her if the need arose.

The gardener was in his early forties and had worked for them for the past four years. He was a quiet man who kept to himself, took his work very seriously, and didn't mingle with any of the other staff. Lizzie had spoken to him on a few occasions, but his English was about as limited as her Spanish, so their conversations had never been lengthy. However, his eyes reflected kindness, and for some reason, she believed he could somehow relate to her situation.

Flossie came back in with the rag and laid it gently across her face. Lizzie was almost certain she detected some empathy on the woman's face, but it was gone as quickly as it had come, and she didn't put much stock in it. She would never forget Flossie's words: "Make no mistake where my loyalties lie."

She drifted into a fitful sleep and didn't awaken until she heard Grant's footsteps stomping down the hall. She glanced over at her alarm clock and noticed it was after 2:00 in the morning. *I wonder what kind of research he was conducting at this hour,* Lizzie thought sarcastically. When he cracked the bedroom door and peeked in, she feigned the labored breaths of a deep sleep. Her heart nearly pounded out of her chest when she heard him flip on the bathroom light and make his way over to her. He stood over her for what seemed like hours in an apparent attempt to assess her injuries. When he had seen enough to satisfy himself, he turned off the light and closed the bedroom door behind him.

Lizzie heaved an audible sigh of relief and rolled over on her side. *I've got to come up with a plan,* she thought. *How am I going to get out of this? He'll never divorce me, and if I do get away somehow, where would I go?*

She spent the next several hours running various scenarios through her head, but none of them seemed feasible. She didn't have any money of her own, no prospects for a job of any kind, and besides waiting tables, she didn't have any job skills. She knew Maggie would welcome her with open arms, but Lizzie didn't want to drag her into the mess; she knew Grant would surely hunt her down and make life miserable for her and anyone involved. In the end, Lizzie decided she would simply have to ride things out for a

19

while and wait for the perfect opportunity to present itself. She knew it might not come anytime soon, but undoubtedly, the opportunity would come knocking. *And when it does, I'll gladly open that door.*

Chapter 7

It had been an exceptionally long day in Dr. Chatsworth's two offices, and Clara was exhausted. Days like that made her wonder why she hadn't already retired. The nurses had all gone for the day, and she was cleaning out the refrigerator in the staff breakroom. "Good heavens." She sighed. "What do these people's homes look like? There's food in here from a month ago." She tossed out the moldy items and the wrinkled pieces of fruit before wiping down the inside of the fridge with a soapy rag. She pushed the chairs back under the table and stacked the magazines, then pulled on her old gray cardigan and grabbed her purse. All she could think about was a warm bath and a bowl of hot soup.

She was sure everyone had left for the day, so she was a bit shocked to find Dr. Chatsworth's office door ajar and the light on. *That man needs to spend more time with that pretty, young wife of his,* she thought as she continued down the hallway, grateful that her own husband had always valued their time together more than he had valued money. She decided to poke her head in and wave good-bye, but as she neared his office, something in the tone of his voice caused her to linger in the hall. It was so unlike her to invade someone's privacy, and she had never felt the need or desire to eavesdrop before. Dr. Chatsworth was certainly not a jovial or open person, but lately, he'd been even more guarded and distracted, and that was beginning to concern her.

"If they are getting too intrusive, they can be dealt with," Grant Chatsworth spat into the phone. "I told you that before. Why are you allowing them to get so close to our research?" A lengthy pause followed while he listened to the reply from the other end. "We're in this together, remember? If one of us goes down, we all do!"

Clara let out a slight gasp before quickly placing her hand over her mouth. *He's got to be talking about the research for the new medication,* she thought. *Oh, my God! Surely, he isn't doing anything illegal.* Grateful for her crepe-soled shoes, she backed up quietly, until she reached the breakroom. As her mind raced, she stood silently, considering what she should do. Dr. Chatsworth was clearly not aware that she was still in the office. The first thought that ran through her head was to try to overhear more of the conversation, but Clara knew it wasn't a good idea. Unsure of how much longer he would remain on the phone, she loudly pushed some chairs around and noisily shut the door to the lounge, making her presence known.

As she made her way back down the hallway, she was met by the doctor.

"Oh, my goodness," she said, gulping. "Dr. Chatsworth? I had no idea you were still in the office. I hope I didn't bother you with all this racket. These nurses must live like pigs. I've spent the past thirty minutes cleaning out the staff refrigerator."

He wasn't pleased to see her, but nothing in his behavior suggested suspicion. "You really should leave with the other ladies, Clara. It isn't safe to be here alone."

"Oh I'm fine," she continued. "I'm usually the last to leave. I try to wrap up everything so we'll be prepared for the next day."

"I commend you for that, but it isn't necessary. Let me walk you to your car."

The two took the elevator and exited the building, neither of them saying a word on the way.

"I'm right over there," she said, pointing to her ten-year-old Buick. "Have a good night, Doctor."

"You do the same, Clara. See you in the morning."

Clara slid onto the seat and quickly cranked the vehicle. She would have preferred a couple of minutes to pull herself together, but he seemed to watch her every move as he made his way to his own car. Her hands trembled slightly as she adjusted her rearview mirror and backed out of the parking space. *What is he up to?* She wondered. She hadn't ever been particularly fond of him on a personal level, but she'd also never had any reason to doubt his character. Still, something about the phone conversation and the way he'd escorted her out of the building just didn't feel right. The tone of his voice suggested that something was not on the level; even worse, it suggested something illegal. "I do have the key to his office," she mused. *Maybe I'll go in a little early and snoop around. Who knows? I just might find out what the good doctor is up to.*

Chapter 8

By the time the party rolled around, Flossie had tried every home remedy and old wives' tale on Lizzie. As a result of her homeopathic endeavors, the swelling and bruising were gone. It had been a distressing two weeks for Lizzie, and she'd spent most of it confined to her bedroom. Her meals were delivered there, along with her pain medication, and she was not allowed to do anything more strenuous than reading or watching television. Her cell phone and the house line were both kept out of her reach, which left her with little more to do than plot how she would escape and begin her life anew.

Lizzie was more determined than ever before to get away from Grant. She had spent the past week and a half watching from her bedroom and bathroom windows; the vantage points offered various views of the estate and the comings and goings of the staff. Although she was penniless, she had no intention of leaving with any of Grant's material wealth.

"Good morning, Elizabeth," Grant said as he made his way into the bedroom. He had visited her for the past three mornings, a sorry attempt to make amends for his unnecessary brutality. Clearly, he needed his dedicated wife by his side for the fundraising event. After opening the heavy drapes to let the morning sunlight stream in, he turned to face her. "You need to get up, dear. Flossie has a nice breakfast prepared for you downstairs."

"Oh? Does that mean I can actually leave my bedroom?"

Grant ignored the snide remark and continued, "Tonight is an important event. I will be entertaining several generous benefactors. It goes without saying that I expect you to be on your best behavior."

"I'm not a child, Grant," Lizzie said softly. "Where did this all go wrong? We were so happy, so in love, and now I'm just...a prisoner in my own home. I never see you anymore."

He walked to the bed and slid her legs over before sitting down. She was surprised when he reached up and gently brushed her hair away from her face. "I have a very demanding job, Elizabeth. Sometimes it gets the best of me. I'm sorry if I've neglected you. Perhaps a long vacation is in order. How do the Caymans sound? I'll have Clara make the reservations today."

Oh, my God, Lizzie thought, as she would never have seen that coming. She looked at Grant and, for a brief moment, wondered if he really did love her. *Perhaps he is under a great deal of pressure. Maybe...* "That would be nice," she answered.

He stood quickly and patted her hand. "Good. Now go downstairs for some nourishment. I'll see you tonight."

"I'll be ready, but I will need my keys."

"What for?"

"I made appointments at the salon, for hair and a manicure."

"Yes, I saw those appointments marked in your planner. I have made arrangements for a driver to take you, and he will be at your disposal for the day. He will be here in an hour."

"That isn't necessary. I'll be fine by myself."

"I'm still a little concerned about that eye, and I'm not comfortable with you being behind the wheel."

She desperately wanted to scream, to remind him that he hadn't been even a little concerned for the past two weeks, but she didn't dare. They were making progress, and she couldn't withstand any more conflict. "Okay." She smiled sweetly. "If he's gonna be here in an hour, I had better eat and get dressed. I appreciate you being so thoughtful."

He bent down and kissed her forehead, straightened his silk tie, and left the house for his day at the office.

It didn't surprise Lizzie that Flossie had her breakfast laid out on the kitchen table instead of in the dining room. Clearly, it was part of her and Grant's attempt to appease her enough to be the wife the crowd would expect. She didn't acknowledge it but did boast about the breakfast.

Flossie floated around the kitchen, cleaning her pots and wiping down the countertops. "It should be a nice evening," she said without making eye contact with Lizzie. "I'm grateful you are feeling better and will be able to attend."

Lizzie stifled the urge to roll her eyes. "I'm sure it will be wonderful. I expected Antoine to show up before now. He usually checks in the morning before one of his parties."

"He's already come and gone," Flossie said flatly. "He's left me a mile-long list of deliveries, from the florist to the caterers to the orchestra. That man must think I don't have anything else to do! Have you picked out your gown for the evening?"

"There are so many in my closet. It shouldn't be hard to choose one."

"That should have been done over a week ago! I'll have Antoine send Natalie over to make the decision and select which jewelry would be best. I declare, child! You should be aware by now that the dress is only part of it. There are accessories, an appropriate hairstyle, as well as the color of your nails and lipstick. I simply can't do it all!"

"I'm sorry, Flossie," she forced herself to say. "I haven't felt well. I enjoyed my breakfast, but I need to shower and dress before the driver arrives."

Lizzie made her way up the stairs and took a quick shower. She dressed in a pair of leggings and a light cashmere sweater. When she heard the doorbell ring, she grabbed her purse and looked inside to make sure her credit cards were there; of course, they were, for Grant would never want the embarrassment of his wife being unable to pay for anything.

She recognized the driver as someone she had met before, but for the life of her, she couldn't place him. He was tall and thick, like someone who might work as a bouncer or night security. His arms were bulging under a dark suit, and she guessed him to be at least six-four.

He removed his sunglasses but never made direct eye contact with her. "Good morning, Ma'am. My name is Gunnar. Where is our first stop?"

"I'm getting my nails done first, and then I have a hair appointment," she answered, handing him both business cards with the appropriate addresses.

He stood at the open door, and she walked outside with him close behind. He was driving a black Lincoln Town Car with tinted windows. She slid in the back, with her purse tucked under her arm, determined to forego any conversation.

The same young lady had done Lizzie's manicures and pedicures for years, but she knew very little about her. Yen spoke

25

very little English, and it made Lizzie uncomfortable when she failed to understand her, so she kept their conversations to a minimum. Today would be no different. They smiled in lieu of a greeting, and Yen got to work, removing the old polish and running hot water for Lizzie to soak her feet in. She worked quickly and efficiently as Lizzie pretended to read a magazine. Meanwhile, Gunnar set up camp at the nail salon entrance, where he had a clear view of Lizzie.

She scanned the area around her, glancing at the few customers who were there. They were each immersed in phone calls or staring at their iPads, paying her and their surroundings no attention at all. *Damn. I wish I could borrow one of their cell phones,* she thought, then wondered who in the world she would call and what she would say. Lizzie put the magazine aside and rummaged through her wallet to see if she had Antoine's business card. She located it and was relieved to find that it listed his office number and his cell. She thought a trip to the bathroom might give her the opportunity to use someone's phone, but she had no idea what she would even say to him if he picked up the call. *Do I ask him to whisk me away and put me on a Greyhound to some undisclosed location?* She realized that would sound ridiculous and that he would probably think she'd lost her mind. A queasy feeling formed instantly in her stomach, and she thought of Flossie. *I wonder where Antoine's loyalties lie.*

She sat stoically as Yen completed her work, then waited longer than usual for the polish to dry. *Let him wait.* She thought of Gunnar. *I'd love to know what Grant is paying him, and what his orders are.*

Lizzie had to admit that getting back out in the world had done her some good. Even the small talk with her hairstylist had made her feel like a person again. With her blonde locks highlighted and twisted into a lovely up-do, she was actually looking forward to the night ahead. She found an exquisite champagne-colored gown lying across her bed, one she didn't remember purchasing. Beside it lay a velvet box that held a new set of cascading diamond earrings. Such extravagance always made Lizzie think back to her struggling days when she'd had to eke by and pay the rent on a waitress's salary. Instantly, she felt a twinge of guilt.

"I see you found my gift," Grant said, surprising her in the doorway.

"Yes. They are lovely. You really shouldn't have."

"Why work so hard if I can't spoil my wife every now and then? You deserve it," he said as he walked slowly toward her and ran his fingers along her face. "Your hair looks beautiful, Elizabeth. I prefer it flowing over your shoulders, but it's nice pulled up too."

She struggled to make eye contact with him but simply couldn't do it; too much had happened, and even his pricey gifts and his handsome face was not enough to overcome it.

"Clara made the reservations for the Caymans. We'll leave this time next week. That should give you plenty of time to shop for whatever you need."

"How can you take time off now, Grant? I mean, with the research and all…"

"It's the perfect time," he assured her. "The staff will be busy preparing the Facility for the delivery of the primates. The place will be a mess. I've already delegated my surgeries to another physician, so we can both enjoy a nice, much-deserved getaway." He leaned down and kissed her lips, then held her close to him. "I think I'll sleep in here tonight," he whispered in her ear. "For now, though, I'd better get in the shower and get dressed. Our first few guests will arrive in a little less than an hour. I'll see you downstairs."

Lizzie sat down on her bed and struggled to keep the tears at bay. *How in heaven's name am I going to go on vacation with him?* She wondered. *And why does it have to be out of the country?*

Chapter 9

Clara found herself back in the breakroom, cleaning up yet another mess at the end of the day. Although she really didn't mind picking up after the others, her mind was somewhere else. Dr. Chatsworth was up to something, and she was determined to find out what it was. He seemed preoccupied and borderline angry most of the time. Not only that, but never before had he left on a whim, to take a spur-of-the-moment vacation. He had never been concerned about spending time with his wife, and the Caymans seemed a little extreme. The doctor had always spurned the beach and the sun, opting for long preplanned vacations where he could visit museums and examine diverse cultures. Nevertheless, he'd been adamant that she interrupt her normal duties to book the trip. His urgency almost frightened her, and now she was grateful he had left early for the day to attend his fundraising event.

She reached for her purse and the comfortable old cardigan, then started down the hall, stopping just short of Dr. Chatsworth's office. "I know I shouldn't be doing this," she muttered to herself, "but I have to know what's going on." Clara fumbled through the overstuffed purse until she felt her keys. "I'll just take a quick look," she said aloud. "What can that possibly hurt?"

Her hands shook slightly as she slid the key into the lock and turned the knob. She thought of turning on the overhead light but decided on the desk lamp instead. His patient files were locked, but she had the key; she had to pull from them daily, and she really didn't expect to find anything there. She slid into the leather chair behind his desk and checked all the drawers, only to find them locked, just as she expected. She dug into her purse once more and pulled out a bobby pin. She almost smiled at the memory of having to enact such a tool for lock-picking her daughter out of the bathroom when she was little. She pushed the bobby pin in and out of the lock, hoping to open the drawer. Just as she was about to give up, she felt it give, and the middle drawer slid out easily. Just as expected, everything was neat and organized. A few expensive pens were positioned alongside prescription pads, a couple of tubes of Chap Stick, and a leather-bound address book. Clara quickly pulled the book out and held it under the soft light of the desk lamp. As she perused it, she recognized the names of several physicians she dealt with from time to time, but nothing seemed to jump out at her. She flipped hastily through the pages, stopping from time to time to take a second glance, but she was beginning to lose hope of discovering anything of significance. However, when she turned to the last page, she noticed that the binding was coming loose. Making use of the doctor's gold-plated letter opener, she separated the lining from the hardback cover.

Clara let out a nervous sigh when she saw a piece of paper tucked inside, with several numbers on it. She didn't have any idea what they meant though. Some appeared to be local phone numbers and others overseas numbers while some were just a series of digits that could have meant several things. She stared blankly at the sheet of paper for several seconds, trying to decide what to do with it. *I'll photocopy it,* she decided. *That way, I can take it home and try to figure out what all this means if anything.* She gently pulled the paper from the binding and placed the book back in its place before sliding the drawer shut. Clara pulled the cord on the lamp and gathered her purse and sweater. As she was turning to leave, she heard the ominous sound of a key turning in the front office door.

Oh, no! Maybe security saw the light, she thought, but she was quickly overcome by a nervous, uneasy feeling. *No, they would have called first. It has to be someone else, but who?* It was too late for her to exit the office without being seen, so she walked swiftly into Dr. Chatsworth's personal bathroom and stood behind the door, hoping that they would have no reason to look in there since the door was wide open and didn't appear to be hiding anything or anyone. *Good Lord, don't let them have to pee,* she prayed silently.

Heavy footsteps suggested a large man making his way directly to the office. Clara didn't hold her breath, but she breathed as softly as she could, which was difficult in such a panic. Whoever it was, he turned on the bright overhead light and made his way to the desk. She listened to the beeps of his cell phone as he placed a call.

"Yeah, I'm at the desk now," he said.

She attempted to place the accent and strained to recall if she had heard it before.

"All right. Second drawer on the right? Got it."

Breathe, Clara continued to tell herself. *Just breathe.*

"Blue folder, you said? All right. Uh...the fax from NPRC verifies that Ursula released six nonhuman primates at the research lab four days ago. According to their records, the primates are being processed, and their final medical exams are being administered. They should be available for delivery in seven days. That equates to no worries for you as you'll be in the Caymans."

Oh, my God, Clara thought. *He's talking to Dr. Chatsworth. But who or what is NPRC? Or did he say, "NRPC"? No. NPRC. I've got to remember that.*

"Let's just hope your benefactors aren't smart or inquisitive enough to try to verify this fax. That would screw us over way too early in the game." There was a long pause as the caller listened to the doctor on the other end. "Okay. I'll drop this folder off at the gate. No, I won't come in. I've got to get back to the lab anyway. There are still some men there, preparing the enclosures." After another pause, he continued, "Okay. Leather portfolio, in the center drawer. Wait. That's funny. Shouldn't you lock that drawer too? You're crazy to leave anything unlocked. I thought you were smarter than that. We can't afford careless errors, Doc."

Clara could hear the loud, angry voice of her boss screaming through the other end of the line.

"Okay, okay! But I'm telling you, it wasn't locked. Damn. Calm down. Mistakes happen, right? The book is here, right in my hands. I'll drop it off with the fax. Get back to your guests now. You have funds to raise."

Oh, dear Lord in heaven, Clara prayed silently. *What have I gotten myself into?* While she didn't make an audible sound, her mouth moved with each word. Her heart was pounding so hard that she feared the man would surely hear it. Instead, he just turned off the light and left the office, then closed the door behind him. She still didn't dare move a muscle for a while until she was hundred percent sure he was gone.

Slowly, her small frame slumped down the wall, and she found herself squatting on the bathroom floor, her hands shaking so terribly that she was unable to hold on to her purse any longer. She stayed in that position for what seemed like hours but was really only a matter of a few minutes. "Get it together, Clara," she told herself. "Think, girl. Think." After closing her eyes and uttering one more silent prayer, she gathered her sweater, shoved the paper in her purse, and slowly crept into the hall. The security light was enough for her to see her watch, and she decided to wait ten minutes to ensure that the mystery man had enough time to exit the building, locate his car, and head to Dr. Chatsworth's residence. As she waited, though, she thought of another problem: The parking lot was sure to be empty, and if he noticed her car and asked the doctor about it, the doctor would realize she was still lingering around the office long after he was gone. *Oh dear. Once he discovers that the paper is missing, surely he'll put two and two together. I'd better call Iris.*

Clara made her way into the breakroom and picked up the phone. Iris answered on the second ring. "It's me," Clara said nervously, stuttering a bit. "I need you to pick me up at work. Don't ask any questions. Just pull up to the side door, the one where you always drop me off after lunch. I'll be watching for you."

"But—"

"Just do it, Iris. I'll explain why when you pick me up. How soon can you be here?"

"Well, ten minutes, I suppose, but... Clara, you know I can't see well at night. I'm taking a big risk to—"

"I'll see you in ten minutes or sooner if you can. Please don't take too long."

Without giving Iris any time to protest again, Clara hung up the phone, her whole body still trembling. She planned to take the stairs to the first floor and use her employee badge at the side door; that wouldn't set off any alarms. Iris would drop her off at work in the morning, and she could have her car towed to the dealership, claiming that she had to leave it there because it wouldn't start. She was fully confident in her ability to play the role of a flustered older lady who would simply panic when they told her nothing was wrong with it.

Iris was there in less than ten minutes, and Clara was waiting at the door as promised. She jumped in the passenger side and shut the door.

"What in the hell is going on, Clara? I'm not sure, but I think I ran over the Williamses' mailbox. They'll think I've been drinking!"

"Iris, please," Clara began. "I'm so flustered. Can we just drive home? I'll tell you at the house. We need to get out of here…now!" she said, nervously darting her eyes around to peer out the windows.

"Clara Samples, honestly. You're gonna be the death of me yet."

The two rode in silence the rest of the way to Clara's. She was grateful for the few minutes to calm her nerves and put things into perspective after such a close call.

Iris Hadley was a good woman. The two had been friends for over forty years since they'd met upon becoming neighbors. They were both widows and enjoyed one another's company every Saturday morning over coffee and almost every evening over a glass of wine. It went without saying that Clara knew Iris could be trusted, and at that moment, she needed a friend. The question was whether or not she wanted to bring Iris in on such a precarious situation.

Iris pulled into Clara's driveway and put the car in park. "You have some explaining to do, lady," she said as she got out of the car.

"I know, Iris." Once again, Clara dug out her keys, grateful that she always left the porchlight on. "Come on in. I'll get us a glass of wine."

Iris turned on the lamps in the living room, slipped out of her shoes, and sat down in one of the wingback chairs. "Might as well bring the whole bottle in here, Clara!" she yelled from her seat. "Sounds like you have a lot to tell me."

Clara had changed into her slippers, which always had a way of making everything better. She placed two glasses on the end table and filled them with Merlot. "I don't know where to begin, Iris."

"You best begin somewhere, sister, preferably at the beginning."

Clara had to laugh. Iris had been such a good friend for so long that she often wondered what she would ever do without her. She was the polar opposite of Clara; perhaps that was why they were such great friends. Iris was pleasantly plump, in contrast with Clara's small frame. She was high-strung and impatient as opposed to Clara's calm and efficient manner. Before retiring, Iris was a hairdresser and thrived on the town gossip, whereas Clara kept mostly to herself outside the workplace.

For the first time since the whole ordeal had occurred, tears welled in Clara's eyes, then began streaming down her wrinkled cheeks. "Oh, Iris," she said, "I've gotten into something I should've left alone. It is so unlike me. I just don't know what I'm going to do."

It was a side of her friend Iris had never seen, and it concerned her. "You're safe now. Just take a few sips of your wine and relax. No need to rush into it. I'll stay as long as you need me."

"What would I do without you, Iris? You've always been such a dedicated friend. I do declare, I have gotten myself into a mess."

"It can't be too bad. You're still in one piece."

The warm wine soothed and calmed her, so she began her tale. "Dr. Chatsworth has been acting awfully strange lately."

"My goodness, honey. How can you possibly tell that? He's such a pompous man. Honestly, Clara, I don't know why you don't just retire. Let someone else deal with him. We could join that seniors traveling club. Jeannette Gentry said they've got six single fellas among them now, real lookers."

"For heaven's sake, Iris. Would you quit thinking about men? The last thing I want is a man to take care of."

"Hey, don't be so pessimistic. Just because you see all those invalids at work doesn't mean there aren't still some healthy ones out there. I'm willing to go out on a limb."

"They aren't invalids...and I don't know how our conversation took this turn. I could be in danger. This isn't a joke."

"I'm sorry. So, the doctor is acting even more arrogant than usual? Continue with your story, honey."

"Well, you know he's a workaholic, always choosing work over time with that sweet wife of his. Yesterday, he up and asked me to make reservations for them to go to the Cayman Islands."

"Okay. So he's finally gonna do right by his wife. Problem solved."

"That's just it. Why now, when he is the busiest he's ever been? The Research Facility is in full swing, and he has a full schedule of patients and surgeries. I had to spend the entire day getting other physicians to cover him. For another thing, he never wants to take a relaxing vacation. He usually has me schedule every detail, right down to the minute, from the most popular restaurants to the most famous museums to the best personal tour guides. This time, he claims he just wants to lie in the sun for several days and eat on the hotel premises. It's out of character."

"Let me get this straight," Iris said. "I had to leave home in the dark, and I'll probably have to reimburse a neighbor for his mailbox, all to pick you up at work like some kind of secret agent, just because your boss wants to catch a few rays with his beautiful wife? You may need to see a doctor yourself, darling…and I don't mean a heart doctor," she said as she swirled her finger around her head.

"No, there is more to it than that," Clara said, feeling exasperated. "The other day, I overheard a very strange phone conversation about the Research Facility. Dr. Chatsworth was very angry. It sounded as though the whole place is a sham."

"You mean it's not on the up and up?"

"Exactly. He's up to something. He left early today because he has this fundraising party at his house. When I finished cleaning the breakroom, I decided to look around his office."

"No! You didn't!"

"Well, I *am* the office manager, Iris, and it *is* part of the office."

"And what did you find?"

"His desk was locked, but I broke into it with a bobby pin."

"Clara Samples, I never knew you had it in you. Hurry now. Get to the good part!"

Clara took a couple of sips of wine before she continued, "At first, I didn't see anything out of the ordinary. I was flipping through an address book when I noticed that the binding on the back cover had been tampered with. I separated it with a letter opener and found a sheet of paper. Here. I have it in my purse." She pulled it out, unfolded it, and handed it to Iris.

"Looks like phone numbers to me," Iris said, "nothing unusual. But why was it hidden?"

"That's exactly my point. Anyway, I figured I'd photocopy it in the office and bring it home, maybe call a couple of the numbers, but before I could do that, a man came in."

"What?! Did he see you?"

"I hid in the bathroom of Dr. Chatsworth's office. I thought my heart would just stop! Anyway, he sat behind the desk and made a call on his cell phone."

"What did he look like?"

Clara shrugged. "Don't know. I didn't see him. He had a slight accent, but I couldn't place it. He was clearly on the phone with the doctor, saying something about monkeys being released to the Research Facility. He was reading from a fax written by a woman with an odd name, it started with a U, like Uma or Ursula. Yes, that was it. Ursula. Anyway, she worked for a place that he referred to by initials. I'm not sure what they stood for, and for the life of me, I can't remember what they were. I know it began with an N. Heavens. I told myself I had to remember that, but I can't pull it outta my head for anything."

"Don't get flustered, Clara. Focus. What happened after that?"

"The man with the accent said he hopes the people at the party don't check on the fax, or else they'll be caught. Verify it, I mean. It must be a fake, but this Ursula must be in on it with them. Apparently, she works for the N place, whatever that stands for."

"That shouldn't be hard to find. How many facilities are there that hand monkeys over for research anyway? What happened next?" Iris asked as she sipped heavily from the wine.

"Let's see," Clara said nervously. "Oh my, it all happened so quickly. Anyway, he told Dr. Chatsworth he would bring the fax by the party and leave it at the front gate. The doctor must have asked him about the book I removed that piece of paper from," she said, pointing to the paper Iris was still holding.

"He didn't!" Iris said, holding the paper up to her chest. "Keep talking."

"The man made a comment about how Dr. Chatsworth shouldn't ever leave his desk drawer unlocked. That caused him to panic, so much that I could hear his angry voice through the phone.

35

The man tried to calm him, then assured him the book was still there."

"Whew," Iris interrupted. "That gives us enough time to get over there and replace the paper."

"No," Clara said sadly. "He took the book with him to the party. Once Dr. Chatsworth notices that the paper is missing, he'll be frantic!"

"We have to find out what these numbers and letters mean," Iris said, concern deepening in her voice. "Surely he won't think you're involved."

"My car is still in the parking lot," Clara said. She then took the time to explain her plan for the following day, but it clearly didn't put her friend at ease.

"What if he decides to go over there tonight to check his office? He'll see your car and come right over! Grab the wine, gal. Let's go to my house and look up some of this information on the internet."

"I don't know, Iris. I'm in so deep already. Maybe I'd be better off not prying any deeper."

"Grab your pajamas and clothes for tomorrow," Iris said, tucking the bottle of Merlot under her arm. "We've got some investigating to do, and you might not be safe here. Maybe tomorrow, after you've fibbed about your car dilemma, he'll feel differently, but for now, you will be much safer at my house."

Chapter 10

A light tap at her door signaled that Grant was ready to go downstairs and greet their guests. Lizzie had to admit that he looked extraordinarily handsome in his black tux. He had somehow found the time to get his hair cut during the day, and his face stretched into a broad smile when he saw her.

"Why, you look lovely, Elizabeth. I don't recall ever seeing that gown before. Can I help you with your necklace?"

"Yes, thanks," she answered. "You look very nice yourself."

He took his time as he clasped the diamond necklace around her neck, taking a few seconds to run his fingers across her back. It gave Lizzie chills, and she struggled not to appear repulsed.

"I've heard the bell ring several times," she said, trying to expedite their entrance to the party. "We must have several guests by now."

"Patrons, Elizabeth. They're patrons. We must always keep that in mind. They are simply investors for my research. Do not get particularly close to any of the women. Is that understood?"

She took a moment to look at him, more closely this time, especially deep into his eyes. "I never get close to anyone, Grant."

"Very well. That is how I like it."

What an odd conversation, she thought, *and I hate when he calls me Elizabeth like that. It makes me feel as though he is speaking to someone else.*

"May I?" he asked, extending his arm for her to hold so he could escort her down to the party.

Lizzie took hold of him and managed to convert her sickened expression into one of grace and contentment. In just the little time she had spent readying herself for the evening, the house had been transformed into the perfect setting for a large soiree. Antoine had outdone himself. The orchestra was playing in the large foyer while hurried wait staff weaved in and out of the growing crowd with drinks and hors d'oeuvres.

Grant instantly transformed into the renowned Dr. Chatsworth as he made his way around to the many supporters anxious to have a moment of his time. It always surprised Lizzie how attentive he was to her when they had guests. His hand was always touching her lightly, and he never failed to introduce her as his "lovely wife, Elizabeth." In years past that had made her feel valued, but she soon discovered it was simply one of her husband's many well-acted roles, a political tactic and nothing more. Nevertheless, Lizzie never failed him, even in the revelation that it was all a performance. She had learned to play the part well, never adding much to the conversation but smiling and nodding in agreement at all the appropriate times. The men always admired her beauty while the women simply acknowledged her presence with little more than feigned smiles.

It's amazing how terribly lonely I feel in a roomful of people, Lizzie thought. She suddenly felt as though she was floating above the crowd, her head swimming with all the events of the past five years. The people around her seemed to be talking loudly, and she struggled to make sense of their words. She felt her body begin to slump heavily against Grant's before the room turned black.

When Lizzie opened her eyes, she was surprised to see her husband and another physician peering nervously over her. She had been moved to her bedroom, her shoes and jewelry removed.

Grant was lightly rubbing a cool washcloth over her face. "Elizabeth? Honey, are you awake?" he asked.

She nodded an acknowledgment before trying to sit up, embarrassment engulfing her. "Oh my. What did I do? I'm so sorry, Grant. The party!"

"It's fine, dear. You fainted, but you're okay. The party will go on without you. I want you to get some rest. Flossie will bring up some tea and crackers. Maybe that will make you feel better. Did you eat lunch today?"

"Well," she said, struggling to remember if she had, "Actually, I didn't. I was rushing to all my appointments and never made the time."

"And there we have it," he said, smiling kindly at her. "You can't skip meals, you know."

"I'm terribly sorry, Grant. I ruined your lovely party. I should have known better."

"None of that now," he said, pointing to the other man in the room. "This is my friend and colleague, Dr. Jean-Luc Phillips.

He was kind enough to help me get you into bed. For now, just rest and eat a few soda crackers. Maybe later, you'll feel up to something a little heavier. Don't worry about the party. Everyone is concerned about you, but they are enjoying themselves. I'll go down and assure them that all is well." He kissed her cheek and pulled the duvet up to her neck. "Let Flossie help you get into a nightgown. I'll see you when the patrons have gone."

Relief swept over Lizzie's body as soon as she heard the door shut behind Grant and the young French doctor. She still felt a twinge of dizziness, but her head was beginning to clear. Her most immediate concern was her general health and wellbeing. It had been a few weeks since she'd felt like herself. Nothing ever seemed appetizing anymore, other than the chicken Flossie fried for her, and her weight loss had been remarkable. Her stomach was empty, and she was sure that was why she felt so queasy.

Luckily, Flossie was there almost instantly with a glass of cold ginger ale and some saltines. She left them at her bedside, then went to pull a gown from Lizzie's drawer. "Do you feel like a warm bath?" Flossie asked. "I'm sure you'd like to have all that hairspray and… What do they call it? Product? I know you need to get all that goop outta your hair."

"That sounds like a dream, Flossie," she answered. "If you'll just start the water, I can handle the rest. I'm sure you have much to do downstairs."

"I'll draw the bath," she said firmly, "but you passed out down there. I can't leave you in the tub alone. Now go on and eat a few of those crackers and get your strength back."

Lizzie nibbled on a cracker and instantly felt better, but the thought of being supervised while bathing was almost too much for Lizzie. "Maybe I'll just wash my face and change into a gown. I'm not sure if I'm up to a bath just yet."

"Suit yourself," Flossie said with a shrug.

She unzipped the evening gown and helped Lizzie step out of it. Lizzie turned her back, unhooked the strapless bra, and let Flossie slip the nightgown over her head; the soft fabric was comforting as it flowed down over her body. She sat on the bed, reached under the gown, and pulled her pantyhose down.

"No need to be modest, child," Flossie said. "I've got eight sisters and three girls of my own. I've seen it all by now."

Lizzie didn't offer a reply. She had never felt comfortable undressing in front of others, and she sure as hell wasn't going to bathe in front of someone. She stood over the sink to wash her face and brush her teeth before climbing back in bed.

Flossie handed her the ginger ale and made room for herself to sit on the side of the bed. She looked Lizzie right in the face and squinted just a bit. "You don't suppose you're with child, do you?"

"What?! You mean pregnant?"

"Yes, that's exactly what I mean. You haven't felt like eating, and you're as puny as an old stray alley cat. You fainted right in the middle of the floor down there. I wasn't born yesterday. I've got eight sisters—"

"And three girls of your own," Lizzie finished for her with a grin. "No, I'm not *with child*. You know Grant rarely sleeps in my bed, Flossie. I just haven't had enough sunlight or exercise. I need to get out a little. I'll be fine, as soon as I get some rest," she said, pulling the cover up and sliding down in the bed, a strong hint for Flossie to leave her alone.

"Very well, then," she said. "I'll leave you be, but don't let me hear the water running in that tub, ya hear?"

"I don't feel like bathing. I'm going to get a good night's rest."

That answer seemed to satisfy Flossie, who quietly shut the door behind her, finally leaving Lizzie alone.

Lizzie reached for another saltine and nibbled on it slowly. *Oh, my God. What if I am pregnant?* She stared at the ceiling while she thought back over the past few weeks, but she was unable to recall her last menstrual cycle. Although she and Grant were rarely intimate, it did happen occasionally, and like a diligent wife, she never denied him the opportunity. As she continued to ponder the possibility, she became convinced that pregnancy was the reason behind her recent symptoms. The smell and thought of certain foods made her nauseous, and in the wee hours of the morning, she often felt faint and dizzy. Instinctually, she laid her hands across her stomach, across the child she swore she would never let Grant know about.

The whole idea of being pregnant significantly narrowed her timeline, requiring that her impending escape plans be far swifter and less precise. She would have to trust all the right people, for there would be no margin for error. For the moment, though, she needed rest most of all.

Her eyes fluttered, and she was almost asleep when she heard footsteps coming down the hall. She assumed that Grant was coming to check on her. She listened intently, but instead of entering her room, he walked into his adjacent office. His voice was muffled, but she could tell he was angry. She heard several heated comments from him before she decided to get out of bed and move closer to the wall to better overhear his phone conversation.

"What the hell do you mean? There's no way I left that drawer unlocked. I'd never be that fucking careless. Is the address book there?" Grant asked, his voice low and threatening. A few moments of silence followed as he awaited a reply. "I need it brought to the house. Leave it with the guard at the security gate and don't come in. We don't need any unnecessary questions." After another brief pause, he continued, "No one here has the intellect or the balls to question the validity of a fax from the NPRC," he said sarcastically. "My reputation precedes me, you idiot. Besides, the fax was written by an actual employee on official National Primate Research Facility letterhead. Just get the fax and the book to the guard as soon as possible, and that page had better not be missing, or heads will roll!"

With that, Lizzie heard him slam the receiver down, her cue to quickly make her way back to the bed. She pulled the covers up to her neck as the sound of his footsteps grew closer and paused at her doorway. She closed her eyes just as he opened the door and looked in on her.

Assured that she was sleeping, Grant closed the door and made his way back to the party and the unsuspecting benefactors.

What was that about? Lizzie wondered. *Perhaps I heard wrong,* she thought, but she knew better. *Could the Research Facility be a bogus venture? But that doesn't make any sense. Grant has an impeccable reputation. Why would he throw all that away? He spent years in undergrad, then in medical school before going through the rigors of his residency.*

41

He was a sought-after surgeon. No, that can't be right. Lizzie rolled numerous scenarios around in her head, but not one of them made any sense at all. *I must have been dreaming,* she finally conceded. *The conversation never happened.*

Chapter 11

Gunnar Azarov drove through the medical center parking area and passed the aging gray Buick in the parking lot. "Must be night security's vehicle," he concluded as he sped out of the lot. He was anxious to drop off the information to Dr. Chatsworth and get back to the men he had left unsupervised at the research area. Even if they started snooping around, they wouldn't know what to make of the information, but he still didn't feel comfortable leaving them for any length of time. Gunnar didn't make much of the unlocked desk drawer; it was careless, but the book was still there. Dr. Chatsworth's rage really wasn't anything new.

The large home on Paces Ferry Road was well lit, and the valets were busy tending to the evening guests. Cornell Sayer was standing post at the guard shack outside the main entrance. He wasn't associated with any of their research business, and Gunnar preferred it that way; something about the man just didn't sit right with him. He was a young, African-American male, probably in his mid-twenties, tall and well-built, and he always had his face in a book. Dr. Chatsworth had told him that Cornell attended Georgia Tech and needed a part-time job to supplement his student aid. Gunnar wasn't impressed with him or his impending aerospace engineering degree. He much preferred to deal with the less educated as that made hiding things a whole lot easier.

"Good evening, Mr. Azarov," Cornell said. "Dr. Chatsworth said you'd be here to drop something off for him."

Gunnar cringed every time the kid said his name. *Why in the hell did Chatsworth have to tell him my name anyway*? He thought. "Yeah, get this package up to him as soon as you can," he blurted. "He's waiting on it now."

"No problem, Sir," Cornell responded. "I'll get one of the valets to run it up to the house on the golf cart right away."

"Can't *you* just take it yourself?"

"I never leave my post when there are guests at the house. Dr. Chatsworth's orders."

Gunnar wanted to insist but reconsidered. "Whatever. Just get the next available person to deliver it. Like I said, he's waiting on it."

The large Russian got back into the Suburban and headed for the research lab. He had taken care of the delivery, and now he would spend the remainder of the night ensuring that the monkey enclosures were being built properly so they would adequately contain the primates when they arrived. He had a bad feeling about the whole thing, a really bad feeling, but he knew from past experience that it was best not to share any doubts with his boss. There were two things Dr. Chatsworth absolutely would not tolerate: misplaced loyalty and incompetent labor. Gunnar had no desire to be accused of either.

One of Flossie's young charges made his way from the front door, over to Grant. It was only the second party he had worked, and he was still quite nervous and unconfident. He was unsure how to interrupt the famous doctor to give him the package, but fortunately, Dr. Chatsworth noticed him coming and broke away from the small group he was talking to.

"I'll take that, young man," Grant said. He motioned for Flossie, who was immediately at his side. "Take this to my office. Just leave it on my desk," he ordered, handing the address book to her.

She nodded and took it directly upstairs.

Grant rounded up the night's wealthiest benefactors and led them into the study. "My apologies, gentlemen. I inadvertently left the latest fax at the office, but a messenger just dropped it off." He made a show of removing Ursula's letter from the manila envelope and passed it around. "As I said earlier, nonhuman primates aren't used as often as rodents in research such as ours, but they share approximately ninety-eight percent of human genes. Almost all primates utilized for research are bred in one of the eight National Primate Research Facilities. This fax verifies that this will be the source of ours. Domestic breeding ensures many things, most importantly that the primates don't have any viruses or bacteria that could adversely influence the outcome of our research."

"Are we talking gorillas here?" asked Austin Jennings, a wealthy businessman. "That seems like quite a liability."

"No, Austin. We are certainly not considering gorillas. Most testing done with greater apes is conducted in a field or zoo setting. That would require greater expertise than our funds allow. Our Facility will deal with both rhesus and long-tailed monkeys. We have employees preparing for them as we speak."

"Interesting," Mr. Jennings said. "And I assume we will be allowed to tour their habitats when they arrive?"

"Certainly. We welcome any visitors…benefactors, that is."

"What is the duration of the trials? How long will it be before we see any results?"

"We have covered this process many times before, Austin. It could take up to ten years before our drug hits the market. We estimate three years of lab testing before we make our application to the FDA to begin human trials. It is not an overnight endeavor, but it will certainly make us all extremely wealthy, not to mention that it will make a significant difference for those living with congestive heart failure."

"I've been reading about accelerated approval programs," Michael Sanford piped in. "Would that be a possibility here?"

Grant was not expecting that question, and it was an idea he certainly didn't want to entertain; the last thing they wanted to do was to hasten the process. "That is particularly tricky, Michael. It is rarely done and, in most cases, is only allowed when there is an unmet medical need. Of course, progressive heart disease is not currently under control. Nevertheless, there are current medications that are being utilized to assist in treating it. I assure you that we are looking into every avenue to get our product out there, but we must be patient and go through all the right channels. Now, gentlemen, let's get back to the party. As discussed, we will meet at the Research Facility next month to update you on our progress. Contributions can be left on that table over there," he said, motioning in the direction of a round, antique table in the corner. "Envelopes are there for you, should you need one."

Each man made his way over and dropped his donation check off before returning to their wives or dates for the evening, ready to mix and mingle now that business was taken care of.

Before leaving the room behind the last of the benefactors, Grant looked over at the antique table and smiled at the pile of envelopes.

Chapter 12

Iris Hadley backed her car out of Clara's driveway and drove four houses down to her place. "I tell ya, Clara, I just feel more comfortable with you being here. Who knows what that crazy doctor will do when he discovers this paper is missing?"

"Iris, that isn't making me feel any better. I just want to know what these numbers represent, but first, I'm starving. What have you got in your refrigerator? I haven't eaten anything since noon."

"I still have some pot roast from Sunday. Want an open-faced sandwich with some gravy?"

"Sounds wonderful," Clara answered before she made her way to the guestroom to hang up her work clothes for the following morning.

Iris busied herself with the gravy while Clara looked again at the piece of paper she'd pilfered from the doctor's book. "Some of these are clearly phone numbers, but others look almost like account numbers. They're long though. Maybe he's got some overseas accounts."

"Ha! That's what it is. He's got an offshore bank account. I saw that once *on All My Children*. One of Erica Kane's husbands hid the majority of his money in a Swiss account so she wouldn't get it in a divorce. Worked like a charm. That ol' money-hungry hussy didn't get one red cent of it."

Clara fought the urge to roll her eyes. "Iris, really. This isn't a soap opera…and for some reason, I really don't believe that sweet wife of his is interested in money."

"Oh, for heaven's sake, Clara. She's young and beautiful, and that makes her high maintenance. Isn't that what they call it these days?"

"You might think so, but I'm telling you she's not that kind of girl. She seemed happy in the beginning, but the last few times I've seen her, she looked almost dejected."

"Well, wouldn't you be too?" Iris threw her hands in the air and whisked the gravy much harder than she needed to.

"Besides, I don't think those offshore accounts are like they used to be. It's harder to stash money in them now. They've come up with restrictions to prevent evading taxes and laundering money."

"I'm quite sure they have. There's no damn way to get around taxes anymore."

"Iris, please!"

"I'm closing in on seventy, girl. I'm entitled to an occasional expletive. Anyway, you say his research is a sham, right? That would be the perfect way to embezzle some money."

"Yep, you're right, but if he gets caught, those countries have to make the account information available to the United States under the latest guidelines."

"How in the world do you know all that? Sometimes I don't even think I know you at all, Clara Samples!"

"I saw a documentary on it recently. Some of us watch more than soap operas."

"Okay, let's think for a minute. They'd pull up any accounts linked to his name. What if someone else is involved, someone no one else knows about?"

"That's a possibility," Clara answered as she reached for the steaming plate of chipped beef and gravy. "Thing is, I don't see the doctor trusting anyone enough for that. I still can't wrap my head around the idea of him scamming these affluent folks out of money. He'd surely lose his practice and his medical license."

"You're right. From what you've said, he's living pretty high off the hog."

"He certainly doesn't have any financial worries and being a surgeon is his identity. He adores the attention and respect. I'm not sure there's any price tag that would make him willing to give up his clout and reputation." Clara ate heartily and finished the bottle of wine with her friend. "I'm afraid to contact any of these phone numbers. With caller ID, it might just come back on us. Let me look up a few things on your laptop," she said.

"I'll go get it from the bedroom. The battery's all charged, so you can just sit right there at the kitchen table and goggle away."

"Google," Clara corrected, laughing at her.

In short order, Iris returned with the laptop. "Here ya go."

Clara tapped away at the keypad, googling Swiss bank accounts. "According to this information, these offshore accounts

48

have a country code, a bank and branch code, and an individual account number. CH is the country code that identifies Swiss banks. Look on that paper. Do one of those numbers start with CH?"

Iris put on her reading glasses and skimmed the sheet of paper. "Well, I'll be dam..." She started, then changed her mind. "I'll be darn! It sure does! He really does have money in a Swiss bank, Clara!" She scanned the remainder of the page. "But there are accounts beginning with other letters too. We may be dealing with several countries here."

"Gimme the next set of letters," Clara said, quickly typing them into the computer.

"Here's one. Let's see...GB."

"That's in Bermuda. Oh my. Is there another one?"

"Yeah, one more. It begins with H."

"Iris, that's in the Cayman Islands! He's going next week. Maybe it's not just a vacation after all. Maybe he's only using that as an excuse so he can deposit those checks from the fundraiser tonight. I-I can't believe it."

"How much money are we talking here? Is there that much money to be made in heart medicine?"

"Yes, Iris. There are millions if not a couple of billion."

Chapter 13

It was after 2:00 in the morning before the last of the guests meandered out of the party. "I'm going up to bed, Flossie," Grant said. "It has been a long night. I'm ready for some rest."

"Good night, Sir," she answered. "It was a wonderful evening."

Grant made his way up to his office and sat down heavily in his chair, then laid the stack of envelopes on his desk. He knew there was no real urgency to check them; everyone had already made pledges, and he was sure those amounts were enclosed, if not more. Overall, it had been a successful event, and he was pleased. No doubt, the introduction of the primates had added an interesting twist for those contributing large sums, just as he knew they would. *Screw Zahir,* he thought. *He is getting just a little too worrisome these days. I need him, but just how much is the question.*

He noticed the address book lying on the desk, right where he'd asked Flossie to put it. She was a dedicated employee, and he paid her well; he knew money was the key to loyalty. If he had learned anything through the years, the power of money was at the top of the list.

Grant picked up the book and flipped casually through it before turning to the back page. He immediately noticed that the binding had been tampered with, and his heart sank when he realized that the paper was missing. It wasn't the end of the world, as he'd had the wherewithal to store the information elsewhere, but it was unsettling to think that someone had their hands on it. That frightened him to his core. He tore the book apart in a rage, desperately looking for the information that was clearly not there. "What the hell?" he barked. He grabbed the phone and quickly called Gunnar Azarov on his cell.

"Yeah?" Gunnar answered.

"It's not here!" Grant yelled into the phone. "The information I need is not here!"

"What are you talking about? I got everything you asked me to. I dropped it off with the guard out front. Didn't someone deliver it to you?"

"Yes, they delivered it to me, but the book has been tampered with, and my information is missing!"

The ruckus woke Lizzie, and she sat up in bed, briefly confused about what she was hearing. Again, she made her way over to the wall to eavesdrop on her husband's latest conversation.

"I told you about that desk drawer being unlocked."

"I *always* lock my desk! Always!" Grant screamed. "Did it look like someone broke into it?"

"Not that I noticed, but then, I didn't look that closely."

"I pay you well to be observant! No one has a key to my desk. Did you notice anyone in the building?"

"Just night security, in the front lobby, as always."

"Was the office dark and locked when you arrived?"

"Yes. Don't you think I would a told you if it wasn't? There was only one car in the lot when I left. I'm sure it belongs to the security guy."

"He rides the Marta train. We've discussed that many times. What'd that car look like?"

"It was an older, gray, four-door sedan, possibly a Buick, but I can't be sure."

"I'll be damned," Grant spat loudly. "That's Clara Sample's car. What the hell was it still doing there? Are you positive no one was in the office?"

"I'm sure. It was locked, and the lights were off. Why would this Clara break into your desk anyway?"

"I don't know. She's an older woman who's worked for me for years." He sighed. "Maybe I did leave it unlocked. I've had a lot on my mind."

"Then how do you explain the missing information?"

"I don't know," Grant conceded. "Maybe someone took it after you dropped it off. Did you give it to Cornell at the gate?"

"Yeah. There's something about that guy, Doctor. I just don't like him."

"Cornell's a good kid. You're just intimidated by his intelligence. He wasn't the one who brought the book to me."

"He said something about specific orders for him not to leave the gate during parties. He was going to get one of the valets to deliver it to the house, on a golf cart, I think."

"Damn it! There could be any number of possibilities. That leaves the valet, the kid who actually handed it to me during the party—"

"My vote is for the old lady or that smartass at the entrance."

"Clara has never been anything but competent. She's worked for me for years. I tell you what. Drive back by the office and see if her car is still there. She could have been hiding."

"We're wrapping up here at the lab now, so I'll head over. Should be less than fifteen minutes. Do you want me to call you when I get there?"

"Yes, call me. I need to know if I have a mole in the office."

Lizzie heard him slam the receiver down, again her cue to jump back in the bed. She lay there silently, hoping Grant had changed his mind about sleeping in her room. She heard footsteps, followed by the door opening.

"Elizabeth?"

She didn't make a sound.

He walked over to the bed, slipped out of his shoes, and lay down on top of the covers.

Labored breaths, she silently warned herself. *Make him think you're sleeping.*

"Oh, Elizabeth," he whispered. "Don't ever be stupid enough to betray me."

Chapter 14

"Elizabeth, honey, wake up," Grant said as he shook her thin shoulder. "I'm leaving for the office. You need to get up and eat. You passed out at the party last night."

Lizzie opened her eyes and allowed his face to come into focus. "Oh my. I remember. Grant, I'm so sorry. I know you must be terribly embarrassed. I was so busy getting ready for the party that I simply forgot to grab lunch. I won't let it happen again."

"I'm going to make you an appointment for some lab work," he continued. "You just aren't at hundred percent lately. Eat a good breakfast, and I'll send a driver to take you to the doctor later today."

"That's really not necessary. I just started my period, and that, mixed with not eating, just left me weak," Lizzie lied. "I need to pick up some things at the mall today though. I think after I eat, I'll be fine to drive myself."

"What do you need? I'll have someone pick it up." he pressed.

"I'm out of some of my makeup, and I need tampons. I'm not comfortable letting someone else purchase that for me. Maybe I'll stop by your office, and we can have a lunch date," she persisted.

"That would be nice, but I never know how my schedule is going to be. I'll probably just have Clara order a sandwich in for me."

"How is Clara?" Lizzie pried. "It's been ages since I have seen her. What a sweet lady."

"She's fine," he answered flatly. "If you start to feel better, I'll send Gunnar over to take you shopping. We can't have you passing out in the mall alone. Surely you understand how dangerous that would be."

Yeah, and I might just make a break for it, Lizzie thought sarcastically. "I'll see how the day goes."

Grant kissed her forehead and left her to ponder the conversation she'd overheard the night before. He was up to something, and whatever it was, it was big. Lizzie couldn't quite put her finger on it, but something about the Research Facility was clearly not on the up and up. *Perhaps I'll do a little snooping later.*

A warm shower did wonders for her, and she dressed casually in jeans, a sweatshirt, and a pair of her favorite sneakers. After breakfast, she wanted to enjoy the outdoors, even if it was just on the estate.

Sizzling bacon and hotcakes welcomed her in the dining room; much to her pleasant surprise, she was able to stomach it. She hoped that would derail Flossie's suspicions of her pregnancy.

"You ate very well this morning," Flossie said as she removed the china plate from the table. "I'm happy to see that. Dr. Chatsworth tells me you need to run a few errands today. Just let me know when you feel up to it, and I'll contact the driver."

"I think I'll spend some time outside this morning. I need some fresh air. The flowers are lovely, and I never even get to enjoy them. I'm gonna grab a blanket and a book. Maybe after lunch, I can pick up the items I need."

"You haven't been well, Lizzie. Why in the world would you want to sit outside on a blanket? You'll catch your death out there."

"Flossie, it's beautiful outdoors. Do you even realize how long I've been cooped up in this house? That's probably what's wrong with me now. By the way, who is that oversized goon my husband has driving me around?"

"Lizzie Chatsworth! I've never known you to be so disrespectful. Do you know how many women would love to have a personal chauffeur?"

"Who is he, Flossie?" Lizzie repeated.

"The young man's name is Gunnar. He works for your husband at the Research Facility. He has always been very respectful. Was there a problem yesterday?"

"No," Lizzie answered stubbornly. "I just don't understand why I need a chaperone. I am a grown woman. Did you tell Grant I was planning on going apple-picking?"

"My conversations with my boss are none of your business."

"Oh? So, it's like that, huh? Well, I'm going upstairs to get a blanket and a book. I'll be somewhere on the estate, should the FBI come looking for me. Honestly, I don't know what is going on around here!" she said as she stalked out of the room like a rebellious teen.

Lizzie grabbed a wool blanket out of the linen closet and randomly selected a book from the library shelf. She heard Flossie banging pots and pans in the kitchen, so she made a quiet exit out of the sunroom.

Outdoors, she felt free for once. The flowers were splendid, and she enjoyed smelling some of them before stopping to remove a small, frightened frog from the swimming pool.

"Morning, Ma'am," the handyman said, startling her briefly. "What brings you out today?"

Lizzie had to laugh when she thought about how strange it was for her to be walking around her own property. "It's Lonnie, right?"

"Yes, Ma'am, it is."

"Well, good morning to you. I just needed a little fresh air. There's nothing like the outdoors." She studied his face for a moment. She guessed he was probably in his late thirties and looked as if he might have come from a background very similar to her own. He had sandy blond hair and dark eyes, an average build, and wore a thin, gold wedding band.

"I have to agree with you there," he said warmly. "The wife and kids love this time of year. It's perfect for camping—not too hot and not too cold."

"Camping? That's nice. Where do you camp?"

"Usually up in Blue Ridge. It's beautiful up there."

"I agree. It's been nice talking to you, Lonnie," she said, pointing to her blanket. "I'm going to find someplace to relax and read. Enjoy your day."

"You too, Ma'am," Lonnie said, then returned to his work.

Lizzie wanted to glance back at the house because she felt sure that Flossie was watching them talk, but she didn't dare. She walked away from Lonnie and wound her way through the many flower gardens before deciding on a place out of sight of the kitchen window. She unfolded the blanket and spread it across the thick Bermuda grass, then sat down and got comfortable with her book. It was impossible to read, though, because her mind was not on it.

She needed to find a way to contact her sister. She was sure Lonnie would loan her his cell phone if she asked, but she needed to have a plan in place before she worried Maggie. Lizzie also wanted to know what was in the office and what Grant was so concerned about. *Can I really just escape this sorry excuse for a marriage and go on with my life?* she wondered. She had heard of people doing that, but they usually had money or connections, and she had neither.

She struggled to remember her last phone conversation with Maggie. It had been months since she'd talked to her sister, and she was terribly ashamed of herself for that. It just always angered Grant so much for her to talk about her past and her family, and it just seemed easier to let it go. The two sisters were very close growing up. Their mother died of breast cancer when Lizzie was only two; if not for the few photographs, she would have had no memory of her. Their father was both a mom and dad to the girls, and after their grandfather passed away, their grandmother moved in with them. In spite of the losses of loved ones, Lizzie and Maggie had enjoyed a wonderful childhood filled with love. Then death struck again, taking their beloved grandma, followed by their father. At that point, they sold the small farm and went their separate ways: Lizzie headed to Atlanta while Maggie married and moved to Biloxi. The two kept in touch for a while, but after Lizzie married Grant, it just seemed harder and harder. She missed Maggie's boys, her twin nephews who were so full of energy and delight. *Those boys would've loved the farm*, she thought.

Lizzie was confident that Maggie would welcome her, but she didn't want to be a burden by invading their family life. She would need some money of her own. Grant was lenient with her spending, but she was only given credit cards, so all of her purchases could be monitored. If she left, he would surely cancel them all immediately. They did have a joint account, but she wasn't even aware of where the checks were stashed. Besides, as soon as she withdrew money, he would be aware of it.

Then she had to consider their vacation to the Caymans, in less than a week. There was no way to get out of it, but a week wasn't enough time to plan her getaway and the rest of her life. *Why the hell does Grant want to go to the Caymans anyway?* She silently fumed. *He hates just lounging around.* She pondered that for a moment, and then a thought dawned on her: *Clara! He had her book the trip. I wonder if Clara thinks something is suspicious too.*

56

Lizzie closed the book and folded up her blanket. She decided she'd have Flossie call the goon so she could do some shopping, then surprise Grant at work with takeout. If he wasn't in, she would just have a little conversation with his head nurse.

"There's no need to go in with me," Lizzie told Gunnar when they pulled up to the drugstore. "I just have a few personal items to get."

"The boss says you've been ill, and he wants me to make sure you're okay," Gunnar answered, already tired of playing babysitter for the doctor's wife.

"Very well then," she answered. Inside the store, she intentionally made quite the scene as she fumbled through the various brands and varieties of feminine hygiene products. "What do you think? With or without wings?" she asked her annoying escort, just to embarrass him.

Feeling quite out of place in the aisle, Gunnar just shrugged and looked impatiently at his watch.

Lizzie smiled as she picked up a box of tampons; a few left in her bathroom trashcan would surely throw Flossie off the trail. "I need to go to the mall next. My husband and I are taking a vacation next week. I will be purchasing clothes and makeup, but feel free to tag along."

Gunnar didn't offer a response and simply shadowed her every move.

After spending freely, Lizzie handed him her packages. "That'll be all for today, except that I need to stop by Houston's. I'd like to pick up a couple of grilled chicken salads and surprise Grant at work."

"He doesn't like surprises. I'll have to call him in advance," Gunnar mumbled. "He's a busy man."

Lizzie put her finger over her lips. "Oh no, you mustn't." She smiled sweetly. "I promise you that nothing would make him happier than a surprise lunch with his wife. Don't you agree?"

Gunnar looked a little uneasy but said nothing. He cooperated and stopped by Houston's, and she picked up the salads before they made their way to his office of the day.

"Dr. Chatsworth here," Grant barked into his office phone.

"Yeah, it's Zahir. We need you at the Research Facility right away. It seems one of the new employees has been snooping in the files. I told you I didn't trust him."

"You'll have to handle it. I'm in my Buckhead office, about to head to the hospital for a consultation with another physician. I can't hold your hand all the damn time, Zahir. Man up and handle it."

"You need to come now," Zahir insisted. "He has the information about the release of the primates and wants to know when the US Department of Agriculture is going to do their initial inspection. He apparently has connections there. If he contacts them, it could mean trouble. I told you the guy's too intrusive, and now I think I see why."

"I'm on my way, but don't let him out of your sight."

Grant slammed the phone down in its cradle with almost enough force to shatter it. Not only was he angry, but he was also quite uneasy. It was too early in the game for things to start unraveling. *Perhaps hiring someone with such impeccable credentials wasn't such a good idea after all.* He gathered his jacket and briefcase and headed out of the office just in time to run into his wife and Gunnar Azarov.

"Why, good afternoon, sweetheart," Lizzie gushed. "I know you said you're busy, but I'm feeling better and thought I'd surprise you with lunch," she said, pointing to the bag containing their salads. "I even got your favorite, warm bacon dressing."

Grant's face turned crimson with frustration, and he struggled not to lash out at her. "Not now, Elizabeth. I'm on my way out. There's an emergency I need to handle at the Research Facility."

Clara rounded the corner just in time to see Lizzie. "Why, hello there," she said, smiling at the pretty young lady in front of her. "It's so nice to see you again, Mrs. Chatsworth."

"You too, Clara," Lizzie said.

Grant could feel his head pulsating and knew his blood pressure was skyrocketing, but publicly scolding his wife would only draw more attention. "How many salads did you bring, dear?" he asked kindly.

"I brought one for each of us, but I understand that you have commitments. I'll just put them in the refrigerator at home."

"Actually, I was going to suggest that you have lunch here, with Clara," he said. "That is, if she doesn't have any lunch plans for the day," he said, turning his attention to Clara. "I could actually use Gunnar to drive me to my meetings."

"I'd be delighted," Clara said.

"Yes, me too," Lizzie exclaimed. *It couldn't have worked out better if I'd have planned it myself,* she thought, grinning from ear to ear.

"Great. Gunnar will be back within the hour to pick you up, Elizabeth. Wait here for him," Grant ordered, giving her a look that strongly suggested she obey and stay on the premises.

"I'll be here," she said, smiling innocently at him.

Chapter 15

Grant burst through the front door of the Research Facility, furious that his daily routine had been interrupted by a problem. Zahir should have been able to handle himself.

Jean-Luc rounded the corner in time to intercept him before he made it to Zahir's office. "It's that new lab tech you hired from Duke University. Zahir caught him going through some papers on his desk about the transfer of the primates to this Facility. He reprimanded him, but the guy continued to question Zahir about the validity of the information. He said something about some inspection by the Department of Agriculture," Jean-Luc said. "He's also questioning some of our studies and the conclusions our research has led to. It is quite unsettling, Doctor."

"Are you talking about Albert Tinsley? The young white kid who just started?"

"Yes, Sir, he is the one. Zahir and I were just discussing him with you the other night. He is far too inquisitive, even about areas that do not fall within his area of expertise."

"We'll get to the bottom of this," Grant said fiercely. "Where is he now?"

"Waiting in the breakroom. Zahir demanded that he leave his office."

"Have Zahir meet us there," Grant said, motioning for Gunnar to follow him, "and send the other employees home for the day."

"Now?" Jean-Luc asked. "We're quite behind already, especially on preparing the primate enclosures."

"Damn it, Jean-Luc! I don't have time to handle all this! What do I pay you guys for anyway? Have them take a two-hour lunch then, beginning right now!" Grant spat, glancing down at his watch. "I want everyone off the premises. Do you understand?"

"Yes, Sir, I do," he answered, then was gone as quickly as he had come.

Grant stomped down the hallway with Gunnar on his heels. The two bypassed the elevator and tackled the stairs rapidly.

Albert Tinsley was waiting impatiently at one of the round tables in the employee lounge. "I'm very glad to see you, Dr.

Chatsworth," he said, standing up and extending his hand. "There are some things going on here that you should be aware of."

Grant ignored his outstretched hand and motioned for him to take a seat. "Yes, I understand you've been going through some documents not meant for your eyes."

"Well, I was simply going to Dr. Chavan's office to discuss some concerns when I came across a fax from NPRC, verifying the release of several nonhuman primates to this Facility."

"Yes," Grant continued. "And why would that concern you, Mr. Tinsley? You were hired as a laboratory technician and nothing more."

"I understand that, but this is not my first rodeo, Doctor. Everyone knows the Department of Agriculture does regular inspections of any research lab and their animal suppliers. I have yet to see the reports from those inspections."

"Mr. Tinsley," Grant said, speaking slowly and with intent, "this is far from a rodeo. Do you see any fucking clowns running around here? Is anyone wearing a cowboy hat or leather chaps? Hell no! You know why? Because this is no fly-by-night circus. We will have over four billion dollars invested in this drug before it's over. Do you have any idea how much four billion dollars is? We're not talking peanuts, you ignorant son-of-a-bitch."

Albert looked as though he was going to crumble under the pressure but quickly regained his composure. "I don't believe this drug application will ever reach that magnitude," he said calmly. "Frankly, it will never make it to human trials."

Grant felt his blood begin to boil. "And what carries you to that conclusion, Albert? Are you suggesting that you know more than some of the top research scientists in the world? You are merely a lab tech with an undergraduate degree. Don't be a fool."

"This drug is simply a combination of several drugs already on the market. You cannot mix a beta blocker, ACE inhibitor, diuretic, etc. all in one pill. The side effects will be lethal. The changes in liver function and increased blood sugar levels alone would kill someone with an already compromised immune system," Albert said defiantly.

Grant turned to Gunnar and nodded. "You're in way over your head, Albert. You should have left well enough alone."

61

"And let investors waste their money? This effort is going to crash and burn. Maybe I do know a little more than those famous scientists you have enlisted."

"You are right about one thing," Grant said, a faint smile crossing his face. "You know a little more than I thought you did."

Gunnar made a move toward Albert and, for the first time, fear was evident in his expression. He sidestepped Gunnar and slid a chair in between them. "What are you doing? You can't be serious, threatening to physically attack me. This is crazy!"

"Who have you shared this information with?" Grant demanded.

"No one," Albert insisted, his voice cracking, "no one at all. Who would ever believe me anyway? The only person I tried to talk to was Zahir, and he kept putting me off. I don't want any trouble. I'll just leave, and you'll never hear from me again."

"Do you think we can take that chance with all this money at stake?"

"But why? I-I don't understand. You have plenty of money without this."

"Yes," Grant said, stifling a laugh, "I do have a great deal of money, but I don't have billions."

"You will never get away with it. It's a house of cards. If someone like me can figure it out, it's only a matter of time before someone else does."

Grant glanced at his watch. "Enough of this," he said. "I'm late for my meeting at the hospital."

Gunnar pushed the chair to the side, grabbed Albert Tinsley in a chokehold, and strangled the life out of him until his thin body fell to the floor with a *thud*. "What do you want me to do with him, Boss?"

"Throw him in the trunk. You can dump him in the Chattahoochee on your way to pick up my wife."

Chapter 16

"Bring those salads back here, dear," Clara said, turning to walk to the breakroom. "I'm sure there's still some tea in the refrigerator."

"That sounds wonderful," Lizzie said. She took the salads out of the bag and set them on the table. "It has been quite a while since I've seen you. How have you been?"

"Oh just fine. My job keeps me busy, and that's helpful. My house is a lonely place with my Harold gone."

"I'm sure it is, Clara. I don't know what Grant would do if you retired."

"That day will probably come sooner rather than later. The old gray mare just ain't what she used to be," Clara said with a laugh. "I overheard you telling Dr. Chatsworth that you're feeling better. Have you been ill, dear?"

Lizzie looked down at her salad and picked through it with her plastic fork. "I am just closed up in the house all the time. I think I need to get out more. But yes, I haven't felt very well for the past few weeks. In fact, I fainted at the party last night. I'm sure Grant wasn't very happy about that."

"Oh dear. Have you had a physical lately? You do seem thinner than when I last saw you."

"Everyone has been telling me that. I just… Well, I…" Lizzie's eyes filled with tears, and she wiped them away with the brown napkin that came with her lunch. "Clara, I'm so sorry. Really."

Clara reached across the table and placed her hand over Lizzie's. "Sweetheart, it's okay. You can talk to me if you need to. I've been trusted with many-a-secret through the years."

"Is there anyone else in the office? Are we…safe?"

"Everyone has gone for the day. We are only open a half-day in this office. Dr. Chatsworth will spend the afternoon at the hospital. You seem frightened, Lizzie. What's wrong?"

Lizzie turned to look over her shoulder, then got up and looked down the hall. "It's Grant," she whispered. "Have you noticed anything strange lately?"

"What do you mean?" Clara asked, leaning closer to her.

"He's up to something, and I'm sure it's not good."

Clara stood up and closed the breakroom door, then sat back down next to Lizzie. "What do you know, dear?"

For an instant, Lizzie regretted trusting her. She inhaled quickly and stood to leave the office.

"Wait! I know what you mean. I'm frightened too, Lizzie."

Lizzie all but collapsed with relief in the nearest chair. "I'm not sure I'm even safe anymore, Clara. He has taken my phone, and I am under constant guard by that brute of man who drove me here."

"I think he's running some type of Ponzi scheme with his investors. At first, I had great faith in his new medicine. After all, your husband is a very skilled doctor. Lately, though, I've overheard several angry phone conversations."

"I have too!" Lizzie exclaimed, grateful to have someone to talk to. "At first, I almost believed I was dreaming it, but I heard some troubling things last night. He said something is missing from his office."

"Oh dear Lord," Clara said, wringing her hands. "I sneaked in his office last night after he left. He's gonna find out it was me. I just know it."

"I don't think he suspects you. Please tell me. What did you find?"

Clara quickly recapped the night's events, followed by her suspicions about the Cayman trip.

"What am I going to do, Clara? There's no way I can get out of that vacation, not this late. Do you think he'll hurt me?"

"I don't believe he will. He's in pretty deep now, and he surely won't want to send up any red flags to the people funneling him money. The best I can figure is that the account is in someone else's name. We need to find out who that person is."

"He hit me two weeks ago."

Clara gasped and held her hand over her mouth. "He did?"

"Yes. Grant has never done that before. I am never allowed to leave the house on my own, and I'm watched constantly by the staff. Everyone is on his payroll. I have to get away from him."

"Where will you go? It could be dangerous. He doesn't want anything to cast a bad light on him now. It will certainly adversely affect his flow of donations."

"I have a sister in Biloxi, but I don't have a way to get in touch with her. I don't want to drag her into this either. How can I get out of this trip?"

"You could certainly fake an illness. That would give you a chance to think some things through."

"Yeah, but he's a doctor, Clara. He'll know if I'm not really ill or, at the very least, have me admitted into the hospital." *Not only that, but he'll surely discover if I'm pregnant,* Lizzie thought but dared not say.

"What if you catch a stomach virus?"

"And how would I feign a stomach virus?"

"There are things that induce vomiting and even drugs that cause diarrhea."

Lizzie placed her hand over her abdomen. "Clara, there's something else."

"What, dear?" Clara asked, arching a curious eyebrow at her.

"There's a possibility I might... I could be pregnant. I can't take a chance of ingesting any medication right now."

Clara shook her head, then closed her eyes. "Let me think. There is ipecac syrup, an easy way to make yourself throw up. They even use it on toddlers, so it is fairly safe. It's not easily found in stores anymore though, so that may be another dead end. An old home remedy is mixing mustard with warm water. I'm not sure how effective it is."

"I'm certainly not allowed in the kitchen. That wouldn't work."

"You could always stick your finger down your throat. The gag reflex works every time."

"But there is the chance he won't go without me. That would really look bad, a man leaving his wife when she is sick."

"I wouldn't worry about that. If he's going there to deposit money like we suspect he is, wild horses won't keep him away."

The ladies heard the front office door open, and Clara quickly opened the breakroom door and sat back down. She began talking loudly about some random subject, followed by a hearty laugh.

Lizzie leaned forward and whispered, "I need a phone, Clara. I don't know if or how you can, but please get one to me."

The ride back to the estate was a silent one, and Lizzie was grateful for that. She had a great deal to process in her mind and not

65

having to make conversation was a plus. At least Clara had confirmed that she wasn't crazy; the conversations she'd heard were real. *But why? What is he up to? Why would Grant steal investors' money when he could possibly discover a new heart medicine on his own? Her* mind spun with unanswered questions, and she wasn't sure what he was involved with, but something so suspicious and of such magnitude surely explained his recent anger and resentment.

She decided to go through with the trip to the Caymans. At the very least, it could offer her some insight as to what he was up to. He certainly wouldn't take her to the bank with him to deposit funds in an offshore account, so she would have some time alone at the hotel. At that point, she'd have access to a computer for the first time in weeks. She had no desire to go with him, but it was a chance she had to take, a getaway that might ultimately lead to her real getaway from a man she no longer wanted to be with.

Chapter 17

The next week seemed to fly by. Lizzie desperately wanted to find a way out of the impending vacation but knew it might be a chance for her to find out more. She spent an hour outside every day, pretending to read and enjoy the brisk weather and blooming perennials. She interacted with each of the staff members equally, feeling them out as potential allies. Lonnie, the friendly handyman, was only around a couple of days a week when he was needed. He loved to talk about his family and seemed like a good-hearted guy, but she was sure she could most trust their gardener.

Santiago spoke in broken English at best, but he understood the basics. He delighted in showing off his plants and landscaping and felt comfortable with Lizzie, but he tried to steer clear of too much conversation. He didn't interact with the other staff, and Lizzie never saw Flossie so much as speak to him. In her book that was a plus.

On Wednesday, Lizzie moved her blanket toward the west end of the property and positioned it under a large magnolia tree. It was still within the confines of the black, wrought iron fence but out of sight of the house and the guard shack. She prayed that Santiago would somehow make his way over to her.

After forty-five minutes, he surfaced in his utility cart, filled with sticks and pinecones. "Great afternoon to you," he said.

Lizzie offered him a smile, then stood slowly. "Do you have a phone?" she asked, holding her index finger and thumb up to her ear and mouth.

"Cell phone? Yes, I have," Santiago answered.

"Can I?" she asked.

He fumbled in his jacket pocket and pulled out his cell. "Yes, yes."

Lizzie placed her index finger over her lips and made a shushing sound.

He nodded in acknowledgment and walked back to his cart. "Will be back soon," he said as he drove away.

"Oh, my God," Lizzie said to herself.

"I actually have my hands on a phone. Now…who do I call?" She scolded herself for not having planned things more efficiently. She thought of calling Maggie but didn't want to worry her just yet. There was always Antoine, but she wasn't sure what she should ask for. Besides that, she'd already been outside for forty-five minutes, and that didn't leave her enough time to go into everything. *Clara!* she thought. *I'll call Clara, but she's at the office, and someone else might answer the phone.* She had to take the chance. After all, she never called Grant's office, so she was sure no one would recognize her voice. Not only that, but Santiago's cell phone number on the caller ID wouldn't rouse suspicions. She quickly punched in the numbers.

"Cardiology, Dr. Grant Chatsworth's office. How may I assist you?"

"Yes, I am trying to reach Clara Samples."

"She is with a patient at the moment. Would you like to hold or leave a message?"

"I'll hold please."

"May I ask who's calling?"

"Yes. This is her neighbor," Lizzie answered, struggling to remember Iris's name.

"Very well. She will be with you shortly."

Perspiration beaded on Lizzie's forehead, and she felt her armpits dampen. *Please hurry*, she thought. She could see Santiago in the distance, picking up more pinecones, and she knew he'd be back any minute.

"Hey, Iris. What's going on?"

"It's me, Lizzie," she said in a whisper. "I'm using a staff person's cell. Do you have any news for me?"

"Not right now, Iris," Clara said without missing a beat. "I'm busy at the office. I'm sorry you're sick. Can I get you anything?"

"I still need that cell phone, but we're leaving Saturday, and I won't be able to use it there anyway, so no great rush. Clara, I need some way to get my hands on some cash. Can you work on that?"

"No problem. I'll pick that up for you on the way home. Hope you get to feeling better, Iris. See you tonight."

"Thanks, Clara. I'll be in touch." Lizzie disconnected the call just as Santiago pulled up. "Thank you so much," she said. "Please keep it a secret," she continued, pointing at the phone.

"No problem. I no tell," he assured her.

Chapter 18

Lizzie reluctantly placed her packed luggage outside her bedroom door for Rufus to pick up and take down to the waiting car. She had been dreading the vacation to the Caymans but couldn't find a way to get out of it.

"Are you ready to go?" Grant asked as he paused in the doorway to her room.

"Yes. Everything is packed. It'll be nice to have a few days in the sun with my husband."

"I had Clara pick up ample sunblock for you, and she insisted I give you these two threadbare paperbacks to read while we're away. She said the author is one of your favorites, and these are two of her best. Honestly, I don't know where this woman purchases her books. She must get them for a dime at yard sales or thrift stores. At any rate, put them in your purse," he said, handing over the books. "Remind me to pick up a Nook or Kindle for you when we get back. There's no sense in you straining your eyes on crusty yellow pages."

Lizzie didn't recall having any conversations with Clara about authors, so she was anxious to get her hands on the novels to see what their purpose actually was. For all she knew, Clara had written a coded message in them.

Rufus quickly ran the bags to the waiting car and returned to the house in an instant. Lizzie was disappointed to discover that Gunnar would be their driver, but she wasn't surprised; he seemed to be everywhere she was.

The trip to Hartsfield-Jackson Airport was only a short ride, and with absolutely no traffic, it took less than fifteen minutes. Getting through security was always an ordeal, but Lizzie found herself enjoying the experience. So limited were her outings that she actually relished the hustle and bustle of the surrounding travelers. Excited children, hurried businessmen, and elderly couples holding hands brought a smile to her face.

Grant found them a place to sit as they waited. "Do you want something from Starbucks? It will be a while before we board."

"That would be nice," Lizzie answered. "I'll just take what you're having."

She watched as he made his way to the coffee shop. There was no denying his good looks. He was tall and well-built and looked just as professional in a pair of khakis and a polo as he did in his well-tailored suits. *Oh, how looks can be deceiving,* she thought.

Lizzie was anxious to look through the novels but didn't dare take the chance yet, knowing Grant would be back any minute. She was sure there had to be something in the books, or else Clara wouldn't have insisted that Grant give them to her.

Grant returned with two iced coffees and a newspaper. "They say the weather is going to be perfect," he said, handing the beverage to her. "I scheduled a series of six microdermabrasion facials for you at the hotel spa. They recommend that particular number to receive the full benefit of the treatments."

"Grant," Lizzie said, "I'm not sure I want to do that. Won't my face be red and sensitive the whole trip? I was looking forward to spending some time at the beach."

"Don't be so dramatic, Elizabeth. It's not a surgical procedure, and there are only minimal risks."

"Minimal risks? Why would I take *any* risks? I'm going on vacation with my husband, for heaven's sake."

"Have you looked at yourself lately? Frankly, you look like hell. This will help restore the youthful glow in your skin and improve the fine lines around your eyes. You should be thanking me. Do you know how many women would love to have the luxury of spending days at an expensive spa? Sometimes I think you've gotten a little beside yourself since I've given you so much."

Lizzie opened her mouth but decided against a response. It was very early in their trip, and it wasn't worth causing a scene yet. Thankfully, the gate agent announced that they were ready to begin boarding in first class.

Grant reached for her hand, and the two made their way to the plane, looking like the perfect couple going on a romantic getaway.

It was a pleasant flight and lasted just over two hours. An older man was waiting at baggage claim, displaying a laminated sign bearing their last name. A younger, painfully thin man was standing by with their luggage. Grant waved nonchalantly in their direction.

"Yes, Dr. and Mrs. Chatsworth." The older gentleman bowed. "The Ritz-Carlton Grand Cayman welcomes you both. Please follow me." He motioned, then walked slowly toward a waiting limousine. He opened the back door for Lizzie, then went to the other side for Grant, while the younger gentleman loaded the luggage in the trunk. "May I offer you a bottle of our finest champagne, Sir?"

"That won't be necessary," Grant answered formally. "We just want to get to the hotel and have a bite of lunch. Could you call ahead and make reservations for us at a restaurant on the premises?"

"That will not be a problem, Sir. We have six restaurants on-site, all of which are exceptional." He put in a call to the hotel as he pulled into traffic.

"It is so beautiful, Grant," Lizzie said truthfully. "This will be a great getaway."

"It is indeed beautiful, but even on vacation, I have a great deal of work to take care of. I just wanted you to have an opportunity to relax."

Yeah, right, Lizzie thought. *You just want to get your embezzled money into an offshore bank.*

Chapter 19

The hotel was indeed one of the finest Lizzie had ever stayed in, even with Grant. Of course, he had Clara reserve the presidential suite, complete with three bedrooms. *Hopefully, that means he won't want to sleep with me,* Lizzie hoped.

The bellboy delivered their bags while Grant placed a few things in the suite safe.

"Let's go down to lunch," Grant said after he tipped the bellhop and the young man left. "Are you hungry?"

"Starving actually. I haven't had such a big appetite in a while."

"That's good to hear. We'll start with a light lunch. I understand that the restaurant where we have reservations for this evening is wonderful."

As soon as the elevator doors opened, Grant reached for her hand and led her through the lobby.

"Dr. and Mrs. Chatsworth?" the maître d' asked.

How do they know that? Lizzie wondered.

"Yes," Grant answered stoically.

"Please follow me. I have a table overlooking the water. I hope you will find it satisfactory."

"It will do," Grant answered, pulling out the chair for Lizzie.

"Would you care to see the wine list, Sir?"

"No. Sparkling water will suffice."

Lizzie took the menu and looked around at all the beautiful scenery.

"What would you like to eat? I have several calls I need to make back in the room."

She scanned the menu briefly. "I think I'll have the vegetarian wrap. Mmm. Roasted eggplant sounds delicious."

"I'm sure it is," he mumbled. He ordered for her when the waiter returned, opting for the grilled swordfish for himself.

The food arrived shortly, and they ate their meal in silence.

"Can I help you with anything? I hate that you have to work while we are on vacation."

"No, there is nothing you can help me with. Actually, why don't you reserve one of those cabanas down by the water? You can catch up on your reading."

"If you're sure you don't mind, but it's a shame that I'll be the only one enjoying myself, Grant."

"Do you think vacations like this are free, Elizabeth? I have a lot of responsibility, and my work doesn't stop just because I'm out of the office. Go on and enjoy yourself. I'll make sure someone is looking out for you, should you need a drink or a snack. I'll call for you when I get caught up."

Lizzie understood exactly what he was saying: She would be under guard. Even though Gunnar was back in Georgia, there was another man just like him, watching her every move.

When they got back to the room, she quickly changed into her bathing suit and pulled a bright terrycloth cover-up over her head. She slipped her feet into her flip-flops and grabbed the books Clara had sent her, anxious to see if there were any encrypted messages inside. Lizzie leaned over to kiss Grant as she left, but he waved her away as he punched numbers into his cell phone. *Just as well,* she thought as she walked out and closed the door behind her.

****

"Research Facility. How may I direct your call?"

"Transfer me to Dr. Jean-Luc Phillips," Grant demanded.

"Is that you, Dr. Chatsworth?" the ditzy young girl asked. "How is the vacation going?"

Grant desperately wanted to scold her but didn't want to waste the time. "Fine. Put me through to Jean-Luc."

"Certainly," she said, unable to hide her resentment at being snapped at. "Right away."

There were three rings, then one more before he answered. "Dr. Phillips speaking."

"This is Chatsworth. How is everything going? Are the enclosures going to be ready and adequate?"

"I do have my concerns, Doctor."

"That's not what I want to hear. They should be complete by now. I don't understand why we didn't purchase them already assembled."

"I discussed that with you. To have them professionally made would have cost almost $28,000 per enclosure, not to mention that companies providing cages such as those tend to ask questions and want to verify which Research Facility you are with. We should have stuck with rats and mice. This is getting complicated."

"Well, uncomplicate it. It doesn't take a rocket scientist to weld some stainless steel bars together."

"It's a little more complex than that. Each enclosure needs individual ventilation with filtered air. They need perches and benches as well, and—"

"We don't need all that! They're only monkeys, for God's sake. Next, you'll be telling me they need Wi-Fi and central air. Hell, we aren't even keeping them that long."

"There is also the safety issue for the staff and the monkeys."

"Just get it done as inexpensively and swiftly as possible. Can you handle that, or do I need to fly back there?"

"No, Sir, we have it under control. They will be completed on schedule."

"When will the rhesus monkeys arrive?"

"They are en route from Mumbai to Charleston. They are on schedule now but could arrive early or a little late, give or take two days either way. It was a very costly endeavor, Sir. Many had their hands out along the way."

"How many hands?"

"Zahir has been handling that part, but his contact in India got the primates from Kashmir, then had to transport them to the port in Mumbai. There was a payoff via the port authority and on the cargo ship. There were also contacts made in South Carolina."

"Who is acquiring them once they arrive in Charleston?"

"Four men will pick them up in the evening hours. That's not a concern."

"*Everything* is a concern. Tell Zahir I will call him this afternoon. I have a few contacts to make here in the Caymans. They seem very interested in investing. Have there been any inquiries about Albert Tinsley?"

"No, Sir. No one has called, at least not to my knowledge."
"Very well. I'll be in touch."

****

Lizzie was amazed when she saw her cabana as she'd really only expected little more than an umbrella stuck in the sand. Instead, the cabana was equipped with a crisp, white canopy to protect her from the sun, two teak lounge chairs, a DVD player, magazines, soft drinks, and a fruit platter. "Heaven," she said to herself.

A young island woman stopped by to offer her an alcoholic beverage, but she quickly turned it down.

She could hardly stand it anymore and hurried to retrieve Clara's books from her beach tote. She flipped through the pages frantically and was sorely disappointed when she didn't discover any notes in the margins or any text underlined as if to pass on some secret message. *There has to be something,* she thought. *Why else would Clara insist on me bringing these?* Lizzie removed each of the bookmarks to make it easier to flip through the pages. *I am missing something. I just know it.* Exasperated, she set the books to the side and opened a fresh bottle of orange juice. As she sipped it slowly, the thought hit her like a brick: *The bookmarks! It has something to do with the bookmarks!*

She reached for them. Each was laminated, with a long red tassel. There was a quote on both of them, but it wasn't of any significance. She ran her finger along one and decided it was just a little thicker than necessary. *Hmm. Something inside maybe?* she thought. Lizzie looked around but couldn't find anything to cut along the seam, and she didn't want to take the chance of tearing what may be inside. She flagged the young attendant down.

"How may I assist you, Mrs. Chatsworth?" the attendant said, instantly at her service.

"I was wondering if I might have a small knife and fork for my fruit."

"No problem, Ma'am. I'm sorry they weren't already here." She shuttled off and returned quickly with the utensils. "My name is Camila. I will be close by should you need any further assistance.

We also have a pub menu with some wonderful appetizers and snacks. I will be happy to get anything you want."

"Thank you, Camila. I appreciate your help. This should be all for now."

Lizzie carefully used the knife to cut along the edge of the laminated bookmark. It separated easily, and she pulled out the cover with the quote on it. When she separated the front and back, she spotted three $100 bills folded very tightly inside. She quickly cut into the second bookmark and found another $300, along with a small piece of paper containing Clara's cell phone number and e-mail address. "You little sneak," Lizzie said with a laugh. "At least I can count on Clara." She hid the bills in the pocket of her tote, between the tissues in a pack of Kleenex. *Now I just have to find a way to call her,* she thought. *She is up to something.*

Two hours later, Camila returned to the cabana. "Your husband, the doctor, has called for you to return to your room, Mrs. Chatsworth. I told him I would let you know right away."

"Thank you, Camila," Lizzie answered. She began to gather her things. "I have enjoyed myself so much. Please call me Lizzie."

"Yes, Ma'am. I will. Enjoy the rest of your day."

Grant met Lizzie at the door. "I need you to shower," he demanded, without even bothering to greet her first. "We are having dinner tonight at the home of a potential investor."

"But I thought you said we had reservations at—"

"Just get cleaned up, Elizabeth. I'm entitled to change plans as necessary," he snapped.

"I'm not sure I have anything appropriate to wear to a business dinner. I brought a black dress. Would that be okay?"

"No, not black. I made an appointment at the hair salon for you in an hour, and the concierge is contacting a local boutique to send over a few selections. For now, just shower," Grant said, then turned his attention back to the research packet he was preparing for the evening ahead.

Lizzie felt a sense of dread, knowing she was participating in a fraud of some sort, but she did as she was asked and showered. After dressing in Capris and a cotton top, she grabbed her purse. "I assume the hair salon is here?" she asked.

"Yes, downstairs. I'll let them know you are on your way." Grant looked up from his work and smiled at her. "You got a little sun today. Your cheeks are glowing. It looks nice."

"Thank you. It's been a while since you've noticed me."

"Why must you always say something sarcastic? I'm sorry I have been so busy, but tonight will be enjoyable. It is at one of the largest privately owned homes on the island, over 48,000 square feet, from what I understand. Try not to act surprised."

"I won't embarrass you, Grant. What does this man do to own such a large home?"

"He's from old money, stretching generations back. He headed the Department of Art History at the University of Cambridge. Smart man."

"Is he married?"

"Yes. His wife's name is Devan. I don't know much about her, but we'll meet her tonight. Now off you go," he said, standing to kiss her. "Tonight will be fun, Elizabeth. You can pick out a beautiful dress, and we'll enjoy the evening together."

Yeah, fun. Just another evening of scamming good people out of their money, she thought.

Her experience at the salon was a pleasant one. They did her hair beautifully and applied her makeup to perfection. Even Lizzie had to admit that she looked stunning. Grant was equally pleased when she returned to the room. He had already chosen the dress, one that was very becoming.

"You look very handsome, Grant," she said. "I'm looking forward to this evening."

"Me too," he said, "more than you know."

Chapter 20

Harper Adams was busy filing the remaining charts, grateful that she only had to work a half-day. It had been a peaceful week with Dr. Chatsworth out of the office. She had plans to enjoy lunch with her mother, and then they would visit the DeKalb Farmer's Market to do some grocery shopping.

"Hey there, Harper," Iris said, her arms full of a bag of Chinese takeout. "I came to surprise Clara with lunch."

"Oh, hello, Iris. You must have forgotten. Wednesdays are half-days in this office. You and Clara could have gone out to lunch."

"My goodness! I'm getting older, you know, and my memory sure ain't what it used to be. Oh well. No sense letting sweet and sour chicken go to waste. I'm here now. Where is she?"

"Cleaning up that breakroom she loves to complain about," Harper said with a laugh. "You can go on back."

"I'll do that," Iris answered, opening the door that led to the back.

Clara was busy wiping down the counters and looked up with surprise when she saw her friend. "Iris, what are you doing here? You know I only work a half-day today."

Iris gave her a coded look. "I'm so sorry. I can't believe I forgot about that! I was getting a manicure down the street and decided to surprise you with lunch. I suppose it worked out for the best. We won't have to rush."

Clara gave her a skeptical look and peeked inside the bag. "What have we got here?"

"Sweet and sour chicken, one of your favorites, as I recall."

"Egg rolls?"

"Of course, but beggars can't be choosy, you know."

"All right. Let me just make sure everything is complete up front. I'll be right back."

Harper was gathering her things when Clara entered the front office.

"Is everything in order?"

"Yes, Ma'am," Harper answered. "The files are put up, and the deposit is in the drawer for you. I don't mind dropping it off at the bank if you want me to."

"That won't be necessary. Go enjoy lunch with your mom. I'll see you tomorrow."

"Bye, Ms. Clara. Enjoy your Chinese."

Clara returned to the breakroom and looked at her friend a bit suspiciously. "Everyone is gone now, Iris. What is this all about?"

"Remember Rusty Barnes, that young man who just graduated from the University of Alabama and moved back home?"

"Yeah. He's right around the corner on Benton Avenue, but what does that have to do with us?"

"Turns out he's quite the computer genius. He said he could do some sort of intervention for us on the computer in Dr. Chatsworth's office."

"What? Do you mean hacking?"

"Yeah, I think that was what he actually called it, now that you mention it. At first, I thought he was talkin' about a coughing spell."

Clara laughed. "Hack into the doctor's computer? Iris, that's completely absurd. I can't believe you'd bring someone else in on this. Have you been drinking?"

"Of course not! I did put a bottle of Chardonnay in the refrigerator before I left though. I thought we might need it after this."

"We can't do that. The doctor will know someone's messed with it."

"According to Rusty, he can do it without leaving a digital signature, I think he called it. He said we can mark the e-mails we read as 'keep as new,' and no one will be the wiser."

"Iris, you don't have any idea what you're talking about. Just last night, I had to show you how to log off of your own laptop. Also, what makes you so sure Rusty won't tell anyone that we're reading my boss's e-mails?"

"As it turns out, I babysat him a few times and have some pretty cute photos of him taking a bubble bath. I could always threaten to put them on Facebook."

"I'm not even going to humor that with a response. This is a Ponzi scheme involving millions of dollars, and you blackmailing him with pictures of a baby's ass! Seriously, Iris."

"Clara Samples, you just said 'ass.'"

"Oh, for heaven's sake. Where is he?"

"He should be here any minute. Let's go up front and wait on him."

Just as promised, Rusty was there within minutes, looking more than a little uncomfortable. "Nice to see you again, Ms. Samples," he said. "Ms. Iris said you two are doing some detective work for the doctor's wife while he's away. I hope she doesn't find out he's being unfaithful."

Clara glared at Iris out of the corner of her eye. "We hope that too, Rusty. We appreciate your help."

"No problem. I'm late for an appointment, so I need to get started. Where is his office?"

"Right back here," Clara said, leading the way. "How does this work?"

"I just need to install this program and see if I can get you in. I can't make any promises. Some firewalls are more stubborn than others," he warned, but within a mere five minutes, Rusty had them signed in to the doctor's e-mail.

"We sure do appreciate this," Clara said nervously.

"Rusty, you know this must remain our little secret, right?" Iris said. "Don't tell a soul."

"I won't, Ms. Iris. Good luck to you."

Clara walked him to the front door and returned quickly. "Just what do you expect to find, Iris? He wouldn't be foolish enough to put anything on his computer."

"Folks do it all the time. Don't you watch the news? Just look at the e-mails and see who they're from. Hurry! The suspense is killing me."

Clara scrolled down the list of e-mails and saw nothing out of the ordinary; most were from doctors Dr. Chatsworth consulted with about various surgeries. Then she spotted a name that did not ring a bell. "There are several from Rayne 326. I'm not sure who that is."

"Open one up and see what it says."

"Hmm. Let's see. All the subject lines are blank. That's a bit odd. Let me pull this one up." After a few mouse clicks, her eyes grew wide. "Oh, my!"

"What? What does it say? Read it, Clara."

"It says, 'Enjoy the islands, but try not to get intimate. I'll be waiting for you when you get back. Be careful making the drop.'"

"He's really having an affair, Clara! I didn't see that coming."

"I can't believe it. Honestly, I don't see how the man makes the time. What do you suppose 'drop' means?"

"I bet she's talking about the deposit at the bank in the Caymans. Whoever this Rayne is, they're in it together!"

"Let me pull up another one. This one is from Dr. Zahir Chavan. I've heard that name before. I think he works for the Research Facility. It came in just a few minutes ago."

"Go on and read it," Iris coaxed.

"Thanks for handling the problem. I did all I could, but at least we won't have any further difficulties. A roommate continues to call, trying to locate him. Not sure how to proceed. Waiting on your direction. Hmm. What could that mean?" Clara asked, scratching her chin as she stared at the e-mail.

"It means they've actually taken somebody out, Clara! I do declare, the good doctor has resorted to murder!"

"No one has been murdered," Clara answered sharply, though she was quite skeptical herself. "We have to get off this computer. We're in over our heads, Iris. If lives are at risk, I don't want us to be next on the hit list. Just let me figure out how to mark this as new so he won't know we pulled it up." Clara tapped the keys as Rusty had instructed, then logged off and quickly turned off the computer. "I'm not doing this again, Iris. I mean it. We are playing with fire. Neither of us knows enough about computers to be hacking into one. I watch *Dateline*. They can find out anything from a computer, including who pulled up e-mails and from which computer they were read from. I don't like it."

"Okay, okay. We won't mess with the computer again. Let's go through his files. I wonder who this missing person is."

"Maybe he's an investor who started figuring things out or an employee at the Research Center."

"If he's a wealthy investor, I'm sure someone more significant than a 'roommate' would be looking for him," Iris said.

"You're right there. Let me see if I can find any information on the employees," Clara said, rummaging through files in the office.

Both women were startled by the ringing of the phone.

Clara grabbed her chest, then had to laugh at herself. "This is getting silly."

"Are you gonna answer it?"

"No. We're closed. Let the machine get it."

The machine clicked on, followed by the message that Harper had recorded. The beeping and a young woman's voice sounded from the recorder: "Yes, um...I am trying to reach Dr. Chatsworth. My roommate is working for him as a lab technician. He hasn't returned to our apartment in two days, and he hasn't called. I am a little concerned and just want to know if the doctor has heard from him. His name is Albert Tinsley. I can be reached at 404-786-9942. My name is Christi Cates."

"Did you hear that?" Iris squealed. "They killed that boy! We have got to get in touch with her. Do you remember the number?"

"Calm down a minute," Clara said, grabbing the nearest pen. "Let me play the message again." She jotted down the phone number and deleted the message. "That's enough for today, Iris. Let's get the hell outta here."

Iris cleared her throat. "You said 'hell.'"

Clara rolled her eyes. "Just come on." She grabbed her purse and the day's deposit, grateful to flee the deserted office. "I've got to make this deposit at the bank, and then I'll be right over," she said as they made their way to the elevator.

The doors whooshed open, and a large man in sunglasses exited before they got on.

"Have a nice day," Iris said.

"You too," he mumbled, just loud enough for Clara to recognize the accent; it belonged to the man who'd been in Dr. Chatsworth's office the night she had rambled through his desk. Clara grabbed Iris's arm as soon as the elevator doors closed. "Listen closely. Meet me in the parking lot of Walgreens down the street. I'll leave my car there and get in with you. Don't say a word. Just meet me there."

Iris opened her mouth to speak, but the elevator doors opened before she could get a word out.

Clara spoke to the security guard who was sitting at the desk in the lobby, and the ladies walked to their cars.

By the time Clara sat down in Iris's car, Iris was frantic. "What's going on now, Clara? I don't get you sometimes!"

"The man who came out of the elevator when we were getting on is the same man who was in Dr. Chatsworth's office the night I was hiding in the bathroom."

"How do you know? I thought you said you didn't see him."

"I didn't, but I heard his voice. He has some kind of accent. That was definitely him."

"Okay, if you say so, but why are we in the parking lot of Walgreens talking about it?"

"Because we have to follow him."

"What?! You know I'm not a very good driver, Clara. What if he gets on the expressway? I have a big problem with merging on the interstate."

"Oh, for heaven's sake! We have to take your car because mine was left in the parking lot that night. He may remember it."

"But he won't remember *you* because he apparently didn't see you. You drive. My nerves can't take it. Fred always drove when we went any farther than ten miles from the house. If you wanna be a renegade, you're gonna have to get behind the wheel. I refuse to go through the humiliation of purchasing another mailbox."

"Okay, Iris. I'll drive, but let's get back to the office and get a look at him when he comes out."

The two ladies staked out at the Waffle House across from the office for a little over an hour. Finally, the man walked out the front entrance and got in a black Lincoln.

"We should have brought hats, Clara. He just saw us get off the elevator."

"Don't worry. He probably thought we were seeing another doctor in the building. No one pays attention to old ladies."

"They apparently do in that senior travelers club I was telling you about. Four of the six single men have already been spoken for."

"Iris, just hush," Clara said, her patience wearing thin. "I can't be thinking about your matchmaking right now. I've got to concentrate on following this guy and staying out of sight."

The women followed the stranger back to the Research Facility and waited across the street for two hours until he exited again. This time, he was dressed in black from head to toe: a black sweatshirt, black jeans, and a black baseball cap. Black sunglasses even covered most of his face.

"This can't be good. He looks like he's working for the Secret Service," Clara exclaimed as she slowly pulled Iris's Honda out, watching carefully for oncoming traffic.

The two women kept a safe distance as they made their way downtown, past Georgia State University, until their mystery man pulled into an apartment complex on Marietta Street. Clara drove past, turned around in a parking lot, and pulled into a parking place on the street. They waited again while he sat in the car.

Twenty minutes later, a young lady, probably in her mid-twenties, walked up to check the communal mailboxes. She used a key to open one of the boxes and remove her mail. Then, after adjusting her heavy backpack, she started for the apartment entrance.

"He's getting out," Iris whispered. "He's picking up his pace. We can't let him hurt her. We have to get out of the car."

"We can't yet, or we'll blow our cover. Let's see where this leads."

They watched in silence as he walked up behind the young woman, startling her and causing her to turn and face him. Just as the women were convinced he was going to follow her inside, a couple of college students walked up the sidewalk.

"Hey, Christi!" Clara heard one of them yell. "Wanna grab some pizza with us?"

"Sure," she answered, happy to make a quick departure from the ominous stranger and make a beeline toward her friends.

"Christi? That *has* to be the young woman who called the office," Clara said. "Oh my. I wonder if he was going to hurt her."

"We have to warn her. Let's follow her."

"No, not yet. Let her go. She's safe with her friends for now. Surely, he won't attack her in a pizzeria in broad daylight, with all those witnesses around. Let's just see what the guy does when she's gone."

The large man in black walked over to the mailboxes, then made his way back to the Town Car.

Clara was just about to crank the Honda when she realized he wasn't going anywhere. "I bet he's going to break into her apartment," she said to Iris. "We have to call the police."

"But we aren't even sure which apartment it is. I say we follow him."

"Absolutely not, Iris! I'm calling the police," Clara insisted as she pulled out her cell phone. "We can make an anonymous report about a suspicious prowler. Write down his plate number, Iris."

Chapter 21

The limo driver was waiting for them when they exited the hotel. Grant and Elizabeth Chatsworth looked like a power couple, handsome and beautiful, young and happy. At least that was what everyone thought when they met them, and that was exactly how Dr. Grant Chatsworth wanted it. He once thought he loved Lizzie, but now he had to wonder if that attraction was really only driven by lust. At any rate, she always made a good impression. She was kind, sweet, and pretty, and she helped to round out the package.

The majestic estate soon came into view, and even Grant had to admit that he was impressed. The driver slowed at the gate long enough for it to open to its full girth. The driveway was long and winding, showing off the beauty of the grounds. They came to a stop right in front.

A butler opened the large mahogany doors as they exited the limousine. "Welcome, Dr. and Mrs. Chatsworth," he said, offering a bow instead of his gloved hand. "Dr. and Mrs. Solomon are awaiting you on the back portico. Please follow me."

The foyer looked more like the lobby of a five-star hotel than a private residence. The group continued through the expansive living area. Large windows overlooked the breathtaking view of crystal-clear water.

The Solomon's were sitting at an antique wrought iron table, with glasses of white wine in front of them. They both stood instantly at the sight of their guests.

"Welcome to our home," Dr. Solomon said, reaching out his hand to Grant and then his wife.

"I'm so glad you could make it," his wife said genuinely. She hugged them lightly and kissed both of their cheeks. "Please sit down. What can we offer you to drink?"

"Wine would be fine with me," Grant answered. "Is that okay with you, Elizabeth?"

Lizzie thought of asking for water or juice but instead nodded in agreement; she didn't want to bring any attention to herself or her potential condition. "You have a lovely place here, Mrs. Solomon," she said. "What a tremendous view!"

"Please call me Devan," the woman said kindly. "We are very happy here. I'll show you around after dinner, while the men are discussing business."

"I would like that very much," Lizzie answered. She studied Devan closely. She was a beautiful woman, probably in her mid to late forties, with light brown hair and blonde highlights. She had large, green eyes and well-tanned skin. She was tall and lithe and seemed warm and unpretentious. If the situation had been different, perhaps they would have been friends.

"So, how was the trip over?" Dr. Solomon asked.

"Very nice. The island is remarkable," Grant answered. "How long have you lived here, Doctor?"

"First, please call me Henry. I've never been very fond of being called Dr. Solomon. It makes me feel a little boastful."

"Very well," Grant answered. "Henry, what brought you to the Caymans?"

"So many things lured me to this place, but I would be dishonest if I did not mention the limited tax liability," he said with a laugh. "This home has been in our family for many years and was left to me when my father passed away. In the Caymans, one pays no property, income, capital gains, or inheritance taxes. The view is splendid as well."

Grant chuckled. "I am also a fan of no taxes. I've just never been able to get out of paying them. I imagine you are saving a mint on property taxes alone."

"No doubt there," Henry said, just as a new bottle of chilled Chardonnay arrived. "A toast," he said, holding up his glass, "to new friends and new ventures."

"Salud," Grant said, raising his glass with the others. "To new friends and new ventures."

The bottle of wine was almost gone when a young woman in a starched maid's uniform arrived at the table to alert them that dinner would be served.

"Thank you so much, Anna," Devan said. "We'll be right in."

The four made their way into the house and to the dining room.

"What amazing paintings," Lizzie said as she studied one of the largest ones.

"Why thank you," Henry said. "That is one of my personal favorites. My wife is quite the artist."

"I didn't know you painted," Lizzie said, turning to Devan. "You are quite talented."

"Apparently, my professor thought so as well," she answered. "He married me as soon as I graduated."

That brought laughter from the group as they made their way to their seats. The young woman who had led them inside filled their glasses with water and red wine. Again, Devan graciously thanked her.

"Anna has chosen one of our favorites for dinner tonight," Henry said. "She is really an amazing cook. We will enjoy local cuisine, fresh-caught mahi-mahi with a chili sauce made up of tomatoes, onions, peppers, and vinegar, served with callaloo, a Caribbean spinach. I hope it is to your liking."

Lizzie was impressed by the way the couple treated their "help," as Grant so rudely referred to them back home. They seemed more like family than employees. On the contrary, Grant would never admit to his guests that Flossie had chosen the evening meal. The food was wonderful, the conversation flowed easily, and Lizzie immediately liked the couple, even if the doctor was involved in some sort of shady dealings with her husband.

"What are you doing tomorrow, Elizabeth?" Devan asked. "I would delight in showing you around the island."

"I would like that very much," Lizzie answered. "However, Grant has been kind enough to schedule me a few sessions at the spa."

"Oh dear, you don't need to spend your vacation in a spa," Devan insisted. "There is far too much beauty here to spend your time inside."

"I'm sure there is," Lizzie answered, feeling uncomfortable and aware that she would somehow feel Grant's wrath later when they returned to the hotel.

"I'm sure your husband wouldn't mind," Henry said. "What do you say we send the ladies out for a day of shopping tomorrow, Grant? I happen to know of a great golf course, and you may make a few more friends with potential interest in your Facility."

That was all that Grant needed to forget about Lizzie's microdermabrasion facials and the youthful glow he thought she needed. He patted Henry on the back and agreed with a resounding, "Of course! I've never been one to deny my wife of shopping," he bragged. "Elizabeth, those appointments can easily be broken. I made them for you simply because I didn't want you to be bored and alone. I have a great deal of work to do on this vacation. Go and enjoy the island tomorrow, dear. I insist."

Chapter 22

Clara put in a call to the Atlanta Police Department and reported a suspicious person. Knowing they would arrive within minutes, she backed up, then eased the car onto Marietta Street.

"We have to warn that young girl," Iris insisted. "She isn't safe, especially if they killed her roommate. Why on Earth would they kill someone? What could be that critical?"

"I'm not sure. There are a lot of unanswered questions, and I'm not comfortable with any of the answers. We need to find out who that man is."

"I have an idea. You know Candy Thomas, the old lady who works at the pharmacy?"

"Yes," Clara said, nodding, "but if you're calling her 'old,' what's that make us?"

"We're not old, honey. We're just a bit aged, like a fine wine," Iris said with a smile. "Anyway, Candy's daughter is a 911 operator. She could run this car tag and tell us who the driver is."

"I don't like it. We are bringing in too many people."

"Just let me call and ask. She won't know why we're looking into it."

"Do you think she'll ask any questions?"

"No. She just loves to brag about that poor, homely daughter of hers. I'm tellin' you, Clara, that poor girl will never marry. An unattractive woman needs a great personality to supplement the ugliness, and she doesn't have either, bless her heart."

"Oh, for heaven's sake, Iris. That is the cruelest thing I've ever heard you say."

"I'm only sayin' that Candy will be flattered if we ask a favor of her plain Jane daughter. She'll be proud to know the girl can be of use to somebody."

"Fine. If you say so. Let's go home and find the pharmacy number."

"No need. I have it right here on one of my prescriptions," Iris said as she rummaged through her purse. "Here it is. I'll call her now."

Clara held her breath; she was willing to go along with the plan, but she certainly didn't like it.

"Good afternoon, Dr. Fletcher. This is Iris Hadley. Is Candy working today?" After a brief pause, Iris continued, "Thank you. I'll hold." She rolled her eyes at Clara to show her growing impatience. "Hey, Candy. This is Iris, Iris Hadley. Yes, Ma'am. Doin' just fine. Does that beautiful daughter of yours still work at the Police Department?"

It was Clara's turn to roll her eyes at Iris. She never felt comfortable turning Iris loose, especially in a precarious situation like the one they were facing.

"Well, good, good. I'm sure she'll be married to one of those handsome detectives before you know it. Mm-hmm. I know it! You ain't whistling 'Dixie,' honey. I know how men are these days. It's just sinful, I tell ya. Hey, speaking of sinful, I think I've got a bit of a problem. Yeah, a stalker."

"Oh, God," Clara whispered. "Have you lost your mind?"

Iris just waved her hand in Clara's direction and continued with her tall tale. "I tell ya, honey, I spot him every time I leave Bible Study, and I can't even work in the yard without him riding by. Oh, for goodness sake, Candy. No, I'm not afraid of him. I just wanna know more about him before I lead him on. You know how it is these days. One can never be too careful. Anyway, I was just wondering if that sweet daughter of yours could run his tag for me—hush-hush, of course." She paused again, looking over at Clara and crossing her fingers. "Oh, that would be simply marvelous! Yes, I have it right here. Let me see. It's WZT 3909. Did you get it? Read it back to me just to make sure."

Clara could feel the perspiration forming on her forehead as she pulled into Walgreens to get her car.

"Okay, Candy. Thank you. I'll call you back in ten minutes."

"Iris Hadley that is the last time I trust you to do anything. A stalker?! Are you kidding me? Was that the best line you could come up with?"

Iris looked hurt, and for a second, Clara felt guilty. "I had to have a believable story, Clara. You are getting more and more ungrateful in your old age."

"I don't mean to sound unappreciative, but this is a very serious matter. Lives could be at stake here, not to mention people's money. I should have left well enough alone and kept this all to myself or butted out in the first place."

"Well, you can't leave well enough alone now. You know too much, and you'll never forgive yourself if you don't look into it further."

"I suppose you're right. Do you want to meet me at my house?"

"The wine is chilling at *my* place, remember?"

"Okay. I'll be there shortly."

Clara pulled up to her house and went inside. She could smell the spaghetti sauce simmering in the crockpot, so she unplugged it and went down the hall to her bedroom to change out of her nursing uniform and into a sweat suit and sneakers. She loaded the crockpot into the trunk of her car, along with a loaf of French bread and a box of noodles. It wasn't necessary to drive to Iris's house, but she didn't want to lug the hot crockpot several houses down.

Iris had changed into a house dress and was rummaging through the refrigerator, trying to find something for dinner. "Mmm. Do I smell spaghetti sauce?" she said, peeking over the top of the refrigerator door. "Oh, Clara, I have been craving your sauce."

"Well, here it is. Get some water to boil for the noodles. I'll turn on the oven and butter the bread. We have a lot to talk about."

Just as Iris filled the pot with water, her cell phone rang. "Hello? Yes, Candy. Oh that was fast. Let me get a pen. Okay, go ahead."

Clara watched as she wrote down the information.

"Thank you so much, and thank your gorgeous daughter for me. Bye-bye now."

"I can't stand the suspense any longer. Who is it registered to?" Clara asked.

"It's registered to Cardiac Care Research Facility on Piedmont Road."

"That's the Research Facility. That only tells us he works there, which I assumed already. We need to call the girl who's missing her roommate. Can I use your cell phone, Iris? It shouldn't show up with a name, and if she calls it back, she won't catch me at the office."

"Sure. Here," Iris answered, handing over her phone. "I'm really worried about that girl."

Clara punched in the number and waited anxiously as it rang.

Finally, a young lady answered. "Hello?"

There was a lot of background noise, and Clara figured she must still be out with friends. "Hello. Is this Christi Cates?"

"Yes. Who's speaking?"

"I'm calling about your roommate, Albert Tinsley."

"Really?" she said, her voice growing frantic. "Hold a sec'. Let me just step outside."

Clara waited for several minutes until the noise seemed to dissipate into the distance.

"I'm here. Do you know where he is?"

"No, I'm sorry. I don't. When was the last time you saw him?"

"It's been a couple of days. Albert always checks in with me. He hasn't even been to the apartment to sleep or shower. I'm so worried. I'm sorry, but who did you say you are?"

"Um, I... Well..." Clara hadn't anticipated the question. "I got your message at the doctor's office and thought I would call. Dr. Chatsworth is out of town for the next week."

"Oh," Christi said, her voice faltering. "I was hoping you'd have some news."

"Tell her she's in danger," Iris whispered, poking Clara in the ribs. "Tell her!"

"Christi?"

"Yes?"

"I need to see you. Can you meet me somewhere?"

"But I thought you said you didn't have any information. Why would I meet you?"

"Because your life is in danger."

Chapter 23

The morning sun shone brightly through the hotel room windows, and Lizzie awoke with a smile on her face. She threw the covers back and hopped out of bed to take in the breathtaking ocean view.

Grant walked in just as she was pulling on her robe. "Good morning," he said, his voice light and unstrained for the first time in months. "Did you enjoy yourself last night?"

"Yes! The Solomons are very nice people."

"They certainly are. Isn't that home unbelievable?"

"I've never seen anything like it," Lizzie answered. "Why are you up so early?"

"Henry and I have a golf date, remember? We have to get out there before it gets too hot. I understand that Devan won't be here for a couple of hours, so I have taken the liberty of ordering your breakfast and morning coffee. Room service should be delivered any minute now." He looked down at his watch. "Just relax in the room. You have plenty of time to leisurely enjoy your breakfast and shower for your day of shopping. You have your credit cards, but I left about fifty dollars in cash on the dresser, should you need to tip anyone. There's a ten in there, and the rest are fives."

"Thank you," Lizzie answered, shocked that he was actually willing to leave her alone. *He must really be seeing dollar signs,* she thought. "I guess I'll see you this afternoon."

"We are meeting for cocktails later at the Solomons' place. We'll meet back up then," he said. He walked over and kissed her full on the mouth, followed by a peck on the cheek. "Have fun, Elizabeth."

"You too," she said with a smile.

As soon as Grant was out the door, Lizzie ran for the bathroom. She took a quick shower, dressed, and was applying her makeup, with her hair up in a towel, when room service arrived. Grant had ordered eggs Benedict, one of her favorites, along with fresh fruit, coffee, and orange juice. She took the time to eat her breakfast, then finished getting ready for the day ahead. Lizzie had noticed a Wi-Fi room off the lobby, furnished with a few computers, and she intended to take advantage of her unsupervised time.

Just as she was slipping on her sandals, the room phone rang. "Hello?"

"Hey, honey," Grant said. "Did your breakfast arrive?"

"Yes. I am just starting to eat now. You ordered my favorite."

"I was sure you would approve. We just arrived on the greens, so I decided to give you a quick call."

"I appreciate that. I'm going to read the paper while I enjoy this food, and then I thought I'd take a long, hot bath and read some more of Clara's book."

"See you this afternoon then," Grant said, then hung up the phone.

Lizzie was thankful she'd caught his call, and she no longer felt so rushed. She was the only one in the computer lounge, probably because everyone else had brought their own laptops and electronics. She pulled Clara's e-mail address out of her pocket but decided it would be best to make a new Hotmail account for herself; she didn't want Grant finding any messages sent from her usual account. It only took a few minutes to establish the new account, and she made sure the e-mail address didn't reflect anything that would link her to it, just in case Grant ever came across it somehow. She quickly typed a message to Clara, asking for any new information and thanking her for the money. She waited for a reply but didn't get one right away.

Finally, just as she was about to e-mail her sister, Clara responded to her message: "Things are getting crazy here, Lizzie. That big brute who came into Dr. Chatsworth's office the night I was hiding in the restroom was seen here again. Iris and I followed him to an apartment of a young girl. Perhaps I should start at the beginning…" Clara's e-mail was lengthy and very detailed, filling her in on the young girl's call to the office, she and Iris hacking into the e-mails, and them spotting the large man at the young girl's apartment.

Lizzie was frantic. She knew they were taking too many chances and could be in danger, and she didn't like that one bit. From what Clara told her, she had talked the young girl into spending the night with a friend but had plans to meet her for lunch that day, and Lizzie feared that they might be followed.

Clara's e-mail continued, "Don't worry about the money. I make the daily deposits for the office and just started keeping some cash out for you. It won't ever be a big windfall, as most people use insurance and Medicare, but the co-pays tend to add up. Don't worry about them finding out. It'd take months for them to catch on. I thought you could use the cash to possibly catch a cab and follow Dr. Chatsworth."

Lizzie finished reading the e-mail and quickly typed a reply: "The large man you are talking about sounds like Gunnar, who has been my chauffer recently. I don't trust him but know little about him other than that he is fiercely loyal to Grant. Please be careful where the lab tech is concerned. That sounds extremely dangerous. I'm not quite sure how to find the names of the Research Facility employees, but I'm going to go back to the room now to look at some of Grant's promotional material. Unfortunately, I need to get out of this computer room before someone notices me here. I'll find out all I can on this end. Just promise to be careful, and make sure you're not followed when you meet the young lady for lunch."

Lizzie left the computer lab without being noticed and made her way to the gift shop. She purchased a bottle of Tylenol and some breath mints and charged them to the room, just in case she missed a call and had to explain to Grant why. Then she hurried back to the room to dig through any material she could find.

Unfortunately, he had taken his portfolio and briefcase with him, so she went through his suitcase with the precision of a prison guard. She found $4,000 in cash but little else. She was sure he must have put anything of any significance in the safe, and he was the only one with the code. *Another dead end,* she thought, *and who is Rayne?* It had never occurred to her that Grant could be having an affair, but it made perfect sense. They were rarely intimate and were only growing further apart. She wasn't angry about that; in fact, she didn't care at all. She simply wanted to be free of him.

Devan called the room to alert Lizzie that she was waiting downstairs, so she zipped the suitcase back up and headed to the elevator. She was surprised to find herself so looking forward to the day.

Devan was sitting in a small convertible, talking to one of the bellhops. Her hair was pulled back in a ponytail, with a bright fuchsia scarf tied in a bow around it. Lizzie liked her. She was unpretentious and down-to-Earth, a quality she hadn't noticed in anyone in such a long time. Devan waved her right hand frantically when she saw Lizzie, making her laugh.

"Wow. Nice car," Lizzie said as she slid into the bucket seat.

"Why, thank you. It's a Jaguar, a little ostentatious, I suppose, but it drives like a dream. Is there anything in particular that you would like to do today?"

"Anything is fine with me. I appreciate you taking time out to show me around. Grant is always so busy."

"That is so sad, dear. Henry was like that until he retired. It got a bit lonely, but I have my painting, which tends to take up a great deal of my time. I saw you admiring our artwork last night. Are you a collector?"

"No, not me. I suppose Grant is somewhat of one. He invests in many things that won't lose their value. But me? I just prefer pieces that draw me in. I know very little about art history, but your pieces are lovely." Lizzie felt silly the instant the words flowed from her mouth. *Grant would be absolutely mortified by me admitting that,* she thought.

"We have a nice little museum here on the island. It mainly hosts work from local artists, but it hasn't ever disappointed me. Would you like to stop by, Elizabeth?"

"Sounds delightful," she said, "but please call me Lizzie. I've never preferred Elizabeth. Grant just insists on it."

"Then off we go, Lizzie," Devan said as she flipped on the radio. "Like the Beach Boys?"

"Most definitely!"

Devan drove the sports car around the winding island roads like an expert while Lizzie relished the wind flowing through her hair and the sun shining on her face. The salty, fresh scent of the ocean was like a dream.

A small clapboard building came into view as Devan slowed to a stop. "Nothing fancy," she said as she opened her door.

Lizzie took an instant liking to the place. It was painted white, with a lavender trim, and it leaned a little to the right as if daring someone to push it over.

"Good morning, Jess," Devan said to the energetic woman hanging a painting on one of the walls. "Morning to you, lady. Who is this you have with you?"

"This is my friend Lizzie. She is visiting from Atlanta, Georgia."

"Well, give me just a minute, Lizzie," she said as she pounded the nail in the wall one last time to hang the painting. "Nice to make your acquaintance. Please look around at your leisure. We are hosting several local artists right now, and all are magnificent."

"Thank you," Lizzie said. She made her way to the first small room, its walls overflowing with various works. "Oh!" She gasped quietly as she took in each of the dramatic paintings. She walked slowly from room to room, relishing the time to examine all the intricate details and swirling colors. After she had made her way through each of the rooms, she found Devan sitting at the counter with Jess, sipping on a cup of coffee. "Oh my. Did I take too long?"

"Certainly not," they both said in unison.

"Rarely does anyone take such an interest. Do you have a favorite?" Jess asked.

"I could never choose just one. They are all so remarkable."

"Would you care to purchase one?"

"They are up for sale? I was under the impression that this is just a museum, for display."

"It technically is, but the artists also sell their works here. They have to make a living somehow."

"I will have to consult my husband, but there are many I am interested in."

"I bet I know which one you like the most," Devan said. She then led her back into the first room she entered. "It must be this one. You looked at it for over twenty minutes."

"Did I really?" Lizzie asked, a bit embarrassed. "I'm so sorry."

"Why are you sorry?"

"I'm sure you are a busy person, Devan. I guess the time just got away from me."

"The painting is a gift from me," she said kindly. "The artist is one of my favorites too."

"Oh, I could never accept such a gift," Lizzie said quickly. "Really, it's too much."

"We are not at the Metropolitan Museum of Art," Devan said with a laugh. "This painting is merely $100."

"That can't be right," Lizzie insisted. "There's so much detail that I almost feel like I'm inside the painting when I look at it. Such a low price would be cheating the artist."

"Have it delivered to the house," Devan said, turning to Jesse. "I insist. Now come along. It's lunchtime, and I'm starving."

Lizzie felt a sharp pain in her chest as she thought of Grant seeing the painting of an older woman throwing kernels of corn to her chickens. He would be livid, but she couldn't possibly hurt Devan's feelings. Fearing the worst, she put on her sunglasses to hide the tears forming in her eyes.

"I'm not exactly showing you the exclusive side of town," Devan joked as she pulled up to a small tiki hut, "but it's the best food on the island."

As she made her way to the counter, the smell of fish frying took Lizzie's mind off her concerns about Grant's wrath over the painting. "What do you recommend? It all smells so delicious."

"I recommend everything."

Lizzie laughed as she scanned the menu that was scribbled on an old chalkboard. "I can't decide between the conch fritters or the fried snapper."

"That's an easy one," Devan said. "Get them both."

"Are you serious?" Lizzie asked, gasping.

"Why not?"

"You're right, Devan. Why not?" She turned to the server and said, "I'll have the conch fritters and the fried snapper."

"Throw in a roasted corn for her too, Tom…and I'll have the same."

The two women made their way over to the wooden picnic table and sat down.

"So… Tell me about yourself," Devan said.

For several seconds, Lizzie just sat there, dumbfounded. She searched her mind for something to say, but for the life of her, a thought wouldn't form.

"Are you okay, Lizzie?" Devan asked, squinting with concern.

"Yes, I'm fine," she managed to get out before the tears started to fall. "I just... I have no idea why I'm crying. I'm so sorry. I've been a bag of emotions lately, I guess."

"Why are you apologizing? I didn't mean to pry. I just want to get to know you. There's something about you, something that makes me want to befriend you."

Lizzie wiped the tears away with the back of her hand. "It's just... Well, it's been so long since anyone has asked me about myself. I just don't feel like myself anymore, so I have trouble answering that, I guess."

Devan reached her hand across the table and placed it lightly on hers. "Sometimes we women get so overshadowed by our husband's aspirations and accomplishments that we lose sight of our own. You aren't alone, Lizzie. Believe me."

The awkward moment was interrupted, much to Lizzie's relief, by the arrival of the food.

Lizzie ate until she thought she would explode, then patted her tummy. "Mmm. I think that was the best meal I've ever eaten," she said, "with the exception of our housekeeper's fried chicken." As soon as the words came out of her mouth, she regretted them; they jolted her right back to the day when Grant had dragged her to the bedroom by her hair and punched her in the face. The conch fritters now took on a sour taste, and she suddenly felt ill. "Please don't tell my husband I ate all this fried food. You know how doctors are about that sort of thing."

"Did you enjoy it?"

"Very much."

"Then screw him," Devan said defiantly.

"Just please don't say anything. He wouldn't be happy about it."

"I won't say a word, Lizzie. I promise. It's none of his business anyway."

The women rode in silence back to the Solomon estate, back to the exorbitant life of wealth and luxury. The butler met them at the door and led them back to the pool area where the men were already seated.

"Good afternoon, ladies," Henry said, jumping to his feet to greet his wife with a kiss. "How was your day?"

"Delightful," Devan said with a smile. "I have made a wonderful new friend who shares my love of the arts."

"Great news! Dr. Chatsworth made many new friends himself," he said, pointing to Grant, who was deep in conversation with several other men dressed in golf attire.

Anna brought both ladies a frozen cocktail, then led them to a table decked out with crackers and fancy cheeses.

"What's wrong, Lizzie?" Devan asked.

"Nothing. I'm fine," she answered as she glanced over at Grant, who had yet to acknowledge her arrival. "Maybe I should have just had you to drop me off at the hotel. I'm a little tired."

"Oh, no, you don't!" Devan joked. "You aren't leaving me here with all these men." She looked over at the handsome man who had gained the attention of their friends. He seemed intelligent and ambitious, so she didn't understand what was wrong with Lizzie, his wife. She fought the urge to bring his neglectfulness to his attention. *One day, that woman is going to find someone better,* she thought.

Henry walked back over to them and took Lizzie by the arm. "Come on over and allow me to introduce you, dear," he said.

Devan joined them as they mingled through the crowd.

"Hello, darling," Grant said, finally noticing her. "Did you have a nice day?"

"We certainly did," Devan spoke up. "If at all possible, I'd love to show her some more of our lovely island tomorrow."

"We'll see what tomorrow brings," he said, wrapping his arm around Lizzie's waist. "You look tired."

"I'm fine."

"Gentlemen, this is my lovely wife, Elizabeth," Grant said. They all introduced themselves and continued to mingle throughout the grounds. "Shall we call it a day?" Grant asked.

"I'm sure you're tired too," Lizzie said. "Whatever you want to do is fine with me."

Grant led her by the waist, back over to their hosts. "It has been a great day, Henry," he said. "The course is one of the best I've played."

"Glad you enjoyed it. I see you have a few interested investors out there. Would you care to make a presentation to us before you head back to Atlanta?"

"Perhaps I would. I'll get back in touch. For now, I suppose I should get my wife back to the hotel for some rest."

"I'll have the car pull around," Henry said, looking a bit perplexed. "I look forward to your call."

The ride home was a solemn one. Lizzie couldn't help but wonder if he somehow knew about the fried food. Even more than that, she dreaded being alone with him.

The short ride back to their hotel was over before she knew it, and she just stared as Grant slid his keycard through the slot to gain entry to their suite. She walked in without saying anything and went over to sit on the sofa.

"What did you do today?" he asked rudely.

"Devan showed me a very nice time. We went to a local art museum and—"

"Did she pummel you with questions?"

"What? Certainly not. Why would you ask me that?"

"I can ask you anything I damn well, please. You are my wife."

"She was gracious and friendly," Lizzie said flatly. "I thought you'd be pleased and in a good mood since you've landed some more interested investors."

"They are so damn arrogant," Grant continued in a rage. "They must have asked me a thousand questions. Who gets that fucking inquisitive about a sure thing?"

"Grant, they aren't doctors like you. Perhaps they just didn't understand. Investors need to be confident in their rate of return. Surely you understand that."

"Ha!" Grant said sarcastically, followed by a loud, feigned laugh. "Rate of return? What do know about that, Elizabeth? Did your daddy get a rate of return on those nasty goats of his?"

Lizzie stood and pointed her finger in his direction. "How dare you make fun of my father? He was a good man. He never talked to me like you do."

"Nor did he provide for you as I do!" Grant barked, grabbing her finger and pushing her back onto the couch. "I will not stand for you talking to me in such a disrespectful manner."

"Respect goes both ways, Doctor!" Lizzie shouted, standing again and walking toward the bedroom.

Grant spun her around to face him. "Let's get something straight, Elizabeth. You will respect me!"

"It's Lizzie. My name is Lizzie."

Grant slapped her hard across the face, then once again for good measure. "You will answer to whatever I choose to call you."

Chapter 24

Clara and Iris left thirty minutes early for their lunch meeting with Christi Cates; they wanted to ensure they weren't followed to the local Cracker Barrel restaurant. It was crowded, as usual at the lunch hour, so they mingled around and shopped in the country store while they waited on her.

Christi arrived early and appeared anxious as she walked through the door.

Iris flagged her down from the back, near the restrooms. "Go in the ladies' room," she told her. "I'll stand guard, to make sure no one suspicious comes in behind you."

The young girl did as she was asked, and Iris stood to watch over the door while Clara checked in with the hostess to get a table for the three of them. Five minutes passed before Iris led their young guest to the table.

"What's this all about?" Christi asked, getting straight to the point. "I'm really not comfortable with this, and I'm missing class. If you don't know anything, you're wasting our time."

"I'm sorry," Clara said. "This is all so crazy, but I had to talk to you. I work for Dr. Chatsworth, in one of his offices. I'm not sure what's going on at the Research Center, but it isn't on the up and up. I am afraid something might have happened to your friend."

"I was afraid of that," she said, her hands shaking slightly as she picked up her glass of water. "Initially, he was so excited about the position, flattered that he was selected for it. He moved here solely for that purpose. I completed my undergrad studies with him at Duke, so when he found out I was here, he asked if I needed a roommate. There was only a two-bedroom apartment available at the complex when I moved in, so I took it. It was really out of my price range, so I was grateful that Albert could split expenses and rent with me."

"You say he was excited and flattered *initially*?" Clara said. "Did something change that?"

"Yes, I'm afraid so. He started noticing things that just didn't seem to make sense. He said they weren't following standard protocols for facilities such as theirs. He completed several internships during his undergrad studies, and he said Cardiac Care was cutting corners. He brought it to their attention on numerous occasions, but I guess his concerns fell on deaf ears because nothing ever changed. Albert wanted to quit, but he had just incurred the expenses of relocating and couldn't afford to leave the job."

"You said in your message that he normally stays in close contact with you."

"Albert always calls. We're just friends, but he always lets me know when he's gonna be late or out for the evening. He'd never leave me to worry like this over his whereabouts. I'm sure something is very wrong. Did you say you think something happened to him?"

"Oh dear," Clara said. "Something is going on over at that Research Facility. I'm afraid Albert may have asked too many questions, and they didn't like it. One of the men who works there was following you."

Christi gasped. "What?! Who?"

"Do you remember the man who approached you at the mailboxes at your apartment, when your friends came up and asked you to go out for pizza?"

"Yes. He made me very uncomfortable. How do you know about that?"

"Because we were following him."

Christi grabbed her purse, her face mirroring distrust. "Fine, but why were *you* at my apartment?"

"Please don't be afraid of us, Christi," Clara said calmly. "I'm trying to get to the bottom of this, just like I know you want to, for the sake of your friend. I was at the office when you left your message, and I knew something must have happened to your friend. When we were leaving that day, that large man was just coming into the office, even though it was closed for the day. We decided to follow him. It just so happened that the big goon went to your apartment."

"I'm not sure who to trust. I don't mean to be disrespectful. I just need some time to think about this. I'll stay at a friend's house until I find out where Albert is. Can I have a number to contact you?"

106

Clara pulled out a pen and wrote her cell and home numbers on a paper napkin. "You can trust us, honey. Just promise me you'll be careful."

Christi nodded at them both and walked out of the restaurant.

"I have to get back to work," Clara told Iris. "I'll drop you off at home. Just to be safe, don't call the office today. I'll let you know if anything else happens."

Chapter 25

"Why do you make me do that, Elizabeth?" Grant demanded. "Why do I have to hit you for you to understand me?"

Lizzie held her hand over her face, the heat still radiating from the blow.

"Just go lie down," he commanded hatefully. "Now you'll have to stay hidden away like a defiant child for the remainder of the trip. Just look at your face!"

Tears sprang up in her eyes, but she refused to let them flow; she wouldn't give him the pleasure or the satisfaction. Lizzie got up and walked into the bedroom, slipped out of her clothes, and squirmed in between the sheets. She adamantly refused to give him even an ounce more of pleasure at her own expense. The time had come: She had to get away at any cost. Just a few more days and they would return to Atlanta. Then she would leave, and he would never find her or their baby.

She listened intently as Grant talked on his cell phone.

"Put me through to Zahir immediately," he spat into the phone.

Lizzie quietly reached into the nightstand drawer and pulled out the complimentary memo pad and hotel pen. She scribbled "Zahir" across the page and listened for any more names he might mention.

"What's happening there, Zahir?" she heard him ask. "Did Gunnar take care of our little problem?"

"Problem?" That has to be the young man Clara told me about, she thought.

"So he wasn't able to get to the roommate?" Grant continued. "That's not good. I don't like loose ends. Do we have an arrival date on the primates? Good. I'm happy to hear that. I have several potential investors here, but they are too damned inquisitive. I'll make a presentation to them in the next day or so. If they bite, they bite. If not, I'm not too concerned. They may just end up being more trouble than they're worth if you know what I mean."

A few moments of silence followed as Grant listened to Zahir go through a recap of the day's events.

"Tell the employees he just quit and nothing more. If they have any sense at all, they'll keep their mouths shut. No, I'm holding off on the deposit. I've got a bad feeling. I don't have to be here to do that anyway. It won't pose a problem. What is Jean-Luc working on?" He paused just long enough for Lizzie to write the other name down. "All right. I'm going to find an office supply place somewhere on this tourist trap of an island and put this presentation together. I'll be home early," he continued. "Not much reason to be here any longer. Do you feel comfortable with the men transporting the primates from Charleston? We don't need any problems there. Good. See you in a couple of days."

Lizzie quickly placed the memo pad between the mattress and box spring and laid her head on the pillow.

"I'll order dinner in for you," Grant said from the doorway. "Don't get out of bed. I'll have them bring it in for you. I'll dine downstairs."

Lizzie didn't answer. When she heard the suite door close a few minutes later, she closed her eyes. When she opened them again, it was almost noon; she hadn't even heard room service deliver her meal.

She could hear Grant moving around as she sat up in bed.

"I'm going to have a company run some materials off for me," he said. "Then I'm giving a presentation at the country club. Do not answer the phone, and under no circumstances are you to leave the room. I will have lunch brought to you. If I'm later than I anticipate, dinner will be sent up as well. Do you understand, Elizabeth?"

"Yes."

"Very well. You can start packing too. We are leaving in the morning. I can't even take a vacation without you ruining it."

Grant had been gone less than ten minutes when the phone rang. Lizzie was sure it was a trap, so she simply let it ring, refusing to be caught in his cat-and-mouse games.

She got up and made her way into the bathroom to assess the damage to her face. It wasn't nearly as bad as the last time he had hit her, but her cheek was already bruising and swollen. *At least it wasn't my eye,* she thought. She ran a hot bath for herself and soaked until the water went cold, then dressed in a pair of shorts.

She thought of going downstairs to e-mail Clara but didn't dare, realizing it was far too risky. Instead, she went out on the balcony and watched the tourists enjoying the waves.

A light knock sounded at the door, then grew louder.

Room service, she thought as she made her way to answer it. When she cracked the door, much to her surprise, she found Devan Solomon standing there. "What are you doing here? Grant will kill me."

Devan pushed the door open enough for her to enter. "What is going on, Lizzie? What happened to your face?"

"It's nothing. I fell last night."

"You can't be serious. Please talk to me."

"Devan, you have to leave. You will only make more trouble for me."

"Please just let me help you."

"You can't. I'll be fine. We're leaving tomorrow."

"Your husband is making a presentation this afternoon. Let's go have lunch and talk about this."

"There is nothing to talk about. Grant is under a lot of pressure. He has two offices and this Research Facility to contend with. He is burning the candle at both ends, and it's taking a toll on him."

"And hitting you makes it better?"

"It's not like that. Really, you need to leave. If he finds out you've seen me like this... Well, he'll be very angry."

"Angry enough to hit you again?"

Lizzie sat down on the couch and burst into tears. "Don't you understand? You being here isn't good for me!"

"Okay, okay. I get it, but please just let me stay a few minutes. I won't judge you. He's probably at the country club by now, and they'll keep him busy."

Lizzie patted the couch beside her. "Sit down. I'll be fine in a minute."

"I've never been in the presidential suite. This is very nice. I'm glad we had some time together yesterday."

"Me too. Do you ever get to Atlanta?"

"I don't get to the States very often, but I do like it there. I like to shop in New York around Christmastime."

"Yes, me too. I love Rockefeller Center, with the ice skaters and beautiful decorations."

"See? You're smiling," Devan said soothingly. "If you could do anything you wanted, what would you do?" she asked.

Lizzie closed her eyes and thought. "I would talk to my sister, Maggie."

"I'm sorry. Did she pass away?"

"No. She's fine. I just don't get to talk to her much anymore."

"There's no time like the present. Just pick up your phone and call."

"She's probably busy. I'll call her later."

"Don't put it off, Lizzie. Just call her. I'll feel better if I know you talked to her."

"I-I don't have a cell phone."

"What?! For the love of God, you've got to be kidding me. Here. Use mine and call your sister. I'll go out on the balcony to give you some privacy." She handed her phone over to Lizzie and, as promised, sat outside on the balcony while she phoned.

Lizzie was nervous, not sure what she would say if Maggie even answered.

"Hello?" It was Maggie's voice, that sweet, Southern voice Lizzie had missed so much.

"Maggie? It's me, Lizzie."

"Lizzie?! I'm so happy to hear from you. How are you?"

"I'm okay. How are the boys?"

"Driving me crazy," she said with a giggle. "Why don't you come and visit them?"

The tears started, and Lizzie cleared her throat in an attempt to mask her emotions. "I'd like that very much."

"Lizzie, are you all right? You sound upset."

"It's Grant," she finally said, her voice cracking. "I have to get away, Maggie. I'm afraid."

"I'll come get you," Maggie quickly said. "I can be there in the morning. I'll have one of my friends watch the kids."

"No, no, that's not necessary. We're in the Caymans right now, but we're flying home tomorrow. I'm not sure when I can get away, but I'll make it happen. Would it be okay if I stay with you for a while?"

111

"You know you don't have to ask. We have a guesthouse out back, with plenty of room. Are you going to be okay?"

"Yes, I'll be fine, but please don't call me, Maggie. Also, if you hear from Grant, don't tell him I called you. Promise?"

"That sounds pretty serious. You're scaring me, Lizzie."

"Just promise me, Maggie."

"I promise."

Chapter 26

Christi Cates parked in the Georgia State University parking deck, grabbed her backpack, and started to walk to her evening class. So many thoughts were running through her head that she wasn't sure how she was going to concentrate on the professor's lecture.

The old ladies seemed harmless enough to her, but they sure did know a lot about the guy who had followed her. She just wasn't sure how they could help her find Albert. At the very least, they would hold her back, so she decided against contacting them again.

Christi opened the door to the staircase and made her way down to the next level. As she did, she heard the door open above her. She hated parking decks, especially at night. She pulled out her pepper spray and broke into a jog until she reached the bottom floor. She opened the door marked with an enormous "1" only to be met by a large man. Her first instinct was to spray the mace, but his hand grabbed it before she could bring it up to his face.

"Hey! Hold on there," the young black man said with a nervous chuckle. "Do you pepper spray everyone who uses the same staircase as you?"

"I'm so sorry," Christi said. "I wasn't expecting anyone to be there."

"No problem. At least you're prepared. Women can never be too careful."

"So they say," she answered uneasily. "Again, my apologies."

Grateful for the cool night air, she exited the parking area and started her walk up Decatur Street, toward the Urban Life building. Her heart was still racing from the encounter with the young man, and she had to laugh at herself. She'd been feeling terrified since Albert's strange disappearance, and the two ladies hadn't *helped. Damn Albert anyway. All he had to do was call.*

As she neared the intersection of Decatur Street and Piedmont Avenue, a man stepped out from behind a telephone pole. "Going to class, Christi?" he asked in a deep, accented voice.

"Who are you?" she demanded, then turned to sidestep him and cross the street.

"Oh, no, you don't," he said quietly. In a blur, he grabbed her arm and began to lead her down Piedmont. "You're coming with me. Albert wants to see you."

"Let go of me, mister!" she screamed.

A few students glanced her way but continued on to their destinations.

He lifted his shirt to show a large, shiny handgun tucked in his waistband. "You don't want me to shoot you right here, do you?"

Christi had seen enough crime shows to know he would be a fool to gun her down there, in plain sight of so many witnesses. On the other hand, if he managed to get her into a dark alley or a car, she was sure she wouldn't live to tell the tale. She elbowed him in the gut as hard as she could; it didn't have much effect, other than to startle him, but it gave her the head start she needed. She ran down Piedmont and took a left on Gilmer Street, allowing the backpack that was weighing her down to fall to the sidewalk. She was putting more and more distance between herself and the crowd heading to class, but she couldn't do anything about that. She ran between cars in a parking lot and sank down behind a large SUV, hoping to lose him.

"Christi? Where are you?" she heard him calling as his heavy boots clomped around the lot.

She held her breath until she felt her lungs would burst. Just when it sounded like his boots were headed in another direction, an old Toyota pulled into the lot, circled around, then parked adjacent to her. A young girl, no older than twenty, opened her door, gathered her belongings for class, and got out of the car. She looked at Christi curiously when she noticed her crouching there.

"Please," Christi whispered. "Don't say anything. Just keep walking."

She clearly startled the young woman, and waving her away with her hands wasn't working.

"Are you okay?" the girl asked.

Christi's head dropped, knowing the girl was leading the man right back to her.

"No, she isn't okay," he said loudly. "This is not her day."

The girl reached for her chest to indicate she'd been startled yet again, then quickly made her way back to the safety of her Toyota.

114

"No you don't, honey," the man with the accent said. "You just happen to be at the wrong place at the wrong time." He reached for her and wrapped his arm around her neck, putting her in a headlock. An attempt at a scream was quickly muted by gasps for life-sustaining air.

As the girl's body fell limp, Christi was jolted back to her senses, gathering her wits enough to make another escape attempt. She made her way out of the lot and was heading back down the sidewalk when she saw him running toward her. Christi knew she'd never be able to outrun him, her only chance was to cross Gilmer and head to Courtland Street where there would be more people. She glanced back one more time and saw that he was quickly closing the gap between them. She jumped off the sidewalk and started across the street just as she heard brakes squealing, followed by a loud *thud*, a noise that resonated when the MARTA transit bus hit her small body and threw it twenty yards down the street.

****

"Clara," Iris said, looking up from her beef stew that the two women were enjoying for dinner, "turn the TV up. There's some kind of breaking news, and I wanna hear it."

Clara reached for the remote and turned the volume up on the small set in Iris's kitchen.

"Fox 5 breaking news... A body, found by a group of rafters has been recovered from the Chattahoochee River. Details at 11:00..."

Chapter 27

Maggie sat at her kitchen table, nursing the scolding-hot mug of coffee and worrying about her sister. Ever since Lizzie's marriage to Grant Chatsworth, the two had lost touch, often for months at a time. That had always bothered Maggie, but something had made her feel that Lizzie's life was better, or at least easier when her past was not involved.

She had never really liked the handsome doctor, but he seemed to make her sister happy, and that was all Maggie could ask for. Somewhere throughout the years, her life had become so busy that she pushed worrying about her little sister to the back of her mind. She always knew Lizzie would contact her if she ever needed her. Now she'd done just that, and it didn't sound good at all. Maggie wanted nothing more than to drive to Atlanta and bring her sister back with her, but something in Lizzie's voice had told her that wouldn't be the best idea. "She sounded so terrified," Maggie said, and a shiver ran through her body as she recalled the phone conversation. *"Don't tell Grant you have heard from me… Promise me, Maggie." Why would he not want Lizzie to talk to her own sister? Is Lizzie's life in danger?* Maggie made up her mind then and there that if she didn't hear from Lizzie in two more days, she would go and get her herself.

She got up and poured the remaining coffee in the sink, then placed the cup in the dishwasher. She glanced at her watch as she would continuously for the next two hours. Maddox and Mason, her twin sons, had just started preschool at the Presbyterian Church, and she always worried that she'd be late to pick them up. It was only two days a week, but it got the four-year-olds out of the house and allowed them to socialize with other children. She knew that was important, for they would start school soon enough.

The old house was starting to grow chilly, so she walked through the living room and adjusted the thermostat. She and her husband Leland had a beautiful home, one that had been handed down through the Knox family. She fell in love with the place the instant she saw it. The large antebellum home had wraparound porches and high ceilings, fabulous wooden floors, and expansive rooms. They had recently remodeled, but none of the upgrades compromised the historical appearance of the home.

Maggie reached into the desk drawer to grab the key to the guesthouse, wrapped a shawl over her shoulders, and made her way out back. The small cottage was rarely used, but Mabel, their housekeeper, still cleaned it twice a month. Although it certainly wasn't what Lizzie was accustomed to, it was an adequate and quaint space, and Maggie was sure she would like it.

The fresh scent of Pine-Sol greeted her as she opened the door, letting her know it was cleaning week for the living space. The cottage was only 800 square feet, but the open floor plan made it seem larger. The den opened to a well-equipped kitchen, and large windows let the morning sunlight stream in. The walls were painted white, and the bright yellow couches cheered the space up. A small half-bath was located off the den, and two small bedrooms were intersected by a Jack and Jill bath.

Maggie checked the bedrooms and found them to be spic and span. She had recently purchased new duvets and sheets for both rooms, so there was really nothing she needed to do to prepare it for Lizzie. *Maybe a few fresh flowers and some groceries will give it a homey feel for her,* she thought.

For now, she could only wait and pray that her sister would be safe. Maggie had no idea what was going on, but she would certainly feel better when her sister made it to Biloxi.

Chapter 28

Lizzie had never been happier to see the large mansion. It had been a long, eerily silent flight home, and she just wanted a hot bath and her bed. She was exhausted.

Rufus met them at the door as soon as the car came to a stop.

As he grabbed their luggage, Flossie was right behind him. "There are warm sandwiches on the dining room table for you," she told Grant and Lizzie.

"Let's get something to eat, Elizabeth," Grant said, anger amazingly absent from his voice.

She wanted nothing more than to go upstairs, but she did as he commanded.

His mood had suddenly lightened, and he even took the time to pull her chair out for her.

Flossie pretended not to notice the bruising on her cheek as she filled iced tea glasses for them both.

"I suppose I'll make a trip to the Research Facility this afternoon. The primates are supposed to come in today."

"That's exciting," Lizzie quickly added, pretending to care.

"It will allow us to begin the animal-testing portion of our research, which will carry us closer to our goal. I'm expecting several men from the Caymans to invest. The trip did not turn out to be a total waste of time and money after all."

"I'm glad to hear that. I need to return one of the outfits I bought though. Can I have my car keys, Grant?"

"Not just yet, Elizabeth. I want to keep an eye on you for a week or so. That fainting spell really made me nervous," he said. "Just stay around the house this week. Hopefully, you will feel better soon. Flossie, come pick up these plates now. We're finished."

Flossie was there in an instant and began removing the dishes. She offered something sweet for dessert.

"No, there won't be any need for that," Grant said. "We ate far too much in the Caymans. Don't plan on me for dinner either, I'll be late. We'll be having a dinner party Friday night. Would you like to cook, or should I have Elizabeth contact Antoine for catering?"

Please pick Antoine, Lizzie prayed silently.

"How many guests are you expecting?"

"Sixteen, including Elizabeth and me."

"And what sort of menu do you have in mind, Doctor?"

"I'm not sure. Forget it. I'll just have Clara contact Antoine. I do know we'll need light hors d'oeuvres and a bartender. It's probably best that he handle it all."

"Very well," Flossie answered. "Have a nice day."

Lizzie stood and pushed her chair in. "I think I'll start unpacking," she said.

Grant kissed her cheek. "Just rest, dear. Flossie can take care of that or have someone else do it for you."

"I don't want anyone else touching my things," Lizzie wanted to say but kept quiet about it. "Maybe I'll finish those books Clara sent. Please thank her for me and ask if she has any more."

"I told you I'd buy a Kindle for you. I don't want you reading out of those worn-out, hand-me-down paperbacks when we can afford better."

"That would be nice," she answered. "I'm going to take a bath. I'll see you later tonight."

"Don't wait up, Elizabeth."

****

Grant's cell phone rang before he could get to the Research Facility. "Yeah?" he answered impatiently.

"Good afternoon, Sir," Zahir said. "Am I to assume you are back in the country?"

"Yes. I'm actually heading your way now. Tell me there isn't another problem."

"Well, nothing that cannot wait until you arrive. I'll meet you in the lobby."

"Very well," Grant answered, frustration already boiling inside him. If he had it to do over again, he wouldn't have hired any of them. They were like children he had to lead around by the hand, and he was ready to strangle them all.

He parked in his reserved space right up front, gathered his briefcase, and made his way to the main entrance. The young receptionist was the first person he saw, and she waved wildly, offering a cheery hello. Grant had never been a fan of the girl; he felt she was far too young for the position, and her perkiness grated on his nerves. Nevertheless, Jean-Luc had insisted they hire her because she knew just enough about computers to handle what little data entry they gave her but not enough to recognize any discrepancies. Either way, Grant felt a sense of dread every time he heard her mousy voice.

"Good afternoon, Doctor," Dr. Zahir Chavan said as he made his way across the lobby. "Your trip must have gone quite well. I've received numerous calls from your new comrades in the Caymans, concerning our work and research. They seem to be quite interested."

"They are a little too intrusive for my taste, but I suppose that's called for where money is concerned. I take it you gave them what they asked for?"

"Certainly. They seem most excited about the arrival of the rhesus monkeys."

"So they've arrived? Can I see them?"

"They should be here within the hour. They had to load them during the night hours to avoid being seen. Importers can only bring live nonhuman primates through ports of entry that have CDC quarantine stations. It was quite a concern in Charleston as it is such a busy port."

"Any problems getting past the port authority?"

"None that we are aware of. I understand that the primates are all quite large. We have six males and two females."

"And the cages are ready?"

"Yes, construction is complete. We have everything required for their diet, including roots, fruit, seeds, bark, and pine needles. They should be fine."

"Glad to hear it. Now, what is this problem you need to talk to me about? I'm not sure I even want to hear it."

Zahir took a deep breath before he began. "It's...Albert Tinsley."

"What about him? I thought we remedied that."

120

"His body was recovered from the river. He has been taken to the Fulton County medical examiner's office for an autopsy."

"Shit. When did they find him?"

"Last night."

"Then I don't really see a problem. By now, he's got to be badly decomposed. More than likely, they'll chalk it up to accidental drowning or jumping to his death. I'm not concerned. Other than tying him to us by his employment here, there is no cause for concern."

"Doctor, they'll know he didn't die from drowning. He was…dead already, so there won't be any water in his lungs."

"The current can force water into the lungs, even if someone is not breathing. Either way, I'm not worried. I don't believe they'll suspect foul play, and if they do, we'll be the last people on the list."

"Very well then."

"I'm going up to my office," Grant said. "I'll be there, should you need me."

"I'll alert you as soon as the primates arrive."

****

Over three hours later, the ventilated box trucks arrived with their cargo. The four men chosen by Zahir to make the trip were exhausted. The primates were transferred from the temporary cages to their new living quarters quickly, and all seemed to be in fairly good health, considering their long, dark journey taken in the belly of the cargo ship. That was the good news, but the bad news would inevitably have to be delivered to Dr. Chatsworth.

Zahir and Jean-Luc walked together to his office, both dreading the encounter and knowing he would be anything but happy. Their short knock on the door was followed by his curt order to enter.

"I take it the primates were delivered?"

"Yes, Sir, they were," Jean-Luc answered, uneasily shifting his weight from one foot to the other.

"Well, spit it out. Why do you look like someone just ran over your puppy?"

"The primates appear to be in good health, except for being dehydrated and hungry. The problem is that Miguel was bitten twice on the forearm during the transport."

"Son-of-a-bitch! Zahir, didn't you tell them all to take proper precautions?"

"We went over the safety instructions, again and again, Doctor," Zahir said quietly, clearly defeated.

"Were they all made aware of the fact that these particular primates carry the Herpes B virus?"

"Yes. They were warned many times to be extremely careful."

"How deep are the bites?" Grant asked.

"The incisors broke the skin and went fairly deep. Instead of cleaning the wounds thoroughly when it happened, he simply wrapped his arm with a dirty towel they found in the truck."

"You've got to be shitting me! The odds of him not contracting the virus are virtually nil."

"What do we do now?" Jean-Luc asked. "If he suffers symptoms and goes to the hospital, we will be fined excessively and imprisoned, to say nothing of what would happen to our research. This is very bad, very bad indeed."

"You aren't kidding, it's bad. Go downstairs and clean and sanitize the wound. Put some antibiotic cream on it and give him a bottle of antibiotics and a couple of Tylenol. You two keep a close watch over him the next couple of weeks. Hell, it could take up to a month for symptoms to appear, but I don't think that will be the case. If the bites are that deep and went a long period without being flushed and treated, he will be ill fairly soon if he contracts it. Assure him that we can treat him, should he get sick. I doubt he's responsible or wealthy enough to carry health insurance, or else he wouldn't have been picking up monkeys in the middle of the night. Reassure him we'll treat him free of charge and tell him not to waste his money at a doctor or hospital."

"I'll get on it right away, Doctor," Jean-Luc said.

"You do that... and Zahir, I need to see any information you faxed to our friends in the Caymans.

I need to be abreast of any and all correspondence."

"I'll have it to you in a few minutes," Zahir answered, grateful to have a reason to leave his boss's office.

Chapter 29

After the last of the patients had gone for the day, Clara sat down at the front desk and went through the daily deposit. She was thankful that she could add over $200 in cash to Lizzie's pot. It was growing every day but still hadn't quite reached the $2,000 she was aiming for. She got out a new deposit slip, made the changes to the deposit total, and then picked up the office phone to call Iris.

"Hello?"

"Hey there. It's me. Have you heard from Christi yet?"

"Not a word. It's a little concerning. I figured it'd only take her a day or so to figure out she can trust us. She shoulda phoned by now."

"You're right. I don't like it."

"I think I'll give her a call. Even if she doesn't wanna talk to us, at least we'll know she's okay."

"Good idea, Iris. I'll wait at the office. Call me when you get her."

Iris dug through her purse and retrieved the girl's number.

After several rings and just when she was about to hang up, a deep voice answered, "Yes?"

The male voice took Iris by surprise, and for a moment, she didn't respond at all. "Oh! I must have the wrong number. Sorry," she finally said.

"No, wait. Who are you trying to reach?"

"Christi, Christi Cates."

"Are you a relative?"

A feeling of dread washed over her. "Not exactly. I'm just…a friend. Is she all right?"

"This is Detective Pitts, with the Atlanta Police Department. There's been an accident, Ma'am. She was hit by a bus and taken to Grady Memorial Hospital."

"Oh, dear! Is she going to be okay?"

"I can't tell you one way or the other. She's at the best trauma center in the state. At the moment that's about the best news I can give you."

"Why do you have her phone?"

"It was found a couple of blocks from the scene, in her backpack."

"A couple of blocks, you say? From the scene? I'm afraid I don't understand."

"Witnesses saw her running down the street before she darted in front of the bus. She must have dropped the backpack along the way. Identification inside the bag led us to her identity."

"I see," was all Iris could think to say. "Thank you for your time, Detective Pitts." She hung up and immediately dialed Clara. "You aren't going to believe this."

"What is it, Iris? Calm down."

"It's Christi. She was hit by a bus."

"Oh, my goodness! Is she okay?"

"No, I don't think so. She's been taken to Grady, but that's not the worst part. She was running, even dropped her backpack a couple of blocks before she was hit."

"How do you know that?"

"A detective answered her cell phone. This smells bad, Clara. I bet that man was after her. We have to go visit her."

"I'm not sure if now's a good time. I'm sure her family is there with her."

"I'm going. You can come with me or not."

"Okay, okay. I have to make the daily deposit, and then I'll be home. Give me thirty minutes."

Clara sat at the desk for a few minutes, running the story through her head over and over again. She and Iris were getting too close. She knew if they visited Christi at the hospital, there was a very big chance they would be seen by someone who was involved. It was too risky. She decided instead to call the hospital and ask about the young woman's condition. She pulled out the large Atlanta phone book, looked up the number, and called.

"Grady Memorial Hospital. How may I direct your call?"

"I'm calling to inquire about a patient's condition."

"Name please."

"Christi Cates, with a C."

Clara could hear the woman running her fingers across the keyboard. "Hold, please. I am transferring you to the Intensive Care Unit."

Clara waited patiently as she listened to the soft music meant to entertain her while she was on hold.

There was only a short delay before a charge nurse answered the call. "ICU, Nurse Emerson speaking."

"Yes, Nurse Emerson. I'm calling to ask about one of your patients. Her name is Christi Cates."

"Are you a relative of Miss Cates's?"

"No, I'm not," Clara answered, fully aware that the honest answer would limit what the nurse could tell her. "I'm a family friend, though, and I'm quite concerned about her."

"I'm sure you are. Christi is stable at the moment. Her brother Justin has been contacted and is trying to get a ride here from college. Hopefully, he'll make it soon."

"That's good news. I somehow misplaced Justin's number. Could I possibly get it from you?"

"I suppose I can give it to you, Ms...?"

"Harkins, Mrs. Harkins," Clara answered. Her hands shook uncontrollably; she'd never been as comfortable telling fibs as Iris was. She was surprised, however, that she never missed a beat when coming up with the false name.

Nurse Emerson rattled off Justin Cates's cell phone number, and Clara quickly ended the call.

"Oh, good heavens! I'm really losing my mind!" she said to herself as she gathered up her belongings and made her way to her car. "None of this can possibly end well."

She stopped by the bank, picked up a bucket of chicken and two sides from KFC, and drove to Iris's house. She had no doubt that her friend would be waiting right by the window, watching for her to pull up.

Clara wasn't even completely out of the car before Iris came bolting out of her house. "What took you so darn long? I've been calling the office," she said.

"Iris, I told you I had to stop by the bank, and I picked up some dinner. Help me get it out of the car."

Iris did as Clara asked but clearly wasn't happy about it. "I figured we'd just grab a bite *after* we go to the hospital."

"We can't go to the hospital and visit that girl, Iris. If you don't watch out, we'll both be up there in Grady with her. Let's sit down at the table. I want to talk to you."

The heavy meal helped to calm Iris and make her a little more reasonable. "I say we go talk to this Detective Pitts, the one who has her phone. We need to tell him she could be in danger."

"Let's think this through first. What do we really have to tell him? I followed a stranger because I recognized his voice while hiding in my boss's bathroom and felt he might be a killer because we hacked into my boss's e-mail? Think about it, Iris. It doesn't sound good. There's also the fact that we haven't seen him do anything illegal."

"Yes, but we saw him drive to Christi's apartment."

"But he didn't do anything but walk up to her then. Her friends showed up, and she went out for pizza. He could've been there to ask about Albert Tinsley's absences from work, for all we know. Going to the police might backfire. It could bring attention to us, and we don't need Dr. Chatsworth to find out what we're doing. I agree that she's in danger, but I think our best bet is to contact her brother."

"Brother? How do you know she has a brother?"

"I called the hospital and claimed to be a family friend. They gave me his number. Apparently, this Justin is a college student, too, and he's trying to catch a ride here to check on her."

"Call him!"

"What are we gonna say, Iris? I don't want to alarm him."

"The girl needs someone with her, Clara. Maybe we can help him get here. Gimme the number, and I'll call him myself."

"Oh, no, you don't! *I'll* make the call. None of this is going well, and I'm not comfortable with any of it, but I do agree that Christi needs someone with her right now. Nobody should be alone in the hospital." Clara found the number and, against her better judgment, made the call.

"Hello?"

"Is this Justin Cates?"

"Yes," he answered, concern apparent in his voice. "Who's this?"

"Everything is fine, dear," Clara answered quickly. "I got your number from the hospital. I know your sister and wanted to see if we can help you get here to see her."

"Oh okay. I'm at West Georgia College right now, but a frat buddy is gonna drive me to Atlanta in the morning. I talked to my professors and plan to stay for a couple of weeks. I guess I'll just stay at Christi's apartment."

Clara didn't like the idea of that, but she didn't want to tell him so just yet.

"How did you say you know my sister?"

"Justin, this is all going to sound a little strange, but I work for a cardiologist in Atlanta. I'm a nurse. Your sister called our office when she grew concerned about her roommate, Albert after he failed to check in with her for a couple of days. He works for my boss as well. I also had a bad feeling about her roommate, so the two of us met to discuss it. I don't want to alarm you, but your sister may be in danger."

"In danger? Can you go to the police then? And someone should be with her."

"That's the thing. We don't have any proof, and right now, going to the police could have...an adverse effect."

"I don't understand," Justin said. He sounded awfully young, and it tore at Clara's heart.

"I don't expect you to trust me," she said kindly. "I'll be happy to meet with you when you get here. Just please don't say anything to anyone right now. The most important thing is to be there for Christi."

Chapter 30

Lizzie took a long, hot bath and a two-hour nap. She was exhausted from the trip but knew that now, more than ever, she had to focus on what she needed to do. She glanced at the clock on her nightstand and noticed it was after 4:00; Santiago and the other house staff would be leaving soon. Flossie, on the other hand, had her own quarters off the left wing of the estate.

She was just throwing on a pair of jeans when the doorbell rang. She pulled a sweater over her head and walked down the winding stairway to see who the visitor was. If they had gotten past Cornell at the gate, then their business was legitimate.

Lizzie was thrilled to hear Antoine's voice as he greeted Flossie, then looked up the staircase to address her. "My, my! Aren't you a sight for sore eyes, Lizzie?" he said with a smile. "You are just as brown as a berry. It looks like the vacation agreed with you."

"Yes, it was a nice getaway." She smiled, turning her head to hide the bruising. "Are you here to plan the dinner party?"

"I am indeed. Fortunately, I had a last-minute cancelation. It seems there's a bad stomach bug floating around the city, which worked to your benefit. Where would you like to meet? The dining room as usual?"

"Let's sit in the living room this time," Lizzie said, waving her hand in the direction of one of the many sitting areas in the home.

"What can I bring you?" Flossie asked. "I have some fresh lemonade."

"That sounds delightful," Lizzie answered. "Would you care for some, Antoine?"

"Yes, thank you."

The two made their way into the living room and made themselves comfortable with Lizzie on the sofa and Antoine in a wingback chair. He noticed the bruising on her cheek and was about to ask about it when he heard Flossie coming with their drinks. Lizzie put her index finger over her lips to silence his inquiries. Flossie laid the silver tray in front of them on the coffee table. It contained a delightful array: a pitcher of lemonade, two glasses, and a plate of cranberry oatmeal cookies. Once she poured their glasses full, she let herself out. They listened intently until her footsteps were silent.

"So I take it the vacation was not that wonderful?" he asked sarcastically. "Lizzie, what's going on?"

"He's under too much pressure, Antoine. I've been resigned to my fate, but now it's worse than it's ever been."

"You can't let that man beat on you, child. Just divorce him, move on, and never look back."

"I don't think Grant will take too kindly to that. Antoine, I need to get out of here."

"You mean *escape*? Girl, you better take him to court and get you some money," he said, his waxed eyebrows jumping up and down on his face.

"I don't care about the money. I just want out of here."

"You only *think* you don't care about the money, Lizzie. How will you survive? Where will you go?"

"I'm pretty sure I'm going to my sister's. I just have to find a way to get out of here. He has me on lockdown like a prisoner."

They could hear Flossie coming back down the hall, and Antoine quickly changed the subject. "So, there will be sixteen guests? Do you have a preference for the menu?"

"I always leave that up to you, and you've never let us down," Lizzie answered.

"I brought some extra ice for the lemonade," Flossie said as she made her way into the room. "I just made it, and it hasn't had time to chill in the refrigerator."

Antoine glanced up at her, then lifted his pen over his paper. "I'm thinking chilled seafood for the hors d'oeuvres, shrimp cocktail, fresh oysters on the half-shell, and a variety of cheeses. Assorted breads as well, of course. Does that suit you?" he asked, looking at Lizzie while clearly dismissing Flossie.

The strong hint did not go unnoticed, and Flossie certainly had a distaste for the man.

The situation struck Lizzie as comical and she found herself struggling not to giggle.

Flossie left the room in a silent huff, but neither of them was confident she was out of earshot.

Antoine pointed to his right ear as if to suggest she was somewhere nearby, eavesdropping on their conversation. "Let's see here..." he said. "Let me calculate what all I will need." He scribbled a note on his pad and showed it to Lizzie. "Don't trust her," it read. "She could be trouble."

Lizzie nodded.

They discussed the party menu for another thirty minutes, interrupting periodically with notes to one another.

"Don't just up and leave," he wrote. "You'll only regret it in the end. You deserve something out of this. Can I recommend an attorney?"

"No," Lizzie wrote. "Right now, I need to get out of this situation. It's dire, and I'm afraid."

Antoine stood and fanned himself with the notepad, clearly distressed. *"I wish I could help you,"* he mouthed.

The squeak of Flossie's crepe-soled shoes was present once again.

"Thank you for your time," Lizzie said nonchalantly. "My husband is always pleased with your services. I understand you will be arranging for the bartender as well?"

"Certainly. Everything will be handled promptly. I have a list here for your maid," he said, the twinkle in his eyes evident.

"I think I just heard her nearby," Lizzie said, smiling at Antoine's mischief. "Flossie? Are you out there?"

"Yes, I am here," she answered, clearly perturbed by being summoned. "What do you need?"

"I have some checklists for you," Antoine said, waving the papers boisterously in the air. "Once again, I will have a florist and a company drop off centerpieces and tablecloths, and of course the food will be delivered prior to my arrival."

"Let me see that," Flossie snapped. "Taking care of your job certainly interferes with my own."

"Oh, forgive me. I'm always available to be here to check the items in, but that will up my fee. Dr. Chatsworth suggested you could handle this minor detail. I'd be happy to let him know if you can't."

"You will do no such thing!" Flossie said angrily. "There is no need to worry the busy man. I'll make sure it's handled."

131

"Very well," Antoine said sarcastically. "Enjoy the remainder of your day." With that, he flitted off through the foyer and out the front door, leaving Lizzie struggling not to burst into laughter.

Chapter 31

Clara was standing at the fax machine as she waited on a new patient's medical record to arrive from his out-of-state doctor. Although it was still early on in her work day, she was ready for it to end. She desperately yearned to hear something about Christi Cates. Finally, the pages began spurting out of the machine, and she gathered them as they fell. She heard the office door open but knew that Harper would handle it, so she continued to place the incoming documents in the file.

"Good afternoon. How can I help you?"

"Hello. I'm wondering if I might have a few moments with Dr. Chatsworth. My name is Detective Pitts."

Clara felt the hair on her neck stand up, but she refused to turn around. Instead, she just placed the last faxed page in the file and stepped into the hall. She wanted to ensure he didn't see her face, just in case they crossed paths at the hospital.

"Just a second," she heard Harper say. "I'll see if I can find him."

Clara skirted into a patient's room to take her vitals, making herself unavailable for any inquiries from the young receptionist. When she came out, she saw the back of the detective as he walked toward the doctor's office with Harper.

Dr. Grant Chatsworth looked up nonchalantly from his computer, stood, and offered his right hand to the police officer, who discreetly displayed his badge. "Good afternoon. I have a long list of patients today, Detective, but how can I help you?"

"I won't be long. I just need to ask you a few questions about Albert Tinsley. I understand he was an employee of yours?"

"Yes. Is there a problem?"

"When did you last see Mr. Tinsley, Doctor?"

"It has been over a week ago, I believe. I was out of the country last week, but I understand he hasn't shown up to work in several days. Is he in some kind of trouble?"

"One might say that. We recovered his body from the Chattahoochee."

"Oh, no!" Grant said, his eyes squinting with concern. "I hate to hear that, but it certainly explains his absence from work. We've heard of so many drownings lately."

"Well, it's rare this time of year, especially with the weather getting cooler. Not many folks are out rafting and swimming."

"I appreciate you letting me know. I'll make sure to call his superiors at Cardiac Care Research, where he was employed."

"Do you know of anyone who might have wanted to kill him?"

"Excuse me? I was assuming he drowned. Are you saying someone murdered Albert?"

"Drowning was our initial assumption as well until we got the M.E.'s report. It appears he was strangled, then thrown into the water."

"Was he in the water for very long?"

"Yes. Unfortunately, he was very bloated and had suffered a great deal of decomp."

"Hmm. I'd imagine that would make a cause of death somewhat difficult to determine."

"Not exactly," Detective Pitts said. "Due to the decomposition, some of the usual signs of strangulation weren't present, such as petechial hemorrhaging, but the damage to the hyoid bone left no question. Our M.E. tells us it was almost definitely a homicide."

"Mr. Tinsley hadn't worked for the Research Facility for long. He was a recent recruit. We knew very little about his personal life."

"I understand. However, we were sure you'd want to know."

"Certainly. We appreciate you taking the time to stop by, Detective," Grant said, standing once again to outstretch his hand and end the conversation.

"I may be back in touch, should we have any further questions. Do you have a card?"

"Harper can give you one out front. Have a nice day."

Detective Pitts paused briefly to pick up a business card before exiting the doctor's office. He wasn't quite sure what it was, but something about the doctor rubbed him the wrong way. He got the feeling that the doctor didn't want to accept the strangulation theory.

At any rate, there was certainly no reason to suspect that the murder had anything to do with Albert Tinsley's employer. Nevertheless, the detective had learned long ago never to underestimate the power of his gut.

Chapter 32

Justin Cates grabbed his duffel bag and jumped out of his frat brother's red '66 Mustang. Waving good-bye, he mouthed a silent thanks and walked into Grady Memorial Hospital. A volunteer at the central information desk told him the floor for the ICU and pointed him in the direction of the elevators. He'd missed his parents on many occasions, but this had to top them all.

Grady was one of only a handful Level One trauma centers in Georgia, and it was always filled with hurried visitors and medical staff. The crowd simply made Justin feel more alone.

A beefy man with very large hands held the elevator door for him as he raced to get on. Justin squeezed through a group of nursing students and hit the button for the ICU floor, the elevator's first stop. He stepped off and followed the appropriate signs until he reached double-doors equipped with an intercom button.

"Nurse Emerson. How can I help you?"

"Hello," he stammered, sweat forming on his forehead. "I'm here to see my sister."

"What's your sister's name, Sir?"

"I-I'm sorry. Her name is Christi Cates."

"I'll buzz you in."

An annoying, piercing noise sounded before one of the double-doors cracked open to let him through.

Justin was met by a middle-aged woman with a stern but empathetic look on her face. "I'm Nurse Emerson, the charge nurse. You must be Justin?"

"Yes, I am," he answered nervously. "How is my sister?"

"There hasn't been much change. She's still in a coma, but surgery relieved the fluid on her brain, and the swelling seems to be subsiding. Follow me. I'll take you to her."

Justin wiped his forehead and tightened his grip on the old duffel bag. He hadn't been to the hospital since his parents' car accident several years earlier. Christi was all he had left, and he struggled to fight off the fear of losing her too.

He followed the nurse until she turned into a room across from the nurses' station. Justin stood at the door, fear encompassing his body, paralyzing him and forbidding him from entering. The sound of the respirator breathing in and out for his sister was the first thing to cause him grave concern, followed by the many beeping and blinking machines monitoring her vitals.

Nurse Emerson turned around and encouraged him to come to Christi's bedside. "It's okay, dear. She isn't in any pain."

"She... God, she's so swollen," was all he could say.

Christi didn't even resemble herself. Her head and body were bloated and badly bruised. She had scrapes and cuts all over her arms, and her head was shaved in several places so the doctors could stitch up her wounds. Her eyes were closed, and she appeared to be in a deep slumber.

"Come here, Justin," the nurse urged. "Come hold her hand. I'll bring you a chair. Talk to her. We don't know for sure if she can hear you, but studies show she probably can."

He willed his feet to move and made his way over to his sister's side. Tears began to spill over as he reached for her hand. "Please," he pleaded. "Please come back to me, Christi."

The nurse brought in a chair for him, then let herself out and left them alone for over fifteen minutes. She knew the boy needed time alone to process his sister's accident.

Nurse Emerson hated to do it, but she had promised the detective she would contact him when Christi's brother arrived. She reached him on his cell phone, and he assured her he was only a few blocks away.

She tapped lightly on the door before entering the room again. She found Justin sitting beside the bed with his head down, his sister's hand in his own. "Justin," she began, "I'm sorry to bother you, but a detective is on his way to speak with you. He has a few questions for you."

Justin looked up at her, his eyes weary and sad. "That's fine," he answered. "I'll be right here. I'm not going anywhere till she's okay."

It took Detective Pitts less than ten minutes to get to the hospital, park his vehicle, and ride the elevator up to ICU. Even after years on the job, he still had a bad taste in his mouth for hospitals. It wasn't the blood and guts; rather, the antiseptic smell and sadness seemed to encompass him whenever he visited one.

Nurse Emerson buzzed him in and waved him down the hall when he came through the doors. "He's back there with her," she said, her face reflecting compassion for the two young people.

He knocked twice, then let himself in. The tear-stained cheeks were the first thing he noticed, and the usual knot formed in his throat. "Justin?" he asked.

"Yes, Sir?" he answered, standing awkwardly and offering his right hand.

"I'm Detective Pitts," he said, extending his own hand. "I'm sorry to bother you at a time like this, but I just need to ask you a few questions about your sister, son."

"Not a problem."

"Have you talked to her much prior to her accident?"

"Yep, sure. We talked briefly almost every day. It's just the two of us now. Our parents were killed in a car accident a few years back."

"I'm sorry to hear that. Witnesses said your sister was running from someone just before she was hit by the bus. Was she having problems with anyone, a boyfriend perhaps?"

"No, she didn't have a boyfriend. She was busy with an internship and working on her masters. Do you think someone was trying to mug her? I've told her so many times to take day classes. It isn't safe for her to walk around downtown at night."

"We considered that, but she dropped her backpack a couple of blocks before she got to the scene of the accident. If someone was trying to rob her, they would have taken the backpack and fled. Not only that, but there was a homicide in a nearby parking lot that same night."

"I know she always parked in the campus parking deck," Justin said. "It's cheaper with her student ID. Do you think it's just a crazy person, some psycho out to hurt women?"

"Perhaps. We are looking into every angle. Is there anything else you can think of?"

Justin thought about telling the detective about the call from Clara but decided against it. She had warned him that involving the police too early might make things worse, and by her voice, she seemed like a nice enough lady. "There is one thing," he added. "My sister was very concerned about her roommate. She said she

138

hadn't heard from him in a few days, which is sorta out of character for him."

"Roommate?"

"Yes. Totally platonic and everything. They did their undergrad studies together at Duke. It made me feel better to know he was staying with her, more comfortable to know she wasn't alone."

"What is this roommate's name?"

"Uh…Albert, I think. His last name starts with a T, but I can't think of it right now."

"Albert Tinsley?" the detective asked, shocked by how the pieces were falling together.

"Yes, that's it. How do you know?" Justin asked, unease washing over him.

"We found his body in the Chattahoochee River. He was murdered."

Justin's face turned white, and he slumped back in the chair. "Oh, my God. My sister *is* in danger. I guess that lady was right."

"What lady? What are you talking about?"

"Some lady called me and said I need to be with my sister. She said something about not having any proof, but she's sure Albert was hurt or something. I-I-don't-know, Officer. I can't even think right now," he said, shaking his head. "This is all too much."

"Justin, this is very important. Did the lady give you her name?"

Justin tried to recall the conversation, but what stood out the most was that the lady didn't want him to talk to the police. *Maybe she doesn't think they can be trusted either*, he worried. He knew he had her name and phone number in his bag, but he wasn't ready to share it just yet. "I'm really not sure. I just know she got a message from my sister that she was worried about her roommate. The lady believed Albert was in danger. I don't know her."

"How did she get your number then? Is she a friend of your sisters? It's really important that you try to remember."

Justin struggled to recall the details of the conversation. *"I think going to the police right now could have an adverse effect,"* he remembered her saying. He wasn't sure why she felt that way, but there had to be a reason for it. Justin didn't know why he trusted

139

the woman, but something in her voice had sounded sincere, like a loving grandmother's plea, and he wasn't about to share her name with the detective just yet. "I was very worried about my sister when she called, so I honestly don't remember much about the conversation, Detective. I just figured she's concerned about my sister, so I thanked her and assured her I'd be here this morning. Maybe she'll call me back."

Detective Pitts rubbed his chin, concern apparent on his face. "Would you mind if we have a look around Christi's apartment?"

"I guess it's okay. I can't imagine her having anything to hide."

"I don't want to worry you, but I'm concerned that the death of Albert Tinsley could be tied to your sister's accident. We have to find some common thread."

"Will she be safe here? I'd like to be there when you go through her apartment, but I'm also afraid to leave her here alone. She won't be able to call for help if she needs it," he said, his voice cracking.

"I'll have the Department send someone over to sit outside her door. Her connection with Mr. Tinsley is enough to warrant it for now. She'll be safe here." The detective looked at his watch. "It's almost noon. It'll take me at least an hour and a half to get someone over here, so what do you say we meet at her apartment around 3:00? That will give you some time to grab a bite to eat."

"What about her car? I mean, is it still in the parking deck?"

"That would be my guess. We haven't had it towed or anything. Her keys should be in her backpack, which is back at the station." At that point, it dawned on him that the young man didn't have any way to get around Atlanta. "Listen, let me check into it, and I'll come by and pick you up here around 3:00. Just wait at the front entrance."

"Thanks, Detective. I appreciate it," Justin said as he turned his attention back to his injured sister.

Detective Pitts let himself out quietly.

Justin waited until the officer was gone before stepping into the hallway with his cell phone. He slowly punched in Clara's number, hoping she would answer.

"Hello?" she whispered.

"Um, is this Clara?" he asked suspiciously.

"Yes. I'm at work. Is this Justin?"

"Yes, Ma'am. I can call at another time if—"

"No, no, it's okay. Let me go in the breakroom. I don't want anyone to hear me. It's lunchtime anyway." There was a brief pause before she spoke again. "Okay, I'm here. Did you make it to the hospital?"

"Yes, and a detective just came by to see me. He said Christi's roommate was murdered. They found him in the Chattahoochee River."

"Yeah, a police detective was at our office this morning too. He must have delivered that same message to my boss."

"They're gonna post a guard at Christi's door. They also want to go through her apartment. I said it's okay, because I know she doesn't have anything to hide."

"Listen, Justin. Make sure they look for anything that has to do with Cardiac Care Research Facility where Albert Tinsley worked. Your sister said he was concerned about the goings-on there. Apparently, he questioned the wrong people."

"Okay, I will. Anything else?"

"Yes. Don't mention my name. I work for Albert's boss but not at the Research Facility. It could put me in danger. Besides, I'm doing a little investigation of my own."

"No offense, but you sound like an older lady. You might not be safe yourself."

"None taken. I'm no spring chicken, but I can hold my own. I don't like the idea of you staying at Christi's apartment though. We followed a guy there who wasn't very pleasant. It isn't safe."

"I understand, but my options are limited. I need to be near the hospital."

"I'm ten minutes away, and I have two extra bedrooms. If you aren't comfortable with that, I've got some money to pay for a hotel room. It's a gift. You don't have to pay it back."

"Detective Pitts is gonna pick me up in a couple of hours. I may have the nurse keep an eye on Christi while I go down to the cafeteria and grab a bite. I'll call you after we go through her apartment."

"Okay. Just remember to look for anything related to Albert's job…and please keep my name out of it."

Justin ended the call and walked back into Christi's hospital room. Things were getting a little crazy, to say nothing of dangerous. He was still unsure why he was trusting a woman he'd never actually met, taking her word over the authority of the detective. Something in her voice just sounded so sincere, and he had to trust his instincts.

A quick glance at his watch told him it was after noon, and he hadn't eaten breakfast. With the lunch hour now upon him, he found Nurse Emerson and made her promise more than once that she would keep an eye on his sister's room while he grabbed a bite from the cafeteria.

Justin hurried to the elevator, punched the appropriate floor, and made his way to the busy dining area. He decided on a burger and fries to go, grabbed a soda from a nearby machine, and headed back to ICU. Nothing seemed to have changed in his fifteen-minute absence, so he settled back in the uncomfortable plastic chair and ate his lunch, seldom taking his eyes off his ailing sister.

Justin pondered all that had happened in the past twenty-four hours. He was unsure of exactly who to trust and what the true story was, but he knew one thing: It wasn't safe to stay at Christi's apartment. He decided that after he went on the search with the detective, he would call Clara. At the very least, he wanted to meet with her. *After all, how dangerous can it be to meet up with an old lady? Maybe she'll offer me milk and cookies,* he thought and smiled for the first time since his arrival.

Chapter 33

Harper caught Dr. Chatsworth as he was coming out of a patient's room. "I'm sorry to bother you, Doctor, but Dr. Chavan needs you to call him at the Research Facility. He said it's not urgent, but he does need you to phone him at your earliest convenience."

"Very well," he muttered as he placed the medical file back in the slot on the wall.

Harper tried desperately not to roll her eyes at the arrogant doctor. He rarely said more than two words to her, but as of late, she'd considered that a blessing; it was better for him to be distant than to berate his staff as he had so many times in the past. *I don't know how his wife can live with him*, she thought. *By the time I got through with him, he'd be the one needing a doctor.*

Grant walked into his office and sat behind his desk. It had been a long time since he'd felt so tired. Between the office, surgeries at the hospital, and his obligations to and at the Research Facility, he was completely overtaxed. Even when his body was at rest, his mind was still reeling with all that was going on in his life. He debated placing the phone call but decided it might be important.

"Dr. Chavan speaking."

"Yeah, it's Chatsworth. What's the problem now?"

"Our guy, Miguel, is already displaying some symptoms of Herpes B. I wasn't expecting it this soon."

"I'm not surprised. You said the bites were deep, and the idiot clearly didn't clean them when it happened. What symptoms are presenting?"

"At the present, he has some vesicular skin lesions near the site of exposure, and he's starting to exhibit some flu-like symptoms."

"Son-of-a-bitch," Grant said, seething into the phone. "Is he there with you?"

"Yes. He's not happy about being ill but clearly, doesn't realize the gravity of the situation."

"Let's try to keep it that way. Find a room in the Facility to make him comfortable. Start him on five milligrams of ganciclovir intravenously, every twelve hours. Let's see what the next couple of days bring. Don't let him go home, or his family may insist that he go to the hospital. We can't take that chance."

"I'll do that right away, Sir."

"How are the primates adjusting?"

"Not very well, Doctor. Almost all of them are engaging in SIB."

"Forgive my ignorance," Grant said snidely, "but could you clarify what that means?"

"Self-injurious behavior, mainly self-biting at this time."

"Damn. What's next? Why the hell are they biting themselves?"

"Most likely it's just the trauma of the move. The nonhuman primates utilized in the US for research are bred here specifically for that purpose. On the contrary, these wild animals were basically abducted from the wild and shipped here over a period of almost three weeks. They are accustomed to traveling in large troops of twenty or more primates. The separation from companions, disruption in their routine, and the anxiety over the personnel handling them is quite a disruption for them."

"So what's the plan to calm them down?"

"We are administering guanfacine orally, twice daily. That should be of some assistance. We are also attempting to house them in compatible groups or pairs. We don't want them to wound themselves severely. It won't look good to the investors."

"No, it certainly won't. How badly have they already harmed themselves?"

"Most of the bites are minor. Only a few have broken the skin. However, we have to get them calmed down. We are working on that now, but the men who transferred them are now frightened to handle them, especially after Miguel became ill."

"Do what you can to ease their minds. We can't let them walk away now. This situation is not a good one. Is Gunnar Azarov there?"

"No. He's out trying to get some information on the woman who lived with Albert Tinsley." Zahir didn't dare share the mishap with Christi Cates, knowing that would be more than his boss could handle at the moment.

144

"All right, Zahir. I have other problems to solve. I'll stop by tonight on my way home."

With that, Grant Chatsworth hung up the phone. Normally, the conversation would have upset him, but he was too tired for that. He glanced down at his watch, picked up the receiver again, and phoned his house.

"Chatsworth residence."

"Good afternoon, Flossie. Is Elizabeth nearby?"

"Yes, Sir, she is. She just met with the party planner. Let me catch her before she goes upstairs."

"Hello?"

"Hey there, Elizabeth. I understand you met with Antoine."

"Yes. He had some good suggestions as always. The dinner party should be a success."

"That's what I like to hear. Don't forget to make your hair and nail appointments for the morning of the dinner."

"I won't. Will you be home for dinner?"

"I don't believe so. I have a surgery this afternoon, and I plan to stop by the Research Facility on my way home. Go ahead and enjoy dinner without me."

"Okay, Grant. See you when you get here."

He hung up the phone without a good-bye, exited his office, and made his way to the next patient's room.

****

Lizzie grabbed her wool blanket and book and made her way outside again. It was starting to get a little too chilly to justify reading on the lawn. She knew she would have to make her move soon. She passed Lonnie, who was putting the cover over the pool, signaling the end of summer. She offered a wave but continued to move along, certain that Flossie's prying eyes were on her every minute. She wound her way farther from the house and laid out her blanket, hopeful that Santiago would soon come by.

It wasn't long before he rode up on his cart. "Morning to you," he said softly.

"Good morning, Santiago," she answered, smiling kindly at him.

"You need phone?" he asked, reaching for his cell and showing it to her.

Lizzie clasped her hands together in delight. "Oh, yes! Thank you so much," she answered as she reached for it.

"I know," he said. "I no tell."

She closed her eyes and let out a sigh. "Thank you. Thank you so much."

He cranked the cart and turned his attention back on the property. "I be back soon."

Lizzie knew she had to call Maggie first; her sister would surely be concerned after their last conversation, and she had to set her mind at ease.

"Hello?"

"Maggie, it's me. How are you?"

"I'm fine, Lizzie. Thank God, it's you. I've been worried to death. Where are you?"

"Still in Atlanta, but I'm working out a plan to get out of here."

"Working out a plan? Just leave."

"Unfortunately, it isn't that easy. I'll have to explain it all later. I've only got a few minutes. We're having a dinner party Friday night. If I'm not here for that, Grant will surely freak out. I'll make a break for it a day or two later. Don't worry about me. I'll be there as soon as possible."

"Oh, Lizzie, I am so frightened. Why don't you just let me come get you?"

"I don't want him to have any idea that I'm with you, Maggie. Please just trust me and don't worry. I'll be there soon. I love you."

"I love you too, Lizzie."

With that, Lizzie ended the call and held the phone close to her chest. It was amazing how much freedom she felt just by having the cell in her hands. She vowed she would never again let herself fall captive to such a situation at the hands of such a tyrant of a man. Next, she quickly punched in Clara's cell phone number.

"Hello?" she whispered.

"Clara, it's me. I know you're at work, so I'll talk quickly. Have you gotten any money?"

"Yes, close to $3,000 now! How can I get it to you?"

"That's a problem. I don't have any idea. If you send any more books, Grant won't give them to me. He says he wants to buy me one of those Kindles because he doesn't like me handling dusty old paperbacks."

"What about a new, signed hardback of Sue Grafton's latest novel?"

"What? She isn't coming to Atlanta anytime soon. How do you plan to get a signed copy?"

"Do you think Dr. Chatsworth would recognize her signature? I'll sign it myself and personalize it to you. I think Ms. Grafton would approve. She's the best mystery writer out there, and this is a pretty exciting mystery we're living right now."

Lizzie had to laugh. Clara was always one step ahead of her, like Angela Lansbury herself. "But there's a problem. I'm afraid $3,000 won't fit in a bookmark."

"You've got a point there," Clara answered, her voice registering defeat. "Wait! I've got an idea, a brilliant one from the doctor himself. I can put it in the binding, behind the front and back covers, then just re-glue them. Just pray he doesn't look too closely."

"That's pretty risky. I don't know if we should try it."

"I'll show it to him at work briefly and make sure to proudly flash a copy of the inscription. Then I'll gift wrap it. Surely, he won't be suspicious enough to unwrap it, especially if I wrap it right in front of him, in the breakroom."

"Yes, but why would you give me a gift?"

"No particular reason. I'll just tell him I stood in line for two hours to get it for you."

"Okay. I guess it's worth a shot. Thank you so much, Clara. I'll never be able to thank you enough."

Chapter 34

Justin Cates stood nervously outside the hospital as he waited on the detective to pick him up. His insides were churning at the thought of leaving Christi alone in the ICU, but he felt the strong need to be with Detective Pitts as he went through his sister's belongings.

It wasn't long before he heard a horn blaring and saw the investigator in his sister's used blue Kia. He hurried over, threw his bag in the back seat, and jumped in the passenger seat. "I see you found her car," he said.

"Yep. Campus Security had already located it for us when we got there. I have to hand it to those guys. They're on the ball. I can't imagine that their job is easy, with the campus being in the middle of the city."

"Me either," Justin muttered, his mind a million miles away. "How far is my sister's apartment from here?"

"Not far at all. It's on Marietta Street, fairly close to the college."

The two men rode in silence until they pulled into her complex. "I was going to ask the apartment manager to let us in, but her key should be on this keyring. I doubt she has a security system. Few apartments do, unfortunately. We'll just check it out."

Justin followed him up the stairs, to the apartment door.

Detective Pitts looked down at the key chain. "A no-brainer. We've got a car key, this small one looks like a mailbox key, and that leaves us with one option for her place." He slid the key into the lock and turned it easily. "I don't hear any beeping," he said to Justin with a grin. "Looks like we're in."

They slowly made their way in, only to discover that the den had been ransacked. The sofa cushions were ripped apart, and stuffing was strewn throughout the room. The DVDs were all opened and thrown about, along with various pictures and open drawers.

"Shit! This doesn't look good," Pitts said. "I wasn't expecting this. Don't touch anything, kid. I'll have to call in a CSI unit."

Justin felt a sudden urge of panic. "CSI? Detective, I really want to get back to the hospital if it's that serious. I'm worried about Christi."

"She's fine. One of my men is with her now. Let me check out the rest of the place."

Justin followed him around, first into his sister's bedroom, then into Albert's. They had both been scoured, but Albert's seemed to have taken the brunt of it.

"Looks like they were after something. My guess is it had to do with Albert. What do you think?"

"I remember my sister sharing concerns about his work," Justin lied. "He didn't believe things were being handled properly."

"Really? I don't remember you sharing that with me before."

"I've been so worried about Christi that it was difficult for me to think. I remember now. She was a little worried about him quitting and moving out. She was strapped with her part of the rent already. I guess I didn't think much about it at the time."

Detective Pitts gave him a skeptical glance but understood that the man had been through a great deal. Losing his parents at such a young age and then such an unexpected accident for his sister was taking its toll. "I'll tell ya what, Justin. Why don't you take your sister's car and find someplace to stay for the night? There isn't anything you can do here, and to be honest, we need you to clear out so we can take some prints and photographs. I'm afraid if there were any clues as to Albert's death and Christi's accident, they've already been discovered and removed."

Justin took the keys from Detective Pitts and walked back to the car. The shock of the apartment being torn apart was sinking in, and he was grateful that his sister was still alive. Something sinister was going on, and he hoped the police could get to the bottom of it so Christi could recover and move on with her life.

Unsure of where to go from there, he drove down the street, pulled into a gas station, and phoned Clara. She was still at work but gave him her address and made arrangements for him to go to her house at 6:00 p.m. The two of them could talk that way, figure out their next plan of attack. Justin typed the hospital into his phone GPS and drove back to visit Christi for another couple of hours.

****

Gunnar Azarov was in a panic. *How in the hell did the girl survive being hit by a bus?* he thought. He was certain the accident would prove fatal, but he was wrong. He was so certain, in fact, that he had simply walked calmly away from the scene. In everyone's haste to get to her, he had gone unnoticed. Now she was still alive and could surely identify him. *I'll just have to get to her before she can flap her lips. I've done it before, and I'll do it again.*

Stopping at a local florist, Gunnar picked up an arrangement in a cheap vase to deliver to the hospital. He handed over forty dollars, requested a small card, then scribbled something illegible on it. Nodding in lieu of a thank-you, he exited the business and walked the two blocks back to his car.

The hospital was conveniently located in the middle of the city but was in the midst of gridlock traffic and the swirling activity from the childrens' hospital and Georgia State University. Grady Memorial, known as one of the largest public hospitals in the US, not only served as a Level One trauma center, but it also cared for the city's indigent and prison population. Gunnar chose to park a few blocks away, then walked briskly to the main entrance.

An older lady, sitting behind an information desk, smiled kindly at him, voicing her approval of the flower arrangement. "You're sure trying to cheer someone up with that," she said. "Do you need a room number, dear?"

"Yes, I'm just a delivery man, but I'm looking for Christi Cates's room."

She lowered her reading glasses to the edge of her nose and slowly typed the name into the system. "Oh, dear," she said sadly. "I'm afraid Ms. Cates is in ICU. They don't allow flowers there."

Gunnar struggled to hide his impatience. "Perhaps I can find a family member who would like to take them home. I'd hate for the arrangement to die without someone being able to enjoy it."

"Why, that is very thoughtful of you," she beamed. "Just take the second set of elevators on your right. It'll take you right up to ICU. You can't miss the ICU waiting area."

"Very well," he muttered. He caught the elevator, exited on the appropriate floor, and intentionally bypassed the family waiting area. He was certain that no one would accept the flowers, but he hoped to attain some information on her condition. He pressed the call button and waited for a response, just as Justin Cates walked up behind him.

"ICU. How can I help you?"

"Yes, I'm a flower delivery man. I have some flowers for Christi Cates."

"I'm sorry, Sir. We don't allow flowers in this area. Would you like to leave the card for the patient?"

"No, that's all right."

"Hey," Justin interjected. "Those are for my sister? What a coincidence. I'll be happy to take the card back."

"Uh, yeah...sure," Gunnar answered, fumbling for the card. "Sorry, she can't have the flowers."

"That's okay. She's in a coma right now and can't enjoy them anyway. I'm sure someone else could enjoy them though. There are lots of sick folks here."

"Right. I'll find someone," Gunnar mumbled as he turned and walked away.

Justin put the card in his back pocket, walked back to visit Christi, and prayed for a miracle.

Chapter 35

At least she hasn't come out of the coma, Gunnar thought as he sat in his car, staking out the front entrance of the hospital. It had been almost three hours, and Christi's brother hadn't exited yet. Gunnar wanted to know where he was staying because after riding by the girl's apartment, it was clear that police would be tied up there for some time. Fortunately, he had found the few notes Albert Tinsley had scribbled regarding his concerns about the Cardiac Care drug development and their unethical actions of acquiring the rhesus monkeys.

He knew it was a good thing they had taken care of Albert when they had because the detective was undoubtedly putting the pieces of the puzzle together quickly. That made Gunnar nervous. His own concerns over his boss's choices were growing. Dr. Chatsworth had his hands in too many projects to pull off something of that magnitude. Drs. Chavan and Phillips weren't capable of taking the reins themselves, and it was only a matter of time before the whole house of cards came tumbling down.

Gunnar's frustration was peaking when he finally saw the young man coming out of the hospital. Justin looked around to get his bearings, then followed the sidewalk to a small, private lot, where he had left Christi's car. Gunnar maneuvered easily through the traffic and pulled over next to the curb to watch his prey. His greatest attribute was a keen ability to track and acquire information on individuals in question. Those skills had kept him continuously employed since he arrived in the US from Russia.

Justin placed a call to Clara before cranking the car. He filled her in on his sister's condition and the fact that the APD had placed officers strategically by her door. The two agreed it was in his best interest to stay the night at Clara's.

Just as she had promised, the ride to her home was almost exactly ten minutes from the hospital.

Gunnar was at least fifty yards behind Justin when he pulled into Clara's driveway, so he pulled over along the curb and observed. As the young man got out of the car, two women shuffled out to greet him. *I've seen those old women before*, Gunnar thought.

Now, where was that? It nearly drove him mad as he searched the memory bank of his mind. Then he spotted it: the old Buick he'd seen in the parking lot of the doctor's office the night the paper from the book went missing. "Well, I'll be damned," he said to himself. "It's the doc's head nurse!"

Gunnar's initial reaction was to phone Dr. Chatsworth right away, but that would force him to explain his mishap with Christi Cates and the sudden appearance of her brother. He knew that would only send his boss into a rage. He decided instead to spy on them and see just exactly what they were up to.

Iris and Clara led Justin into the house. They had a large, home-cooked meal for him spread out on the table, so the three sat down to eat. It wasn't long before the whole story came tumbling out of the ladies.

Justin felt a sudden shiver of fear run up his spine. "I wish I had known all this was going on," he said. "I coulda transferred to Georgia State and roomed with her myself. Now look at the predicament she's in."

"Don't get worked up, honey," Iris piped in. "Let's just concentrate on her getting better. That's the important thing."

"Yep, first things first. I have her cell phone in my duffel bag. I wonder if I should try to call some of her friends and let them know about this. Someone sent her flowers today, but they wouldn't let her have them back in ICU. If I had been thinking straight, I would have brought them over here for you to enjoy, Ms. Clara."

"What a sweet thought, dear, but the last thing you need to worry about is lugging some flowers around."

"Yeah, it was the oddest thing," Justin started.

"What was?" Iris asked, leaning forward in hopes of a bite of juicy information.

"Oh, it's probably nothing, but the delivery man was so, um…just weird for that job."

"How do you mean?"

"He was huge and had a Russian accent, looked more like a wrestler or bodyguard or something. I recognized it because one of my friends is from Russia. His dad talks the same way."

"Oh no," Clara said. "Please tell us everything. Exactly what did he say?"

"Well, not much of anything. He was pleasant enough, just seemed a little rushed and frustrated. I asked him for the card, and he gave it to me."

"What did it say?" Iris asked.

"I never opened it," Justin said. He retrieved the card from his back pocket. "Let me see," he answered as he took the time to tear open the miniature envelope. "Holy shit! Oops. I mean...oh, God," he said as his hands began to tremble.

"Tell us!" Iris all but screamed.

"It says, 'Get well soon. Your friend, Albert.'"

Both of the women's hands flew up to their mouths as they audibly gasped.

"That's it. I'm calling the police," Clara said. "I left the cordless phone in the living room. Let me go get it. This is getting out of control. We can't wait any longer. We have to tell them what we know."

Clara made her way down the hall, located the phone, and was just about to place the call when Gunnar Azarov kicked in the back door. "What are you ladies up to?" he asked snidely. "You should have minded your own business."

"Hide, Iris!" Clara screamed as she ran down the hallway.

Justin motioned for Iris to get down in the corner of the kitchen as he attempted to run toward Clara's voice.

"Oh, no you don't," Gunnar said, wrapping his right arm firmly around Justin's neck, rendering him immobile. "You're swimming in a mighty big pond here, fella. We can't have you making waves like that sister of yours did."

"She didn't do anything," Justin said, gasping. "It was all Albert."

"Let him go!" Iris screamed from the corner. "You'll pay for this. We're going to the police."

"Not what I wanted to hear," Gunnar said calmly as he removed a handgun from inside his jacket. "Not what I wanted to hear at all, old lady."

Justin squirmed ineffectively against the enormous man's grasp, trying to throw the hefty Russian off-balance before he could fire the weapon. It didn't work, and the sound of the shot temporarily deafened Justin.

154

Thankfully, Iris had grabbed the old cast-iron skillet that Clara used every Sunday for cornbread; it deflected the bullet, causing it to ricochet into the outdated wooden cabinets. Before Gunnar could react, Clara hit him over the head with a large waffle maker, causing him to collapse onto Justin.

"Help!" Justin gasped as he attempted to get out from under Gunnar's weight. Between Iris and Clara and Justin wiggling like a wounded worm, he was soon freed.

"Lord have mercy," Clara sighed. "Is everyone all right?"

"Yes, we're still here," Iris said. "We better get this guy tied up before he pulls another weapon on us."

"There's not much need for that," Justin replied. "He's gone."

"Gone? What do you mean?" Iris asked. "You'd better tie that big old lug up. Get him something, Clara. He could come to any minute, and he won't be happy!"

"No, Ms. Iris," Justin insisted. "He's gone...as in dead."

"I'll be damned, Clara. You've killed the man! How are we gonna explain this one?"

"Oh, my," Clara said, her hands shaking terribly. "You've been pressuring me to get rid of that old waffle-maker for years, Iris, and I told you they just don't make 'em like they used to. I guess I was right. It took all I had to lift it high enough to hit him."

"Well, you knocked the fire out of him. Now what?"

"If we talk to the police, they'll go straight to Dr. Chatsworth. I can't take that chance, especially because it will put poor Lizzie in greater danger. I just sent the money-filled book home with him today. If he knows I'm involved, he'll certainly put two and two together, with us exchanging reading material and all. They won't arrest him on the spot. This whole thing is going to take a lot of investigation by several different agencies."

"So what are you saying?"

"We have to give Lizzie a chance to make her escape."

"And what do we do with this guy in the meantime?" Iris asked. "Not that I really care, since he called me an 'old lady' and all, but he's gonna start stinkin' like high noon after a while."

"First, Justin, you have to get out of here. We can't have you involved." Clara rambled through her purse and pulled out some cash. "Here," she said, thrusting it toward him. "Go find a room

155

near the hospital. We'll handle this. Just forget you ever talked to either of us. It's in your best interest. You may want to stop by a mall and purchase a turtleneck sweater. That bruising's gonna be pretty bad by morning. Now get out of here. Go."

"I can't just leave you here with a dead body," Justin said nervously. "I think we need to go to the police. This could get worse."

"Worse than a dead giant Russian on my kitchen floor? I don't think so. Besides, who's going to report him missing? I have a strong feeling he's the one who dumped poor Albert in the Chattahoochee. I think he's Dr. Chatsworth's strong arm. Just help me for a minute, Justin. Let's go through his pockets for an ID."

Justin pushed, pulled, and rolled the dead body until they found a sham of a driver's license and an obviously implausible passport. "These are fake," he said. "I'm no expert, but fake IDs are prevalent among college students trying to get into bars. This isn't even a decent one. There's no way it's real."

"Okay," Clara said. "If he doesn't have a real ID, then he simply doesn't exist. Got that? Now go. Please."

Justin pulled a set of keys out of Gunnar's jacket pocket. "Looks like he's parked somewhere nearby. We've gotta get rid of the car too."

"We can handle the grand theft auto, son. You go get a room."

He embraced both of the women and quickly left the house. *This can't possibly end well*, he thought. *What a piece of shit I am for leaving them.* Then another thought entered his mind: *Then again, I'm sure if anyone can handle this, Ms. Clara and Ms. Iris can.*

****

Clara fell into one of the kitchen chairs and fanned herself with a dishtowel. "Oh, Iris, I've really done it this time."

"It's gonna be okay," Iris assured her. "Let's not get in a rush. We need to think this through. Actually, I have an idea."

"Of course you do." Clara didn't want to ask, but she did. "What is it?"

"Remember when my Fred was so sick there at the end?"

"Yeah. Losing our husbands was a terrible blow, but it hardly relates to this."

"Well, I bought a hydraulic lift from the used medical supply store. It helped me get him in and out of the tub and bed."

"Are you suggesting we put this corpse on it?"

"Why not? I still have that thing in the garage, and it cost me good money. I don't see any reason not to. Don't get so prim and proper on me now, Clara. You're the one who killed him."

"Good grief, Iris. What are we going to do with him then?"

"Well, I wouldn't recommend leaving him here in your kitchen, if that's what you're thinking!"

"Of course not," Clara said defensively. "I just haven't thought of anything yet. Besides, how on Earth do you propose we get that lift down here? It won't ever fit in either of our cars."

"It has wheels. How do you think I got it around the house? It's not really that heavy, just bulky. They put it together for me, but I don't think we have time to figure out how to take it apart and put it back together again. It'll be daylight soon enough."

"Oh, dear," Clara said, her nerves beginning to get the best of her. "We still have to find his car and put it in the garage. How will we ever get rid of that?"

"I say we put him in his trunk and drive the whole kit and caboodle into the river. You said yourself that no one's gonna report this big ol' whale missing. That doctor of yours is going to want to distance himself as much as possible from this situation. He'll have a lot of explaining to do if he contacts the police about this man's disappearance. Besides, this puts Christi out of harm's way, to say nothing of us!"

"There is some truth to that," Clara concluded. "You drive my car," she said as she picked up the Russian's keys. "I'll take his car back and put it in the garage."

"I knew you would see it my way," Iris said, patting Clara on the shoulder. "Now let's not waste any more darkness."

The two rode around for less than a minute before spotting the dark Lincoln. It was pulled over next to the curb, fortunately away from any residences.

Clara grabbed her garage door opener from the visor of her own car, quickly exited, and jumped into the other car. It cranked easily, and she drove around the block before pulling into her garage. She hastily shut the garage door and met Iris as she pulled in behind her. "Now what?"

Iris held up her own keys and dangled them in the air. "Let's walk down to my house and roll that lift back here."

"What will we say if someone sees us?"

"First of all, it ain't nobody's business. If anybody asks, we'll just say you have a friend who may be interested in buying it, so they're coming to your house next week to check it out. That's legal, you know. I do own the thing outright."

"But why would we roll it up the street in the dark?"

"Because you work during the day, remember? Hello? The clock is ticking. Quit your blabbing and let's get going."

Against her better judgment, Clara agreed. There didn't seem to be a better plan, and Iris was right about time being of the essence. The two walked quickly down to Iris's house and rolled the large contraption down the driveway and into the street. Luckily, the wheels were rather quiet, and they didn't seem to draw any unwanted attention from nosy neighbors who were probably enjoying dinner. They made it back to Clara's garage without even running into a passing car.

"Thank God," Clara said, heaving a sigh. "This is just getting crazier and crazier. I never dreamt I'd be part of something so foolish."

"Now is not the time for that, Clara," Iris said sensibly. "We have work to do. We can dwell on that at a later time. Help me get this in the kitchen."

The ladies worked swiftly and efficiently as Iris wrapped the straps around Gunnar's torso and lifted his dead weight. His height worked against them, but they were able to wheel him out to the car. It took them several attempts, but they finally managed to load him into the trunk of the large, luxury automobile.

"Oh, dear Lord in heaven, please forgive me," Clara said.

"You said yourself that going to the police would endanger Lizzie," Iris reiterated to her friend. "Now get off the pity pot and let's dump this man somewhere."

158

Clara brushed away the tears flowing down her cheeks and turned to face her friend. "We have to wipe the fingerprints from the car. We can't drive this car into the Chattahoochee. The only areas I'm aware of aren't that deep. It's just not feasible. Besides, it would leave telling tire tracks."

"Well, we can just dump his body in there," Iris suggested.

"That won't work. We'll need the lift. Wherever we leave him, he'll have to remain in the car."

"What about just abandoning him in a known drug area. Somebody else will find him and think the big brute was killed by a drug dealer. We could even plant some drugs on him."

"Really? And just where are we going to get drugs to plant on him, Iris?"

"Don't you have some? You're the nurse."

"No! I don't have any drugs. I don't even write prescriptions."

"Well, I have some prescription Tylenol."

"Seriously, Iris. You're scaring me."

"Well, it is 9:30, after all, and I missed my nap today. You're lucky I'm still awake."

"Still awake? I may never sleep again!"

"Well, wherever we dump him, it can't be too difficult to drive to. I have my limitations, you know. As you know, I can't merge on the interstate, especially in the dark, and I've got trouble getting in and out of parking spaces. Then there's—"

"Stop! I'm well aware of your driving limitations, Iris. We need to think, really think. Leaving him somewhere to be found isn't such a bad idea. It would bring attention to the Research Facility, since the car is registered to them, and Albert Tinsley worked there before he was killed. Surely that would raise a red flag for the Police Department."

"And without tying him to us."

"As long as he didn't place any calls before he kicked in my door, which is yet another problem we have to deal with."

"If he placed a call, someone would be here looking for him by now. No one would think two old women could have killed the overgrown bully."

"You have a point there, Iris. We have to get rid of his cell phone, too, before it starts pinging off towers or whatever they talk about on those *Dateline* mysteries."

Iris reached for his phone, wiped it off with a dishtowel, and wrapped it in another one, just to be safe. "We can throw this out the window when we get farther from the house."

"Good idea, but we have to think about any surveillance videos we may pass when we're going down the road. Let me think," Clara said, putting her face in her hands. "Oh, I'm just at a loss. Let's wipe the car down really well. I'll grab a pair of gloves for when I drive it to wherever we go."

"I'll meet you in the garage," Iris said as she grabbed a couple of dishcloths.

The two wiped down any areas of the car that they thought they might have come in contact with, and Iris threw the gun in the trunk beside Gunnar.

Clara got behind the wheel. "Well, this is where the rubber meets the road," she said sadly. "Iris, follow me in my car, and we'll just drive until I find a spot that I believe is fitting. I'll stay away from any main roads and the highway."

Clara backed down the driveway and started toward the worst section of town she could think of. Taking back roads that Iris could easily maneuver, she drove for at least thirty minutes until she spotted an old, abandoned business that had once sold used tires. She pulled around to the back and said a silent prayer that no debris there would give her car a flat. Two old ladies stranded in that part of town would be a recipe for disaster. She turned the headlights off, killed the engine, and walked hurriedly to Iris, who was waiting nearby. As soon as she got near the car, Iris jumped out and got in the passenger seat.

"Looks like this is where it ends," Clara said as she buckled her seatbelt.

"I didn't think you'd ever stop. There musta been fifty places just like this. Why'd you come so far? Do you even remember how to get back home?"

"Yes, Iris, I know how to get home. I had to put him far enough away so no one will ever tie him to us."

"Well, I'm sure they'll find no connection between us and a closed used tire business on Bankhead Highway!"

"Then we were successful," Clara said defiantly. "I'm just ready to get home. I'm exhausted, physically and mentally, I still have a damaged back door, and of course, I have to show up for work tomorrow with a smile on my face."

Chapter 36

Lizzie was eating dinner alone in the dining room when Grant got home. He had already removed his coat and tie, and his shirt was unbuttoned at his throat. He looked tired.

"How was your day?" Lizzie asked kindly.

"Exhausting," he snapped, stating the obvious.

"Why don't you sit down with me and have some dinner?"

"I think I'll do that. I'm going to fix a stiff drink, then have Flossie bring my plate in." A few minutes later, Grant returned with a scotch on the rocks and sat down at the head of the table.

Flossie came in with a plate of steaming food and a glass of ice water. "Enjoy, Sir," she said.

He muttered his thanks before taking a long swig of the copper-colored liquor.

Unsure if any conversation would encourage an argument, Lizzie continued to eat in silence.

"I left a present for you in the library, from Clara Samples."

"A present?"

"A novel…and thank God it's a new one this time, not one of those mildewed paperbacks she's always sending over here. Apparently, she waited in line to get it autographed for you. She even wrapped it."

"How kind of her. She is such a sweet lady."

"I don't like her getting in our personal business. She can be very nosy."

"I think she's just lonely. Besides, everyone likes to keep the boss's wife happy."

"Maybe, but don't encourage her to continue with this gift-giving."

"I won't. I'll send her a thank-you note and let her know I'm really too busy to read right now. That should take care of it."

"Very well. Do you have a gown picked out for tomorrow night?"

"Yes, a new one I've never worn before. It should be lovely with the new earrings you gave me a few weeks ago."

"You wore those to the last party."

"Yes, but I didn't have a chance to mingle and show them off. I fainted, remember?"

"I certainly haven't forgotten that. Fine, wear them again, but make sure you eat a decent lunch tomorrow to ensure we don't have another fiasco."

"I will. My appointments start at 11:00. Can my driver be here by 10:30?"

"I'll have to call him. He's been hard to get in touch with the past couple of days."

"Okay. Thank you. I'm getting my nails done first, then my hair and makeup. Who all will be attending the dinner?"

"Just the usual corporate types, along with their wives. Hopefully, the evening will end early."

"You look so tired, Grant. Aren't you sleeping well?"

"Yes, but I never seem to get enough rest. I'm drained, Elizabeth."

For a brief moment, Lizzie pitied him. He was such a brilliant man, but there was never enough for him: never enough money, never enough investments, never enough glory. She studied his face and, for the first time, noticed fine lines around his eyes and mouth. The whole scam was taking its toll on him. She wanted to reach out and plead with him to stop, to plead with him to be content with saving lives and being a husband, but she knew it was of no use. The wheels were already in motion, and the outcome was predetermined.

Grant placed his fork across his plate, signaling he had eaten his fill. "I'm going to sit in the library and have another drink. Good night."

That was her clue that their conversation was over. "I'll grab that book before I turn in," she said casually. "I'm sure she picked one of my favorites." Lizzie walked beside him to the library and picked up the wrapped novel. "I'll make sure I mail that note tomorrow while I'm out," she assured him. "That should be the end of the book exchange."

"Very well," he said before making his way to the crystal scotch decanter.

There were times when Grant felt remorseful for the way he shrugged Elizabeth off, but he was simply tired of his life and

163

everything to do with it, including his wife. In the beginning, being a surgeon had been a high he'd only dreamt of, but now it was all-consuming and exasperating. Elizabeth was beautiful and sweet but far beneath being his intellectual equal. The spark was gone, leaving him wondering if it had ever really been there at all. His home was all anyone could hope for, but he just wasn't enjoying it anymore. He wanted to relax and simply live. He wanted to dine at fine restaurants with the love of his life and spend his nights in a warm hot tub, drinking champagne. He was tired of early morning patients, last-minute surgeries, and vacations during which he had to pretend to enjoy sex with a woman he had never really loved. "No more pretending," Grant said to himself. "To the future," he said aloud as he raised his scotch in the air. "To another life." He picked up his sports coat and pulled his cell phone from the inside pocket.

"Dr. Chavan here."

"Zahir, it's me," he said bluntly into the phone. "Where the hell is Gunnar?"

"I'm not sure, Sir. He hasn't answered any of our calls. He said something about visiting a sick friend earlier in the day," Zahir lied, anxious to come up with any story that would lead Dr. Chatsworth away from the truth. "I'm sure he will phone soon."

"How's our Herpes B patient doing?"

"Miguel is not faring well. That's another problem. Something will have to be done soon. He's spiraling downward."

"There isn't much we can do. If he's not responding to treatment... Well, his prognosis isn't good. What are his current symptoms?"

"The disease has spread to his central nervous system. A variety of neurological signs are developing, including ascending flaccid paralysis. He is in and out of consciousness."

"That means it won't be long now. He'll die from respiratory failure very soon. Have Gunnar dispose of the body, but tell him not to use the fucking river this time. We don't need another body surfacing, associated with us in any way. What about the other men who transferred the primates?"

"They have all left, Sir. They were frightened of the primates and refused to deal with them. Gunnar put a great deal of fear in them about discussing our Facility or ever returning again. Being illegals, I don't believe they will be a concern in the future. They are too frightened of the INS for that."

"Who is handling the feeding and handling of the primates now?"

"Jean-Luc has been handling those duties and is attempting to train some of the other staff. It would be most beneficial if the investors make their tours here soon. The primates are posing a problem, and it's one we are not equipped to handle."

"Very well," Grant mumbled, pausing to take a long sip from his scotch. "I'll schedule a Facility tour sometime next week. After that, we'll no longer allow visits from the investors. We'll dispose of the primates accordingly."

****

Lizzie lay awake in bed until she heard Grant turning in for the night. Her heart was racing, and her mind spun about the thoughts of the money hidden in the book. She peeled the wrapping paper off slowly and quietly, then pulled the glued bindings back to retrieve the cash Clara had squirreled away for her. After debating where to hide money, she decided to stash it in the cardboard applicators of her tampons. The thought of someone looking there was laughable, especially Grant. She repaired the book as well as she possibly could but not before running her finger over the signature Clara had forged. Lizzie couldn't help but think that the humor of their personal mystery would not be lost on suspense writer Sue Grafton. She placed the novel in her nightstand drawer and soon drifted off into a fitful sleep.

"Good morning, Elizabeth," Grant said, shaking her slightly. "I'm leaving for work."

Lizzie opened her eyes and looked up at her husband. "Okay. I'll see you tonight. Have a good day."

"I haven't been able to contact Gunnar," he said flatly. He handed her car keys to her, keys she hadn't had in her possession for weeks. "You'll have to drive yourself. I don't like this situation at all, so you need to tend to your appointments and return home quickly, with no other stops between. I hate the thought of you fainting someplace, particularly behind the wheel, but I've no other option right now."

Lizzie tried not to look shocked; the thought of driving again was almost too good to be true. "Oh, don't worry about me. I only have two stops and shouldn't be gone long."

"Flossie will have your cell for you when you leave. Make sure to answer it when it rings. I don't want to worry unnecessarily."

"Of course," she answered. "Have a nice day, Grant. I'll see you tonight."

He looked as though he wanted to say something more but instead turned and walked out of the room.

She heard his footsteps as he walked down the stairs, and as soon as he hit the last one, she got out of bed and jumped in the shower. As the warm water soothed her body, her mind pondered all the places she could go while she was out, all the plans she could make for her escape. Then a frightening thought hit her: *Maybe this is simply a test. Someone will surely be watching me. Maybe he even has Gunnar on call to tail me.*

Chapter 37

Clara could not possibly fall asleep after committing accidental manslaughter and abandoning a dead body but knew she had to shower and show up for work. She couldn't risk changing her routine at all. She and Iris had somehow gotten the damaged back door closed and locked, and at least that allowed her to arm her alarm system for the night, which gave her some sense of comfort. Iris had gone home around two o'clock in the morning, and Clara hoped she'd been able to get some semblance of sleep herself.

Harper beat her to the office, but luckily, Dr. Chatsworth hadn't arrived yet. They had a busy day ahead as most Fridays were. Thankfully, she was able to busy herself with many duties and tasks, which seemed to calm her nerves. Clara was gathering up the patient files for the day when the doctor came in, grunted some type of greeting, and walked to his office.

Clara poured a cup of steaming coffee and delivered it to him just as she did every morning. "Good morning, Dr. Chatsworth," she said with a smile. "Busy day today, but you don't have any surgeries."

"Mm-hmm," he mumbled with a snort, his mind clearly preoccupied with other things.

Clara wanted to ask him if he'd delivered the book, but she didn't dare; she could only trust that it had all worked out and that Lizzie had the money safely tucked away. "Your first patient will be in Room Seven, whenever you're ready," she added before quickly skirting out of the room.

Grant leaned back in the chair and sighed heavily. *How much longer can I keep this up?* he thought. He ran numbers through his head, wondering how close he was to his goal, wishing he could just take the money and run. The dinner party would surely produce a substantial sum, hopefully, enough to hasten his exit, but they were far from the billions he had in mind when the whole ordeal began. Grant had not anticipated all the problems he was running into, nor could he possibly have predicted the inadequacy of the other doctors. He could settle for much less, but he still needed to ensure that he would never want for money. He couldn't leave until he knew he was set for life. He reached for the phone, sighed, and dialed, not at all looking forward to the conversation he was about to have.

"Zahir speaking."

"What's the update on Miguel?" Grant snapped without even offering a greeting.

"It won't be long, Sir. With Gunnar not answering our calls, I'm not sure what to do with him, in the event... Well, you know, Sir."

"Jesus. Listen, Zahir, and listen carefully. You and Jean-Luc will have to handle this situation. I'm having a dinner party tonight and can't be disturbed, nor will I be available to handle this latest disaster that should have been avoided in the first place. Get the staff together and clean this cluster-fuck up. I want the Facility in top-notch shape, the damn monkeys contained and on their best behavior, and the lab displaying miraculous research in the art of drug development. I will schedule a visit from our investors for next Wednesday, and they had better see and hear only what we want them to see and hear. Do you understand?"

Dr. Zahir Chavan had heard his boss upset many times in the past, but this was almost frightening. He clearly meant what he was saying, and Zahir knew there was much at stake in the venture. More than ever before, he had to step up to the plate, or he was sure he'd be the next to be pulled from the river by local rafters. "Yes, I understand, Doctor. You will not be disappointed. Everything will be ready for visitors Wednesday, and they will be impressed."

"For your sake, I hope you're right," Grant answered, then hung up. He was through walking them through everything step by step. They had to start pulling their weight, as he was paying them well to do, or he would walk away from it all and leave them holding the bag, a very empty bag, at that.

****

Lizzie had showered, dressed, and eaten her breakfast. She was feeling better, as her morning sickness had subsided, leaving her feeling alert and healthy.

Flossie gave her the keys, along with a stern glance, yet another reminder that she wasn't to veer off schedule.

Lizzie pulled on a jacket and left the keys on the dining room table. "I think I'll take a walk around the yard first," she said to Flossie.

"It is much too cool for that today, Lizzie," Flossie insisted. "You will catch a cold."

"Actually, I've felt much better since I started spending time outside. I think the fresh air and sunlight do me good. You should try it sometime."

"Fresh air? In Atlanta? I hardly think so." Flossie sneered before turning back to her work.

The air was brisk but not too cold for Lizzie to enjoy the immaculate grounds. October always signaled cooler weather in Georgia, but it often alternated with warm days, a reflection of summer trying to hold its own. It would be Halloween in a couple of days, and she wondered if Maggie's twins had their costumes ready. She couldn't wait to see them, and the mere thought of seeing Maggie caused tears to form in her eyes.

Lizzie put her hands in the jacket pockets and walked slowly around the estate. It was a beautiful place, really, but it had just never felt like home to her. She vowed that her new life wouldn't include a household staff. She would have an eat-in kitchen, bake cookies and treats for the holidays, and would never let a nanny raise her child. *My child...* Her hands instantly went to her belly, and a feeling of uneasiness quickly engulfed her. She no longer had to fear for only herself; she had to protect her unborn child as well. She would need prenatal care as soon as she got settled, and she had to ensure that she stayed hidden, so Grant would never find her. It was unrealistic to think he wouldn't consider her running to Maggie. After all, she was Lizzie's only family. There was the cottage out back, and she could stay well-hidden there, at least until he was found out by his investors. *"Maybe,"* she thought naïvely, *"he won't even come after me at all."*

There was no sign of Lonnie, which surprised her since Flossie always had everyone working extra hard prior to a planned event. She shrugged, hoping he was enjoying the mountains with his family before the colder weather set in.

She had almost finished walking the perimeter when Santiago drove up on his cart. Today, it was filled with bags of beautiful autumn leaves he had raked from under the old oaks. "Mornin' to you," he said with a smile. "Gettin' cold outside."

"Yes, it is. The leaves are beautiful."

"Yes, Ma'am. Very nice. All colors," he said, pointing to the overflowing bags. "You need phone?" he asked, reaching in his pocket. "I no tell no one, not ever."

Lizzie closed her eyes and smiled at him gratefully. *What a kind man. He must know what a desperate situation I am in*, she thought. "Just a minute," she told him as she took the phone from his hand. "I will hurry."

"No problem, miss. You need me to get you phone? I worry for you."

"No, no," she said quickly. "I don't want you to get in trouble. I will be okay."

He nodded at her and drove away in the cart.

Lizzie stood beside a large magnolia tree and dialed Maggie.

"Hello?"

"Maggie, it's me."

"Thank God! I'm so worried, Lizzie. Please tell me you're on your way."

"I told you I have to be here for a dinner party tonight. I'll get away in the next couple of days. It could take up to three days, but I'll call you when I arrive in Biloxi. I'm taking the bus from Atlanta, I'm not sure of the timeline, but I'll be there."

"The bus, Lizzie? I'm so frightened for you. Please be careful."

"I have to go now. I hope the boys have a great Halloween. I love you, Maggie."

"I love you too."

Hearing Maggie's voice always made her emotional, but she didn't have time for that today. She had too much to do, and she couldn't allow herself to ruin it all by bringing suspicion on herself. Against her better judgment, she dialed Clara's cell phone.

"Hello?" Clara whispered.

"It's me," Lizzie whispered back.

"Oh, thank God. Just give me a second to go in the breakroom. He's in a conference with another doctor at the hospital. I just don't want anyone else to overhear me."

"Okay." Lizzie waited until Clara was able to speak again.

"Oh, Lizzie, so much is going on. Please tell me you got the money."

"I did. I don't know how I can ever thank you. I'll be leaving in the next couple of days, so I probably won't phone you again. I don't want to put you in any more danger."

"Are you going to your sister's?" Clara asked, deliberately leaving out the story about Gunnar, for fear of scaring her.

"Yes. I'm going to take the bus from Atlanta. Grant will never suspect that I'd ride a bus."

"I wish I could take you, but I'm afraid he may be suspicious of me now."

"It's okay, Clara. I'll be fine. You have done more than enough."

"If he goes to the police or the media, they may post your picture on the news. Anyone riding the bus will surely recognize someone as beautiful as you. I have an idea."

"Oh no, Clara. I can't take any more chances."

"Just hear me out. I have a dear friend who owns a sandwich shop right down from the bus station on Forsyth Street, J&L Subs. Her name is Daisy. She's there every day and never has trusted the employees to handle the cash register. Stop by there first. I'll leave a bag for you. Just get it and go into the restroom. It'll have a wig, a few more dollars, and an outfit that won't draw attention, something like I wear, maybe from the Alfred Dunner line. That's hip for us older ladies. Buy five pieces, and you can mix and match twenty outfits out of it," she said with a laugh.

Lizzie thought of refusing but decided that Clara was probably right. She had been right so far, but something in Clara's voice concerned her. She seemed afraid or at least very tired. At any rate, she ended the conversation and waited on Santiago to return.

As if he knew when she needed him, he drove up on the cart with yet another bag filled with debris from the yard.

"Thank you," Lizzie said. "I just want to thank you."

"No need," he said, then looked over his shoulder and around the yard. "Ms. Chatsworth, I don't know how to say just right. My English is no good," he started but looked uneasy about continuing.

"It's okay. What is it, Santiago?"

"I was planting, um… How you say? Pansies? Um…flowers for cold weather. I see the doctor hit you when you were in kitchen. I hear Flossie tell everyone to watch you and no let you go anywhere. I worry for you."

Lizzie looked up at him, stunned. "I'm afraid. I want to run away, but I can't trust anyone."

"I take trash to dump on Monday mornings. You hide in back of truck, under blanket, by 9:00 a.m. I take you to my house. My wife help you."

"Oh, my God," Lizzie said, her voice cracking. "I have to go now," she said, panicking when she realized how long she'd been gone from the house. "I'll be in the truck, Santiago. I *will* be there, one way or another…and thank you."

Chapter 38

Lizzie made her rounds to the manicurist and the hairstylist as quickly as she could, making minimal conversation with them. There was very little she could do prior to Monday morning, except to stay under Grant's radar. She made it back to the estate in record time, parked her Lexus in the garage, and returned her car keys to Flossie, who was overwhelmed with the constant flow of deliveries for the evening. "Let me take care of that, Flossie," Lizzie suggested kindly.

"I've got it," Flossie said resentfully. "I just don't understand why that man can't handle his own deliveries. It seems to me it should go along with the job." Flossie mumbled a few choice words under her breath and hurried to the kitchen.

With her hair and makeup done, Lizzie didn't dare go outside and chance messing either of them up. Instead, she went upstairs to her room and laid out her gown for the evening. The guests would be arriving soon, and she wanted to be right on point with her appearance. She was approaching the day of her departure, and she didn't want to do anything that would upset Grant or leave him suspicious.

A short while later, she heard Grant speaking to Flossie, followed by his footsteps coming up the stairs. He paused in the doorway of her room. "I see you're almost ready," he said.

Lizzie looked up at him and noticed the weariness in his eyes. "Yes," she answered. "Maybe everyone will leave early so you can get some rest. Perhaps you can stay home tomorrow and relax a little."

"It's not really feasible for me right now, but it might be just what the doctor ordered. I didn't get any rest in the Caymans, so I may take the weekend off. There are a couple of new restaurants I've been wanting to try out. What do you think of a date night?"

The suggestion shocked Lizzie, but she tried not to show it. "That would be nice. I gave my keys back to Flossie. I know you were worried about me driving today, but all went well. I ate a nice lunch and feel much better than I did a couple of weeks ago."

"That's good to hear," Grant said. "I have just enough time to shower and dress. I'll stop by to get you on my way down."

Lizzie spent the next forty-five minutes going through her bedroom, deciding which items to take with her. She was basically limited to one small tote bag; anything larger would surely bring unwanted attention. She slid the pictures of herself and family from the photo album and wrapped a rubber band around them. They were undoubtedly her biggest treasure. Grant hadn't allowed her to bring much of anything from her studio apartment, so there was little she would regret leaving behind. Most of her jewelry was in the safe in Grant's office, but she didn't want it anyway. Realizing that was probably a foolish choice, she did decide to take what few items were in the jewelry box in her room. She couldn't rely on Maggie and Leland to take care of her financially, and the pieces were quite valuable; leaving them behind would be a stubborn decision and now wasn't a time to be proud. She decided she'd stuff the items in a sock just before she made her way to Santiago's truck on Monday morning.

A tap at the door alerted her that Grant was ready. As usual, he looked handsome and well put together, and all signs of fatigue were well hidden behind a façade of contentment. She tucked her arm in his, and the two walked down the winding staircase to the growing crowd below.

The estate was swirling with activity, the same group of waiters walking discreetly among their guests with trays of expensive wines and canapés, while a small orchestra played softly in the backdrop. It never ceased to amaze Lizzie that their parties always seemed to come together with such perfection. The couples were mingling with one another, but all stopped to watch as she and Grant made their grand entrance. She completely understood how her husband had them fooled. After all, she had been fooled herself.

Grant made his way to each of the guests, addressed them by name, and introduced Elizabeth as his wife and inspiration. She smiled sweetly at them, extending her thin hand to meet theirs and trying desperately to block out their faces and identities. It was hard to accept what Grant was doing to them, but there was little she could do about it.

"Elizabeth," one of the women said as she made her way over to her, "I am a friend of Devan Solomon's and she told me to let you know she enjoyed your visit to her home."

The thought of Devan brought a warm, comfortable feeling to Lizzie, and she reached out to grab the woman's hand. "Oh, she is such a delightful person," she said. "I so enjoyed our day together. Devan is also a very talented artist."

"Yes, indeed she is," the woman said. "Forgive me. My name is Lyla. My husband is J.P. Harvey."

"Where is J.P.?" Grant interrupted. "He is here, isn't he?"

"Yes, Dr. Chatsworth. I left him over there, with the Cornwalls."

"I'll be right back, darling," he said, giving Lizzie a light pat on the arm before he walked away. "I haven't seen J.P. in quite a while."

Lizzie turned her attention back to Lyla. "The Solomons' home is breathtaking. Have you ever visited her in the Caymans?"

"Yes, a couple of times. Indeed, it is exquisite. You have a beautiful home too."

"Thank you," Lizzie said. "How do you and Devan know each other?"

"Through the arts. J.P. loves to invest in fine pieces, and Devan and Dr. Solomon are always happy to educate us on their value. I know very little about it myself."

"Same here," Lizzie said. "But I do enjoy viewing lovely pieces. She took me to an art museum on the island, and I thoroughly enjoyed it."

"There are several nice places here in Atlanta. J.P. is on the board at the High Museum of Art. Perhaps you'd like to go with me one day."

"That sounds nice," Lizzie said, just as Grant returned with Lyla's husband.

"Good evening, Mrs. Chatsworth," J.P. said, extending his hand. "It's an honor to make your acquaintance."

"Yours as well," Lizzie answered. "I understand that you are on the board of directors for the High Museum of Art."

"Yes. Unfortunately, I don't have as much time to contribute to it as I have in the past, but I can't bring myself to give it up."

"I've invited Mrs. Chatsworth to go with me one day. I'm sure you can arrange a private tour," Lyla said.

"No doubt about it," J.P. said with a wide grin. "It would be my privilege."

Lizzie looked at Grant out of the corner of her eye but couldn't quite decipher if he was pleased or disgruntled. Either way, she wouldn't have to deal with it for much longer.

The conversation was cut short when they were summoned to dinner. Everyone seemed to enjoy the meal, and, thankfully, the night came to a quick close. Grant had spent about a half-hour with the men in the library and seemed quite pleased when everyone had gone. *They must have left hefty checks*, Lizzie thought sarcastically.

"I'm going to meet Zahir and Jean-Luc for a nightcap," Grant said, pulling on his navy-blue blazer. "Go ahead and turn in. I'll see you in the morning."

"I thought you were going to relax this weekend."

"It's just a nightcap, Elizabeth. I won't be performing surgery."

Lizzie sensed a change in his demeanor and decided to let it go. Besides, she really didn't care where he went. *He could have drinks with his mistress, for all I care.* "See you at breakfast," she said.

She made her way up the staircase to her bedroom and was reminded of how the last party had ended for her. She was grateful to be able to soak in a hot bath without having to worry about Flossie hovering over her. She started the water in the tub and undressed, then laid the gown across one of the chairs in the bedroom. She took the time to wash off the excessive layer of makeup, then began pulling bobby pins out of her updo, one by one. She removed the cascading diamond earrings and put them in her jewelry box so they would be readily available for her when she left on Monday morning. "Delightful!" She sighed as she climbed into the steaming water, laid her head back, and wet her hair.

Unsure of how long she had soaked in the tub, Lizzie got out, dried off with one of the large, plush towels, and slipped into a silk gown. She was sitting at the vanity when she heard the drawers opening and closing in Grant's desk in his office next to her room. *That's strange*, she thought. *He just left for drinks. Perhaps he forgot something.* Reaching for her night cream, she took her time as she rubbed more than an ample amount on her face.

The sounds continued from the study: papers rattling and filing cabinets being opened and shut.

Lizzie opened her door and walked down the hallway to check in on Grant. The door was shut, so she knocked lightly but got no response. *That's odd*, she thought. She tapped again, then noticed that the light under the door went out. For a second, her heart began to race. "Grant? Are you in there?"

She didn't hear anything.

Someone had to be in there; after all, she had heard someone and seen the light go out. *It's not Grant*, she suddenly thought. *Oh, my God. Who is in there?*

She walked quietly back toward her room and picked up her pace as she neared the staircase. "I'll just make it to the phone in the kitchen and alert Cornell at the gate," she said to herself. Reaching for the bannister, she started quickly down the stairs.

She was halfway down when a tall man, dressed in black from head to toe, grabbed her from behind. His hand was over her mouth, and his breath was heavy and warm on the nape of her neck. "Don't make a sound," he whispered. "Don't mention that anyone was here. Do you understand?"

"Yes, yes, I understand," she whispered back, tears stinging her eyes.

"I've been watching you. I know what you're planning. If you mention anyone being in your husband's office, I'll see to it that you never leave this house."

"Okay," Lizzie whispered back. "I won't say a word."

Just as quickly as he had grabbed her, he was gone. Lizzie held on to the bannister and leaned against the wall. She felt weak and was breathing so heavily that she feared she would hyperventilate.

"What in God's name is going on here?" Flossie said as she came into view at the bottom of the staircase, wearing her robe and with her hair tied up in a scarf. "Lizzie, what's the matter? You look like you've seen a ghost."

Lizzie stood up straight and tried to calm her breathing. "Nothing, Flossie. I'm fine."

"You most certainly are not. What was all that racket?"

"I, uh… Well, I was just going to the kitchen for a glass of milk and lost my footing at the top of the stairs. I almost fell."

"You coulda killed yourself, girl! Lizzie, you must be more careful. Do you want me to bring the milk to you?"

"No, that won't be necessary. I'm going to bed. I don't even want it anymore."

"Very well then. I'll see you in the morning."

Lizzie made her way back to her room and sank into the bed. *Who could that have been?* she thought. *And how does he know about my plans?* Clearly, he didn't want to hurt her, or he would have. *What did he take from the office?*

Her body was still trembling from the whole ordeal, but she got up and went into Grant's office. She turned on the light and looked around. Nothing appeared to be out of place. The drawers were all shut, and the desk was clear of any loose papers.

"What are you doing in here, Lizzie?" Flossie asked. "Dr. Chatsworth doesn't allow anyone in his office. You know that."

"Oh, my God," Lizzie said, grabbing her chest. "You scared the hell out of me."

"Why are you in here?"

Flossie's interrogation was unsettling to Lizzie, and she didn't appreciate it. "I live here, remember?"

"Yes, I know, but the doctor has made it painfully clear to everyone that this room is entirely off-limits. We don't even clean it unsupervised."

"I thought I heard him. I came to check that's all."

"Well, he isn't in here, so let's turn the lights out. You can go to bed."

Lizzie wanted to say more, to lash out at Flossie and make her resentment known, but she knew it would only cause more problems, something she couldn't afford with her escape just over the horizon. To be honest, Flossie frightened her. Her loyalty to Grant proved that she was protecting him, and Lizzie was sure the woman was fully aware of what he was doing. "I'm going to leave my door open. I'd like to see him when he gets home," she said. "I've been worried about him. He seems so…tired."

"Yes, which means he needs his rest. Let him be and go on to bed, Lizzie. I'll shut your door. He'll be downstairs for breakfast in the morning."

Lizzie did as she was told. *How strange*, she thought. *How strange that Flossie wants to keep me from Grant, my own husband.*

Chapter 39

Drs. Zahir Chavan and Jean-Luc Phillips were waiting in their usual booth in the dimly lit bar when Grant Chatsworth came in. It was after 11:00 p.m. on Friday evening and they were all exhausted.

Grant nodded to both of them before sliding into the booth. A cute redhead delivered Grant's usual, a finely aged scotch on the rocks, and he gave her a smile and slight wink. "Thanks, Andie," he said. "Keep them coming."

"I certainly will, handsome," she answered, flashing a beautiful, white smile before walking away, keenly aware that the good-looking doctor was following her with his eyes.

Zahir thought of telling Dr. Chatsworth that the woman was trouble but decided against it. There was far worse misfortune at the moment.

"Okay, fellas. Spill it. How's it going?"

"Miguel is nearing the end, as we expected. He's in and out of consciousness. I'm confident that he isn't even aware of his surroundings," Jean-Luc said.

"Who is with him now?"

"My cousin," Zahir piped in. "It is just a matter of time."

"Have you heard from any of his family? Have any of the men who transferred the primates returned?"

"There haven't been any calls, and we don't anticipate any," Jean-Luc answered. "We understand his family is still in Mexico. They don't know about any of this."

"That's one positive in this whole mess," Grant said sarcastically as he swirled his scotch around in the glass before swallowing it all.

It was only a few seconds before Andie returned with another round for all of them. Grant didn't offer any recognition this time, and she walked away looking disappointed.

"What shall we do with the body, Sir?" Zahir asked.

"I don't want him put in the river. We can't afford another body floating to the top, even though it would be difficult to establish the connection between us."

"If his body is found, the medical examiner will surely discover the bites from the primate, to say nothing of the vesicular skin lesions around the wounds. I hate to say it, but we should amputate the arm before disposing of the body," Zahir whispered nervously.

Grant was sipping from his drink and almost choked. "You're kidding, right?" he asked rudely.

"No, Sir, I am not. His lungs will be heavy from the congestion, but that could be caused by any number of things. The arm will be the one concern that will surely give us away."

"Jesus! Do not...and I repeat...do *not* cut the poor son-of-a-bitch's arm off. Shit, Zahir," Grant said, shaking his head in disgust. "I'm not as concerned about the arm as I am the whole damn body. Once that virus crossed the brain barrier, it filled his brain with infected yellow puss. His organs will be a mess. Our only hope is to put him somewhere where he'll decompose before anyone finds him."

"What about a fire?" Zahir pressed. "That would surely deplete any evidence."

"You have to be careful there too," Grant insisted. "If the fire is extinguished before it gets hot enough, it could simply preserve the organs. There is no room for error on this one, Doctors. Also, where the hell is Gunnar? I haven't heard from him in days, and he hasn't answered my calls."

"We do not have any information on him," Jean-Luc said, making sure to leave out any details about Christi Cate's accident. If Gunnar had left the country or gotten into some kind of trouble, maybe Dr. Chatsworth would never have to know about his latest screw-up. If the two doctors failed to tell him about it, it would make their lives much easier. They had already decided that they wouldn't bear the brunt of Gunnar's botchery anymore. "He hasn't shown up at the Research Facility or called in a couple of days."

"I knew from the get-go that he's no more than a fly-by-night mercenary," Grant said, lifting his glass toward the cute waitress to call for a refill. "We can manage without him. He may have gotten a better offer from some other part of the world. That type has only one allegiance, and that's the almighty dollar. One thing we don't have to worry about is him selling us out. The last thing he wants is to be blackballed from the mercenary business."

Zahir and Jean-Luc both heaved audible sighs of relief. They had felt from the beginning that Gunnar was a loose cannon. He could have simply walked away from any of the crimes he had committed. Gunnar didn't have any allegiances to anyone or anything, and there was certainly no love lost between them.

Maybe he will float up in the river, Zahir thought, *and it might not be such a bad thing.*

Chapter 40

Lizzie had gotten little in the way of sleep the night before. She just lay awake, worrying about the stranger in Grant's office and the reaction she had gotten from Flossie when she wanted to wait up for Grant. She knew she needed more rest, but it was clear she wouldn't be getting it anytime soon. There was just too much on her mind.

She pushed the heavy duvet back, climbed out of bed, and opened the drapes to let the bright sunlight flood into her bedroom. She decided on a quick shower rather than another bath. The hot water felt good on her weary back and shoulders, but her mind insisted on traveling back to the man in black. There was something vaguely familiar about his voice, even though he clearly attempted to disguise it in harsh whispers. Lizzie was so shocked at the time that it was hard to recall any details. She remembered that he was about six feet tall, lean, and strong, but she didn't even catch sight of him as he ran away. *Odd*, she thought. *What was he getting from Grant's office, and how does he know I'm trying to escape?*

Lizzie kept her shower short, dressed, pulled her hair into a ponytail, and went down for breakfast. She was hoping Grant would be downstairs already. She had an uneasy feeling and she wanted to make sure that he wasn't on to her.

Grant was sitting at the dining room table with his coffee, reading the *Atlanta Journal Constitution.*

"Good morning," Lizzie said.

"Good morning to you," he responded. "How are you feeling?"

"Fine. Have you eaten breakfast already?"

"No. Flossie is just about to bring it out. She said you almost fell last night."

"I simply lost my balance. It was nothing, really. I'm just clumsy, I suppose."

"Well, enough is enough. I'm going to schedule a physical and full lab workup for you next week. I should have insisted after the fainting spell."

"I appreciate that, Grant," Lizzie said. "I have been feeling better since I've been reading outside, but the weather won't allow that any longer. Hopefully, a physical will get to the bottom of this."

Grant turned his attention back to the newspaper while Flossie came in with their breakfast. The smell of food no longer made Lizzie nauseous, and her appetite was growing by leaps and bounds.

"Do you think you'll have any room left for a big dinner tonight?" Grant asked, glancing over at her empty plate. "I was going to make reservations at one of the new restaurants I mentioned."

"Sure." Lizzie smiled. "There's plenty of time to build my appetite back up."

He laughed playfully at her, something he hadn't done since they were dating.

If only things could have worked out differently between us, Lizzie thought regretfully.

"Excuse me, Doctor," Flossie said as she returned to the dining room. "Cornell Sayer just phoned and said there's a Detective Pitts at the front gate. He would like to speak with you."

"Very well. Tell him to send the detective up. I'll meet with him here."

"Would you like me to go upstairs?" Lizzie asked.

"That won't be necessary," Grant said. "I don't have anything to hide from my wife."

Flossie greeted the detective at the front door and led him back to the dining room. "Can I get you a cup of coffee?" she asked politely.

"Yes, that would be nice," the detective answered as he sat down across from Lizzie at the oversized table. "My apologies," he began. "I'm afraid we haven't met."

"This is my wife, Elizabeth," Grant said curtly. "What can I do for you this morning, Detective?"

"It appears that one of our patrol units has located a Lincoln Town Car, abandoned on Bankhead Highway. It is registered to Cardiac Care Research Facility. Do you know anything about it?"

"No, I'm afraid I don't. You must understand, Detective, I operate two offices, perform surgeries in two different hospitals, and run the Research Facility. I'm a very busy man. I hardly have time to keep up with company vehicles."

"That's a valid point. It hasn't been reported stolen as of yet. However, I am confident you can scratch it off as a total loss. Whoever stole the vehicle certainly did a job on it."

"What does that mean exactly?" Grant asked arrogantly.

"It was stripped of anything of any value. Chop shops utilize virtually everything from a new car these days. It is essentially perched up on cinder blocks behind a failed business."

Detective Pitts's radio made a loud static noise before a voice resonated over the air, "Excuse me, Sir. We have a Signal 33S in the west end, with a Signal 48, possible homeless man."

"My ETA is about twenty minutes. I'll radio for the address when I leave my current location."

"Ten-four, Sarge."

"I'll have to take a rain check on that coffee. Seems we have a structural fire at the moment. You can contact the Police Department to obtain a report for your insurance. I'm sure they'll be impounding what's left of the vehicle soon."

"I'll do that," Grant said, standing to shake the officer's hand. "So a homeless man set a fire?" he asked nonchalantly.

"I'm not sure who started it, but it appears a homeless man is dead at the scene. Just another day in the big city," Detective Pitts said as he shrugged his shoulders.

"Looks like my day off has been short-lived," Grant said sarcastically to Lizzie. "I don't know what those buffoons are doing at the Research Facility, but it seems as though they require more of my energy than being a surgeon does. I'll make a reservation for 7:00 tonight, but I'll have to let you know if I'll be able to make it," he added as he got up from the table and made his way to the front door.

Lizzie strode quietly beside him, gathered his coat from the closet, and handed it to him. "No problem," she answered. "I was just hoping you'd have some time to rest."

"That's impossible these days. I'll be in touch," he said, leaning down to kiss her cheek before grabbing his keys from the pewter bowl by the door.

Chapter 41

Grant pulled up to the Facility in short order, luckily beating any Saturday event traffic in Atlanta, which could have been bumper to bumper at any given time. He sat behind the wheel for a few minutes, trying to mentally lower his blood pressure before confronting his staff.

Fortunately, the perky, young receptionist was off, so he didn't have to deal with her silliness. The main entrance was locked, but he had his key with him. He was grateful that the alarm system wasn't activated, meaning there were some staff on site. Grant made his way back to the laboratory and found several technicians in white lab coats, looking tediously through microscopes and documenting their findings. It was an impressive setup if he could say so himself. A great deal of time and funding had been spent on it, and although the drug would never be approved or even reach human trials, they had some damn good ideas. If he could have spent all his time on the development of a new drug, it was possible he could do great things, but that was out of the question, and it really didn't even interest him.

A Peruvian woman in her mid-thirties looked up from her work. "Good morning, Doctor," she said as she removed her glasses. "What brings you out on Saturday?"

"Just stopping by," Grant answered casually. "Is Dr. Chavan or Dr. Phillips here?"

"I haven't seen them, but they don't always stop by the lab when they come in on Saturdays. Perhaps they are back with the primates."

"I'll go take a look. How are things progressing?"

"Very well. I only work on the weekends, but I am seeing much progress."

"Glad to hear it," Grant said, attempting to sound upbeat and on top of things, even though he was neither. "Nice to see you again," he added, struggling to remember her name but quickly giving up on that.

He made his way through the building, back to where the primates were held. He could hear them screeching long before he entered the section containing their cages. Grant had never been fond of animals and certainly detested any that were loud or boisterous. It was feeding time, which seemed to be the reason for their shrieks, so he stood in the backdrop and observed the two men placing straw and fruit in their cages. The food seemed to keep them busy and temporarily silenced their irritating shrills. Grant noticed Zahir coming in to supervise the feeding, and he motioned for him to meet him outside.

It wasn't long before Zahir made his way into the corridor, outside of the primate habitat. "What brings you out today?" Zahir asked.

"I just had a visit from a police detective. Was our monkey boy burned up in a structure fire today?"

"All is well, Sir. The abandoned building and body were burned very badly, long before any sirens were heard. You can trust that neither his identity nor his cause of death will ever be determined."

"I am glad to hear that, but that's only one bullet we've dodged. Apparently, Gunnar's Town Car was found abandoned in a seedy section of town this morning. Thank God they stripped it of everything, or we'd be trying to conceal the fact that Albert Tinsley's body was stashed in it at one time. My next question is where the hell is Gunnar Azarov?"

"I wouldn't worry about him," Zahir said abruptly. "We might be better off without him. He was a loose cannon as you Americans like to say. He was beginning to make me very nervous."

"I can't argue that," Grant conceded. "However, we don't need his body surfacing so we're forced to explain why we employed a damn mercenary."

"Good riddance," Zahir continued. "Good riddance of Gunnar, the Lincoln Town Car, Miguel's body, and even that nosy Albert. Hopefully, now we can concentrate on why we are here in the first place."

"Indeed. The laboratory looks good, the Facility is immaculate, and the primates are impressive, Zahir. You look tired though. I realize you and Jean-Luc have been working as hard as I have. Take the weekend off," Grant said sincerely. "I'm going to take my wife to dinner and spend tomorrow watching the movies that have been piling up on our DVR. Some rest will do us all good."

Zahir looked at his boss as if he had three heads. Dr. Grant Chatsworth had never done anything but push his employees to the maximum, and it was quite the contrary to hear him suggest a respite. It could only mean one of two things: Either he sincerely believed they were due some must-needed rest, or else he was about to bolt with the money. Either way, it left Zahir with a bad feeling in his gut.

Chapter 42

Clara and Iris spent their Saturday morning combing through the newspaper and watching the local news.

"I don't see anything, Clara," Iris said, her brow furrowing in frustration. "The discovery of a body in an abandoned vehicle surely woulda warranted at least a small blurb, even here, don't you think?"

"I suppose you're right," Clara answered, "but it's possible they haven't found the car yet."

"Let's just take a ride over there," Iris suggested. "We can see if it's still there."

"No way," Clara said, looking at her friend in astonishment. "The killer always goes back to the scene of the crime. They might be expecting us, and I want no part of that welcome wagon."

"I'm not proposing we go back behind the building, Clara. I'm not that foolish. I'm simply suggesting that we ride by the scene, just to see if any cops are there."

"We'll stick out like a sore thumb. What business could two old white women have on that side of town?"

"If I didn't know better, I'd say you sound like a racist, Clara."

"No, I sound like a *realist*," Clara said flatly as she folded up the paper. "It hasn't made the paper, so there's no sense in worrying about it today. Besides, we wiped all our fingerprints from the car, and I don't see how they could possibly tie us to the crime."

"I wonder how Justin and Christi are doing."

"We have to let that go also, Iris. We've just got to trust in the good Lord that Christi will recover and that the two of them have a long, healthy life."

"Well, I don't see how one phone call could possibly hurt."

"No, Iris…and I don't mean, maybe. Now ride with me to take these items over to Daisy at the sub shop. I'm so worried about Lizzie riding that bus."

"People do it every day. She'll be fine."

"She'll be on the run. I'm sure the first place her husband will look will be the bus station. He's no fool, and he knows she doesn't have any other means of transportation."

"Do you honestly think he'd even consider the possibility that she'd board a Greyhound? He's too uppity for that to even cross his mind."

"I don't know, Iris. I'm just on edge. Hopefully, the items in this bag will help hide her identity."

"Let's get going then. I'm still tired from missing all that sleep the night you killed that… Well, never mind."

"Iris, I do declare. I don't think I can turn you loose anywhere. If you don't learn to hush that mouth, you're going to get us caught."

Iris refused to participate in any further banter with Clara. They were both exhausted, to say little of the stress the past couple of days had put on them, and she didn't have the energy to keep arguing with her friend. "Okay. Let's go on over to Daisy's place. I'm ready for a long bath. I'm turning in early tonight."

"Me too."

The two women were almost to J&L Subs when Iris couldn't stand it any longer. "What's in the bag?"

"Just a disguise I threw together. She is a very beautiful young lady, and if the police or media start showing her face around, surely someone will remember her. Not only that, but Lizzie will definitely be out of her element on public transportation. I'm terribly concerned about her. I wonder if Dr. Chatsworth will look for her."

"It all depends," Iris answered, wrinkling her forehead in thought. "You didn't answer my question though. *What's* in the bag?"

"A gray wig, some large sunglasses, a floppy hat, and an outfit more suitable for our generation. If she keeps the shades on, most of her face will be obscured."

"Poor child," Iris said. "She's going from riches to rags. I don't envy her."

"Somehow, I don't think she's worried about leaving the money."

"Well, sometimes it's worth it to walk away, I s'pose, especially if your man keeps throwing bodies in the river."

Clara steered her car through the alley and around back, then parked as close as she could to the building. "If there's one thing I hate worse than the traffic in this city, it's the parking situation downtown. We better get in and out. I don't need another parking ticket."

Their friend Daisy was manning the cash register, just as they suspected she would be. She offered a quick wave but was busy ringing up a customer, so Clara and Iris slid into an empty booth.

"Might as well get some lunch," Iris suggested.

"Good afternoon, ladies," Daisy said. "If you wanna order anything, it's on the house. The pastrami is to die for."

"Pastrami gives me heartburn," Iris said. "That reminds me, Clara. We need to stop at Walgreens on the way home and pick up some Tums."

Clara ignored the comment. "I'll take the turkey on wheat, Daisy. How are you today? Looks like you have a big crowd."

"Not so big. The weekends are never as busy as the weekdays. I get a lot of business people during the week, the lunch crowd. Iris, do you want to try the turkey too?"

"Sure. Why not?" Iris answered blandly.

"I'll be right back, ladies." Daisy put the order in at the grill and quickly reclaimed her position at the cash register.

Clara had known Daisy for at least twenty years. The two had been in the same Sunday school class since Daisy had moved to Atlanta to be closer to her daughter. She was a quirky lady, very small in stature, with a glowing red dye job and teased hair that never seemed to shift out of place. Her whole life revolved around the restaurant, and Clara figured she would die if she was ever forced to retire.

The sandwiches arrived quickly although neither woman had much of an appetite.

Clara motioned Daisy back to their booth. "Thanks so much for passing this on, Daisy," she said as she handed over the brown paper sack. "Lizzie should be in Monday morning sometime, though I'm not quite sure when. Will you let her use the restroom to change?"

"Certainly. That's not a problem. She can go out the back, at the end of the hall, just off of the women's restroom. No one will notice the change. I don't know what you've got going on and don't really wanna know," she said matter-of-factly, "but you've been a

191

good friend, and I'm glad to help." With that, she was off, flying back to the cash register to resume her daily tasks.

Clara and Iris both offered a wave before ducking out of the sub shop and heading home.

Chapter 43

Maggie Knox had been a bundle of nerves since she'd first heard from her sister in the Caymans. Other than the fact that Lizzie wanted to leave a bad situation, she knew little else about what was going on. Maggie was somewhat apprehensive about sharing it with her husband, but she knew Leland would be fair and empathetic about her sister's difficult circumstances. He had never let her down before, and she didn't expect him to now.

When she talked to him about it, Leland did bring up one very valid point, one Maggie hadn't considered. Although the guesthouse was an ideal place for Lizzie to stay, it was far from a feasible hideout. Grant Chatsworth was not an ignorant man, and their home would be one of the first places he would look. After all, Maggie was the only family Lizzie had left, and she felt certain that any friends Lizzie had when they married were long gone by now.

"I have a client over in Ocean Springs who's leaving town for a few months to visit his ailing mother," Leland said one evening. "I'm sure I could make some type of arrangement with him. I could inquire about renting for a while, but at the very least, I'm confident he'd welcome a house sitter. It's right on the bayou. It isn't a huge place but nothing to sneeze at either. It's also very secluded. It's over off Iberville Avenue, and the road dead ends into a cemetery. Evergreen, I think it is."

"I'd worry to death about her being over there by herself. It's so isolated, Leland."

"Maggie, Ocean Springs is as safe as it gets, and it's just across the bridge. Besides, we don't know the whole story yet. Her husband may not even come looking for her at all."

"Okay. Can you talk to your client tomorrow? We had better be prepared, just in case."

Leland talked to his client, Colton Marshall, who was delighted at the prospect of having someone stay in his vacant home for such an undetermined amount of time. He only asked that Lizzie pay for the utilities and water. Colton graciously agreed to keep the details under wraps and left the key under the mat for Maggie to check the place out. Sunday was the perfect day for her to look around because no one would have any idea yet what Lizzie had planned.

Maggie decided to leave Leland behind with the kids and go alone. She had so much on her mind, and the last thing she wanted to do was share it with anyone. She hoped her nerves would settle down when her sister finally arrived safely in Biloxi.

Leland was right: Not only was Ocean Springs a pretty place, but it was also a safe one, just over the bridge from Biloxi. Maggie passed all the casinos and seafood restaurants that advertised specials on shrimp and oyster po' boys. She always enjoyed crossing the long bridge and never took for granted the serene beauty and peacefulness of the water below. She passed the eclectic art shops, drugstores, and the large chain grocery store before noticing the Krispy Kreme doughnut shop coming into view; that was the landmark that indicated she would make a left on Iberville Avenue.

The red light gave her just enough time to ponder whether to stop for a pastry and a cup of warm coffee. *A no-brainer,* Maggie thought. *A steaming cup of black coffee and a fresh glazed donut will certainly calm me down a bit.* She opted to go inside instead of going through the drive-thru, and she took her time savoring the treat.

Maggie glanced down at her watch, realizing she could no longer prolong visiting the house. It was less than a mile before she saw the street numbers on the mailbox. The U-shaped brick driveway made it possible to enter from one of two ways. She placed the minivan in park and got out to look the place over.

The house was a smaller version of a Southern antebellum, white with dark green shudders, with a wraparound porch and silver tin roof. The front yard, although relatively small, was well-kept and manicured. Maggie walked up the cement stairs leading to the front porch and retrieved the key from under the mat. She was greeted by an expansive foyer and wide hallway with heavily varnished hardwood floors. It was very similar to her own house, albeit not quite as large. Heavy window treatments hung from the oversized windows in the living room but were pulled back to allow in the sunlight. She walked over and looked out at the tall grass that concealed the bayou in the distance. A large white heron stood just at the water's edge, perhaps waiting to discover his next meal. The house wasn't decorated sparsely but wasn't overdone with unnecessary furniture either, making it appear roomier. Maggie hadn't asked Leland anything about the owner, but he was apparently a single man with good taste. There were a couple of framed photographs: what appeared to be friends on fishing trips and one displaying a young man and his mother.

Maggie slowly made her way through the house, taking notice of the updated kitchen and recently remodeled baths. It was a three-bedroom, two-bath home, practically sparkling from a recent cleaning. There were two fireplaces, one in the living room and another in the master bedroom, and each appeared to be in working order. She walked out on the back porch through French doors that opened off the living room. There, she discovered a beautiful outdoor space with a charcoal grill and table with four cushioned chairs. The bayou could be seen in the distance, along with a long, narrow dock and a boathouse. The entrance to the cemetery Leland had spoken about could be seen to the left of the property. Although Maggie felt at peace when she visited her grandmother and her parents at their resting places, cemeteries generally made her feel dreadful; she hoped Lizzie would be okay with one right next door.

Unsure of how much time had passed, Maggie decided to make one last sweep of the property to see what supplies she would need to pick up for her sister. The basics were all there: clean towels and sheets, chopped firewood, and kitchen utensils. A quick trip to the local grocery store would provide Lizzie with all she might need.

Maggie made the trip to the store and was back within thirty minutes. She placed navel oranges, tangerines, grapes, and bananas in a large bowl on the kitchen counter. She found a delicate crystal vase in one of the cabinets and filled it with water and the bouquet of flowers she had found in the Floral Department. The refrigerator had a few condiments in it, but she had purchased a gallon of milk, fresh-squeezed orange juice, a dozen eggs, sandwich fixings, a variety of cheeses, a loaf of bread, and a couple of bottles of nice wine. She also placed a few cans of soup in the pantry, along with a canister of mixed nuts and a bag of chips.

Next, Maggie made her way to the master bathroom where she placed a basket of deodorant, shampoo, conditioner, a new hairbrush, toothpaste, and a toothbrush. She wasn't sure what toiletries her sister would be able to bring with her, as she had to make a quick and clandestine getaway.

Maggie made one last walk-through of the home, set the alarm, and closed the door behind her. All that was left to do was wait and pray that Lizzie would soon arrive safely.

Chapter 44

Lizzie had slept very little over the weekend as she was too encumbered with anxiousness about meeting Santiago Monday morning at 9:00. Grant left early for work Monday, and she had told Flossie the night before not to wake her for breakfast because she wanted to sleep in. She had spent much of the previous night deciding what she would take with her. Lizzie decided to place her treasured items in a pillowcase for easier concealment. Her photos were the first things she packed, followed by a few pairs of clean undergarments, all the jewelry that was readily available to her, and the money Clara had embezzled for her. She had also taken the time to write a short note for Daisy to pass on:

Dear Clara,

Words cannot express how much I appreciate all you have done for me. In fact, this escape plan could not have been pulled off at all without your help. The money you've given me will certainly come in handy, and I pray that you don't get caught for taking it for me. As you know, I am headed to Biloxi to be with my sister. If anything urgent should happen that I need to be aware of, you can reach my brother-in-law at Bevins, Knox, and Jenkins law firm, where he is a partner. I trust that you and your friend will be careful. You have done all you can, Clara. Let the authorities do the rest.

Respectfully Yours,

Lizzie

She quickly placed the letter in an envelope and stuffed it in the pillowcase before strapping on her Cartier watch. It, too, could be sold if money became tight. At 8:45, Lizzie made her way down the stairs, out one of the back doors, and to the garage where the property maintenance vehicles were housed. She was very careful and didn't notice anyone who might have spotted her.

The old brown truck Santiago used for trips to the dump was parked in the garage, and she welcomed the stained blue tarp in the truck bed. She climbed onto the back bumper, stepped over the tailgate, and plopped her body into the truck.

Grateful for her oversized down jacket, she gathered her long, golden mane into a black stocking cap, pulled the pillowcase near her chest, and snuggled under the cold plastic tarp, nestled among the bags of debris.

Fortunately, the wait wasn't long. She heard the shuffle of his work boots, then listened intently as he cleared his throat to warn her of his presence. "Ms. Lizzie?" he whispered.

"I'm here, Santiago," she whispered back. "All is well. I made it."

"Thanks to God," he whispered back, then hopped in the truck and cranked the sputtering engine.

The frigid air blew swiftly under the tarp, and Lizzie shivered from the cold of both the weather and the metal truck bed. She struggled to hold the old piece of plastic down around her small frame. She envisioned where they were as they wound their way down the curvy drive. She felt the truck coming to a stop as Santiago approached the front gate, and she held her breath.

"Good mornin', Mr. Cornell," Santiago said. "Today is cold outside."

"Yes, indeed it is," Cornell Sayer answered. "I suppose you're headed to the dump, huh? It's about that time, eh?"

"Yes, Sir. Monday mornin's is for getting rid of lawn things, pine cones and sticks."

Lizzie continued to hold her breath but gasped loudly when a gust of wind pulled the bottom of the tarp up over her sneakers. She shifted quickly to recover it and hold it down with her feet.

"Just a second, Santiago," Cornell said.

Lizzie could hear his footsteps as he made his way back to the rear of the truck. She was sure her heart would simply burst when he lifted the tarp, ever so lightly, right near her head. The two made eye contact. Lizzie didn't say a word but pled with him with her eyes, which were now filling with tears. He winked at her slightly before placing the tarp back over her face, but not before she noticed the black gloves, the same ones that had been wrapped around her mouth a couple of nights earlier when he'd ransacked Grant's office.

"All's clear, Santiago," Sayer said. "Just thought you were about to lose your tarp, but it's secure." He hit the side of the truck, and Santiago pulled out of the drive and onto Paces Ferry Road.

Chapter 45

Lizzie wasn't sure how many miles they had driven before Santiago pulled the truck over to the side of the road. She heard him shut the driver door, then saw his face as he removed the tarp from her body.

"So sorry, Ms. Lizzie. I know you're cold. I could not pull over for a long time. I did not want someone to see. Please get in front. Truck is very warm for you."

Lizzie was so chilled that it took a couple of minutes for her to get her stiff body to cooperate and stand. She stepped over the tailgate and onto the bumper, and Santiago reached for her hand and helped her to the ground. She quickly made her way to the warmth of the truck cab.

"Take off gloves. They are cold. Hold fingers to heat," Santiago said kindly. "I so sorry, Ms. Lizzie."

"Oh no, don't be sorry," she assured him. "Thank you, Santiago."

"I was scared Mr. Cornell was seeing you."

"He didn't," Lizzie lied. "He wouldn't have let us leave if he had." She rubbed her hands together in front of the heat vent and smiled. "We did it, Santiago! Thank goodness I'm free!"

"I take you to my wife right away. She has coffee for you."

Lizzie felt the sting of her tears—they were tears of relief and tears of the unknown. Her journey was far from over. In fact, it had just begun.

The two rode in silence for about ten minutes until Santiago pulled into the driveway of a small cinderblock house.

A short, stout, Hispanic woman met them at the door and spoke hysterically to Santiago before hugging Lizzie and touching her face. "You okay now, you poor child. I take good care of you. Come, come," she said, motioning inside the house. "I get you warm coffee. You feel better soon."

"This is my wife, Mariana," Santiago said as he led Lizzie to the kitchen table.

His wife was already pouring a large mug of steaming black coffee, which she quickly handed to their guest. "Drink, drink," she said, motioning hurriedly with her hands. "You so cold, child."

Lizzie blew on the liquid, then slipped slowly, grateful that it heated up her frozen insides as it went down. "Thank you, Ms. Mariana. Thank you so much."

Santiago's wife busied herself at the stove while he spoke. "My wife is preparing large breakfast for you. You get warm and rest. My brother will arrive in an hour to take you wherever you want go. I must go to dump limbs and leaves, then return to work."

Lizzie swallowed the coffee that was in her mouth before she felt the heaving sobs coming from her body. "Santiago, how can I ever thank you? You have truly saved my life."

"No thanks for me. You be safe, and that is enough. I must go now, or Flossie will wonder."

Lizzie fought the sudden urge to hug him and instead buried her face in her hands and sobbed.

Mariana stepped away from the stove and wrapped her thick arms around her shoulders. "Enough, child," she said as she wiped her apron across Lizzie's wet face. "You will be fine. My brother-in-law see to it. Now eat," she said as she passed over a plate of flour tortillas filled with scrambled eggs, chorizo, and refried beans.

Lizzie ate until she thought she would burst, and that seemed to please Mariana to no end.

The loveable Latina refilled Lizzie's coffee cup an immeasurable amount of times, then gave her a brown bag that she assured her contained a hearty lunch for the road. Next, Mariana led her through the small house, back to a bathroom, where she handed her a warm washcloth. "Wash your face now. No more tears." She turned and walked out, closing the door behind her.

Lizzie paused to look at herself in the mirror and was mortified by her own disheveled reflection. She was so thin and pale, almost ghostly in appearance. She wondered how long she had looked that way. The wet washcloth felt good against her face. Lizzie hoped Maggie wouldn't notice just how sickly she looked. She knew she'd have to visit a doctor right away so she could start taking the prenatal vitamins.

She heard the front door open, then close, and she overheard a male voice speaking to Mariana in Spanish. She rinsed the cloth off and folded it, then placed it on the edge of the bathroom sink. Lizzie made her way down the short hallway to the living room.

Mariana grabbed her hand and pulled her close. "This is Eduardo. He take you where you want to go. He is good man, Lizzie."

Lizzie reached out her hand to meet his. "It's nice to meet you, Eduardo. Thank you very much for your help."

"I'm happy to do it," he said in fluent English, much to Lizzie's relief. "My brother, Santiago, has been very concerned about your safety."

"You speak English very well."

"Thank you," he answered with a smile. "I have been here for over twenty years. My brother and his wife have only been here five. I understand that you want to take the bus to see your sister?"

"Yes, but I need to be dropped off down the street at a sub shop owned by the friend of a friend if that is okay."

"Sure. No problem. Like I said, I am here to help. Are you ready to go?"

"Yes," Lizzie answered. She turned to Mariana and hugged her tightly, burying her face in the woman's stout shoulder before reaching for her pillowcase.

"No, child. That won't do for the road trip. Let me get you something else," Mariana said. She rambled around in the kitchen cupboard until she found a small tote bag. "Put things in here," she said, smiling kindly. "You will be okay, child. I pray many times for you. *Vaya con Dios, Mija!*" she insisted, shooing Lizzie toward the front door with her hands.

Eduardo held the door open for Lizzie as she got into the truck, waving good-bye to Mariana while assuring her that she would eat the lunch she had packed for her on the road.

"So the sub shop is near the Greyhound terminal on Forsyth?" Eduardo asked.

"Yes. It's called J&L, and my friend said it's just a couple of blocks from there."

"I know the place. Is that little bag all you have with you?" he asked as he motioned toward it.

"Yes," she answered somewhat sheepishly, trying to hide her embarrassment. "I'm sure Santiago told you I'm leaving unannounced, so to speak."

"He did, but do you need anything else? I can make another stop if you need me to."

"No, thank you. I can get whatever I need when I arrive at my sister's. I'll be fine."

It was only a short ride before Lizzie was saying good-bye, stepping out of the truck, and starting her life anew. She thanked Eduardo profusely and offered him some gas money, which he kindly refused.

Lizzie took a deep breath before entering the shop. Although she had never met Daisy, it was quite easy to spot her. She was busy at the cash register, so Lizzie got in line with the other customers.

"Good morning...or early afternoon, I suppose," Daisy said as she looked up at Lizzie. "What can I get for you?"

"My name is Lizzie," she said, just above a whisper. "My friend Clara left something here with you."

Daisy's eyes lit up, and a broad smiled formed on her small face. "Yes, dear. I have it right here behind the counter. Just have a seat in that far booth, and I'll be with you shortly."

"Okay. Thank you," Lizzie said, then walked to the booth and slid in.

Daisy rang up the remaining customers and said something to the cook behind the counter before making her way over to Lizzie. She slid into the booth and passed a large paper bag over to Lizzie. "This is all Clara gave me. It's my understanding that you are to change into whatever's in there, then exit out the back. There's a ladies' room right down that hallway, and if you follow the hall, you'll find an exit door back there, out of sight. I took the liberty of packing you a sandwich for the road. I hope you like pastrami. Ours is to die for," she bragged.

Lizzie smiled. "I love it."

"Good luck to ya. Don't really know what the story is and don't really care to, but it sounds like you're running away from something. Long story short, any friend of Clara's is a friend of mine." Daisy didn't wait for a reply, nor did she give Lizzie time to thank her. She simply jumped up and went back to her work.

Lizzie slid out of the booth, with the paper bag in hand, then hurried back to the restroom. Even though her hands were trembling and her heart was racing, she had to let out a quiet laugh when she saw what Clara had packed for her. She quickly put on the relatively baggy clothes, followed by the gray wig, floppy hat, and large sunglasses. She stuffed her own clothes in the paper sack, went out the back door, and tossed the bag in the dumpster; the clothes she threw away were very expensive, but she didn't want anything to remind her of the life she had led for the past five years. *Maybe a homeless person will find them and wear them*, she thought with a smile. *Wouldn't Grant just love that?*

She walked the two short blocks to the Greyhound terminal and made her way through the crowd outside. Lizzie had never traveled by bus before, and she was afraid she might be stuck at the station for hours before the next one left for Biloxi, like people always seemed to be in the movies. She was pleasantly surprised not only to find a kiosk that took her cash and spat out a printed ticket but also to learn that her ride would depart within the hour. Avoiding any eye contact with the security cameras, even though her eyes were well hidden behind the obnoxious shades, Lizzie purchased a newspaper and sat down on one of the gray metal benches. The station was alive with commotion, some people departing for their destinations and others returning from long trips. Small children begged for snacks from the numerous vending machines, and others ran around and around the benches, driving their mothers crazy.

Lizzie looked blandly at the front page but didn't see anything of interest. She pulled the ticket from her bag and glanced at it. It would be a long ride, almost nine and a half hours in all. If she had her own transportation, she could make the trip in five hours. That was surely a concern because if Grant realized she was missing early on, he could beat her to the bus station in Biloxi. The bus was scheduled to make two stops in Alabama, one in Montgomery and another in Mobile. No matter what, it was bound to be a long and grueling day, and it didn't help that she was pregnant and had started off the morning being smuggled in the back of a rusty old pickup.

204

Lizzie desperately wanted to use the payphone and was surprised to see such a relic there, but she didn't want to draw any attention to herself; she feared that Grant might demand to see the surveillance tapes later on. She was in a good spot now, clearly out of sight of the cameras. She busied herself with the newspaper, reading the comics until the boarding call came for her bus. When she boarded, she made her way to the back and settled in next to the window, clutching her bag tightly. It was almost noon, and she wondered if Flossie had tried to wake her for lunch.

A young girl, probably in her early twenties, sat down beside Lizzie. She offered no greeting and attempted to cover a recently bruised eye.

Grateful not to have to offer any conversation, Lizzie quickly turned away and looked out the window. After days of struggling for rest, she was now exhausted. She laid her head against the cold glass and drifted into a deep sleep.

Chapter 46

Flossie was relieved to have a break from Lizzie and decided to let her sleep as late as she desired. She was tired of babysitting her and thought of her as nothing more than a spoiled, vulnerable child. *It's beyond me why Dr. Chatsworth keeps her around*, Flossie thought. *"She is more trouble than she's worth. Surely, the man could find some less annoying eye candy to accompany him to parties.*

The holidays were nearing, which meant there was a great deal of work to be done in the house. Flossie would spend the day polishing the silver trays for upcoming events at the estate, then meet with the staff to ensure that everything was in impeccable shape, both in and outside the home. Her job was never really done, and just when she thought she had some downtime, it seemed something else popped up on her never-ending to-do list. That was really good news though; it meant Dr. Chatsworth could not possibly manage without her, and she relished that thought. *I'm really the woman of the house, not Lizzie*, she thought snidely. *And it won't be long before he sees it.*

Flossie gathered up her silver polish and polishing cloths, then assembled all the pieces she needed to clean. She saw Santiago tending to the grounds, watched as Lonnie replaced bulbs in the pool house, and heard Rufus running the buffer over the marble foyer. *Everything is coming along just fine,* she thought.

The ringing of the doorbell temporarily derailed her work, but when she heard Rufus turn off the buffer, she knew he was taking the time to answer it. As Flossie began rubbing the smelly paste across a silver platter, she heard the fast-paced clicking of stiletto heels.

"Hello there, Mother," an unpleasantly familiar voice said flippantly as she tossed her sleek hair extensions over her shoulder. "Polishing the good doctor's silver, I see."

Flossie turned so quickly that she came close to losing her balance. "What the hell are you doing here, Jameeka? I've told you time and time again not to show up at my place of employment."

"Not to worry, Mother. I was simply in the neighborhood and thought it only fitting to stop by and–"

"To stop by and try to get a look at my handsome boss? Or is it the college boy down at the gate?"

"Why would you even suggest such a thing?" Jameeka asked, flashing a wicked smile. "I don't need to throw myself at anyone," she continued, running her hands seductively down her figure and spinning around to show off her sinfully tight, short skirt.

"Lizzie is upstairs, you fool," Flossie hissed. "Get on outta here, and don't come back, ya hear?"

"Don't get so defensive. You act as though *you're* the doctor's wife when you're really nothing more than his maid. You might be polishing his silver, Mother, but someone else is polishing his—"

"Get out!" Flossie whispered fiercely.

As Jameeka turned around to leave, she was met by Rufus, who was coming through the kitchen to get a new buffing pad from the storage closet. "Leaving so soon, Miss Jameeka?" he asked.

"Why, yes, Sir, I am." She smiled meekly. "My mother is quite busy, so off I go," she said, waving good-bye to Rufus and blowing her mother a kiss.

Flossie was clearly upset, and Rufus knew better than to ruffle her feathers any further. He got what he needed from the closet and went back to work.

That girl is the devil, Flossie seethed. *If she had half an opportunity, she'd wiggle her way into the doctor's bed,* she thought. Her hands were shaking with such fury that she wasn't able to stabilize the platter enough to apply the polish. "I won't let her ruin a good thing," she said to herself. "I will not let that happen!"

It was then that Flossie did something she had only done on rare occasions: She raided Dr. Chatsworth's liquor cabinet. It was early in the day, but she convinced herself that a quick shot or two wouldn't hurt anybody. She bypassed Rufus and made a beeline for the study. After moving several decanters around, she found a nicely aged Chivas Regal and poured a large splash into an iced tea glass from the kitchen. *I work too damn hard,* Flossie thought. *Even I deserve a break every now and then.*

She took the scotch and walked down the hall, avoiding Rufus and that godforsaken loud machine. She was relieved to reach her living quarters. Although her apartment was modest, it was more than adequate, and she had never denied that she enjoyed living on the premises. She placed the glass on her only coaster, removed her apron, and flopped down in the recliner. "So that sickly little wife wants to sleep in today, huh?" she said with a laugh. "Well, maybe Miss Flossie will take a nap too. I sure as hell deserve it more than her pampered ass does!"

Chapter 47

Lizzie felt a light tapping on her arm and forced herself to wake up.

"Ma'am," the young passenger beside her whispered, "we've made it to Montgomery. I didn't know if you need to get off for a snack or just to stretch your legs."

"Thank you," Lizzie managed, still groggy from such a deep slumber.

"Um, you... Well..." the girl stammered.

"What is it?" Lizzie asked as her eyes focused on the woman beside her.

"Your wig. It's, uh...kinda crooked."

"Oh!" Lizzie said, quickly adjusting the mass of gray curls. "It's a long story."

The young woman reached up and touched the bruise on her face. "I suppose we both have a story or two."

"What time is it?" Lizzie asked as she straightened up in her seat.

"We've been on the road a couple of hours. We have a twenty-minute layover."

"I was sleeping so soundly."

"You must have needed it. My name is Sandi," she said, allowing herself to make eye contact for the first time.

"It's nice to meet you, Sandi. I'm, uh..."

"No problem," she said, smiling back at Lizzie. "Sandi isn't my real name either."

The two troubled women smiled at one another.

"It's nice to make your acquaintance, whoever you really are," Lizzie said. "Are you hungry?"

"A little, I suppose."

"How about a pastrami sandwich? I have an excess of food here."

"I'd appreciate it. I didn't really bring a lot of money with me." She smiled sheepishly.

Lizzie watched as she devoured the sandwich. For the first time, she realized she wasn't alone in a nightmare that happened to countless other women every day. She wasn't happy about that, but it did make her circumstances a little easier to bear. "Where is your final destination?"

"I'm getting off in Mobile. I have some family there, and things should be a lot better for me."

"I'm happy to hear that." Lizzie smiled. "I think I'll just stay on the bus for now."

"Yep, it's probably best for both of us. You should take another nap. I'll be awake to keep an eye out for you. If you're leaving a situation anything like mine, you'll need to stay awake when you're alone."

"I appreciate that," Lizzie answered, but she wondered if the peace of sleep would come again.

The crowd soon made their way back to their seats, and the bus merged onto the highway once again.

Lizzie's mind drifted to Maggie. She hoped her sister wasn't too worried about her as she traveled. *What a relief it will be to see her after all this time*, she thought. *I bet the twins have gotten big.* She checked her watch and wondered what was going on at the estate. She was sure Flossie had noticed she wasn't in her room by now, but she hoped the nosy woman would just assume she was lurking around the estate somewhere. That would buy her a little more time.

Chapter 48

Detective Pitts was sitting in a coffee shop with a steaming cup in front of him when his cell phone rang. "Pitts here. What's up?"

"Yeah, Nettles here. Seems a body was dumped over off Bankhead. I'm gonna have to pass it over to you. My boy's got a temperature, and the wife can't get off to take him to the doctor. Ain't that some shit? Says they're having some important state tests for her students this week. I don't understand why everybody can't just go to school online these days, what with everything else being on the damn interwebs."

"Doesn't she teach first grade, Nettles? I mean, it'd be a stretch for first-graders to school online when they can barely type, don't ya think? I believe that online shit is for people who already have the basics down pat. And it's internet, by the way."

"Screw you, Pitts. Anyway, I've gotta take the kid to the pediatrician. He'll probably catch ten other illnesses while we're in the waiting room. I hate being around all those snot-nosed kids."

"Has it ever dawned on you that maybe the other parents feel the same way about your kid?"

"Let me guess. You're on your first cuppajo, aren't ya?"

"Pretty much. Anyway, tell me about this body. How long has it been there?"

"Probably less than a week. Robbery appears to be the motive. No ID. His pockets are turned inside out, but he's wearing a pretty expensive suit though. I'm surprised some wino didn't steal that too. Doesn't appear to be from that neighborhood. Caucasian, and from what I hear, he's a pretty big son-of-a-bitch. Patrol units are there, and the M.E. is en route."

"All right," Pitts answered as he slugged the remainder of his first cup of morning coffee. "Where is it?"

"Behind Fat Cat's Used Tire and Appliances. It's closed now, but you remember the place, right?"

"I'll be damned. We just found an abandoned Lincoln over there a few days ago, registered to that Research Facility over off Piedmont."

"Hmm. Ain't heard of it."

"Yeah, well, something just isn't right about it. I haven't figured it out yet, but I'm getting closer. I'll head over there now. ETA is five."

"Thanks, pal. I owe you one."

"Right. When the hell are you gonna start paying up?" Pitts asked. When he got no answer, he disconnected the call.

He laid four ones on the table and gathered his coat. From the first time since he'd met the arrogant cardiologist, his gut felt queasy. It was as if he'd eaten a bad cup of chili and washed it down with stagnant beer.

Pitts made it to the scene in his estimated five minutes and swerved through the growing group of onlookers. The body had been rolled down the embankment behind the business. Thanks to the cooler weather, it hadn't yet suffered any major decomposition. Travis Upshaw, the M.E. on duty, was squatting beside the corpse, with a perplexed look on his face.

"What've we got, Travis?" Pitts asked as he made his way down the embankment, cursing all the way.

"Appears to be blunt-force trauma to the head, best I can tell," he muttered, his brow furrowed quizzically.

"So somebody knocked him over the head? It's not the first time, and it won't be the last."

"Yeah, but this is a big dude. If I was gonna rob him, I'd have shot him from a distance. Look around. What the hell was he doing out here? This suit must've cost a couple of grand, but they left it and took his shoes. They must have been expensive too. If they carjacked him, they would have used a gun."

"I agree. Something's fishy, and it's not just the way this guy smells. I guarantee he's connected to that doctor who's running that research place over off Piedmont. He's one of those rich, know-it-all, sons-of-bitches. You know the type."

Travis switched gears and looked up at the detective. "Don't care for him much, do ya?"

"How'd you guess? Trouble just seems to follow him. In our business, where there's smoke, there's usually fire."

"I have to agree with you on that one. There's no identification on this guy, and I won't be surprised if we don't get anything back on the prints. He looks Scandinavian, possibly Russian."

"Somebody's gonna be chasing their tails for a while then. I'll canvass the scene, see if I can come up with anything, and then meet you at your office. Maybe we'll get lucky, and you'll find something else on the autopsy."

Travis nodded an acknowledgment, then motioned his crew to place Gunnar in a body bag and onto a gurney that was wheeled into the morgue van.

Detective Pitts gave instructions to the crime scene techs, then vaguely scoured over it himself, not expecting to find much. His gut told him the man was dead before his car was parked behind the building. More than likely, the local thugs took everything of value from his body, then dumped him down the embankment. What Pitts really wanted to do was to have a few words with that surgeon.

Chapter 49

Justin Cates sat in the uncomfortable hospital chair with his head propped up against the wall. According to the doctor, his sister's condition was improving, but she still hadn't awakened. He had spent the past several days in turmoil, struggling with his decision to leave Iris and Clara alone with Gunnar's body. He hadn't heard from them, which was to be expected, but he longed for some communication that would put his mind at ease. He got the newspaper every morning and listened to the local news every time it aired, but nothing had been released about two older ladies being arrested for murder. It would have been big news, so the simple fact the media hadn't sunk their teeth into it had to mean no one was the wiser of the crime.

Just as Justin glanced down at his watch, he heard the sheets rustle and noticed Christi's hand reaching for him. "Oh, my God! Christi? Christi, you're back," he said excitedly as he jumped up from his chair.

Her eyes fluttered briefly before fully opening and fixating on her brother's face.

"Stay right there," he ordered as if she would get up and walk away. "I'm gonna get Nurse Emerson. Oh, my God!"

Justin squeezed his sister's hand firmly before exiting the room and running down the hallway to the nurses' station. "Nurse Emerson, Nurse Emerson!" he shouted, startling her from the work she was completing on the computer.

"Justin, what in the world is it? Calm down."

"It's Christi! She's awake. Her eyes are open. Come quick!"

Nurse Emerson followed a fast-paced Justin as they returned to her room, then smiled down at Christi. "We've been waiting a long time to see those beautiful eyes, young lady. Your brother has been very worried about you."

Christi smiled up at Justin and placed her hand on her throat. "I'm so… I'm th-thirsty."

"What just a minute," the nurse instructed as she held Christi's eyelids open and ran a penlight across them. "Let me contact the doctor. I don't want to give you anything just yet. Justin, talk to your sister. I'll call her physician and be right back."

"You're gonna be okay, Christi," Justin encouraged. "You're in the hospital."

A look of confusion crossed his sister's face as he brushed the hair away from her eyes.

"Don't ask her too many questions right now, dear," Nurse Emerson said as she returned to the room. "We don't want to overwhelm her." She put a small dropper of water in her mouth, and the two watched as Christi swallowed.

"More," she pleaded. "More."

"Let's give it a few minutes," the nurse said kindly. "The doctor is on his way. He needs to evaluate you."

Christi gave her a look of confusion, and her eyes began to flutter.

"Is she okay?" Justin pleaded. "Don't leave us again, Christi."

"She must be very exhausted," the doctor said as he entered the room. He removed the stethoscope from around his neck and listened to her heartbeat. "Very good. I'm glad to see you awake, Christi," he continued. "Can you squeeze my hand?"

She squeezed, albeit weakly.

"Nice. Good job."

Her eyes began to close slowly, and then her labored breaths suggested a deep sleep.

"Is she gone again?" Justin asked dejectedly. "I thought she was coming back."

The doctor pulled a stool up and sat down, then motioned for Justin to take a seat in the chair nearby. "Your sister has been through an extremely traumatic event. She won't recover overnight, but this is an extremely good indication that there is little if no permanent brain injury. The swelling was relieved quickly and did not return, and I'm confident in a full recovery. However, that being said, she won't be walking out of here tomorrow. Her progress may take days or even months, and she will need you to be very patient with her."

"I can do that," Justin promised the doctor. "I'll do whatever I need to do to make her better."

"First of all, you need to get some rest yourself. An exhausted caregiver is not an ideal one. There are a few things you need to be aware of. When she awakens again, don't bombard her with questions. It will only overwhelm and frustrate her. She may never have any memory of her accident or even the days leading up to it. Tell her things if you want, but don't ask her questions. Talk to her about the weather, sports, anything that might interest her. Don't expect her to be able to remember everything right away. Keep noise, visitors, and touching to a minimum, so as to not confuse her. Basically, just reassure her that you are here for her, speak to her about where she is, the day of the week, that type of thing. I believe Christi will progress quickly and make a full recovery." The doctor stood and rolled the stool out of the way. "I'll be close by, son. Just remember to get some rest yourself. You can't take care of her if you don't take care of you."

As soon as the doctor exited the room, the tears began to fall, and Justin laid his face in his hands.

It took all that Nurse Emerson had not to put her arms around him. "She'll be okay. She needs her rest now. Why don't you go get something to eat? You've been sitting up here for so long. I know you must be famished."

Justin looked up at the nurse he was becoming so fond of, then wiped his nose on his shirtsleeve. "Maybe I will," he said. "Just make sure that police officer stays on his post."

Chapter 50

Lizzie was able to sleep until the bus pulled up to the station in Mobile, Alabama. She said a heartfelt good-bye to the battered woman beside her, known only as Sandi, a name that wasn't even her own. The two women hugged tightly, an embrace that offered unspoken hope for better tomorrows for each of them, and then Lizzie was left alone. She gathered up the tote Marianna had given her; that was another sweet woman she would most likely never see again. She adjusted her wig and sunglasses and exited the bus among the crowd. They were transferring to another bus that would, thankfully, be the last leg of her long, grueling trip.

Careful to keep her head down and avoid looking directly at any of the security cameras, she quickly dipped into the nearest bathroom. She went through her bag, disposed of any leftovers, then wet a couple of paper towels and rubbed them across her face. Her appearance was so different with the wig on that she had to smile at herself. She wondered what Maggie would think when she saw her. *She must be worried sick,* Lizzie thought. *I need to find a way to phone her.*

After taking some time to gather her thoughts, Lizzie exited the bathroom. She looked around the bus station, which was not nearly as large as the one she had left in Atlanta. She spotted a row of pay phones, the old-fashioned kind she hadn't seen many of since her childhood. It required coins, so she took out two singles, purchased a bag of chips, and retrieved her change.

Lizzie quickly dropped in two quarters and punched in Maggie's number.

"Hello?"

"Maggie, it's me."

"Lizzie! Thank God. Where are you?"

"In Mobile. We have a layover before I transfer to another bus. I should be there in a couple of hours."

"That's wonderful news. I've been so concerned. We have a place for you to stay, temporarily at least. It's across the bridge, in Ocean Springs. Leland feels it will be safer than our guesthouse, in case Grant comes looking for you."

"That's not a bad idea," Lizzie said. In spite of the sleep she'd gotten, a wave of exhaustion washed over her. "I don't know if he's aware of my disappearance yet, but I know he won't take it well. He doesn't like his ego to be bruised as you know."

"Yes, I know his reputation is very important to him. I just hope he hasn't beaten you to the station," Maggie said. "He very well could have, you know."

"It's possible, but I don't believe he has. He's got so much going on right now that I'm on the back burner. I don't think he'll believe I've actually left him, not this quickly anyhow."

"Leland's paralegal is going to pick you up at the station. He's a nice young man and knows nothing of the story. He isn't even aware that you're my sister. He'll be outside in a silver Honda Civic when you get there."

"I have a gray wig on, and some clothes that... Well, they aren't exactly of our generation," Lizzie said, attempting a laugh. "Tell him not to look for me. I'll find him in the parking lot. I won't phone again."

"I'll be at the house in Ocean Springs when you get there. I love you, Lizzie," Maggie said, her voice cracking with emotion.

"I love you too. Don't worry. I'm almost there. I just can't wait to see those nephews of mine. They owe their aunt lots of cuddles!"

"I'm sure the twins will be happy to see you too. I know I will!"

Chapter 51

A loud knock at the door awakened Flossie from her sound sleep. It took several seconds for her to get her bearings before realizing she'd been napping in her room. *Oh God,* she thought. *What the hell am I doing, drinking and sleeping on the job?* "Just a second," she said through the door as she quickly put on her apron and tied it around her back.

"It's Rufus, Ma'am," he said softly.

"I hear ya," she said rudely as she opened the door and eyed him suspiciously. "What's the problem?"

"It's Dr. Chatsworth. He's on the phone for you. I've been looking everywhere."

"Well, he can just wait a minute," she spat. "I don't feel well today, and I needed a catnap. What time is it?"

"It's 4:30, Ma'am."

"Hells bells," Flossie muttered, hoping Rufus couldn't smell the stale liquor on her breath. "Which phone is he on?"

"In the front parlor, Ma'am."

"Call me Ma'am one more time, Rufus, and we're gonna have a problem."

"My apologies, but he's been holding for some time now."

Flossie refused to discuss the matter further with him; he was simply an employee of the house, her inferior, and he knew nothing of the inner workings of the estate. She brushed by him, her shoes squeaking as she walked rapidly to the parlor. The cordless was lying on the coffee table, waiting for her. "Yes? This is Flossie."

"What's going on there, Flossie?" Grant demanded. "I've been holding for over five minutes."

"I'm terribly sorry, Doctor. I was cleaning out a supply closet and didn't hear the phone. Rufus was unaware of where I was."

"Why didn't Elizabeth answer?"

"She's napping, Sir," Flossie lied with ease. "That poor child hasn't felt well in several months. Is there a problem?"

"I have to make a quick trip back to the Caymans. It appears there are more interested investors, and I need to make another presentation. My flight leaves at 9:00 tonight, and I have to go by the Research Facility before I leave."

"What can I do to help?" Flossie asked, gathering her thoughts swiftly.

"I'll send a driver by in the next hour. If Elizabeth is ill, I'll need you to pack a bag for me. You probably know better than she does anyway. I won't be gone more than two days, but pack for three, just to be on the safe side. Besides a couple of suits, I'll need something casual, suitable for golf. Make sure my clubs are ready as well."

"Not a problem, Sir. I'll get on it right away."

"I'm going to make an appointment for Elizabeth to see a doctor tomorrow. Will you see to it that she makes the appointment?"

"Indeed I will," Flossie said.

She was grateful when he ended the conversation so she could catch up on what was going on in the house.

She made her way up the staircase and stopped by Lizzie's bedroom first. The bed was still unmade, but Lizzie's purse was on the bedside table, giving Flossie a sense of relief. *She must be somewhere on the grounds*, she thought. *I'll deal with her later.* Her next stop was the doctor's room, where she gathered the items from his closet and laid them out on the bed. Grant Chatsworth was right: She knew more than anyone when it came to what he needed.

In less than five minutes, his toiletries were packed, along with a carry-on and a zippered garment bag with his dry-cleaned clothes. Rufus carried it downstairs and had it waiting by the door for the driver, along with his prized golf clubs.

Flossie walked into the kitchen, made herself a sandwich, and ate it quickly. *Now, where is that crazy Lizzie?* she wondered. The keys to the Lexus were in the kitchen drawer, so she was sure there was no way the doctor's wife had left the estate. Flossie grabbed her coat from the mudroom off the kitchen and walked outside. It was getting too cold for Lizzie to read outdoors, and she was sure that was why the stubborn woman never felt well.

"Good afternoon," Lonnie said, looking up from the engine of the old truck Santiago used on the grounds. "What brings you outside?"

"Free country, last time I checked," Flossie snapped. "Have you seen Lizzie out here?"

"No, Ma'am. Can't say I have. I've been working in the pool house for the past couple of hours."

"Where's the yardman?"

"Santiago is on the south end of the property, meeting with a tree contractor. One of the old magnolias is gonna have to come down."

"It's about time. I'll just call down to the gate," Flossie said snidely. She didn't trust the young white man, but his employment wasn't up to her. He hadn't ever given her a problem, and while she had a bad feeling about him, he had no reason to lie about seeing Lizzie.

After Rufus met her at the back door to let her know the driver had picked up Dr. Chatsworth's luggage, Flossie padded up the stairs to check Lizzie's room once again. Everything appeared to be in place. Her clothes from the night before were in the hamper, and her designer makeup was still spread haphazardly across her vanity. *Must she always be so sloppy?* Flossie silently fumed.

The absence of Lizzie's Cartier watch on the nightstand brought her pause; Lizzie rarely wore it unless she was leaving the estate. Flossie opened the small jewelry box on the dresser and gasped audibly when she noticed that it was empty.

But her purse? she thought. *Surely, she wouldn't have left without that.* She grabbed the expensive designer bag and rummaged through it until she felt a wallet. She pulled it out, opened it, then smiled as relief washed over her. Inside were several credit cards and a few dollars in cash, all Grant ever allowed for tipping and valets. Flossie sifted through the cards one by one and she only realized her goose was cooked when she didn't discover Lizzie's driver's license. *Damn! If Lizzie sneaked away, she wouldn't use her credit cards. She knows that would lead Grant right to her,* she thought, putting two and two together, *but she'd need her driver's license as identification.* "That ungrateful little bitch," Flossie said snidely. "She's run away! Now, what the hell am I gonna do?" She paced back and forth across the room, her mind flipping from one awful scenario to the next. With her boss gone, she would have at least a couple of days to find the woman.

221

Flossie went into the doctor's study, picked up the phone, and dialed the guard shack.

"Security. Cornell speaking."

"I'm calling from the main house. Have there been any deliveries today?" she asked nonchalantly.

"No, Ma'am. The postman dropped off the mail, but other than that, the only activity was your daughter's visit."

Anger over her daughter's unscheduled visit engulfed Flossie once again. If Jameeka hadn't shown up, she never would have needed the drink that sent her reeling into that long nap, and she would have noticed anything unusual. "Are you expecting a delivery?" he asked.

"No. I mean, well... I have some buffer pads on order for Rufus, but it can wait." *The old bat finally realized Lizzie is missing. Has her shitting bricks*, Cornell thought with a grin. "Oh yeah, I almost forget," he added. "There's a tree contractor on the premises. Actually, he calls himself a tree surgeon. Santiago is meeting with him, something about a magnolia that's scheduled to come down. He has the proper credentials. Also, a driver came by to pick up Dr. Chatsworth's luggage, but the doctor phoned prior to his arrival."

"I already know all that!" Flossie spat into the receiver. "I don't need to hear every detail of your job. I have more than I can handle with my own duties. Just do your job out there." With that, she disconnected the call and walked downstairs to where Rufus was still busying himself with the floors. She motioned for him to turn the machine off.

Noticing the wild look in her eyes, he complied instantly. "Yes, Miss Flossie? What can I do for you?"

"Was anyone with the driver who picked up the doctor's luggage?"

"No, Ma'am. Cornell buzzed from the guard shack when he let the driver through, so I met him outside with the luggage. He was alone. Is something wrong?"

"No, nothing's wrong," Flossie said rudely. "Have you seen Lizzie today?"

"No. As a matter fact, I haven't. I know she wanted to sleep in this morning. I've been busy with these floors though. Perhaps she's reading outside."

Flossie's face reflected the panic she was desperately trying to hide.

"What is it, Ma'am?" Rufus asked.

Flossie motioned for him to follow her into the parlor. "Lizzie's missing," she whispered. "I think she's left the doctor."

"What?! You can't mean that, Flossie. I'm sure she's somewhere on the property. No need to worry."

"Don't be so naïve, Rufus," she said with a combination of disdain and alarm. "Come upstairs with me." When they entered Lizzie's bedroom, Flossie closed the door. "Her jewelry is missing," she said, opening the small jewelry box to prove her point.

"Oh, no! Someone could have stolen it. Do you think someone has taken her?"

"Hell no. Nobody has taken that woman! She's left Dr. Chatsworth, I'm telling you. Look," she said adamantly, "she even took her driver's license. If someone took her and her jewelry, they certainly would have taken all these credit cards and the cash as well, and they'd have no need for her license."

"I see your point," Rufus said quietly, wringing his hands with worry. "We have to tell Dr. Chatsworth before he gets on that plane."

"Oh, no, we don't!" Flossie said, louder than she intended. "We'll do nothing of the sort. We have to find her before he gets home."

"But how, Miss Flossie? If he finds out we kept this from him, it could mean big trouble for all of us."

"It will only mean big trouble if we let her get away," she hissed back at him.

"With all due respect, Ma'am, she is a grown woman. We aren't supposed to watch her like a child."

"You clearly have your head up your ass, Rufus. Don't you see what's going on around here? She's a liability for the doctor. It's our job to protect him."

"I don't know about all that," Rufus continued, his pride clearly taking a punch. "I just do my job. I don't know anything about him or his business."

"She must have been planning this all along," Flossie said. "She's never asked me to let her sleep in before. I should have known. Let's think, Rufus. How could she have left the estate?"

"I'm sure Cornell would have seen her. Is her car still here?"

"Yes, in the garage. First things first. I'll check around the house for any clues, and you walk the grounds. Talk to those men who work outside. Somebody had to see something."

Chapter 52

By the time the bus pulled into the station in Biloxi, Mississippi, Lizzie was exhausted. Between the long hours of travel and the stress of what she'd done, and her body was almost limp with weariness. She waited for most of the crowd to disperse before gathering her bag and exiting the bus. It was dark out, which was certainly how she preferred it. Sidestepping the throngs of people entering the station, Lizzie made her way around the outside of the building and into the parking lot.

The area was well lit with security lights, making the silver Honda Civic relatively easy to spot. She walked past it a couple of times, just to ensure that it was the right one. Lizzie tapped lightly on the passenger door, and the young driver leaned over to unlock and open it for her. "Hi there," she said uneasily. "Are you the paralegal from Bevins, Knox, and Jenkins?"

"Yes, Ma'am, I am," he said, smiling warmly at her. "I'm Kenny, Kenny Deveaux," he continued, extending his hand in greeting.

Lizzie placed her hand in his and returned the smile with a little uneasiness. "Thank you for picking me up," she said, feeling awkward for not offering her name. She reached up and touched the mat of gray curls atop her head. "I suppose I look ridiculous," she said wryly.

"No need to explain," Kenny said nonchalantly as if picking up a strange woman in disguise was something he did on a regular basis. "I understand I'm to drive you over to Colton Marshall's place in Ocean Springs. It won't take long. It's just over the bridge, ten minutes at the most."

"I appreciate it," Lizzie said, finally allowing her body to relax and lean back in the seat.

"Ever been to Biloxi before?" he asked.

"No."

"It's really a great place. Lots of history here, and we've got some nice casinos too," he continued as he pointed in the direction of the large hotels to their right. "We get about every headliner out there eventually."

Lizzie knew he was trying to be kind by making conversation, so she nodded in lieu of offering any small talk. It was indeed a pretty place, and she shifted in her seat to take in the wharf and small shrimp and fishing boats, each with its own character and personality. They passed several seafood restaurants that reminded her of the day she and Devan had ordered both the conch fritters and fried snapper. That was a good day, and now she could allow herself to enjoy the memory of it. The bridge Kenny had spoken of came into view soon, along with the waterway.

"It's lovely," she said. "The water is beautiful."

"It never gets old, crossing this bridge. Many people are frightened by long bridges, but I think this one is peaceful."

"The lights from the hotels and surrounding homes make it seem so serene."

"Yes, that's true," Kenny agreed. "It's pretty during the day, but I prefer it at night."

The two rode in silence until he pulled into a driveway.

"Here we are," Kenny said. "I'll walk you to the door. I understand Mr. and Mrs. Knox are here. You'll be fine. They're nice folks."

Lizzie nodded and got out of the car. The excitement of finally being reunited with Maggie was almost more than she could stand, and she struggled against breaking into a run.

Kenny stood at the bottom of the stairs until she reached the front door, to make sure she got inside safely. "Nice to meet you, Ma'am. Take good care of yourself."

"You too," Lizzie stammered. She waited until she heard the car door shut before she knocked on the door.

Maggie opened it instantly, grabbed her arm, and pulled her into the home. "Oh, Lizzie! Thank heavens," she said between sobs. "I've been worried sick." Maggie alternated between holding her sister close and stepping away to get a better look at her.

Lizzie pulled the wig off her head and let her blonde locks flow over her shoulders, finally resembling the sister Maggie knew so well. "It's so good to see you, Maggie. So much has happened. I'm just grateful to be here," Lizzie said, her voice failing her.

"Come over here," Maggie insisted, leading her by the hand to the sofa. "Leland, get her something to drink, perhaps a hot tea. Oh!

226

What am I thinking?" she asked. "This is Leland, Lizzie. You've never met my husband. The last time we saw each other, I only had the twins with me."

Lizzie looked over at the man putting a kettle on the stove. He was just as she had expected: handsome and clean cut; with kind eyes; thick, brown hair; and of average height and build

"Nice to meet you," he said, offering her a timid grin. "I've heard so much about you that I feel as though we're old friends."

"Thank you. Thank you for this," Lizzie stammered. "It's not only embarrassing but also a little overwhelming."

"There will be no talk of that tonight," Maggie insisted. "You must be exhausted. What in heaven's name do you have on?" she asked, laughing.

"This little ensemble is a gift from a friend," Lizzie said, finally able to chuckle at her odd appearance. She looked down at her outfit and the wig lying on the sofa beside her and realized just how ridiculous she looked. She reached for the small bag beside her. "This is all I brought with me. I didn't want anything more. I'll need some clothes, but I do have some money. Maybe you can pick a few things up for me."

"We won't worry about that tonight," Maggie said kindly. "There are plenty of men's t-shirts in there for you to sleep in. You look like you could use something warm to eat, as well as a long, hot bath. Do you think you'll be able to sleep?"

The thought of a meal, a bath, and a decent night's sleep sounded wonderful. "Yes, yes Maggie. For once, I'll be able to sleep."

****

After eight hours of uninterrupted sleep, Lizzie awoke to the soft light of day filtering through the thin white sheers. The memory of her escape the day before caused her to sit straight up in bed in a panic. Surely Grant would be aware of her absence by now, and he wouldn't be happy about it. *Will he show up at the door any minute?* She pulled the comforter up to her throat and lay back among the feather pillows. *No, he can't possibly find me here,* she thought. *He doesn't know anything about this house.*

Lizzie allowed her breathing to slow back to a normal rate. Just when she had decided to get out of bed and start the coffeepot, she heard a key turning in the lock. There was no time to run or even to jump out of the bed, so she simply curled under the covers and held her breath.

"Lizzie? It's me, Maggie," her sister chirped. "Good morning, sleepyhead," she continued as she stood in the doorway of the bedroom. "Were you able to sleep?"

"Like a log," Lizzie answered, patting the space beside her in bed. "Come sit with me. You are so beautiful, Maggie. My God, it's been so long."

"I have a few things for you," Maggie said, laying a pile of bags beside the bed before curling her feet up under herself and sitting down. "I guessed you're about a size four. Am I right?"

"Close enough. Thanks so much."

"I know we have a great deal to talk about, but let's not delve into all that now. Why don't you pick out something to wear? I'll start some breakfast. You don't look like you've been eating right, Lizzie. That concerns me."

"It's just nerves, Maggie. My appetite has been shaky at best, but I'm safe now. I'm here with you," Lizzie said, reaching for her sister's hand and giving it an affectionate squeeze.

"Okay," Maggie said, standing up and clapping her hands. "There are toiletries in the bathroom, along with a clean washcloth. I'll be in the kitchen."

Lizzie took her time washing her face, brushing her hair, and pulling it back into a ponytail. She slipped into a pair of leggings and pulled a soft cashmere sweater over her head. For the second time that morning, her mind drifted to Grant, and she felt that sudden surge of panic.

"Lizzie? Are you coming?" Maggie called from the kitchen.

"On my way!" she yelled back, then took her time making her way to the kitchen, stopping along the way to look the house over. It was a beautiful place, and obvious care had been taken in its restoration. It had character, and Lizzie loved it.

Maggie was standing over the stove, turning the sizzling bacon and sliding fried eggs onto a plate. "There's juice in the fridge," she said before motioning to one of the cabinets. "The glasses are in there."

"Thank you so much. I..." Lizzie started before her voice faltered. "I thought this day would never come."

"Don't get emotional, Lizzie," Maggie insisted. "You're safe now. Just sit down at the table, and we'll talk," she said as she placed hot food in front of her sister. "Great house, isn't it?"

"Definitely. Tell me about the owner."

"He's a client of Leland's. He's spending time with his ailing mother, but that's about all I know. His name is Colton Marshall, and other than being a client of my husband's, he has absolutely no ties to us."

"Meaning Grant won't put two and two together and search for me here."

"Exactly! Do you think he'll even look for you, Lizzie? Do you think you're in danger?"

"I'm not sure, but it's not good, Maggie. He's into some bad things, the most disturbing being a multimillion-dollar Ponzi scheme. If he thinks I know anything about it, he'll surely spare no expense to find me."

Maggie reached for Lizzie's hand and shifted her chair a little closer. "Lizzie, tell me everything...and I mean everything. Don't leave out a thing."

Chapter 53

Flossie hadn't slept a wink the night before, and when the sun peeked over the horizon, she knew full well that Lizzie Chatsworth was gone and not coming back. She would have to tell the doctor and felt the uneasy anticipation in her gut that she would inevitably be held responsible. The illuminated red light on the clock radio reflected 6:00 a.m., so she got out of bed and dressed for her grandest performance to date. The staff had not yet arrived, so she went through the motions of going to Lizzie's bedroom. As expected, the room remained the same as the day before, and Lizzie was not in it.

She walked to the adjacent room, Dr. Chatsworth's home office, and picked up the phone. Flossie knew his cell number by heart, even though she could count on one hand the number of times she'd had occasion to use it. The call would surely awaken him, and that would not make him happy; however, it was Flossie's hope that she'd appear on top of things by noticing Lizzie's absence at such an early hour.

"Yeah?" Grant growled sleepily into the phone.

"Yes, Dr. Chatsworth, this is Flossie."

"What's going on? Do you know what time it is?"

"Yes, Sir, I do," she said softly, maintaining her composure despite the undeniable urge to fall apart. "We have a problem."

"What kind of problem?" he asked crisply, his voice suddenly sounding much more alert.

"It appears Mrs. Chatsworth is missing."

"Elizabeth?! What the hell are you talking about?" he spat into the phone. "What do you mean, she's missing?"

"She was not in her bed this morning, Sir. I check on her every morning when I get up, and she's... Well, she's not here."

"You called me in the Caymans to tell me you can't find my wife? Jesus, Flossie. She's probably in the bathroom or out under one of those damn trees, reading some musty old paperback like I told her not to. Just look around for her."

"Sir, I've got a really bad feeling. Her jewelry and driver's license are missing."

"What?! You can't be serious. Son-of-a-bitch! Did she take the Lexus? I'll report it missing."

"No. It's in the garage, and the key is in the kitchen."

"Did Cornell see her leave?"

"I haven't spoken to him yet, but he doesn't arrive until 8:00."

"When did you see her last?"

"Lizzie was in bed most of yesterday," Flossie lied, maintaining her composure. "She was complaining that she didn't feel well. I was going to make sure she saw a doctor today, but—"

"Was the alarm set last night?" he demanded.

That question threw Flossie temporarily off her game; the alarm company would surely have the time it was turned off, had Lizzie left in the middle of the night, so lying about it would be a death blow to her little charade. "Rufus worked late," she said, searching for a plausible story. "I went to bed before he finished buffing the floors. I didn't feel comfortable giving him the code to the alarm system."

"What the...?" Heavy sighs emanated from Grant's end of the line.

Flossie held her breath, waiting on the tirade that was sure to follow. What came next surprised her.

"I can't say I'm all that concerned," the doctor said. "I certainly won't lose any sleep over her being out of the house, but we have to find her. She could destroy me."

"I understand, Sir," Flossie quickly responded. "Just tell me what to do, and I will see to it that it's done."

"She's probably taken off to see that sister of hers. Elizabeth never was able to let go of that sentimental nonsense, that poor, white-trash life she left behind. Is there anything out of place in my office, Flossie? Anything at all?"

Panic once again surged through Flossie. She had failed to share her concern about the night she found Lizzie at the top of the stairs, then again in Dr. Chatsworth's office. Flossie had simply demanded that Lizzie go back to her bedroom and reminded her that her husband's office was off limits. If anything was amiss after that, it would be her fault too.

"Flossie? Are you there?"

"Yes, I'm here. I'm actually calling from your office. I was just doing a quick scan of your desk, Doctor, but nothing appears to be out of place or tampered with. It's just as you left it."

"I suppose I'm giving her far too much credit," Grant said. "Maybe I'll call the sister, maybe I won't. In a few weeks, she'll come crawling back, groveling, and missing the charmed life she was living."

"So what am I to do, Sir?"

"We have to keep this under wraps, Flossie. Don't discuss it with anyone. Should anyone ask, she is not feeling well, and we don't want her disturbed. She's looked like hell lately anyway. It's too cold for her to be sitting out there on a blanket with those books anymore, so none of the grounds crew should be looking for her."

"Very well," Flossie said in agreement. "Mum's the word."

"I'll be home tomorrow, and we'll go through her bedroom with a fine-toothed comb. If she's up to something, she won't get away with it. I can't help but wonder, though, how the hell she left the estate without being noticed. I pay those security fools too well."

Chapter 54

"Yeah, Pitts here."

"Afternoon, Detective. It's Upshaw, over at the M.E.'s office. I've got your body up on the table if you wanna head over."

"Your ears must have been burning," the detective said. "I was just about to call ya. I'm over at the jail. I'll see you in a few."

"I'll be here."

The ride over was a quick one. It was just before 3:00 in the afternoon, and the slew of county and state workers hadn't begun to leave their offices for the day, so city traffic wasn't so congested yet. Pitts pulled around back and entered through the loading dock door. He smiled at the attractive brunette as he passed her desk and wondered if he would ever get up the nerve to ask her out.

"Good afternoon, Detective," she said as she offered an inviting smile. "Where are you off to in such a hurry?"

"Upshaw's got a case of mine," he answered. "I'll catch you on my way out."

She let out a girlish giggle and went back to her work. Her name was Jessalyn, and Pitts guessed her to be in her mid-thirties, right in his age bracket. According to his connections, she had never been married and didn't have any children; that meant no baggage, an added plus. She was a petite woman, maybe five-four and probably 110 pounds soaking wet. What Pitts liked most about her was that she was always dressed professionally and appropriately, a rarity in his line of work. He was still thinking of her when he got to Upshaw's office.

"Hey, Doc. What ya got?"

"Not a whole lot," Upshaw answered. "Want to come on back?" Travis Upshaw was a very competent doctor, one of Pitts's favorites to work with because he never left a stone unturned.

"I guess so," Pitts said sarcastically. The morgue was not his favorite place, but it sure as hell ranked above hospitals on his list. He followed Upshaw through a labyrinth of pristinely waxed hallways, and they ducked into a room stocked with aprons, masks, and jumpsuits.

"Just grab a mask and apron," Travis said. "This won't take long." The doctor pushed the swinging silver door open with his hip while he put on his gloves. "He's over here," he said, pointing in the direction of the body.

"Damn, he's a big dude," Pitts said.

"Yep, pretty much fills up this autopsy table. Six-six and 264 pounds, to be exact."

"Geez. What killed him?"

Upshaw carefully lifted Gunnar's head from the piece of foam it was resting on and pointed to a wound toward the base of his skull. "Blunt-force trauma, like I figured. Had to have been a freak accident. It got him in just the right place. He probably died instantly."

"That's a pretty broad wound. What do you think caused it?"

"That's a real mystery. I don't believe it was anything like a tool or bat. Like you said, it's a pretty large indentation. The only way to be sure is to find the weapon itself. Did you see anything in the surrounding area that could have possibly caused this wound?"

"It's a dumping ground behind that business. We found everything from bags of garbage to old tires. Now that I know more about what we're looking for, I can take a crew back over there. I have a feeling he was dumped there though. He's too large for somebody to just walk up and conk him on the head, especially at an abandoned business in that section of town. I'd think he'd be on alert in that scenario."

"My thoughts exactly."

"Still no ID?"

"No. We're running the prints, but he looks Russian to me. He's got an eastern Slavic appearance."

"And what's that? Big and blond?"

"Russians aren't always blond, but his skin is extremely white," Upshaw said before lifting his eyelids. "His eyes are gray, something we don't see often. His lips are thin, like his brows, but his cheeks and jawline are broad. The dead giveaway is the nose." He waved his hand over the man's face as if giving a presentation. "Straight and protruding with a thick, rounded tip. I've seen it in every Russian I've ever autopsied."

"And you do a lot of autopsies on Russians, do ya?"

234

The comment brought a chuckle from Travis as he pulled the sheet up to cover Gunnar Azarov's face. "Not so many, but the nose and jawbones are always the same. My guess is he's some type of mercenary. I know that's far reaching, but the expensive clothes and area he was found in suggest something wasn't on the up and up. Have you had any missing persons reports matching his description?"

"Nope, sure haven't, but an abandoned Lincoln was found in that area just a few days ago. Belonged to a Research Facility. The doctor who runs it gives me some bad vibes. He's a condescending little prick."

"Looks like you may have the doctor's chauffeur here. Just a thought, of course."

"You're a good man, Upshaw. Once again, you didn't disappoint. I'll go back to the scene and see if I can find our weapon."

"Get back with me if you find anything. I have a feeling he'll be in the cooler for a while. Oh yeah. Please ask Jessalyn out when you pass her desk. I'm tired of the game you two are playing. Jesus, get on with it already."

Sweat beaded on Pitts's forehead as he neared Jessalyn's desk. He had secretly hoped she'd stepped away for a few minutes, but she was there, wearing a broad, expectant smile fixed on her pretty face.

"How's the case going?" she asked.

"Another dead end," Pitts said with a laugh, "no pun intended."

"That's funny," she said sarcastically.

"Listen, I've gotta run, but I was wondering if you'd like to grab some dinner this weekend." The flash of surprise on her face didn't go unnoticed by Pitts, and for a moment, his stomach knotted up.

"That would be nice," Jessalyn said, sounding quite pleased with the invitation, "but there's only one thing I need to know before I accept."

"Uh-oh. Here we go," Pitts said. "What do you need to know?"

"Actually, I make it a general rule to know the first name of a man before I go out with him."

"So Pitts isn't good enough for ya, huh?"

"First name please."

"Pritchard."

"Excuse me?"

"Pritchard."

"Your name is Pritchard Pitts?"

"Hell yes. That's why everybody just calls me Pitts. It was my mother's maiden name. Apparently, she had a sense of humor."

"Hmm. Pritchard is nice," she said, forcing a smile. "It just doesn't really fit you. Perhaps I'll just keep calling you Pitts."

"I appreciate that," he said. "I'll call you Friday, and we'll make some plans."

"My name's Jessalyn. There's no need to call me Friday."

"Huh?"

"Never mind," she said with a laugh.

Detective Pitts left the morgue with a pep in his step. He couldn't remember the last time he had been on a date, let alone with a woman who had a great sense of humor. Unfortunately, the thought of dinner with a pretty woman was quickly replaced with the reminder of the dead man on Upshaw's autopsy table. *I can't wait to see that arrogant doctor's face when I ask him about this,* he thought.

Chapter 55

Lizzie was unsure of how much time had actually lapsed since she began the story of her last five years with Grant. She felt an odd combination of exhaustion and hope. Being out of the house and away from Grant was almost exhilarating.

"I'm just speechless," Maggie said, her forehead wrinkled with concern. "I am so ashamed of myself for allowing us to drift apart. I should've known my little sister needed me."

"Hey, none of that now," Lizzie scolded, patting her sister's hand. "I should have left long ago. The question now is if he'll allow me to stay away. This won't look good for him or his image, and he has to be wondering how much I know."

"I expected to hear from him by now," Maggie said. "Frankly, I'm surprised, but I won't discount the fact that Grant's not going to make this easy for you. I've been watching my rearview mirror, and I haven't seen anyone following me, but if he's anything like you say, he's bound to show up. If not Grant, he'll hire a private detective. It sounds like he has a great deal to lose, Lizzie. I'm not going to pretend I'm not frightened. This goes far beyond an arrogant husband who doesn't want egg on his face. His reputation and millions of illegal dollars are at stake, to say nothing of his history of violence. If he hit you over eating at the wrong table, God only knows what he'll try to do to you for this."

"That's why I hesitated so long to contact you. The last thing I wanted to do was to put you or your family in danger."

"Don't even think like that, Lizzie. We just have to be extraordinarily careful. Here," Maggie said, reaching into her purse to pull out two identical cell phones. "Leland got these just for the two of us. It's not unusual for this house not to have a landline. Most people have been alleviating them from their budget for a while now. He got these at Walmart, and we just have to continue to purchase minutes for them. They're throwaways, untraceable, with no contracts or accounts or anything to tie us to these numbers. There won't even be a way to find the history of the numbers called. We'll have to communicate strictly via cell phone for a while, because it just isn't safe for me to keep coming back here, in case anyone is spying on me. I'll see to it that you have everything you need, but promise me you won't go outside."

"I won't, Maggie. I give you my word. How long do you think it'll be like this?"

"I'm not sure, but if things are progressing like you said, he's bound to be caught soon. Until then, we have to keep you hidden. He'll probably put a tail on me, hoping I will lead him to you. The other problem is the pregnancy. You've got to see a doctor right away."

"How are we going to work that out?"

"I'm not sure, but I'll get on it."

The lyrics from "Surfing USA" blared out of Maggie's purse, interrupting their conversation.

"Hold on a sec'," she said. "I have to get this." She reached into her purse and pulled out another cell phone. "Hello?" After a brief pause, she continued, "Hey, Mabel. Is everything okay?" Maggie listened intently for a minute, then answered, "It's no problem. Thanks for calling. I'll be home soon, and I'll return the call then. If you're not still there when I get back, I'll see you next week. Thanks for calling." Maggie disconnected the call and looked over at Lizzie. "Well, it looks like the good doctor has finally noticed his wife is missing. That was Mabel, our housekeeper. Apparently, he demanded that she get me to the phone. When she explained that I wasn't home, he ordered her to tell me to call the very minute I get there. His grandmother must not have taught him the same lessons Gran taught us about catching more flies with honey than with vinegar."

The reference to their grandmother brought a smile to Lizzie's face, but it was quickly replaced with concern. "I'm not sure what to make of it, Maggie. Do you think he's on his way here?"

"I don't know, but I suppose we'll find out when I give him a call." She pulled a charger from her purse and handed it to Lizzie. "The phone is fully charged now, but make sure you keep it that way. I'll call you as soon as I talk to Grant."

With Maggie gone, Lizzie was left with her own thoughts. She ran numerous scenarios through her head, none of which had a positive ending. Grant could only conceal her disappearance for so long; after that, he would have to address her absence. *I'm going to drive myself crazy,* she thought. *I just need to wait on Maggie to call me back and see what Grant's intentions are.*

Lizzie got up and walked through the house. It was warm and inviting, and the thought of going back to that oversized mansion in Atlanta made her stomach churn; that place had never felt like home. She walked back into the den and opened the curtains. The view of the bayou was calming, enticing her to go outside and sit on the deck, but she knew better. One nosy neighbor could make things difficult.

"Are those tombstones?" Lizzie asked herself as she looked to the left side of the house. She walked to the far side of the home and looked out one of the guestroom windows. A brick fence with a metal plaque marked the entrance to what looked like a very old cemetery. "What does the plaque say?" Lizzie asked as she squinted to read it. Never before had she seen a graveyard at the end of a street lined with houses. Rather than finding it disturbing, it was comforting to her in some way. The scenery looked like something right out of a gothic movie, with large, looming oaks draped with dangling moss, surrounding aged headstones and family plots cordoned off with intricate wrought iron fencing. Lizzie felt a sudden urge to visit the graves and read the names etched on the markers. A wave of guilt washed over her as she thought of her own family gravesites in the small country cemetery back home. *How shameful that I never insisted on visiting them and leaving flowers in their memory.*

A faint buzzing noise caught her attention, and she realized it was her cell phone ringing in the den. Lizzie trotted down the hallway, quickly scooped up the mobile device, and answered it. "Maggie?"

"Hey, Lizzie. I just got off the phone with your very disgruntled husband."

"Tell me everything," Lizzie insisted as her hands started to tremble.

"He was calling from the Caymans. Supposedly, he was summoned there on the spur of the moment for some type of presentation. Apparently, his housekeeper discovered you, your jewelry, and your driver's license missing."

"That would be Flossie. She's very loyal to Grant. Something isn't right about her. I don't trust her."

"I told him we hadn't heard from you in months, but he clearly didn't buy it. He's convinced you are throwing some sort of tantrum and will return sooner rather than later. He said if you don't return within a month, you'll regret it."

"What do you suppose that means? Do you honestly think he'll leave me alone until then?"

"I believe Grant's convinced that's how long he can cover up your absence. After that, he needs you back to keep up his charade of an ambitious doctor and loving husband. In the meantime, we just need to pray that nothing angers him or he catches wind of your suspicions of his criminal behavior."

"I don't know how to feel, Maggie," Lizzie said with a sigh. "It's almost like the calm before the storm. I want to feel relieved, at least for now, but I'm afraid to. He will never let me be at peace."

"We have to play it safe. Remember our plan. I'll stay away, and you stay in the house. It may be difficult, but we can't risk him finding you. My doctor can see you tomorrow morning. He's agreed to let you come in at 7 o'clock in the morning. He doesn't have any other patients scheduled until 9:00, so you won't be seen."

"What did you tell him?"

"That you are my sister and that you are visiting for a month or so. He's bound by patient-doctor confidentiality and I reminded him of that. He's a lifelong family friend of Leland's parents, and I trust him fully."

"How am I going to get there?"

"I know it may be awkward, but Kenny Deveaux, Leland's paralegal, will take you. He'll leave from his house in the morning, so I don't suspect that anyone will follow him. Make a list of anything you may need, and he can pick it up during your appointment."

"That's kind of strange, Maggie. What in the world does he think about this situation?"

"He's such a nice young man. He's very grateful for the opportunity to work for the firm. Kenny grew up here. He's trustworthy, but we haven't shared any details with him. I know he

240

must have a lot of questions, but for now, he's glad to do whatever we ask. Make sure to give him a list of anything you need—makeup, food, specific laundry detergents or whatever. I'll get you some more clothes tomorrow and get them to you somehow."

"Oh, Maggie, this is so burdensome. I feel terrible."

"Just remember, Lizzie. It won't always be like this."

Chapter 56

Detective Pitts got out of his unmarked car and stretched his long limbs. It had already been an eventful day, but he still wanted to visit the doctor's office before 5 o'clock. He relished the thought of seeing Dr. Chatsworth squirm. He flashed his badge at the security guard behind the desk.

The security man looked up from his *Men's Health* magazine with little interest. "Sign in," he said, pushing a clipboard across the counter. "The office is on the third floor. Just turn left off the elevator."

Pitts scrawled his signature across the paper and caught the elevator. The same young girl he had spoken with before was sitting at the front desk, tapping away on the computer. The waiting room was empty.

"Good afternoon. How can I help you?" she asked, looking up from her work.

Once again, he pulled out his wallet and displayed his badge. "Detective Pitts. I'm here to see Dr. Chatsworth."

"I'm sorry, Detective. The doctor is out of the country," she said, waving her small hand in the direction of the waiting room. "His appointments have been canceled. I'm just here taking care of some paperwork."

"Do you know when he'll be back?" he asked.

"He should be in tomorrow, but let me double-check. He'll be working out of the other office, and I only work at this one." She picked up the phone and dialed an extension.

Before anyone could answer her call, an older lady in a nurse's uniform came from the back. When the nurse's eyes met Pitts's, there was no denying that she was not only startled but borderline frightened. "Oh! P-Pardon me," she stammered. "I didn't mean to interrupt."

"You didn't, Clara," the young girl said politely. "In fact, I was just trying to reach you in the back."

The detective could have sworn he could almost see her heart beating rapidly in her chest. *I wonder what that's all about,* he thought.

"What do you need?" she asked in an attempt to pull herself together.

"Clara, are you all right?" the girl asked.

"Yes, Harper, I'm fine," she said tartly. "Why would you ask?"

"You just seem upset about something. I'm sorry. Anyway, this is Detective Pitts. He's looking for Dr. Chatsworth. I told him the doctor is out of the country, but I'm not exactly sure when he'll be back."

"Dr. Chatsworth is in the Caymans, conducting some business. He's expected back in our Northside Drive office in the morning. Is there anything I can help you with?"

"No, Ma'am. I really need to speak with him directly. Do you work at Cardiac Care Research Facility as well?"

"No. I'm his lead nurse and manage both of his offices, but the Research Facility is completely separate from us."

"I see," Pitts said, studying the older woman's face. She looked kind, competent, and, frankly, well beyond the usual age of retirement. "And what is your name?"

"I'm Nurse Samples, Clara Samples."

"Nice to make your acquaintance, Nurse Samples. I'll try to catch the doctor tomorrow at your other office. I'd appreciate it if you don't share that with him."

Chapter 57

Lizzie woke up at 3:00 in the morning and couldn't get back to sleep. She was worried about her baby and the doctor's appointment. She certainly hadn't been taking care of herself for the past few months, and she knew the stress couldn't be good for her unborn child.

Kenny, the paralegal, was supposed to pick her up at 6:45, but she was standing at the door looking out for him at 5:30 a.m. She had a scarf draped over her head, tied loosely under her chin, but it was far too early to don sunglasses. Lizzie wished she had brought a purse, because she felt foolish with her cash wrapped around her driver's license, tucked carelessly in her back pocket. She had also left her makeup behind, so all she could do was apply some lotion to her face. The dark circles under her eyes were puffy and unsightly, and that embarrassed her.

At exactly 6:45, the silver Honda Civic pulled into the drive, and she rushed out to meet it.

"Good morning."

"Good morning, Kenny. It's so nice of you to get up this early and take me," Lizzie said sheepishly. "I'm sorry you've been given this duty, taking care of me, I mean."

"Oh, I can think of worse things," he said with a smile. "I understand you have a shopping list for me?"

"I feel really uncomfortable asking you to go shopping for me."

"Don't," he said as he looked over to meet her gaze. "Mr. Knox is compensating me well to handle whatever you need. It's not a problem."

"I'm not sure where you can possibly shop at this hour," Lizzie said.

"We have a twenty-four-hour Walmart. It may not have the brands you want, but it has the basics. I shop for my Grandma once a week, so don't feel awkward in asking for…well, any women's items."

That drew a laugh from Lizzie as she pulled the list from her front pocket. "It's not much really, just a few toiletries, some fresh fruit and vegetables, a disposable razor, and some mascara. Any brand will do. Here's the list," she said, handing it over to him. "I'm not sure how much it will cost, but this should cover it," Lizzie added as she peeled a couple of $100 bills from her license.

"Keep it. I was told to use the company credit card."

Lizzie thought of arguing with him but decided against it, knowing she might need the money for future doctor visits.

They pulled into the parking lot with five minutes to spare.

"I'll be back in an hour," Kenny said. "I'll just wait in the parking lot for you. The lights are on, so I'm sure Dr. Redding is already here."

Lizzie reached up and touched the silk scarf on her head to ensure that she was somewhat camouflaged. "Thank you," she murmured as she nervously got out of the car and made her way into the building.

"Good morning," a perky older gentleman said as he opened the glass window separating the office from the waiting room. "You must be Lizzie."

"Yes," she said, so quietly that she almost didn't hear it herself.

"Well, come on back," he said, opening the door for her. "I'm Dr. Redding, Lizzie. It's nice to make your acquaintance. I'll be doing an exam this morning, so I'll give you a few minutes to undress from the waist down. Here is a sheet to cover up with. I'll be back shortly."

Lizzie undressed and sat nervously on the examination table, shivering from the coolness of the office.

A light tap on the door sounded, and the doctor entered. Lizzie studied his old, kind face. He looked to be in his mid-seventies, several years past retirement. He wore round, wire rimmed spectacles and had a light wisp of white hair swept across his balding head.

He extended his hand toward her. "I understand we may have a pregnancy here."

"I think so."

"And why do you think so? When was your last menstrual cycle?"

Lizzie reached into the depths of her memory, but for the life of her, she couldn't recall the date of her last period; she'd had a lot more painful things on her mind than cramps lately. She was already nervous and being unable to answer his questions shook her up terribly. The tears came so quickly that she wasn't even able to fight them. "I'm so sorry," she said between sobs. "I-I just can't remember, Doctor. I've been feeling sick for quite some time, not able to eat, feeling nauseous. I just... I..." Lizzie said, struggling to get a hold of herself.

Dr. Redding reached for her hand and patted it softly. "It's okay, dear. Really. Just lie back so I can take a look at your cervix. Everything will be all right. Just relax."

Lizzie lay back on the examination table, with tears flowing down the side of her face. She closed her eyes and tried to imagine being somewhere else, anywhere else.

"There now," the doctor said, patting her on the leg as he took off the latex gloves. "You can sit up." He washed his hands and handed her some tissues. "You are definitely going to be a mother," he said, smiling compassionately at her. "Your cervix is soft and has changed color, which is normal." He reached for a stethoscope and placed it on her belly. "Nice. Very nice. Listen to this," he said as he handed the instrument over to Lizzie.

She put it up to her ear and heard what sounded like rushing water. "What is it?" she asked.

"That, my dear, is your baby's heartbeat."

Lizzie's gasp was audible. Even with her obvious symptoms, pregnancy just seemed so unimaginable. Her right hand went instantly to her small, rounded belly, and she left it there as if to somehow protect her unborn child. "I can't believe it. It just seems so...unreal," she whispered, more to herself than to the doctor.

"Well, believe it, gal," he said, a broad grin stretching across his wrinkled face. "To detect a heartbeat, you've got to be between eighteen to twenty weeks. We'll need to schedule a sonogram right away."

"Why? Is something wrong?" Lizzie asked quickly.

"The heartbeat is strong," Dr. Redding said compassionately. "The sonogram will tell us much more though. They will measure the circumference of the head, the abdomen, and the femur. It will also check the heart and kidney function. The test can give a more definitive due date. You'll also find out the sex of the baby if you choose to know."

The last comment all but overwhelmed Lizzie. She had rolled the idea of having a child around in her head, but she had never thought of whether it would be a little girl or boy. It made it seem so very real.

Dr. Redding scribbled several notes in her new file. "You'll need to eat right, Lizzie, and eat a lot. You need to gain a great deal of weight. Are you still dealing with nausea?"

"No, not anymore," she said. "At first, certain smells really made me sick."

"Perfectly normal. The best foods for you are eggs, whole-grain breads, colorful fruits and vegetables, and lean meats. Green, leafy vegetables like spinach, as well as sweet potatoes, are great sources of vitamins. The sooner you start eating more, the healthier you'll be. That goes for your baby too."

"I can do that," Lizzie said, feeling better than she had in a long time.

The doctor tore a prescription off his pad and handed it to her. "This is for prenatal vitamins and iron. Get them filled as soon as possible. I'll be in touch with Maggie about your sonogram appointment."

"I can't thank you enough, Doctor," Lizzie said, her emotions beginning to falter again.

"Now, now. There will be none of that. You've received some good news today. Go home and let it sink in."

"How much do I owe you?"

"Nothing but a promise to follow my instructions, dear. It's been taken care of."

Chapter 58

Flossie had been busy in the house most of the day, but she had stopped her cleaning to prepare one of Dr. Chatsworth's favorite dinners. He would be home from the airport at 6 o'clock, and she knew he wouldn't be happy. She hoped a good dinner would lighten his mood. She had sworn Rufus to secrecy about Lizzie's disappearance, and no one else on the staff seemed to even be aware of her absence.

At exactly 6:00, the bell chimed, signaling that a car had passed the front gate and was headed up the drive. Both Flossie and Rufus were standing outside the front door when the limousine approached. The driver opened the doctor's door, then met Rufus by the trunk to hand him the luggage.

"Good evening, Doctor," Flossie said. "I have dinner prepared. Are you hungry now, or will you freshen up first?"

"I might as well eat," he said flatly. "I have to go over to the Research Facility to make sure everything is ready for tomorrow's tour. Let me wash my hands, and I'll be in the dining room directly."

Flossie quickly fixed his plate and put it on a tray, with a glass of water and red wine. She was just placing it on the table when he walked in.

"Have I missed anything else?" he asked. "I mean, other than the obvious."

"No, Sir. All has been quiet. The staff has been busy, and there haven't been any questions."

He looked around as if to ensure that there were no eavesdroppers about. "Come sit down, Flossie. I need to talk to you."

She sat down two chairs across from him and folded her hands in her lap. "Yes, Sir? What can I do for you?"

"Was there any indication of Elizabeth planning an exit?"

"No, Sir. I would have shared that with you immediately had I had an inkling. Lizzie did share with me her frustrations about having a chauffeur. She clearly didn't like the idea of having someone drive her, I don't think she was very fond of Gunnar."

"Was he ever inappropriate with her?"

"No. She just wanted her privacy. She once referred to him as 'an overgrown goon,' as I recall."

"She wasn't too far off," Grant said with a sneer.

"I only knew him by name, Doctor. I could just tell there was no love lost between the two of them."

Grant's face brightened as if a light bulb had just gone off. "You know, Flossie, it's the strangest thing. Both Gunnar and Lizzie are missing. That's a little odd, don't you think? Maybe they left together."

Flossie's face reflected strong disbelief. "I just can't see it," she said. "If that's the case, both of them are Oscar-worthy actors."

"It might explain how she got out of here without using her own car."

"But they would have had to get past Cornell."

"Not if they left before 8:00 in the morning," Grant continued.

"But the alarm would have alerted me had the gate opened."

Flossie and Grant sat quietly for a couple of minutes, both pondering the possibility that Lizzie and Gunnar had somehow devised an escape plan.

Rufus interrupted their thoughts. "Excuse me," he said quietly as he cleared his throat. "Cornell has opened the gate for that detective to enter. He's on his way up the driveway. Just wanted you both to know."

"Damn. Will I ever shake that son-of-a-bitch?" Grant muttered, more to himself than to the others. "Let him on back, Rufus. Flossie, grab a couple of cups of coffee. I'll let him talk as long as he wants to this time because I won't allow him back again."

Detective Pitts refused to wait until the following morning to question the doctor at his office. Something told him that the seemingly innocent older nurse might give him the heads-up, so he drove to his home instead. Pitts wanted to make sure he was the first to share the news about the dead Russian found near the Lincoln belonging to the Research Facility. He was actually greatly looking forward to it.

He was met at the door by an accommodating older gentleman dressed like a butler. He bowed in lieu of offering his hand, so the detective did the same. "Follow me, Sir," Rufus said as he made his way back to the dining room. "The doctor will see you now."

Dr. Grant Chatsworth was obviously irritated by his unannounced visit, but that pleased the detective all the more. It also didn't go unnoticed that the doctor didn't stand to shake his hand and chose to simply nod instead.

"May I?" Pitts asked as he pulled back a chair.

"Yes. Please sit. To what do I owe the pleasure of this impromptu visit, Detective?"

"Well, my apologies for showing up at your home, but I stopped by your office today, and they told me you were out of the country."

"If you were told I was out of the country, then why are you here?"

Pitts fought the urge to grin; he thoroughly enjoyed getting under the doctor's skin. "Actually, I was told you would return to the office in the morning, so I assumed you would arrive home tonight. I just took a chance."

"What could be so urgent, Detective?"

"Remember when I told you we discovered your company's Lincoln on Bankhead Highway?"

"Yes. I recall that conversation and visit well. I have had someone get the police report, and I assume they are also handling whatever paperwork needs to be filed with the insurance company."

Flossie came in with the tray containing the cups and saucers and a silver coffee pitcher. She placed a cup in front of each man and poured their steaming coffee. "Will there be anything else, Doctor?"

"No, Flossie. That will be all. Thank you."

Grant waited until she exited the dining room before he continued, "Do you normally follow up with stolen vehicle reports, Detective?"

"Not particularly, Doctor," Pitts answered, enjoying stringing him along. "However, it's the strangest thing." He paused to take a sip of his coffee but not before blowing on it in an attempt to cool it. "We've discovered a body at the bottom of the embankment at the same business where we found your car."

"My *company's* car," Grant interjected sharply. "And how does this body involve us? Who is it?"

"He appears to be of Russian descent, according to the medical examiner anyway."

"And, as I said, how does that involve me or my company?"

"See, here's where it gets real sketchy. Have you been over on Bankhead Highway lately, Doctor?"

"I can't say I have. I don't have any business on that side of town. Do you suppose he is the man who stole our car?"

"No, not the man who *stole* it. That area has been declining economically over the past few years, businesses closing, drugs running rampant—"

Grant made a point of looking at his watch and interrupted, "Excuse me, Detective, but I just returned from a long business trip overseas, and I need to unpack and prepare for my day tomorrow. This conversation seems to be lasting a little longer than I'm willing to sit through. You can make an appointment at my office tomorrow for a time more convenient for me."

"Why don't we just finish while we're both here?" Detective Pitts suggested, leaning forward to look directly into Grant's eyes. "I think this Russian may have been working for you, Doctor, maybe as a driver or assistant of some kind. I'm just not sure."

"I do not have any Russians working for me or my Facility," Grant spat. "I don't know where you're going with this, but it sounds unjustly accusatory, Detective, and I'm not interested in playing games with you."

"I just find it interesting that a Russian dressed in a $2,000 suit would be found murdered just a few feet from your $50,000 Lincoln Town Car, Doctor, especially in a crime-riddled section of town, behind a failed business, where the only people around are dope boys and prostitutes." Pitts stood and pushed his chair under the table. "I appreciate the coffee, and I'm glad to hear this fella had nothing to do with your business. Frankly, I think he was up to no good, and I intend to get to the bottom of his murder and his identity. Have a nice night. I'll let myself out."

Chapter 59

Lizzie spent the remainder of the morning unpacking the groceries Kenny had picked up for her. She also spiffed up the house a bit. He was thoughtful enough to choose several new magazines for her, and she had just settled down on the couch to read a few when her cell phone rang. "Maggie?"

"Yes. Good afternoon, Lizzie. I was expecting you to call before now. How was the appointment?"

"I really like the doctor. I just can't believe I'm actually pregnant. Grant would just kill me if he knew about this."

"He doesn't know, Lizzie, and we're gonna keep it that way. I wish I was there with you."

"Me too, but I'm fine, Maggie. We just have to keep our distance. I know Grant, and he's not going to take this lying down. I have some jewelry I need you to sell for me. I can't expect you and Leland to pay for everything."

"Let's not worry about that right now. You just got here."

"I would just feel better if I got rid of it."

"One step at a time, little sister," Maggie insisted. "I'm sure you're bored to death over there. It would be nice if there was some way to get you out."

"I'll be fine. I'm not willing to take any chances. I have the television, and Kenny purchased some magazines for me."

"Okay. I have to pick the twins up from preschool. I'll talk to you later."

"I wish I could see them."

"Me too, but we'll get to that. Just relax for now. I love you."

"Love you too," Lizzie said before she disconnected the call.

She walked through the house once again and ended up in a guest bedroom that had been transformed into a home office. She turned on the computer at the desk and waited for it to boot up. It was such a liberating experience to be able to get on the internet. She pulled up the *Atlanta Journal Constitution* and skimmed the headlines, but nothing stuck out to her. She googled Grant's name, and numerous articles popped up about his expertise as a surgeon and his newly established Research Facility. She clicked over to the suggested website for Cardiac Care Research Facility and pulled up every available tab and subject. Lizzie had to admit it was quite impressive and had she not be privy to the scam, she would never have suspected a thing.

Her mind went back to those who had helped her escape. Lizzie was so concerned about Clara. Grant was a very intelligent man, and she was sure it wouldn't be long before he began to doubt Clara's loyalty. Santiago would probably be okay, but she still didn't understand Cornell's odd behavior, rummaging through Grant's office and then letting her go when he spotted her in the bed of the truck. It really made no sense at all.

She also wondered how long it had taken Flossie to realize she was gone. The thought of Flossie panicking over her disappearance brought a brief smile to Lizzie's face. She relished the idea of the housekeeper scrambling for a story as to why she was unaware of Lizzie's getaway.

There was no doubt that Grant was confident she would return home, but he wouldn't wait idly by while she made up her mind. He would have one of his goons staked out in Biloxi before long if they weren't already. Lizzie didn't feel as if she was in danger yet, but as time passed and she didn't return, she knew things were bound to take a turn for the worse.

God forbid he should find out about the pregnancy. Her hands went instantly to her stomach and fear raced through her mind. *I won't ever go back,* she vowed, *and Grant will never get his hands on my child.*

Chapter 60

The past few days had been difficult on Dr. Grant Chatsworth, but he was determined to put it out of his mind for the next couple of hours as he led his wealthiest investors on a tour of Cardiac Care Research Facility. They gathered briefly in the finely polished lobby where they nibbled on expensive finger foods and sipped on finely aged wine and scotch. Grant gave them a brief summation of what their tour would entail and answered any related questions.

It was a larger crowd than he had intended to host, but Grant had made up his mind that it would be the first and only walk-through he would give them. He was ready to dispose of the monkeys; as Jean-Luc and Zahir had both predicted, the animals were becoming a nuisance, far too expensive to house and feed. Grant had also quickly tired of their incessant shrieking. After tonight's little open house, he would also lay off the majority of his lab technicians. They all had exemplary credentials, and it wouldn't be long before they began to wonder why progress was at a standstill. He would promise to hire them back as soon as investors gave their next pledges, and he was certain that would keep them at bay long enough for his bank account to increase dramatically.

Grant watched the expressions on the potential investors' faces as they wound their way through the mazes of hallways, well-equipped laboratories, lavishly decorated offices, and finally, to the large, open space that housed the nonhuman primates. It was apparent that they were impressed, and any mounting concerns over their investments instantly dissipated. Grant then led them back to the lobby where he enjoyed another scotch as he mixed and mingled with them, spending equal time schmoozing each.

Only a few of the wives attended, and Grant immediately apologized for his own wife's absence, citing a recent bout with a stomach bug. They just nodded and smiled and sipped smugly from their cocktails, mentioning that they knew something had been going around in the city. Grant had decided it was best not to share his recent troubles with Lizzie with Jean-Luc Phillips or Zahir Chavan; the three of them had enough on their plates, and he found it unnecessary to share any personal struggles.

The supposed two-hour tour took well over three, and Grant sighed with relief when the last of the investors called it a night. "I think that went well," he said to the other two doctors. "I'll meet you both at the bar. I have something to discuss with you, and I don't feel like spending another minute here."

Both men nodded in agreement as they grabbed their coats and made their way to their cars. It had been a long night for all of them, and a stiff drink in a different atmosphere would be a welcome diversion.

Grant was the first to arrive at the dimly lit bar where the three often met to discuss topics they didn't want anyone else to be privy to.

The sexy redhead who always waited on them, was up front when he arrived and seemed pleased to see him. "Still prefer your booth in the back?" she asked, fluttering her long, false lashes.

"That would be nice, Andie," Grant answered, winking seductively at her.

She grabbed three menus, even though the men never ordered anything but scotch, then led him to the far booth in the corner. Andie leaned forward to give him a glimpse of her large, augmented breasts and whispered something that only Grant could hear.

He smiled mischievously, then cleared his throat in form of a warning. "Good evening, gentlemen," he said, directing his attention to the two men as they slid in the booth. "Get us the usual, Andie," he said flatly. Grant then turned to face his colleagues. "We have a problem. I was going to meet with you both last night, but I didn't want to add any more pressure to tonight's event. It was imperative that the Facility tour went off without a hitch, and it did."

"What is it, Doctor?" Zahir asked.

"Gunnar's body was found down an embankment, in close proximity to where the Lincoln was discovered."

"Body? As in *dead*?" Zahir asked incredulously.

"According to the detective who keeps popping up, he was murdered. I'm at a loss, gentlemen."

Jean-Luc shifted in the booth, and Grant detected a faint trembling in his hand as he reached for the scotch that Andie was

255

handing him. He waited until she was gone before saying, "I'm afraid I don't understand. Who could have killed him?"

"That's the million-dollar question," Grant answered. "And what was he doing on that side of town?"

"He could have been operating some shady drug business on the side," Zahir suggested. "I never trusted that man."

"He was paid adequately for his services with us," Grant added. "He would have been a fool to jeopardize his position."

"Gunnar Azarov had no allegiance to us," Zahir said. "I never felt any loyalty. He killed too easily," he whispered.

"Frankly, I am relieved he's dead," Jean-Luc added quietly. "I was concerned he would end it all for us."

"I denied he worked for us," Grant said, taking a long swig of his liquor. "I'm afraid it's going to come back to bite me in the ass though. That detective is determined to pin something on me."

"How will they tie him to us?" Zahir asked.

"All they have to do is start showing his picture around the Facility or even my home, and someone will unknowingly admit they've seen him. I should have just told the man he was a driver for us."

"Perhaps you can request to view the body in the morgue," Jean-Luc suggested. "You can let that detective know you were told today that one of the drivers was missing, that no one wanted to bother you with it while you were out of the country."

"That's a thought. There's no doubt I'll have to backpedal on this one, boys. Who should I say hired him?"

Both men looked at one another, then back at their boss.

"Tell the officer he was a friend of Albert Tinsley's and I gave him a job," Zahir said.

Grant's lips formed into a thin smile. "I like it, Zahir. I like it."

Chapter 61

The past few days of Lizzie's confinement had taken a toll on her. The fact that Grant hadn't tried to contact Maggie again gave her a renewed sense of confidence, though, and she wanted desperately to get out of the house and take a walk. Unfortunately, Maggie had made Lizzie promise that she would remain inside, and she didn't want to break a promise to her sister. Although Colton Marshall's home was located at the end of the street, Lizzie saw her neighbors coming and going occasionally and understood her sister's concern, so she had complied with Maggie's wishes. She was starting to feel better, and her appetite was growing, so she busied herself with cooking and dreaming about what her life would be like if she was ever truly free of Grant.

The evenings were the most difficult, and she felt very lonely then. With the television on, Lizzie curled up on the sofa in her flannel pajamas and covered up with a throw. She had quickly tired of the sappy love stories, the Lifetime movies frightened her because they reminded her of her own situation, and she wasn't up on any of the recent shows. Lizzie couldn't even remember what she had done back in Atlanta. She hadn't watched much TV and rarely left the house. She realized now that most of her energy had been spent contemplating a feasible escape. *What a sad life I've lived,* she thought.

Pulling the curtains back just enough to look out, she watched the tall grass swaying in the bayou. The small boathouse in the distance had a faint outside light on, one Lizzie had curiously observed since her arrival. *It must remain on for security reasons,* she thought. She noticed a leaning tombstone out of the corner of her eye and was reminded of the old cemetery tucked away at the end of the street. "It's dark out," she said to herself. "Who would notice me?"

Lizzie grabbed a jacket recently purchased by her sister and quickly tore off the tags. She slipped it on, pulled on a wool scarf she found in Colton's closet and grabbed a flashlight from the bedside table. Luckily, she saw her cell phone on the coffee table and stuck it in her pocket, just in case Maggie called. The keys were in a drawer in the kitchen, so she retrieved them and quickly set the security alarm. It was after 9 o'clock, and except for a few lights on in the surrounding homes, Lizzie didn't see anyone outside. As she pulled the door closed behind her, she felt the first twinge of guilt. Maggie would not be happy with her leaving the house, and the fact that it was dark made it an even more unwise decision, but the brisk air felt so rejuvenating on her face that she refused to go back inside.

Colton Marshall's home was the last one on the street, and as Lizzie scurried around the corner of the house, she doubted that anyone would notice her. The full moon illuminated the area almost as much as streetlights would have, rendering the flashlight unnecessary. Lizzie walked through the red brick entryway, pausing to read a copper plaque that she figured to be the name of the cemetery: *"Evergreen." Interesting,* she thought. She followed the main roadway and was immediately engulfed in the beauty of the final resting place for so many. It was lovely and unbelievably peaceful, yet it could have also passed for a scary setting of a horror movie. Large, looming oaks formed a canopy overhead, almost like thin, weathered hands reaching across the sky. Spanish moss hung under the shady boughs of the long limbs.

She walked several yards before she dared to turn on the flashlight. As the road forked, she was greeted by marble crosses, marking the graves of those who had lived long ago. She shined the light on engraved letters and numbers, taking time to read the names and dates of birth and death. This section in the fork of the road was clearly the designated burial place of priests and nuns belonging to the Marianites of Holy Cross. Lizzie had worshipped in a little white brick Baptist church her grandmother had been raised in, but she did have a friend who went to Catholic school. Lizzie always enjoyed hearing about the nuns and their strict, no-nonsense style of teaching.

She bent down and ran her fingers across the date of death. "Wow, 1904," Lizzie whispered. "So long ago. Sister M. Elizabeth," she mouthed. Her friend Ansley had told her that all the nuns' names began with Mary, after the Virgin Mary, which would explain the initial M. Lizzie allowed her mind to drift, and she wondered if Sister M. Elizabeth had cracked her wooden ruler across young, tender knuckles or if she had been a soft-spoken, gentle mentor.

Lizzie stood again and decided to follow the small, curving road around the perimeter of the cemetery. She glanced back at the house one more time before she continued walking deeper into the wooded area. The kitchen light was on, as well as a lamp in the foyer, and all was quiet. The moon gave off a hint of silvery light, just enough for her to follow the one-lane road. Smaller, less ornate tombstones stood amidst the larger, more decorative ones. Lizzie passed a family plot that was cordoned off by a rusted, wrought iron fence that still had remnants of the shiny black paint that had once covered it when it was new. She cut through the damp grass and walked over to take a look. A gate clung desperately to tired, aged hinges, so she pushed it open as carefully as she could. Nervous about encroaching on their eternal resting places, she stepped just inside the plot and shined the flashlight over each stone. It appeared to be a mother and father, along with their son and his wife, all buried in the mid to late 1800s. She wondered if there had been any grandchildren. Lizzie closed the gate back and returned to the path.

Glancing at her watch, she was surprised that almost half an hour had passed. Knowing she shouldn't push her luck on her first secret outing, instead of continuing beside the perimeter and alongside the bayou, Lizzie turned left and cut through the middle of the cemetery to take a shortcut. She listened to the sounds of the night. Toads and crickets sang raucously as she shined her light from side to side.

A small block caught her eye up in the distance, so Lizzie kept her sights on it until she reached it. It was a tiny tombstone, made out of what appeared to be cement, unlike the other markers that were carved from granite, marble, or sandstone. Bending down and resting on her knees, Lizzie looked at the small, broken monument. The body of a sculpted lamb rested atop its base, but the head had long since broken off, maybe from the many hurricanes or perhaps from a caretaker as he tended the grass nearby. The name "Baby Belle" was carved at the bottom, but there was no date of birth or death. Looking around, she didn't see any other gravesites close enough for it to be considered a family plot.

"What's your last name, little one?" Lizzie asked quietly. "And what's your story?" A lump formed in her throat, throwing up a red flag that it was time for her to get back to the house. "I'll be back, Baby Belle. I'll be back to visit you."

Chapter 62

Clara poured Dr. Chatsworth's morning coffee, added two sugar cubes, and carried it to his office.

The doctor, stone-faced as usual, grunted some form of a thank-you and picked up the phone receiver.

She quickly exited the office and pulled the door closed behind her. Pausing briefly, she was able to overhear him asking for Detective Pitts. Clara could have sworn her heart skipped a beat or two. She wondered what was going on. The detective had been in the day before and told her not to share his visit with the doctor. *Why would the doctor be calling the investigator now?* Suddenly certain that Gunnar's body had been found, she stifled the urge to call Iris. *Please don't let them find any prints,* Clara prayed silently as she replayed that fateful night in her head.

"Are you okay?" Nurse Alyssa asked. "You look a little flushed, Clara."

"I'm fine," Clara answered. "I could use a cup of coffee though. I didn't sleep well last night."

"Let me get it for you," Alyssa insisted.

"I'm fine," Clara barked, surprising the young nurse. "I-I'm sorry, dear. I'm just a little tired."

"All right," the girl answered as a look of confusion washed across her face. "Let me know if I can do anything."

What am I doing? Clara thought. *With all I've been through, I can't fall apart now!* She went into the breakroom, poured herself a cup of black coffee, and sat down at the table. *Just keep it together,* she thought, *and no one will ever be the wiser.*

"Pitts here."

"Yes, Detective Pitts. This is Dr. Chatsworth."

The detective smiled to himself. *He's worried,* he thought. *I've got him just where I want him.* He paused long enough to make the doctor antsy before he replied, "What can I do for ya?"

"I spoke with a few employees at the Research Facility last night, and it appears we did employ someone who matches your murder victim's description. According to Dr. Zahir Chavan, he hired this man, under the recommendation of Albert Tinsley, to be a standby driver for us."

Pitts was silent for a few seconds as he allowed the statement to sink in. It was one of two scenarios: Either Tinsley really knew the guy, and they were mixed up in some shady dealings together, or else it was merely a ploy by the doctor, a lie to throw blame on a dead man who couldn't defend himself. Either way, his case was far from over. "And how did Mr. Tinsley know this fella?"

"I'm not quite sure. As I told you before, Detective, I'm a busy man. I have nothing to do with the hiring of drivers, nor do I keep track of company vehicles. I'm sure you can relate to that. Being that you're a detective, I doubt you know where every beat cop is at the moment, nor do you account for all the parking tickets written in this large city of ours."

Pitts forced a chuckle while he rolled his eyes on the other end of the phone. *I hate a smartass,* he thought. "Have you ever seen this driver? Could you identify him?"

"It's my understanding that he was sent to chauffeur my wife a couple of times, but I've never met him myself." As soon as the words came out of his mouth, Grant regretted them.

"So your wife would be able to identify him then?"

"I'm sure she would, but I won't send my wife to a morgue. I'm sure you understand that. However, I can see to it that Dr. Zahir Chavan meets you there at a time convenient to your schedule."

"That'll work," Pitts said. "Have him meet me in the lobby of the Fulton County medical examiner's office at 1:30 this afternoon."

"I'll do that," Grant said flatly. "Since I'm merely the middleman here, I assume this situation can be handled between the two of you?"

"Good day, Doctor," Pitts said then hung up the receiver, grinning from ear to ear. Something about the doctor still didn't sit right with him. Although he understood that his hands couldn't be in everything, Grant Chatsworth was just a little too defensive for the detective's taste. The past had taught him that a defensive person usually had something to hide. *Maybe it's time for me to pay another visit to Christi Cates,* he thought. *It's been a while.*

Chapter 63

Just as he had so many days before, Justin Cates sat by his sister's bedside at Grady Memorial Hospital. Christi was close to being released and anxious to get back to her apartment and her studies. The only thing holding her back was completing her physical therapy and regaining her strength.

Justin had been patient with her and although he, more than anyone, wanted to know the details of her accident, he hadn't pushed her to answer any questions. Her memory only went back to her initial concerns about Albert Tinsley's disappearance, so Justin didn't feed her any information about his murder. He wanted any memory of what had occurred to be her own, not something she heard from him.

He was reading from one of his textbooks when he heard a knock on the door. Feeling safe with the officer still stationed out front, he told the visitor to come in.

"Hey there," Detective Pitts said, offering his hand, then removing his jacket. "Mind if I sit down?"

"No, please do," Justin said, quickly closing his book and removing his schoolwork from the extra chair.

"Where's the patient?"

"She's downstairs, in rehab. She's almost ready to go back to her apartment," Justin said, then frowned with concern. "Do you think she'll be safe? I mean, I realize that cop can't follow her everywhere," he said, motioning to the police officer standing guard outside the door.

"I don't know," Pitts answered. "We're not much closer to finding the guy who did this to her. Has her memory of the accident come back at all?"

"Nope, nothing."

"Not even in little spurts? Sometimes it happens like that, a few pieces of the puzzle if you will."

"She doesn't remember the day of the accident. The last thing she recalls is worrying about where Albert was and why he hadn't contacted her. I haven't had the nerve to tell her he's dead. Christi's still weak, and I don't wanna set her recovery back."

"I understand that, but why does she think she's here?"

"She's been told she was in an accident and was hit by a bus. I haven't given her any more details. I want any memories of that day to be her own, not just hearsay that I put in her head."

"Listen, Justin. It seems we have another murder victim in the morgue. According to the doctor who hired Tinsley, he was a buddy of Albert's. The Research Facility hired him on, at Albert's request, as a driver. Now he's dead too."

Justin felt the perspiration forming instantly on his face, but he couldn't stop it. His face and ears grew hot, and he saw splotches of random light on the hospital wall, like psychedelic amoebas from the pages of his textbook. Detective Pitts's voice seemed to fade in and out, and then his world turned black.

"Justin? Justin! Can you hear me, dear?" Nurse Emerson asked over and over again.

His eyelids fluttered several times before the nurse's face came into focus. Justin sat up quickly and attempted to stand, but Nurse Emerson placed her hand firmly on his shoulder.

"Don't get up now. Let me get a damp cloth. You just fainted, and you're not stable enough to stand."

Justin could see the detective out of the corner of his eye and remembered what had caused him to panic. "Sorry about that," he managed to say.

"No problem, kid. Just take your time. You'll be okay in a few minutes."

Nurse Emerson spoke softly to him as she rubbed the wet cloth over his face and offered him a few sips of water. Both she and Detective Pitts grabbed an arm and lifted him back onto his chair.

The sheer embarrassment of it all kept Justin from making eye contact with either of them. His biggest fear was that the investigator would now grow suspicious of him and somehow link him to Gunnar.

"It's all right," Pitts said as he patted Justin's shoulder forcefully. "I know you're worried about your sister, but she's okay."

That's what he thinks, Justin thought. *I'll go with that theory.* He cleared his throat and sat back in the chair. "Yes, I'm worried sick about her. What's to keep her from being murdered too? As a

264

matter of fact, why is that cop outside the door and not with her now?"

"He walked downstairs with her, but another cop was working in that area, so he came back up. She's fine. We just need to figure out what these two men were up to. Whatever it was, it cost them their lives."

"Have you been back to her apartment?" Justin asked. "Maybe you missed something."

"There's nothing else there. I've made two trips. Anything of importance was taken the day it was ransacked. Where are you staying?"

"At a cheap hotel, and even that is out of my price range. I'm not sure where we'll go when Christi's released."

"Let me see what I can do," Pitts answered as he glanced at his watch. "Look, kid, I've gotta meet somebody in a few minutes. I'll get back with you if I hear anything else. You've still got my card, don't you?"

Justin pulled out his wallet and checked. "Yeah, I've got it. I'll let you know if they release her."

Detective Pitts pulled out his own wallet and slid out a couple of twenties. "I know times are hard for ya. I've been there. Maybe this will buy you lunch for a couple of days."

"Thanks, but I can't take that," Justin said.

"It's nothing. Really. You don't owe me anything back, and I'm not keeping a ledger." He dropped the money on the lunch cart beside the bed and walked out. *Poor kid,* he thought. *Poor, innocent kid.*

****

Dr. Zahir Chavan walked apprehensively from the Research Facility to his new SUV. Aware of how much could be riding on his answers to the detective, he struggled to control his nerves. Although he had the directions memorized, Zahir entered the address of the morgue into his navigation system anyway, just in case his mind began to wander. So much had happened since the inception of the Research Facility, and more than a few times, he'd found himself wishing that he'd never accepted Dr. Grant Chatsworth's offer to be part of it. The whole idea had sounded so well thought out, like such a sure thing, and at the time, Zahir believed he would be a fool to turn down the opportunity. He was told the risks would be minimal and that he would walk away with more than enough money to return to his country a wealthy man, but now, things were beginning to go severely awry, and too many risks were being taken. Not only that, but Dr. Chatsworth refused any input from him or Dr. Jean-Luc Phillips. The whole situation with the Russian could have easily been avoided had Grant put any stock in their gut instincts about the man. At any rate, Zahir was in deep, and he knew he had to find a way to steer the persistent detective away from them and in another direction.

Hoping for a little more time to formulate his deceptive plan, Zahir was disappointed when he pulled up to the morgue in such short order. He chose a parking place in the middle of the lot, grabbed his jacket, and locked the vehicle.

The building was red brick, like so many others in Georgia. He opened one of the glass double-doors and stepped inside. Since the place was taxpayer funded, the furnishings were far less glamorous than that in the pristine, modern office he'd just left. Plastic and metal chairs were placed sporadically throughout the lobby in random order, with no particular rhyme or reason. A few severely outdated magazines were strewn about; their condition didn't suggest the reading would be anything close to current. The floors were polished, but the square linoleum tiles were dated and chipping.

He followed the hall to a woman sitting behind a desk. She stopped tapping on the computer and peered up with a quizzical look. "Can I help you?" she asked.

"Yes," the doctor answered, nodding in greeting. "I am here to meet with Detective Pitts. My name is Dr. Zahir Chavan."

"He called a few minutes ago, Doctor. He's on his way. Have a seat in the lobby if you don't mind."

"Not at all," he answered, "but I do have a meeting in an hour. He won't be very long, will he?"

"He was just a couple of minutes away when he phoned. I expect him any second. I'll let you know when he arrives."

266

"Very well. I'll be in the lobby."

Detective Pritchard Pitts parked his car by the loading dock, as usual, then entered through the back door.

Jessalyn was seated at her desk and threw up her hand in a friendly wave when he came through the door. "There's someone waiting on you up front. Want me to get him for you?"

"No," Pitts answered, winking flirtatiously at her. "I'll get him myself. Will you buzz Upshaw and let him know I'm here? Tell him we'll be back in a couple of minutes."

"No problem," she said. "You can't miss him. He's the only one up front."

Pitts made his way to the lobby and spotted the Indian doctor sitting impatiently in one of the metal chairs. *He's probably worried about dirtying his expensive clothes,* Pitts thought snidely. "You must be Dr. Chavan," he said as he extended his hand and forced a smile. "I'm Detective Pitts. I appreciate you coming out. I'm sure you're a busy man."

"Not a problem," the doctor answered. "I do have a meeting in an hour, however, so I hope this won't take long."

"No, I won't waste your time. Please sit back down for a minute. I have a few questions for you."

Zahir sat back down in the chair while Pitts eyed him suspiciously. He was certainly not what he had expected. The Indian doctor was neat and clean, his nails well-manicured, his designer clothes tailored, and his Italian leather loafers appeared to have been professionally polished. That, however, was where the similarity to Dr. Grant Chatsworth ended. Whereas Chatsworth was tall and strapping, Dr. Chavan was pitifully thin, probably five-four at best. His thinning hair was cropped so closely to his head that one could see his flaky scalp. His smile was far from the dazzling rows of bleached, white teeth Chatsworth flashed at others; instead, his dismal greeting displayed crooked, yellowed, neglected teeth. His air was that of a confident, intelligent man, but he wasn't arrogant or conceited. He was all business, and Pitts respected that.

"I'll cut right to the chase, Doctor," Pitts began. "We have a Russian male back in the cooler, and we think he may have been employed by Cardiac Care Research Facility."

"Why would you make that assumption? What is this gentleman's name?"

"We don't have a positive ID on him yet. That's why you're here. I assumed Dr. Chatsworth would have explained that to you."

"Dr. Chatsworth was uncertain as to the gentleman's employment status with us and asked me to verify if this male could possibly be a missing employee."

"Let's not play games, Doctor," Pitts said bluntly. "We both know this man was one of your company's employees."

Zahir took a deep breath, and just for a moment, the detective expected him to lose his temper. Instead, he stood and ran his hand over what little hair remained on his head. "Detective, we don't appear to be solving any mysteries with this banter. We indeed have a missing employee who is of Russian descent. Before I delve too deeply into this person's personal business, I believe it is necessary for us to see if we are even discussing the same person."

Detective Pitts liked Zahir. He wasn't sure why, and he didn't necessarily trust him, but he wasn't dancing with the investigator, and he appreciated that. "You're right, Sir. I may, in fact, be wasting your time, and I assured you I wouldn't do that. Let's go on back."

Zahir nodded at him and followed the detective as they made their way back to Travis Upshaw's office. Upshaw was busy shuffling through mounds of paperwork on his desk when they arrived. His hair was disheveled as if he had just run his hands through it, and his glasses were barely clinging to the end of his nose. Pitts tapped lightly on the open door.

"What's up, Pitts?" Upshaw said as he glanced up. He stood when he saw the doctor standing behind him. "Hello there. I'm Medical Examiner Travis Upshaw."

"Dr. Zahir Chavan," Zahir said, introducing himself. "It's my understanding that you may have an employee of ours."

"We certainly hope so anyway," Upshaw said, pushing his wire-rimmed glasses back up on his nose. "Sorry. That may not have come out right. I meant I'd certainly like to make an ID on this fella. Let's go on back."

The men walked in a single-file line until they reached the refrigerated cooler and stepped inside.

"Normally, I'd bring him to one of our viewing rooms for official identification, but with you being a doctor, I didn't think you'd find that necessary."

"No problem," Zahir replied. He ran his hands over his arms, trying to stave off the chill of the cooler, then waited patiently as Travis unzipped the appropriate body bag, revealing Gunnar's face. "That's him," Zahir said calmly. "His name is Gunnar Azarov, and we employed him as a driver. May I ask what happened to him?"

"Blunt-force trauma to the head, a homicide. Do you know of any family?"

"No. Unfortunately, I don't. I knew very little about him, in fact."

"Let's take this outside," Pitts suggested. "Besides being cold, I don't like having a conversation in a refrigerator full of dead people."

Travis zipped the bag up, and the three men walked back to his office in silence. He moved a few stacks of paperwork out of two chairs and motioned for them to take a seat.

"What exactly *do* you know about him?" Pitts asked as he made eye contact with Dr. Chavan.

"We hired a young gentleman a few months back. Albert Tinsley was his name. He was a lab technician, highly qualified, with excellent references. Our company was very pleased with his job performance, and Albert was a nice young man. He approached me a couple of months after he started and asked if we might have anything available for a friend of his, someone who was visiting him from Russia. The man had no medical background and no necessary skills that we were aware of, but I did employ him as a driver, a chauffeur, I guess you would say. We called him when we needed him and paid him in cash, off the books. I realize that may not be appropriate in the States, but it seemed to work out for everyone involved—no payroll, no medical benefits, that type of thing. He came in when we called him, and he was paid that day for his services. He dressed professionally, and although he didn't talk much, he was perfect for the job."

"So you didn't do a background check?"

"No. I didn't see a particular need for that. I spoke with the man. He impressed me enough to allow him to drive on occasion,

269

and he came with a reference from a model employee. He always did as I asked. There wasn't ever any problem."

"Is that your normal protocol for hiring?"

"Certainly not. In fact, this was an isolated incident. I am a doctor at the Research Facility and deal predominantly with drug development. I also supervise numerous lab technicians. Prior to this, I haven't ever hired or interviewed any employee without a medical background. You must understand that we are dealing with wealthy investors and large egos. There are occasions when we require a chauffeur."

"Such as in Dr. Chatsworth's case?" Pitts said sarcastically. "I understand from him that his wife was chauffeured by this gentleman from time to time."

"I do believe so, but again, he was not my only employee. There were times when I had others call him to give him instructions. I simply didn't always have the time."

"Did he drive Dr. Chatsworth around?"

"I am detecting some resentment where the doctor is concerned," Zahir stated, a small grin forming on his thin lips.

"That's not surprising. I think your boss is an ass...and I'm sure I'm not alone in that."

The smile turned into a soft chuckle. "Dr. Chatsworth is an extremely gifted surgeon and brilliant doctor. When this drug hits the market, it will save countless lives, and he will be hailed quite the hero, an ass or not."

"So," Pitts said, changing the subject from Grant back to the murdered guy in the cooler, "why do you suppose both Gunnar and Albert were murdered?"

"That, I cannot help you with. Although I found Albert Tinsley to be very smart and capable, I knew very little about him either. I work long hours, seven days a week. I do not have time to socialize. My family is back in India, and I spend what little free time I have to partake in much-needed sleep. I have his address on file in the office, but I never visited him. He came to work, did what we expected of him, and left. Other than asking for a job for his friend, we discussed nothing other than work."

Officer Pitts let out a small sigh. "Did you see much interaction between Tinsley and this Gunnar fella?"

270

"Like I said, Albert worked in the lab, and Gunnar drove on occasion. Beyond that, I'm afraid I can't be of any help."

Pitts thought of discussing the Cates girl and the concerns Albert had shared with her about his job but quickly changed his mind. Either Gunnar or Tinsley were up to some really precarious stuff, or else it was some kind of elaborate cover-up. He couldn't put his finger on it just yet, but Pitts knew he was getting closer, and somehow, the wealthy, good-looking doctor was involved.

Chapter 64

Dr. Redding wasted little time in scheduling Lizzie's sonogram. He was uncomfortable with the fact that she hadn't received any prenatal care in her first trimester, and he was concerned that her situation at home had been a violent one. She was a beautiful young woman but seemed so vulnerable, and she was much too thin to be so far along in her first pregnancy.

Paxton Torres, the sonographer, contacted Maggie with the date for Lizzie's ultrasound, then gave her the directions and proper instructions for the morning of the procedure. Maggie feared she just may burst with excitement.

Lizzie answered on the second ring. She was sitting at the kitchen table, eating a salad topped with grilled chicken, plump grape tomatoes, cucumbers, and a combination of low-fat cheeses when the phone rang. "Hello?"

"Lizzie, it's Maggie," she said breathlessly. "We've got your sonogram scheduled for tomorrow morning. I'm so excited I can hardly stand it."

Lizzie smiled to herself as she chewed the remainder of the chicken in her mouth. "I hope you don't have that poor boy taking me, Maggie. He's got to be uncomfortable with all this, no matter what he says."

"No, he's not taking you," she chirped happily. "He's babysitting the twins. I'm taking you!" she squealed.

"Seriously? *You'll* be with me?"

"Do you think your sister would miss this? I'm borrowing his car, so be ready at 6:00 a.m."

"So we're going in before the office opens again?"

"Just trust me, Lizzie. Frankly, I think you've gotten too comfortable. Just because Grant hasn't shown up at your doorstep that doesn't mean that he doesn't intend to."

"I know," Lizzie agreed. "It's just been so nice to be away from him. I'll be ready when you get here."

"Drink lots of water," Maggie added. "Your bladder needs to be full."

"My bladder is always full these days," Lizzie said with a laugh before she disconnected the call.

She rubbed her hands across her expanding belly and smiled. It had been so long since she'd really had anything to be happy about. Lizzie allowed her mind to drift back to Atlanta, and she wondered what was going on. She knew Grant had to be furious. She thought of the oversized house and of Flossie and her team of housekeepers. Then she thought of Santiago and his wife Mariana. A queasy feeling came over her as she thought of Grant discovering their involvement in her escape. Lizzie shook her head as if to shake the memories away.

The sonogram would answer many of the questions plaguing her about the baby's health, and she was excited about possibly finding out the baby's gender. The dread was quickly washed away with anticipation.

It seemed that 6:00 couldn't come soon enough. Lizzie stood looking out the window anxiously, with a scarf pulled over her head and tied under her chin. She noticed Kenny's Honda pulling into the drive, and she scampered out the door quickly. Maggie had her hair tucked into a baseball cap and the collar of her coat turned up, concealing her face.

"Don't we make a pair?" Lizzie said with a laugh, taking the time to affectionately squeeze her sister's hand. "Will this be at Dr. Redding's office?"

"No, but it's not far away. I brought you a sausage and egg biscuit and some decaf coffee. Does that sound good?"

"Yes, but I ate a boiled egg and had a piece of toast before you got here. I don't think I slept at all last night. I'm so glad you're going with me."

"I wouldn't have missed it."

The two rode in silence for the remainder of the trip. Lizzie was lost in thought, worried about health issues with the baby. It had been quite a while before she had even allowed herself to believe she could actually be pregnant, and it was all a bit overwhelming.

Maggie pulled into a parking spot and turned off the car. "No one followed us," she said flatly. "That's good news."

The two women quickly ducked into the building and found the appropriate office.

"Good morning, ladies," a friendly, young woman said with a smile. "You must be Lizzie," she said, patting Lizzie's arm tenderly. "I'm Paxton Torres, and I'll be performing your sonogram today. Why don't you come on back?"

Lizzie grabbed Maggie's hand and followed the sonographer nervously down the hall.

"Here we go," Paxton said. "I'll leave you alone for a couple of minutes. I just need you to put on the gown from the end of the bed. You can leave your panties on."

Lizzie changed into the gown quickly as though the young woman might change her mind and not perform the test.

A light tap sounded at the door, and Paxton returned. She sat down on a stool and rolled it over to Lizzie, who was sitting on the examination table. She patted the pillow and motioned for Lizzie to lie back. "Is your bladder full?"

"Yes, always these days," Lizzie answered with a smile.

"Good. I hope you aren't too uncomfortable, but it makes things much easier to see," Paxton said as she grabbed a wand connected to the machine. "This may be a little chilly," she said as she squirted gel onto the wand and Lizzie's abdomen. "We're going to do several things today. We'll get measurements across the skull, along the thighbone, and around the abdomen, as well as check basic anatomy. The results will be sent to Dr. Redding, and he'll discuss them with you at length. I'm not at liberty to discuss them with you, so don't be concerned that anything is wrong when I don't give you details."

Lizzie took a deep breath and listened to the swishing of the baby's strong heartbeat.

"There's the head," Paxton said as she wound the sticky wand across Lizzie's stomach. "See the arms and hands?" she continued. "It appears that your baby is being cooperative today. Would you like to know the sex of your child?"

Lizzie felt a sudden surge of nausea and reached for Maggie's hand. "Yes," she stammered. "Yes, I would like to know."

"Looks like you're gonna have a sweet little girl," Paxton said with a smile.

Lizzie stared at her blankly. It never occurred to her that she might have a little girl. Maggie had given birth to twin boys, so for some reason, she just assumed her baby would be a boy too. Relief washed over her like a wave, but then her breath grew labored, and she began hyperventilating.

"Lizzie?" Maggie said, quickly getting to her feet. "Are you okay?"

Paxton handed Lizzie a tissue and offered her a cup of chipped ice. "Don't worry, Lizzie," she said. "You aren't the first to be overwhelmed. This makes your pregnancy more tangible."

"I guess I was just expecting a boy," Lizzie said weakly, "but I'm so excited to be having a girl, an innocent little girl that I'll protect with my life."

Chapter 65

Justin said an early good night to his sister and made his way to Christi's car that was parked far from the hospital, to save a few bucks. His heartbeat hadn't seemed to get back into a normal rhythm since Detective Pitts had shown up with the news about Gunnar. *He's gotta know something,* he thought, *or else he wouldn't have told me about it.*

He cranked the aging Kia and looked at the gas gauge; it was low again. Justin hit the steering wheel with both his hands and sighed heavily. Something had to give soon because he simply couldn't keep up. As he pulled out of the lot, he watched in the rearview mirror to ensure that he wasn't being followed. He was confident that he wasn't, so he went against his better judgment and headed toward Clara Samples' house. He knew she wouldn't be happy to see him, but Justin didn't feel he had any other choice.

He pulled the car to the side of the road a couple of streets over from Clara's, grabbed his jacket, and locked the vehicle. He pulled his hood up over his head and threw his backpack over his shoulder, trying to look the part of a college student nonchalantly walking from the bus stop. Her garage door was down, but he could see lights on in the house. He rang the bell and stood impatiently by the door. "Ms. Clara, it's me, Justin. Please let me in."

He heard her wrangling with the locks, and then the door opened quickly. Just as quickly, she pulled him inside by his forearm. "What in heaven's name are you doing here? I told you not to come back."

"We have to talk, Clara. I know I told you I wouldn't come back, but Detective Pitts came to see me at the hospital. They found Gunnar's body. I think they might suspect me."

"Oh dear," Clara said softly. "Come back to the kitchen. Let me call Iris."

Justin was sitting at the kitchen table with a glass of sweet tea when Iris arrived.

"Oh, thank goodness," she murmured. "I've been so worried about you and Christi!"

"But we told him not to come back, Iris," Clara interrupted. "Someone could've followed you!" she snapped at the boy.

"No one did," Justin said adamantly. "We have to talk about this. They found Gunnar's body, and—"

"I know," Clara cut in quietly as she sat down at the table. "That detective came by our office. I was sure that was why he was there."

"What did you do with the body?" Justin asked.

"We left him in the trunk of his car," Iris said as she paced back and forth across the small kitchen. "We wiped off all the fingerprints though."

"Yeah, but nowadays, they've got all those crazy forensic science techniques," Justin said. "They might have fibers and stuff."

Clara stood up and offered her chair to Iris. "Please sit down, Iris. You're making me a nervous wreck! They may find fibers, Justin, but they have to have something to compare them to. Let's face it. Why would they suspect us? That will only happen if one of us folds or if they saw you with us. That's a link we don't need them to discover right now, which is why you shouldn't have come here."

"I just didn't know what else to do," Justin said, dropping his face in his hands.

"Now, now, dear," Iris said, trying to console the boy, "things are gonna be okay. Let's just all keep our mouths shut, and no one will be the wiser."

"But Christi will be released soon, and we can't go back to the apartment. I'm running low on funds and will be out of that low-rent hotel by the end of the week. Besides, I wouldn't ever take her there."

"That's a problem easily solved," Iris said firmly. "You will both move into my house until all this is resolved. A great aunt of one of your frat brothers has offered you a place to stay after hearing about your plight. That's all you've gotta say, a little fib to cover your butt...and ours."

"We can't possibly do that," Justin said. "I appreciate the gesture, but it's not a good idea."

"I agree with Justin," Clara spoke up. "Our houses are in close proximity, and if they connect me with either of you, it will be too big of a coincidence. Justin, I have some money saved, and let's be honest. What am I ever going to do with it? You and your sister can use it to get an apartment and back on your feet, hopefully away from the city. It'll give you the breathing room you need for now."

"I-I just couldn't. Christi wouldn't like it."

"Christi isn't going to like a lot of things when her memory returns, but she'll just have to accept some of it."

"Clara's right, Justin," Iris said. "We don't know that you're out of danger, even now that Gunnar's dead. Now's not the time to be proud, my boy. Just take the money."

"Maybe just enough to get into an apartment," he stammered. "Christi's gonna be so ticked though."

"Justin," Clara said firmly, "you have to stay away from us. I'm serious. Dr. Chatsworth is my boss, and if he finds out I'm involved, he could have me killed. This isn't a game."

"Don't you think I know that?" Justin said defensively. "My sister was almost killed, and that big guy tried to choke me to death before you killed him with a waffle iron!"

"I'm sorry if I offended you," Clara said, "but we can't get caught for Gunnar's murder."

"It was self-defense," Iris interjected.

"Self-defense or not, we're up to our ears in this," Clara said. "All I know is that Christi is going to recover, and Lizzie has made it safely to Biloxi. It's time for me to retire."

Chapter 66

Grant Chatsworth sat at his dining room table eating dry toast, sipping black coffee, and reading the morning newspaper. It had been a long week, so he was relieved that it was Friday. He had rummaged through Lizzie's room with Flossie and come to the conclusion that she had only left with a few pieces of jewelry and her driver's license. There was no doubt she would be back after her temper tantrum, but he had yet to decide how he would punish her. Grant could mask her absence for a while, but he'd need her back soon, at least until he made his final exit. *Perhaps that will be her punishment,* he mused. *Lizzie will be left penniless after the investors become aware of this deception. The greedy bastards will sue my estate for anything they can get their hands on, and that conniving little bitch will end up poorer than she was when I met her and pulled her out of that trash dump she was living in.* A small, devious smile formed on his lips as he thought of her back in some studio apartment, struggling to keep the utilities on. "You better enjoy it while you can, you ungrateful little brat. You won't have my money for long," he said, then snickered to himself.

The ringing of his alternate cell phone took his mind off of Lizzie.

"Yeah?"

"It's me," Rayne said. "How's everything going?"

"Fine, except for being exhausted. I don't have any surgeries today, so I'll catch up on paperwork at the office and see the day's lineup of patients."

"Just reminding you of my trip to Escaldes-Engordany. I'll be back Tuesday."

"Which ones are you looking at this time?"

"Two penthouses and that flat with the great view."

"Don't make any offers or commitments until you've consulted with me."

"Don't you trust my judgment, dear?"

"Yes," Grant said seductively, "but I'd like to be in on the decision-making too. After all, it's going to be *our* new home."

"So the wife isn't back yet?"

"Nope. Frankly, I'm enjoying the solitude."

"And I'm enjoying the thought that you aren't having to be intimate with her."

"You know that's not an issue, not often anyway."

"If you touch her at all, it's too much."

"Jealousy is not very becoming," Grant said. "Don't take your cell phone, and don't call me from Andorra. We'll speak when you get back. Make sure you don't run into any men over there. I don't enjoy sharing either."

"Jealousy is not very becoming," Rayne teased before disconnecting the call.

Grant folded the paper and took one last sip of his coffee. His mind drifted to Escaldes-Engordany, a small parish in Andorra. He had done a great deal of research into nonextradition countries, but the decision had been a difficult one. Grant had narrowed his search down to Marseille, France on the Mediterranean for its beauty and Croatia for its miles of beaches, uninhabited islands, and the simple fact that his money would go far. In the end, though, he changed his mind altogether after visiting the small country of Andorra, nestled high in the Pyrenees between France and Spain. It was situated in a beautiful setting, offered great skiing and cultural events, and it didn't have an extradition treaty with the United States or even a consulate, for that matter. The government was simply a parliament served by two co-princes, the president of France and the bishop of Urgell. They didn't even have a military to speak of. It was perfect in every way, except that it was taking much too long for him to get there.

The next step would be for Rayne to secure a residence for them and wait for the whole thing to play out. Grant had bought some more time with the investors after the successful open house, and he intended to milk it for all it was worth.

The detective was a pain in the ass, but Pitts didn't know nearly as much as he thought he did. From now on, Grant would simply refer all inquiries and visits from him to Zahir. If Pitts had a problem with it, he could get a warrant, which would be next to impossible. Lizzie's disappearance was just a bump in the road, and if she wasn't back soon, he'd go to her sister's house and get her.

The monkeys would soon be gone, and with the employees temporarily laid off, things were looking up.

Flossie came out of the kitchen with a fresh pot of coffee. "Would you care for another cup?"

"I believe I would," Grant said with more enthusiasm than Flossie had heard in a while. He sat back in the chair and, for the first time in months, allowed himself to relax. Things weren't nearly as bad as they seemed.

Chapter 67

Lizzie put on her flannel pajamas and heated a cup of milk. Her emotions were still reeling from the sight of her infant daughter on the sonogram machine. She touched her belly, something she did often now as if to assure herself that the pregnancy was real. Grant certainly didn't suspect it, and Lizzie couldn't help but wonder how he would feel if he knew. *It doesn't matter. He'll never know about our child, my child,* she thought to herself.

Realistically, she knew that one day, she would have to face him, file divorce papers, and end it all, but she wouldn't ask for a thing from him. She hoped Grant would just dismiss her like a difficult child and go on with his life. There was always the hope and the possibility that the authorities would discover his little scam, but she would have no part in that. Her child was too important to her, and she wanted nothing more than to be free of Grant Chatsworth.

The warm milk felt good going down her throat, and that warmth spread across her chest. It had been quite a long day, but Lizzie was far from tired. Her mind jumped eagerly from one excited thought to the next: the color of the nursery, where she would live, and what kind of mother she would be. She would be a good mother: Of that she was certain. They would bake cookies and pies without worrying about how messy the kitchen got. There would be bubble baths with warm water splashed all over the bathroom, and she would take her little girl to visit her parents and grandmother, even though it had to be the cemetery.

The cemetery. Lizzie's mind switched gears, and she thought of the little girl's grave not far from the house. She, too, had been someone's daughter. *Surely Baby Belle was loved by a mother who had once looked forward to her birth.* "I promised her I would visit again," Lizzie said aloud.

She slipped out of her house shoes and into her sneakers. After grabbing the flashlight, cell phone, and her jacket, she made her way to the door. It had been dark for some time now, but she pulled the heavy drapes to one side to ensure there wasn't anyone outside. Lizzie closed the front door quietly and followed the same path she had before along the narrow roadway. She passed the rusted gate of the family plot she had visited before and looked for the same spot she had cut through between the tombstones. Lizzie continued across the damp grass and shined her flashlight up the small hill in search of the tiny, broken monument. She quickened her pace as it came into view.

There was a chill in the air, and Lizzie's body shuddered from the cold. She silently scolded herself for not remembering to pull a scarf over her head. Maggie was right: She was getting too comfortable. Grant was not the type of man who would forgive, and Lizzie had to bear that in mind. The cemetery was so quiet and serene that it brought a false sense of security.

Lizzie leaned against a plump oak and listened intently. All she could hear were the crickets in the distance. She flashed her light in a slow arc across the circumference of the property but didn't see any movement; she was alone. Shivering again from the cool temperatures, she made a mental note to remember her scarf next time, as well as gloves or mittens, as her grandmother would have said. The memory brought a smile to her lips as Lizzie reached the grave.

She rubbed her hands together, trying to warm them before she ran her fingers over the inscribed name. "Baby Belle." It was just that simple, nothing more, nothing less. Lizzie looked around again for another family member's grave but saw nothing within a reasonable distance. "Why are you alone, little girl?"

Lizzie's eyes started misting over, and she suddenly felt foolish. Of course, it was terribly sad for a child to be buried without having a chance to live a full life, but she didn't know her. *Hormones*, she thought. *Everyone says you get hormonal when you're pregnant. Perhaps it's because I found out I'm having a daughter of my own. Yeah, that has to be it.* Still, Lizzie knew that wasn't the only reason her heartstrings were being tugged. There was an odd sense of connection that she couldn't deny. She ran her finger over the carved lamb's body, then felt the sharp edges where the head had broken off. It made her heart sink. *Maybe that's it.* The small, broken monument would make anyone sorrowful. Lizzie got down on her knees and wiped the tears away. Her mind went back to the times when her grandmother had taken her and Maggie to visit the cemetery where relatives and friends were buried. They had often taken jonquils from their yard to lay across graves, familiar ones and even some of those they didn't know. The young girls had walked among the tombstones, reading the names and studying unique carvings or messages. "The rosebud signifies a child twelve years or younger," her grandmother explained. "The partial bloom signifies a teenager, and the fully blooming rose is an adult." The sisters always found the symbols and their meanings so interesting. They had seen many cherubs and angels on the babies' graves, and they learned that it was a symbol of innocence, but the most fascinating was the granite baby's chair on a young boy's grave. Their grandmother had explained that it signified the unfulfilled life of a child. Lizzie and Maggie stopped by that particular tombstone every visit thereafter.

Most of the babies and young children were buried either with their families or in what was often called a baby land, a place where several little ones were laid to rest when they didn't have a deceased parent to rest beside. Another thing Lizzie remembered was that in older graves, stillborn children weren't ever named. She found that the saddest of all. They were often listed as simply "Son" or "Daughter," followed by a family surname, but sometimes the grave simply read, "Infant."

"You weren't stillborn, were you, Baby Belle?" Lizzie asked quietly. "Even though no one put the date of your birth on here, you lived, didn't you, little one?" Lizzie remained quiet, lost in thought of what little Belle's short life had possibly been like.

The sound of the crickets faded in the distance, and all was quiet and peaceful. Then it started to happen. At first, Lizzie thought she was fabricating it in her mind, so she leaned forward on her knees to see more clearly. It began as a light fog that slowly changed to a faint mist. The world around Lizzie grew darker, almost black, and everything around her began to fade away. She concentrated on the mist, but her heart was beating out of her chest, and her breathing came in deep gulps. Lizzie couldn't distinguish any features, but she could see the outline of a small face, a three-dimensional mist clothed in a bonnet and flowing child's nightgown. The figure hid behind a nearby tombstone and appeared to peek around.

284

"Belle? Baby Belle, is that you?" Lizzie whispered.

The mist faded as quickly as it had come, leaving Lizzie limp. It hadn't frightened her but now she was exhausted and cold and wanted to get back to the comfort and warmth of the house. She stood and brushed off her pajamas at the knee as a shiver ran through her body.

The sound of footsteps nearby was followed by what sounded like the snap of a twig.

"Oh, God," Lizzie said with a gasp. "Someone's here."

She moved slowly and methodically and hid behind one of the massive oaks. She strained to hear movement, but there was only an eerie stillness. She knew it was ridiculous to think she could stand out in the cold all night. *Perhaps it was just my imagination.* Lizzie listened intently for another couple of minutes, then stepped from behind the large tree and crept quickly toward the house.

She was within fifty yards of the cemetery entrance when a hand reached from behind a tree and pulled her by her arm. She gasped, but before she could make a sound, fingers wrapped around her mouth, reaching from one side of her face to the other.

"Shh! Don't scream. It's me, Kenny," he whispered as he removed his hand from her face.

Lizzie turned to face him. "What in the world are you doing? You scared me to death!" She gasped again, then leaned forward and put her hands on her chest. "For the love of God. I think you took ten years off my life."

"What are you doing out here?" Kenny asked nervously. "I stopped by the house to drop off some groceries, but you didn't come to the door. I saw some light out here, and against my better judgment, I figured I'd check it out. I thought you might be hiding from someone."

"No, I'm not hiding. I just wanted to get out of the house for a bit. It's rough being cooped up all the time. Let's walk back," Lizzie suggested, linking her hand through his arm. "We'll talk about it when we get back to the house."

Kenny drank slowly from a tall glass of lemonade while Lizzie put away the groceries. His brow was furrowed into a frown as he voiced his concern. "You shouldn't be out like that, Lizzie, especially at night. Someone could see you."

"It was dark, and I made sure no one was outside," she answered stubbornly. "Maybe it wasn't the best idea, but please don't tell Maggie. She worries enough as it is."

"I don't know your whole story," Kenny began, "but I've figured out that you're hiding from someone. A violent spouse is my guess. At any rate, there's a reason why we're shuttling you around before normal doctor's hours, and you always wear scarves and wigs. I just don't want to see anything happen to you."

Lizzie turned from the refrigerator and sat down beside him at the counter. "You're not too far off base," she said flatly. "It's been a long road, and I'm sorry to be a burden to Maggie and you. I hate that they pulled you into this."

"It's no problem," Kenny said as a smile formed on his lips. "I'm kinda enjoying the overtime, especially at time and a half."

Lizzie chuckled and patted his arm. "Glad I can help then. Just please don't tell Maggie about me leaving the house. It won't happen again."

"I won't say anything," Kenny promised as he stood and reached for his coat. "Here's my cell number," he said, placing a business card on the counter. "Feel free to call me anytime."

"Thanks," Lizzie said. "I appreciate all you've done."

"No problem," he answered as he walked toward the front of the house. "Be careful, Lizzie," Kenny added as he closed the door behind him.

Lizzie plopped down on the couch, sighed, and closed her eyes. Her heart was still racing from Kenny surprising her in the cemetery. She glanced at the clock on the mantel and realized it was almost midnight, well past bedtime for a pregnant woman.

Chapter 68

The wind was howling, and the rain fell in sheets as Lizzie Chatsworth lay in a fitful sleep. The erratic dreams taunted her mercilessly, and sweat formed quickly on her forehead and dampened her golden locks. In her nightmare, Grant was chasing her, but Lizzie was the only one running. No matter how fast she ran, he was catching up to her, with long, careful strides. She was exhausted and kept tumbling over branches and rocks. Finally, a twisted ankle disabled her to the point of being unable to stand. Grant was on top of her quickly, wrapping his large hands around her smooth neck. Lizzie struggled to scream, but no sounds would come, and she could no longer breathe.

She bolted straight up in bed with her hands reaching for her neck as she gasped for air. A nightlight in the master bath suggested she'd only been having a bad dream and that Grant was not actually poised over her. The down comforter was crumpled on the floor, and the sheets were wrapped carelessly around her legs. Lizzie untangled them and walked into the bathroom to splash water over her face. The heavy storm was thunderous, and flashes of lightning illuminated the outdoors in a dazzling display at frequent intervals. It was going to be difficult to get back to sleep.

Lizzie shuffled out of the bathroom, slipped out of her house shoes, curled up in the bed, and pulled the duvet up around her neck. She listened to the rain pelting the house, followed by loud booms of thunder. *Thank goodness we got the groceries in before this storm hit,* she thought. She fluffed her pillows, then closed her eyes.

Lizzie had almost drifted to sleep when she heard a loud banging coming from the guestroom down the hall. It sounded as though someone was knocking on the window panes. Her first thought was to sink down further in the bed, but then reason overtook her; she couldn't hide under the covers like a child. "Why would someone be knocking on a window in the rear of the house? If someone was stranded or needed help, surely they'd ring the bell at the front door," she told herself. Lizzie sat up in bed slowly as if to ensure she was no longer dreaming. The noise resonated throughout the house, making her tremble with fear. She stood as quietly as she could and slipped into her robe, then placed the cell phone in the left pocket.

The banging grew louder as she inched her way down the hall. The knocking was unremitting and, coupled with the claps of thunder, reverberated loudly throughout the house. Lizzie thought of calling 911 on her cell phone, but she didn't want to bring attention to herself. *I should call Maggie,* she thought before quickly changing her mind.

She inched purposefully into the guestroom that had been transformed into a home office. It was pitch-black, but she could make out the heavy drapes that were pulled shut in front of the double-window. Lizzie slid out of her slippers, not wanting to make any unnecessary noise, then moved slowly toward the knocking. She brushed her damp hair away from her face and reached for the edge of the curtain. Just as she pulled it back, a flash of bright lightning raced across the sky and lit the room up as if someone had just turned on the lights. Lizzie screamed when she saw the large limb that had fallen from a nearby tree and was bumping against the window, the source of the knocking and banging.

"Oh, dear Lord," she said with a gasp, feeling like a fool. "It's just a tree branch."

Between the dream and the loud noises, she was wide awake and alarmed. She walked over to the desk chair in front of the computer and slumped down on it. She wouldn't be able to move the limb until morning, so she'd just have to close her bedroom door and hope for some semblance of sleep. Rest would be hard to come by, and Lizzie took measured breaths as she tried to calm down. Another clap of thunder shook the house, and then the computer flicked on. The flash of the monitor startled her, and she reached for her chest again.

"What in the world?" she said aloud to herself as she forced a laugh. *I'm getting way too paranoid,* Lizzie thought. When she reached down to turn the computer off, she noticed that the power button wasn't even on. *That's odd,* she thought. *I hope the lightning didn't mess it up.*

Lizzie reached up to shut the monitor off, but the screen began flashing from one website to another. Her eyes darted from one

288

scenario to the next as she tried to make sense of it all. First, she saw the website for Evergreen Cemetery, followed by the site of the Old Biloxi City Cemetery. Finally, there was a web page referencing the 1840 census. Finally, the monitor shut down and went black.

Lizzie leaned back in the chair, dumbfounded. "The cemetery? How could that have popped up?" She hadn't ever pulled it up on the computer. In fact, the only sites she'd gone to were the *Atlanta Journal Constitution* and a few containing information about Grant and his Cardiac Care Research Facility.

"I need more warm milk," Lizzie said.

As she started to get up from the chair, the screen came to life again, displaying the Evergreen Cemetery site. At that point, it was hard to deny that something was going on.

Lizzie sat back down, rolled the chair up to the computer, and began reading accounts of the area. Ocean Springs had a beautiful history of diverse religions and races, all belonging to a harmonic community and joined together in eternal rest in Evergreen Cemetery. She scanned the different tabs until she discovered the one that would allow her to search the gravesites. Lizzie scrolled through the long, alphabetized list, searching for Belle, to no avail. There was no record of her burial at the cemetery at all. *Perhaps Belle is her last name,* Lizzie considered, but she was unsuccessful in that attempt as well. *Hmm,* she thought. "Maybe there's no record because she was so young," she said aloud.

The computer flashed, then went dark again.

Lizzie pushed the power button, but nothing happened.

A flash of lightning was followed by persistent thunder, but something was odd: The tree limb was no longer knocking on the window.

Lizzie pulled the chenille robe tight around her expanding waist and inched slowly to the window where she cautiously pulled the drapes back once again. The limb was gone. She closed her eyes, then opened them again, as if she had somehow missed the large tree limb that had hindered her sleep. The hair on the back of her neck stood on end while her hand quickly released the curtain. A cool chill seemed to brush by her face, and Lizzie shivered.

"Enough of this silliness," she said to herself. She exited the office and turned the light on in the hallway, along with the one in the living room and kitchen. She turned on the television, conscious that sleep would not be coming anytime soon.

Chapter 69

The morning sun filtered through the window sheers and awakened Lizzie from her sleep. She had dozed off on the sofa at some point during the stormy, creepy night. She rubbed her eyes and reached for the remote to turn the television to her favorite morning news show. Memories of the night before started pouring through her mind as she started brewing her decaffeinated coffee. Lizzie convinced herself that it was undoubtedly a dream.

When her cell phone rang, she realized it was still in the pocket of her bathrobe. "Maggie?" she said when she picked up the call.

"Good morning. How are you feeling today?"

"Just fine," Lizzie answered, trying to feel her sister out to see if Kenny had betrayed her confidence by telling Maggie about her forbidden visit to the cemetery.

"You sound like you just woke up."

"I haven't been up long. I woke up last night and couldn't get back to sleep."

"A baby will do that to you. I had insomnia a lot when I was pregnant with the twins. Did Kenny deliver the groceries?"

"Yes. Thanks so much, but I have some money, you know. I also still have that jewelry I'd like you to sell."

"We'll worry about that later. Listen, Lizzie, I don't want to alarm you, but Grant called last night."

"He did? What did he say?"

"He sounded like he'd been drinking, but I couldn't be sure. He wasn't very happy and told me to remind you that his patience is wearing thin. Grant demanded that you call him no later than noon, or he'll be on his way here to get you."

"Oh, no, Maggie. What did you say?"

"Of course, I denied knowing where you are, but he's no fool, Lizzie. You're going to have to call him."

"I can't, Maggie! I just can't do it. Just the thought of hearing his voice makes me nauseous."

"I don't see that you have a choice. Maybe the phone call will keep him at bay for the time being. If he comes to Biloxi, he's bound to find you, Lizzie. We simply can't get around doctor's visits and delivering food to you. Like I said, he's no fool."

For the first time since Lizzie had arrived, she was truly frightened. She had been foolish to think that Grant would simply forget about her. The holidays were right around the corner, and he would have great trouble explaining her constant absences from all the parties and annual get-togethers. Any questions or inconsistencies would certainly raise doubts among his investors, and he wouldn't tolerate that.

Lizzie almost dropped the phone, then realized her hands were trembling terribly. "I know I have to call him," she conceded. "I just don't know what to say. I'm so afraid. Could you come over, Maggie? It'd be so much easier if you were here."

"I wish I could," Maggie answered, her voice reflecting the sadness she felt, "but the twins don't have preschool today, and we can't forgo the possibility that Grant may already be here. It could all be a ploy to get me to lead him right to you."

"I hadn't thought of that. You're right. Just stay where you are. I'll call him after I have a couple of cups of coffee and some toast and maybe a warm bath to calm me down."

"Don't put it off too long. Noon is his deadline."

Lizzie poured a cup of steaming coffee into an oversized mug and stood at the window, looking out over the bayou. The world was still dismal and damp from the previous night's storm, and the beautiful heron she watched every day was nowhere in sight. *The limb,* Lizzie thought nervously. *Maybe it really was all a dream.*

She left her coffee on the counter to cool and walked down the hallway to the guestroom. Things seemed much different in the daylight, and Lizzie didn't feel any of the nervousness she had the night before as she pulled the drapes open and looked outside. The large limb she remembered so vividly was no longer there, and there was no visible evidence that any had fallen. *Yep, just a dream,* she thought, *just like Grant trying to choke me. I've got to get on a more consistent sleep schedule. I'm just too damn tired to even sleep well.*

Her mind went back to the impending phone call to Grant, and she strode back into the kitchen and sipped from her coffee. Calling him would certainly affirm her location and her contact with

Maggie. Lizzie worried about tying her sister to the whole mess. That was the last thing she wanted to do, but she didn't want to go back to Grant either. Putting off the call would only make him angrier and prolong the inevitable, so she punched the familiar cell number into her phone; she didn't want to hear Flossie's voice answering the one at the estate.

Three rings in, he answered in a hurried voice, "Dr. Chatsworth here."

"Grant, it's me, Lizzie."

"I recognize your voice, Elizabeth," he said curtly.

"I understand you wanted me to call you."

"Don't play games with me. Of course, I did. What the hell are you doing? I will not tolerate this type of boorish behavior. Do you understand me? You're behaving like a child throwing a tantrum."

"Grant, I'm hardly acting like a child. Our marriage has been deteriorating for quite some time. We both need a break. You're very busy, and the time apart will do us some good." Lizzie held her breath as she waited for the explosion that was sure to follow.

"You ungrateful little whore!" he spat into the phone. "I have treated you like a queen. Need I remind you that I pulled you out of the gutter?"

"No, Grant. You have reminded me of that daily. It's hardly necessary to reiterate it again."

"Are you seeing someone, Elizabeth?"

"Of course not," Lizzie answered. "I just needed to get away I couldn't stand being locked up in that house anymore, and, frankly, I was tiring of being your punching bag."

Grant paused briefly before continuing, "Enjoy Thanksgiving, Elizabeth because you'll be spending Christmas in our house. I'll see to that myself!" With that, he disconnected their call.

Lizzie laid the phone down on the end table and collapsed on the couch. Her hands were shaking, but her attempts to release tears failed. She pulled her knees up to her chest and wrapped her arms around them. The mere sound of his voice had brought back all the horrible memories, and she vowed then that she would die before she would ever return to that house.

Chapter 70

Dr. Grant Chatsworth leaned back in his office chair and shook with anger. "How dare Elizabeth talk to me in that manner?" he muttered, seething. "She is nothing without me," he hissed under his breath.

After the initial rage settled a bit, Grant realized he had actually enjoyed her being gone. So many times, her mere presence had annoyed him, and he now relished the peace and uninterrupted quiet in his smooth-running home. On the other hand, she was a critical piece of the puzzle, and he couldn't allow her to remain absent for much longer. He'd let her whine to her sister and pout for a while, then send someone to bring her back. Things were going according to plan now, and whether she liked it or not, she would be necessary around the Christmas holidays, as his investors would be expecting some lavish party at the estate. It would be his last hoorah, the last time he would have to spring for another extravagant spread. Soon after, he would be living the life he had always wanted, and Elizabeth Chatsworth would be left behind to lose it all. The thought brought a wide smile to his face. *You think you're in control now, don't you, Elizabeth?* he thought. *My dear, you have no idea what's ahead of you.*

The sound of his cell phone ringing interrupted his thoughts.

"Dr. Chatsworth," he barked in the phone.

"Yes, Doctor," Zahir said into the phone. "I am phoning to inquire about the release of the primates."

"Release?" Grant snorted. "What the hell are you talking about, Zahir? Surely you don't intend to unleash the irritating little pains in the ass on this good city."

"Certainly not, Sir," he answered, resentment apparent in his tone. "I was told there is a large population in Florida, and I assumed we would just release them back to the wild. It hasn't been that long, and the animals should be able to assimilate to—"

"Ha!" Grant scoffed, cutting him off. "First of all, if there's a fucking rhesus monkey population in Florida, why the hell did we pay to have them shipped from India?"

"They live in the wild, Sir. Capturing them would have brought much unwanted attention."

"I see, but capturing them in the wild and shipping them through an illegal cargo port in the United States wouldn't arouse suspicion?"

"The capture and transport of those primates was extremely well thought out," Zahir said bluntly. "The primates in Florida were transported there many decades ago by a tour operator who thought the public would enjoy them. His idea came from a popular movie here, *Tarzan*, I believe it was called. At any rate, they also carry the Herpes B virus and have become quite the pests to residents. I assume the tour guide never anticipated they would reproduce at such a rapid pace, nor did he realize they could swim or migrate throughout the state so quickly."

"I don't give a rat's ass about the history of migrating monkeys, nor do I care about fucking Tarzan!" Grant screamed into the phone, forgetting briefly that he was in his office with patients within earshot. The all-too-familiar pounding in his head returned, and he rummaged through his desk to find a Tylenol. "Just meet me after work for a drink. We'll discuss the matter then. I'll see you at 7:00."

"Very well," Zahir answered.

Grant stood from behind his desk to go see the next patient waiting for him in the adjacent room. He glanced at his watch and grunted with impatience when he realized it wasn't yet noon. The day promised to be a long one, but at least he only had one more patient to deal with before lunch.

Nurse Clara Samples stood patiently outside the exam room, holding the patient's medical file.

Grant snatched the folder from her hand without any conversation and entered the room. The usual charismatic smile crossed his lips, and he transformed quickly to the well-liked doctor with a caring, authentic bedside manner. *Damn it,* he thought. *I'm so sick of the game, sick of pretending I genuinely enjoy this good doctor shit.* Nevertheless, for the next fifteen minutes, he went through the motions of appearing interested and offering hope to someone who had already experienced the best years of his life. He even patted Mr. Ross on the knee and told him to book his next appointment in six months. "Take care now," Grant said, flashing the winning smile once again. "I'll see you next time, Mr. Ross. Say hello to that beautiful wife of yours." Grant then made his way back to his office, only to find Clara waiting for him outside the door.

"Excuse me, Dr. Chatsworth. I'm sorry to bother you, but I need a couple of minutes of your time."

He thought of denying the request and putting her off until later, but he knew he wouldn't be any happier to deal with her issues then either. "Come on in," he said, opening the door and extending his hand in a gesture suggesting she enter first. "Have a seat, Ms. Samples," Grant said as he walked behind his desk and sat down himself. "What can I do for you?"

"Well, I'll just get right to the point," Clara said, folding her wrinkled hands together and placing them in her lap. "I've enjoyed working for you so much, but I think it's time for me to retire and let someone with a younger mind take my place."

"Are you having any health problems?" Grant asked, his brow furrowing with feigned concern.

"Oh no, nothing like that," she answered. "I'm well past retirement age, and I think I'd like to do some traveling while I'm still able. A friend of mine is a widow, too, and there are a few places we'd like to visit while we can."

Grant got the feeling the conversation had the potential to drone on and on, so he interjected, "You've been a tremendous asset to my practice over the years, Clara. I'm very saddened by your decision, but I certainly understand." He leaned forward, his teeth glittering like perfect diamonds as he smiled pleasantly.

Clara wasn't fooled by his demeanor; she knew the wolf that lay beneath the sheep's clothing. "I appreciate you being so kind. Of course, I will work out a sufficient notice. I figure I can work till the end of the year. That should be ample time for you to find a replacement. I'll be happy to share all I know about the office, but as you're aware, times have changed, and my old mind just can't grasp all this new technology." Clara forced a laugh, then stood and walked toward the door. She hoped he wouldn't be suspicious; for all she knew, he was probably relieved to be rid of her.

"Thank you, Ms. Samples," Grant said as he walked her to his office door. "Again, I appreciate all you've done to ensure that the office runs smoothly. You will certainly be missed."

Clara offered a timid smile and gathered her gray cardigan to leave for lunch. She waited to exhale until she got on the elevator. She grabbed the brass rail, then leaned against the elevator wall. A wave of dizziness swept over her, and she pulled a Kleenex from her purse and wiped it across her face. She wasn't quite sure if it was dizziness or simply relief. Either way, she was grateful Dr. Grant Chatsworth would soon be out of her life.

Once again, Grant sighed and plopped back down behind his desk. Hopefully, he would be gone soon after the holidays and he wouldn't even bother looking for a replacement for his office manager. Grant had to admit that Clara had been a good nurse, and if he wasn't planning to leave, he would have offered her a raise to stay.

He still had two small procedures to perform at the hospital before he could call it a day, but just as he stood to turn off the lamp on his desk, his cell phone rang again. "Chatsworth here."

"Hey, honey," Rayne said seductively into the phone. "Do you miss me?"

"You shouldn't be calling me from Andorra," Grant answered rudely. "We've discussed this before."

"Don't chastise me as though I'm a child. You aren't speaking to Lizzie."

"What's so urgent? I have to be at the hospital in thirty minutes," Grant said, his tone softening.

"I found it, baby," Rayne said with growing excitement.

"What are you talking about?"

"The house! I found the perfect one!"

"I'm on my way to the hospital. Give me a quick overview. I don't have much time."

"Perfect location and within five minutes of Charlemagne Avenue. Stunning views across the valley, and it's surrounded by luscious gardens. Sound good so far?"

"When you put it like that, I suppose it does. Are we looking at a lot of stairs?"

"A three-story with a magnificent mahogany spiral staircase. Of course, there's an elevator too."

"Can't argue with that. Are there decks and patios to enjoy the views?"

"Wraparound decks on every floor and ample space to entertain as well."

"Hmm. Well, I'm going against my better judgment by not seeing it first, but just do it. Your name is on the offshore account, so take the money out and purchase it."

"I wouldn't lead you astray, dear. Trust me."

Grant disconnected the call, and a dark feeling of unease crept over him. *"Trust me"?* he thought. *Two very dangerous words.*

Chapter 71

Lizzie dressed in leggings, quickly becoming her daily go-to outfit. Her small baby bump was expanding at a rapid pace, most likely because she was eating better and providing her little one with much-needed nourishment. With Kenny bringing her groceries almost daily, she was able to prepare healthy, tasty meals, and she shamelessly enjoyed eating for two.

She washed her face. For the first time in months, she noticed some color coming back to her cheeks. Lizzie applied a little blush, then ran the mascara brush through her lashes. She wasn't expecting to see anyone, but preparing for the day seemed to make her feel better.

Trying desperately to erase the conversation with Grant from her mind, Lizzie wiped down the bathroom sink with a Clorox wipe and made her bed. She wasn't quite ready for lunch, so she made her way back into the home office, trying to remember the websites that had flashed across the computer screen the night before.

Lizzie pulled up the internet browser history, but all that showed up was her recent search on Grant. Puzzled, she pulled up the website for Evergreen Cemetery and quickly recognized it. She typed Baby Belle's name back in, another dead-end search, just like the night before. She looked for anyone with the surname of Belle but again found nothing. *Perhaps the records just weren't kept well so long ago,* Lizzie thought. *They didn't exactly have spreadsheets in the 1800s.* Then she immediately remembered another cemetery flashing across her screen the previous night. She couldn't recall the exact name of it but recollected that it was in Biloxi. She typed "Biloxi Cemeteries" in the search bar and immediately recognized one of the names that popped up: Old Biloxi Cemetery.

It was located in an area quite different from the aged Evergreen Cemetery positioned at the end of a quiet neighborhood street. Old Biloxi sat directly across the thoroughfare from the gulf where the water leisurely rolled up to spread across the white sand beach. It, too, was filled with history, with headstones dating back to the 1800s. Pictures of Hurricane Katrina's destruction showed broken, toppled monuments, along with photos of the Historical

Society's valiant efforts to repair the damage. Lizzie enjoyed reading the diverse history of the people buried there. Unlike Atlanta, where cemeteries mostly remained segregated by race and prominence, Old Biloxi Cemetery held an Indian War Congressional Medal of Honor recipient, a Civil War Confederate brigadier general, and the first African-American to hold the rank of archbishop. Others of great distinction and achievement rested among those hardworking but mostly unknown common folks who made up the distinguished past of Biloxi, Mississippi.

Lizzie heard her stomach rumbling, signaling that it was time to fill her belly. She had become so immersed in the cemetery's history that she had lost track of time. She piled a bun high with roasted turkey and cheese, washed some raw celery and carrots, then carried the plate back to the computer. "What am I looking for?" she asked herself aloud. "How does this cemetery tie in with Baby Belle? Help me, little girl. Show me what I'm supposed to find."

She chewed on a piece of celery while her eyes remained fixated on the screen, but she saw nothing. Lizzie laughed out loud and shook her head. "I'm losing it," she snickered as she picked up her plate and walked back into the kitchen.

Still, it was hard for her to let it go. As much as she wanted to dismiss the things that had happened the night before, she knew in her gut that they had indeed happened. She picked up a magazine but soon shut it and placed it back on the coffee table. The memory of she and Maggie laying the handpicked jonquils on the graves when they were children played over in her mind. *Perhaps I'll ask Maggie to bring some fresh jonquils,* she thought, then decided against it, realizing that Maggie might recall the same memory and suspect her of visiting the cemetery. *I'll give Kenny a call later,* she decided. *If he was going to tell Maggie and Leland about me sneaking out of the house, he would have done it by now. Apparently, he's no tattletale.*

Chapter 72

Andie was waiting at the entrance of the bar, her hair draped seductively over her right shoulder and her large breasts protruding from the low-cut uniform. She smiled broadly as Dr. Grant Chatsworth came through the door. "Good evening, Doctor," she said in her raspy voice. "I assume you want your usual booth?"

"Yes please," he answered. Grant offered her little more than a nod but winked when she said she'd be right back with his scotch. For the first time in his career, he was contemplating calling in sick for a few days. The thought was a pleasant one but was quickly replaced by contempt when he spotted Zahir and Jean-Luc moving toward the booth. He was beginning to abhor their meetings. "Evening, Zahir, Jean-Luc," he said as he glanced in their direction. "How was everything at the Research Facility today?"

"Quite pleasant actually," Jean-Luc replied. "With most of the staff on temporary layoff, it was quiet, with the exception of the nonhuman primates, of course."

"You mean the fucking monkeys?" Grant sneered.

Zahir looked around nervously, hoping no one had overheard the vulgar profanity. "Doctor, they need to be taken care of as soon as possible."

"Yes, Zahir, indeed they do. Euthanize them as humanely as possible and dispose of their remains. We are officially out of the monkey business. I allowed you two to talk me into that fiasco, but they've served their purpose. The investors have laid their eyes on them and their expensive little habitats, so we can now be rid of the noisy Herpes-carriers."

"Are you sure you don't want them released back into the wild, Sir?" Zahir asked.

Grant allowed his gaze to linger on the doctor's face for several seconds, making Zahir feel uncomfortable. "Of course I'm sure. First of all, we don't need to incur any unnecessary expenses. Second, we can't risk anyone else being bitten. What is it, Zahir? Are you suddenly working with PETA? Are you some sort of animal rights activist? I said euthanize them, not slaughter them."

"I understand, Doctor. I just want to be certain. It will be handled first thing tomorrow morning."

"I'll need extensive reports from the both of you," Grant continued. "Our last event of the year will be around Christmas, an additional expense to keep our investors writing those pledge checks. Without any staff to supervise or shrieking primates to feed, you should be able to focus your energy on documenting our monumental medical breakthroughs."

The familiar knot started to twist in Zahir's gut. Something about the whole situation didn't sit right with him. Without primates or employees, he wasn't sure how they could carry on with the charade. He was sure the investors would demand more than a padded report every once in a while if they were going to continue investing sizeable sums of money. He shifted in his seat and swallowed hard. "Very well, Doctor. That certainly won't be a problem. Perhaps the early part of December would be a good time for Jean-Luc and I to visit our families."

Grant's brow furrowed, and he cleared his throat. "And leave the Facility empty? I don't like it. As I've said before, there will be plenty of time for that when this is over."

Andie showed up with a tray of drinks, but Grant waved his off.

"I'm exhausted," he said bluntly. "Just leave that one on the table for the others." He stood and reached for his coat. "I'll talk to you gentlemen later in the week. I'm going home to rest. Please keep all phone calls to a minimum. In fact, don't call at all, unless it's absolutely necessary." With that, he threw two twenties on the table and strode out of the bar.

The two foreign doctors sat silently for several minutes.

"You realize he's planning a big exit, don't you?" Zahir asked.

"Yes," Jean-Luc answered, "and he'll take all the cash with him."

"So we know what we have to do?" Zahir continued in a hushed whisper.

Jean-Luc nodded in affirmation as the two men sipped slowly from their aged scotches.

Chapter 73

Grant opened the front door to his Atlanta estate and was immediately greeted by Flossie, who graciously took his coat and offered him a drink. "I'll be in my study," he grunted as he made his way up the staircase.

He was sitting in an armchair in the corner of the room instead of behind the desk like Flossie expected. His face was drained of color, and he looked tired. She handed him a snifter of brandy and a small cocktail napkin. "Forgive me for the intrusion, but you don't look well, Sir."

"That's because I'm exhausted as hell," Grant barked before allowing his expression to soften. "I'm sorry, Flossie," he said as he motioned for her to take a seat next to him. "It's after 10:00. Why are you still in uniform?"

"I've just been busying myself in the kitchen. The holidays are right around the corner, and there's silver to be polished and cupboards to organize."

"You should take a break, especially with Lizzie away," he said, wishing immediately that he hadn't let her name escape his lips.

"May I ask what's going on with her?" Flossie nervously asked.

"The same thing as always. She's being a selfish bitch. I should've known better than to marry a woman who came from nothing," he spat angrily.

"You did give her quite a lot," Flossie said quietly. She wanted to say more, but if she'd learned nothing else, she had learned her place and when to hold her tongue.

"She's throwing some sort of childish tantrum and has fled to the open arms of her sister, who is apparently listening to her sordid, woe-is-me nonsense. I'll let her stay through Thanksgiving, and if she hasn't come running back home begging for forgiveness by then, I'll go drag her ungrateful ass back here."

Flossie stifled the urge to smile. The estate had been so pleasant without Lizzie, to say nothing of having Dr. Chatsworth all to herself. "Very well, Sir. Will there be anything else?"

"No, Flossie. That'll be all. As I said, I'm really worn out and will most likely phone in tomorrow. I need some rest. Could you intercept my phone calls and take messages? Unless it's life or death, I don't want to be disturbed."

"Very well," she said again, then she offered a partial curtsy before letting herself out of the study.

Grant sipped slowly from the brandy, leaned his head back on the chair, and closed his eyes. With Lizzie away, he could work from home on research material without worrying about her snooping around. He would wait until tomorrow to go through his desk. For the time being, he just wanted to go to bed. His head was swimming, and he felt as though he might vomit. He stood, then stumbled into the desk, causing a lamp to fall over.

It was only a second before Flossie was there at his side. "Dr. Chatsworth, are you okay?" she stammered as she offered her arm to steady him.

"Yes, I'm fine," Grant answered defensively. "Apparently, I had more to drink than I thought."

"Did you have dinner?"

"No. I've been too busy."

"Drinking on an empty stomach isn't good," Flossie added as she led him to bed. "Don't worry about anything," she said soothingly. "I'll call your office first thing in the morning. You just sleep in," she said kindly as a plan formed in her devious mind. *Why haven't I ever thought of that before? There really is a way I can have him all to myself.*

Chapter 74

Lizzie sat impatiently on the couch as she watched the evening news. It was after 11 o'clock, and Kenny should have been there almost thirty minutes ago. She walked into the kitchen and grabbed a bottle of water just as she heard the doorbell ring. She caught herself before she turned on the porchlight and glanced out the peephole instead.

"Where have you been?" Lizzie drilled. "I've been worried sick."

"Sorry about that. Jonquils aren't as easy to find as one might think. Then I had to run some errands for my grandmother, and I met an old friend for a beer. We've had it planned for a few days, and I didn't wanna cancel on him at the last minute."

"Oh, Kenny, I'm so sorry. I have to realize that other people have their own lives. Just because I'm locked away in this house doesn't mean everyone else is." Lizzie took the bouquet of yellow flowers from him and laid them on the kitchen table. "Want some water or anything?" she asked.

"No thanks." He smiled sheepishly. "May I?" Kenny asked as he motioned toward the sofa.

"Of course. Please forgive my lack of manners."

"You know," Kenny stammered, "I haven't asked any questions, but I can't stand it anymore. What's with the jonquils, and why are they such a secret?"

"Well," Lizzie started before plopping down on the sofa beside him, "I think I've got way too much time on my hands." Her giggles seemed to put him a little more at ease. "Please don't share this with Maggie, as I don't want her to worry."

"Scout's honor," Kenny said, holding up his right hand to gesture a sacred promise. "It's got something to do with that old cemetery, doesn't it?"

"Yeah. It all started because I was getting a bad case of cabin fever. It was dark, no one was around, and it seemed harmless enough."

"So you started snooping around the cemetery in the middle of the night?"

"Well, when you put it like that, it sounds like I was trespassing. It is a public cemetery, you know."

"Yes, I'm aware of that, but how many other citizens did you see visiting graves in the middle of the night, other than me, looking for you?"

"I didn't do anything wrong," Lizzie said defensively. "I just needed to get out of the house, to get a little fresh air."

"Don't get upset," Kenny said. "I'm just concerned about you. Clearly, you are hiding from someone or something. It just seems like going out alone could be very dangerous. Then again, for all I know, you could be the criminal," he said as a grin crossed his young face. "I'm only kidding, of course."

Lizzie shared a laugh and leaned back on the couch. "Maggie is my sister," she confessed. "I was in an abusive marriage back in Atlanta. I finally got up the courage to escape, for lack of a better word, and I caught the Greyhound here."

"Ah. That explains the gray wig and huge sunglasses."

That made Lizzie laugh again, and it felt good. "Yes. That was quite a getup, wasn't it? A dear, sweet friend helped me with that." She thought of Clara, and a sense of dread washed over her. *Please let Clara be okay,* she prayed silently.

"And how long do you plan to stay locked away in this house?"

"Our plan hasn't been thought out that far. I guess you've figured out by now that I'm pregnant. That's also thrown a kink into the plan."

Kenny shifted uncomfortably on the sofa.

Lizzie realized it might all be too much for him to take in at one time. "Okay, let's get back to the cemetery. Maggie and I used to visit a cemetery with our grandmother when we were little. That might seem odd to some people, but it was enjoyable to us. We visited relatives' graves, as well as, burial places of my grandmother's friends who'd passed on. We often left jonquils from our yard on the tombstones."

"So you want the jonquils to lay on the graves? Why jonquils?" he asked, feigning exhaustion.

Lizzie thought about sharing her interest in the baby's grave but wondered if it might seem too eccentric.

Then she looked at Kenny, and his sweet, innocent demeanor caused her to change her mind. "There's something odd going on," she started as she leaned forward and looked him in the eyes. "Perhaps it's just me and the emotional, hormonal rollercoaster I'm on right now."

"Go ahead," he said, his eyes brightening with interest.

"There's this child buried there. I noticed it the first night I walked around. It got my attention because the carved lamb on top of the tombstone is broken."

"Yeah, the death of a child gets to everyone."

"No…" Lizzie hesitated before continuing, "There's more to it than that. It's as if she wants to contact me." She ran her hands through her hair in a nervous gesture and took a deep breath. "I know it sounds absurd, and for a while, I was beginning to think I'm going crazy, but the night you frightened me in the cemetery I could have sworn I felt her presence. I-I… Well, I swear I actually *saw* her." She glanced over at Kenny, who was wearing a blank expression. *Great. I've told him too much,* she thought. *I need to stop here. If I tell him about the tree, he'll tell Maggie, and she'll have me committed.*

"Okay," he said slowly. "First of all, I don't think you're crazy if that's what you're concerned about. But why do you suppose this child would want to contact you?"

"I don't know," Lizzie insisted. "I was initially drawn to the tombstone because it's so sad, so damaged, but then I noticed it only has a first name with no surname, no birthdate, and no date of death. That's rather odd, don't you think? As I told you before, I've visited cemeteries all of my life. I don't think she was a stillborn because back in the 1800s and early to mid 1900s parents didn't give those babies names. I'm not sure why. Perhaps they didn't want to get too emotionally attached since it occurred much more often than it does now, but tombstones from that era normally just have 'Infant' or 'Baby Son' or 'Baby Daughter' on them for stillborns. I'm sure this baby was born alive."

"Okay, so she wasn't stillborn," Kenny said. "Why wouldn't she have a surname? Is she in a family plot? That might explain it."

"No, she's all alone. I checked the cemetery website and it doesn't provide any information about her."

"There should be records of the date of interment."

"Interment?"

"I'm sorry. It means burial. You're supposed to be the cemetery expert, aren't you? Anyway, I've never walked around Evergreen, but my grandmother often took me to the Old Biloxi Cemetery. Must be a thing for grandmas."

Lizzie gasped. "Really? Tell me everything."

Kenny gave her an odd look but continued, "It's a beautiful place, full of history and directly across from the water. We spent many Saturday afternoons walking through it, and sometimes she even let me frolic in the water for a while."

"That cemetery has something to do with Baby Belle. I can't explain it, and I don't understand why, but there's a connection. I need to find out what it is."

"There's a website for Old Biloxi too. They've kept meticulous records through the years. One of my grandmother's friends works at City Hall and oversees the graveyard archives. She'd be more than happy to help us, but I wouldn't know what to ask her. I mean, we don't even know who Belle is."

"Perhaps she was originally buried there, then someone moved her to Evergreen."

"Are you suggesting someone stole or exhumed her body and placed her in a strange grave back there?" he said, motioning toward the end of the street.

"I don't know what I'm saying," Lizzie answered.

"Let's take the jonquils out to her," Kenny suggested.

Lizzie didn't want to appear unappreciative, but she wanted to deliver them alone. She knew the child had tried to contact her the last time, and she was afraid Belle wouldn't connect with her if someone else came along. "I think I had better go alone," she said, smiling slightly. "Please don't take offense, but this is something I have to do by myself. Can you check with your grandmother's friend tomorrow? Maybe see if one of the families buried in Old Biloxi Cemetery had a child named Belle?"

"I'll do that," he said, standing and pulling on his coat. "Just call me if you need me...and please be careful roaming around in the middle of the night.

If something happens to you without me telling Mr. Knox about this conversation, he'd never forgive me."

"I'll be fine, Kenny. Go home and get some rest. Tomorrow is another day."

Chapter 75

Grant tossed and turned in a fitful sleep. His rest was laced with twisted dreams that awoke him with a jolt. He glanced at the glowing numbers on the clock radio on the nightstand and sat up as soon as he realized it was after 9:00 a.m. He could tell from the way he felt that he was coming down with something. His throat was on fire, and he didn't need a thermometer to confirm a low-grade fever.

"Good morning, Sir," Flossie said after tapping lightly on his bedroom door and cracking it slightly. "Will you be coming down to breakfast, or should I bring it up to you?"

"Come in," Grant said groggily as he pulled the cover up to his chin. "Did you call the office?"

"Yes, Sir. I spoke with your office manager, Clara, and explained that you aren't feeling well and won't be in today. I assured her I'll update her later in the day as to when you might feel up to returning."

"I'll call her after breakfast. She's very proficient and will reschedule everything quickly."

Flossie didn't like hearing the doctor praising anyone else, and she struggled not to let her facial expressions reflect her thoughts. "Very well, Sir. Now, where will you be eating your breakfast?"

"You can just bring it up on a tray. I have a terrible sore throat. Maybe just a bowl of oatmeal will suffice. I'm going to hop in the shower. Maybe that'll make me feel better."

The oatmeal topped with fresh berries was waiting on a tray when he got out of the shower. Although it was what he had requested, it didn't appear very appetizing. Grant pulled on his boxers, along with a pair of flannel lounge pants and an undershirt. He ate one mouthful and quickly decided against eating any more. He reached for his charged cell phone and called Zahir's direct line.

"Dr. Chavan speaking. How may I assist you?"

"It's me, Zahir. I've got a scorching throat and high temperature. My guess is strep. Can you send someone over with some antibiotics?"

"We've got a skeleton crew here, but I suppose I could run it over. It'll be about an hour."

"I appreciate it. Just leave it with Cornell at the gate. He'll have someone bring it up to the house."

"I'll get on that right away. Call me should you need anything else."

Grant disconnected the call without so much as a goodb-ye. His next call was to his office.

Harper answered and quickly transferred his call back to Clara.

"This is Dr. Chatsworth," he began as he swallowed against the fire raging in his throat. "Flossie said she contacted you, but I'm up now and just wanted to touch base with you. I'm sick, most likely strep. Go ahead and cancel my appointments for the week and reschedule any surgeries I have for the next couple of weeks."

Clara had been suspicious when she'd heard from the doctor's housekeeper, but now that she was speaking directly with him, his scratchy voice confirmed the story. Either he was ill or was very good at faking it. Either way, she was glad she wouldn't have to see him at the office. "No problem here. I hope you have a speedy recovery."

"I'll be in touch in the next couple of days. I've been needing some rest. I suppose this will force me to get some." Again, he clicked off the phone without any further conversation.

Flossie came in to take his tray and scolded him for not attempting to eat more.

"I don't feel like I can eat anything right now," he said flatly. "I'm having some medicine delivered to the gate. Cornell will bring it up to the house. I'll appreciate it if you get it here as soon as it arrives."

"I'll do that, Sir. Shall I cut off the lights?"

"Please do. I just want some rest."

For the first time in a couple of years, Grant rolled over and went to sleep without any thoughts of surgeries, money, Lizzie, or shrieking monkeys.

Chapter 76

Justin Cates paid the landlord in cash for two months' rent, then slid the key into the lock of the aging duplex. It was thirty minutes outside the city limits, and with little time to spare before Christi was released from the hospital, he was lucky to find it. At $500 a month for a furnished two-bedroom, one-bath, he couldn't expect much. Fortunately, he was pleasantly surprised. The furniture was dated but appeared clean, and the hardwood floors had recently been varnished. It was small and sparsely furnished, but it would serve nicely as a home until they could figure out what to do with the rest of their lives. He had contacted West Georgia College and dropped his classes for the remainder of the semester; he knew there was no way for him to catch up, and he had no idea what the next few weeks would bring.

His frat buddies planned to deliver his few belongings on Saturday, and he intended to ask them to go to Christi's apartment with him to get what they could of her things. He was much too afraid to go alone, and he certainly didn't want Christi to ever return to that place. Gunnar was dead, but he was unsure of who else they had to fear.

The ringing of his cell phone startled him. "Hello?" he said.

"Justin?"

"Yes."

"This is Dr. Parks. Your sister will be able to leave the hospital tomorrow, but I'd like to meet with you first."

Rather than relief, Justin was overcome with dread. At the hospital, she was safe. Now, he was not confident that he could protect her, and he didn't even know who or what he might have to protect his sister from. "Thank you," he stammered. "I can be there in just a few minutes."

"How about 4:00? I have a few patients to see in the meantime."

"That's perfect," Justin answered, then ended the call. He slumped onto the sofa and put his face in his hands. He felt the tears stinging his eyes, but he refused to let them fall. He had to man up.

He didn't know what size Christi wore and knew nothing about buying girl's clothing, so he decided to purchase a couple pairs of flannel pajamas in a medium size. He knew he could pick them up at Walmart, along with a few groceries at the same time. A glance at his watch told him he had over three hours to get that done and return to the hospital by 4:00.

Christi was sitting in a chair in her hospital room when he got there. Her hair had been washed, and she was wearing a bright yellow jogging suit. She smiled cheerfully at him. "I finally get to leave this place tomorrow," she said, holding up her hand for him to high-five her. "I bet my apartment has an inch of dust in it by now."

Justin swallowed hard and looked down at the floor. *This is gonna be more difficult than I thought.*

"What is it, Justin? Is everything okay?"

"We have a few things to talk about, Sis," he started before being interrupted by Dr. Parks.

"Good afternoon, you two," he said. "Wow! It must feel good to be out of that hospital gown."

"Yes," Christi said, beaming. "Apparently, the volunteers provide a clothing pantry here. I don't know what happened to the clothes I came in with."

Dr. Parks' expression turned somber as he sat down between the young brother and sister. "I'm sure they were cut off of you in the trauma room. You're a very lucky young lady."

"So I've heard," Christi answered. "There are still a few nasty scars though."

"They will fade in time," the doctor assured her. "I am more concerned with your emotional health now. There is an excellent psychologist I'd like you and your brother to see."

Christi gasped for air as though someone had knocked the breath out of her. "What on Earth are you talking about? I got hit by a bus. I made a foolish mistake and was probably distracted by my phone or traffic and just walked out in front of it. I'm getting stronger every day, and—"

"It's okay, dear. Don't get upset. You *are* getting much stronger, and you're quite the fighter, but we need to discuss a few things. Would you mind if an investigator joins us for a few minutes?"

Her eyes glazed over with confusion, and she looked pleadingly at her brother. "Justin, what is this all about?"

"Do you remember how concerned you were about Albert?" he asked her.

Before she answered, Dr. Parks interrupted. "Justin, I think we should invite the investigator in now."

Justin could only nod. His head was pounding, and he couldn't look his sister in the eye.

The detective entered the room and nodded at the two of them. "I'm Detective Pitts," he said softly to Christi. "I've visited your room several times, but you were either asleep or in physical therapy."

"Why? Why would a detective be visiting my room?"

"Can I get a chair, Doc? She might feel more comfortable if I'm sitting down."

The doctor quickly returned with a chair and poured a cup of water for Christi.

"Christi, I certainly don't mean to frighten you or confuse you in any way. Everything is okay, and you are safe."

"Safe? What's he talking about, Justin? Why wouldn't I be safe?"

"It's okay, Christi," Justin reassured her. "Just listen to what he has to say."

"This may be too much for her right now," Dr. Parks chimed in. "It may be too soon."

"No," Christi said emphatically. "What the hell is going on?"

"Do you have any recollection of your accident?" Detective Pitts asked.

"No, not really. I was told I was hit by a bus," Christi answered. "Are you insinuating that the bus ran over me intentionally?"

"No, certainly not," Pitts continued, leaning back in his chair to put more space between them, hoping it might make her more comfortable. "I'm just wondering how far back your memory goes. Do you recall your concerns about your roommate Albert Tinsley?"

"Albert?" Christi murmured softly. "He's my roommate. Is he okay?" she asked, her eyes pleading with the officer. The confusion on her face seemed to dissipate, and it appeared that clearer

314

thoughts were beginning to form. "Something's wrong with him, isn't it?"

"Why would you think that?" Pitts answered.

She wrinkled her forehead and closed her eyes as if willing herself to recall their conversations. "I'm not sure really. He was worried, but I can't exactly remember why. If you know something, please tell me," Christi pleaded. "Albert's a nice guy."

"Don't get upset. Everything's okay."

"No it's not," she said defiantly. "What's wrong with Albert?" she demanded as she turned to Dr. Parks. "Please make him tell me what's going on. I can handle it. I need to know."

The doctor nodded solemnly at Detective Pitts, affirming that he could continue.

"Christi, it's very important that you have your own recollections of what happened," Pitts began. "I'm concerned that if I give you too many details, it will hinder your own memory of what happened, not only the day you were hit by the bus but also your conversations with Albert prior to that. We can take as much time as we need. There isn't any rush, so be sure your memories are vivid." He gave her a few seconds for everything to sink in before continuing, "I understand from your brother that you mentioned Albert being unhappy with his job. You reiterated this to Justin on several occasions. Do you remember that?"

Christi looked at her brother, and he nodded affirmatively that they had indeed had the conversations. She rubbed her forehead, then her eyes before looking up at the detective. "It's right there, but I can't quite remember. Maybe when I go back to the apartment tomorrow, it will start to come back to me."

Detective Pitts cleared his throat and leaned closer to Christi. "Justin has rented the two of you a place on the other side of town. It will be best for you to stay there for a while."

Christi looked blankly at each of them. "The other side of town? What for? I'm a grown woman, and if you won't give me a good reason why I shouldn't, then I'm returning to my apartment," she insisted. "Is Albert is some kind of trouble?"

"Albert is dead, Christi," Justin said, reaching for his sister's hand, "and I'll be damned if you're gonna be next."

Chapter 77

Lizzie sat on the couch long after Kenny had left. Her thoughts rambled back and forth between Grant and her concern for Clara. Lizzie thought of e-mailing her but decided it might put her in some type of danger and decided against it. *Why isn't Grant hunting me down already?* she wondered bitterly. Although she had felt somewhat comfortable the past few days, she knew it wasn't wise to let her guard down. Clearly, he was unaware of what she knew about the Research Facility and his attempts to bilk all the money he could from investors. If that had ever crossed his mind, she was sure he would have come for her right away. *Perhaps he's enjoying his mistress, for now,* she thought, but she knew he would come for her soon. For all she knew, he had someone watching her. As she did so often, she moved her hands to her stomach and prayed she'd never have to share her child with him.

Anxious to get Grant out of her thoughts, she walked over and picked up the jonquils. She smiled at a memory of her grandmother, with her apron tied around her waist. *Such good times.* It was after 1:00 a.m., but that didn't matter to her. The neighbors had long since turned their lights off, so she bundled up and exited out the back door. The crescent moon didn't offer much light, but she was familiar with the area now, and she had a small flashlight. Lizzie didn't spend time looking around. Instead, she made her way briskly down the one-lane road before cutting through the middle of the cemetery.

The crisp autumn leaves had fallen, and they crunched beneath her feet. Using the flashlight sparingly, she shined it toward where she knew she would find the grave she had come to visit. Kneeling on the ground in front of the monument, she scolded herself for not remembering to bring a blanket to sit on. Instead, Lizzie propped herself on her knees and sat on her heels. She had left the green florist paper back at the house, and she fanned the jonquils out across the grave.

Not sure what to expect, she listened to the sounds of the night and held her breath in anticipation. *Nothing.* Lizzie sat silently for several more minutes, but the apparition she was sure she had witnessed before didn't visit her again. She wrapped her arms around her waist in an attempt to fend off the chilly weather and thought of scurrying back to the warmth of the house, but something seemed to compel her to stay. It wasn't a presence but a feeling that there was unfinished business that required her attention.

Lizzie was shocked when she heard her own voice. "I told you I would come back to visit, little girl," she whispered. "There's some type of bond between us, isn't there? I don't know much about spirits, but there must be some reason for our connection. I wish you would help me." She waited patiently, but it was clear there wouldn't be another occurrence. "I'm not afraid of you," Lizzie continued in a kind voice. "I know you aren't trying to harm or frighten me. I just wish I knew what to do for you."

Lizzie's legs were throbbing, and the hard, cold ground was unsympathetic to her shins. "I won't give up on you, Baby Belle," she said finally as she slowly stood. "I promise to bring more jonquils."

Lizzie thought back to Kenny's comment about the absence of a surname. She thought there might be family plot nearby, but it would surely be a distance from her small grave. *Perhaps, because she died so young, her family buried her here, then later relocated to another city and left her behind. So sad.* Lizzie turned on the dull flashlight and walked to the other family sites located at least ten feet from Belle's isolated gravesite. There were four families close to her, and their surnames wouldn't be easy for Lizzie to remember. She tried to lock them in her memory so she could pull up their history on the cemetery website: *Pennington, Wright, Whitworth, and Jordan.* Each family was cordoned off by either wrought iron fencing or stacked stone bricks notating their identified space. Without stepping inside the fencing, she scanned the light across the tombstones closest to her. Nothing seemed to link them to Belle, but then again, she had no idea what to look for. She hoped she would have better luck with the computer back at the house.

Lizzie glanced back at Belle's grave before heading home, and there she was, peeking from behind a thin, young oak. Her face was round, like a chubby cherub. She was wearing a bonnet, with the straps tied in a bow under her chin, along with a flowing white

317

nightgown. Her body was merely a mist, denser in some areas than others, but Lizzie could make out her form. She wasn't an infant; from what Lizzie could tell, she looked to be about five years old. Belle appeared to be weeping, wiping tears from her misty face.

Lizzie struggled not to rush over to her. She didn't want to frighten her away as she wanted the ghostly child to remain with her as long as possible. Lizzie's feet felt like bricks as she lifted them slowly and took a few steps toward the girl. "Please don't leave...and don't cry. I want to help you," she said, grasping for any words that may convince her to stay.

Belle tucked her face behind the oak, but Lizzie was still able to make out the outline of the bonnet.

"I'm not here to harm you," she whispered softly.

The edges of the bonnet became lighter, until they slowly faded away, along with the gown. Just that quick, she was gone.

Lizzie felt a cool breeze that seemed to run straight through her body. She shivered almost violently before turning to go back to the road. Black ravens sat atop every gravestone she passed, and she quickened her steps into a jog before breaking into a full run. She could hear their loud, raucous squawks and felt their wings flapping directly around her as she fled for the safety of the house.

She slipped just at the entrance of the cemetery, losing the flashlight and skinning her knee through the thin fabric of the leggings. She ambled to her feet, flailing her arms at the ravens, whose beaks tugged fiercely at strands of her hair.

Lizzie's hands were shaking badly, but she succeeded in getting the key into the lock of the back door. Somehow, the ravens disappeared as quickly as they had come, and she collapsed on the sofa, shaking with sobs.

When the tears dissipated, she slipped out of the torn leggings and cleaned her gashed knee with a warm washcloth. Then she stumbled back to her bedroom, turned off the light, and pulled the covers up to her chin, hoping daylight would return quickly.

Chapter 78

Sometime during the night, Lizzie fell into a deep sleep, one uninterrupted by bad dreams, loud noises, or random clues. It was her cell phone that finally woke her after 10:00 a.m. "Hello?" she answered, her voice deep from just awakening.

"Are you still asleep?" Maggie asked.

"I was finally able to get over that insomnia. I don't suppose there's much to wake up for anyway," Lizzie answered. "Is everything okay?"

"Sure is. I just wanted to check on you. Do you need anything?"

"No, I'm fine. Kenny is keeping the fridge full for me. I don't know what you're paying that young guy, but he's worth his weight in gold."

"He's a go-getter, no doubt. I scheduled another doctor's appointment for you in a couple of days."

"Another early one, under the blanket of darkness?" Lizzie teased.

"It's not a joke, Lizzie," Maggie answered sternly. "If Grant's up to what you say he is, he hasn't forgotten you. Frankly, the thought of him discovering the pregnancy is a complete game-changer."

The reality of the mark instantly took the wind out of Lizzie, and she gasped audibly. "I'm afraid to go to the doctor. Can't he come here?"

"No, I can't ask him to do that. We're already asking too much of him as it is. Just be careful, Lizzie. I know you're tired of being cooped up, and I wish I could visit more often, but for now, let's just be careful. I love you."

"I love you too," Lizzie answered, her tone much different than before, her reality much darker.

Lizzie opened all the drapes across the back of the house and took a long, steamy shower before bandaging her scraped knee and dressing for the day. She ate heartily and carried her glass of orange juice back to the computer. Although it took great effort, she was able to recall the family names from the plots surrounding Belle. There were several members in each plot, but none reflected any correlation with the young child. She was able to follow rather lengthy lineages of the families, and it would have been rather odd for them to leave out a small child. In short, she came up empty again. She was sure there had to be something in Old Biloxi Cemetery that would give her answers. Hopefully, Kenny would talk to his grandmother's friend and give her a call soon.

Then it hit her: *The ravens. Did that really happen, and where did they all come from?* She had seen them in horror movies and on scary book covers, but she had no idea why there were so many and why the birds had frightened her so. Grateful for the luxury of the internet, she typed "Raven Symbolism" into the search engine. There wasn't any shortage of information, and it appeared that various cultures believed the beautiful, sleek, black ravens represented one thing or another, but most signified the same credibility of the raven's presence.

Ancient cultures alleged that the loud, haunting bird was the link between heaven and Earth. Others believed the raven's appearance implied birth, renewal, and healing, and still, other cultures felt it was merely the haunting symbol of loss. The one that grabbed Lizzie's attention the most was from the Native Americans. Their convictions were that the ravens brought messages from the cosmos. Whereas the ravens had frightened her deeply the night before, she now felt they were somehow pleading with her to stay, to unravel whatever mystery was hidden with Baby Belle's tomb. Perhaps the mystery lay in the child's birth or death, but clearly the cosmos, the ravens, and the deceased child had chosen her to find some semblance of peace and resolution for the matter, whatever it was.

Lizzie went through the lengthy list of Old Biloxi Cemetery, studying each name and the dates of birth and death. Her eyes were burning, but she still found nothing. If Kenny didn't call soon, she would take the chance of calling him herself. She wanted to talk to the lady in charge of the cemetery records.

The phone rang again, startling her.

"Hey, Lizzie. It's Kenny. Hope I'm not interrupting anything."

"Are you kidding? I've been waiting on your call. Did you talk to your grandmother's friend?"

"Yes. Her name is Annelle Buer, and she's amazing. She's willing to give you any history you need. I told her to expect your call."

"What?! You've got to be kidding. I can't tell her who I am, and what in God's name am I going to ask her?" Lizzie felt her heart fluttering and her head swimming. "I don't feel so well. I think I need to lie down."

"Go lie on the couch right now. I'm on my way over. It's not lunchtime, but no one will notice. See you in less than ten minutes."

It was indeed less than ten minutes before she heard the light tap at the door. She let him in and walked back to flop down on the couch. "Sorry about that," she said. "I'm just quite overwhelmed. So much is going on in my life, and my nerves are shot, to say the least."

"Listen, I'm sure the cemetery research has helped take your mind off things, but maybe it's time to let it go now. Someone clearly cared enough to have a burial for Belle, so she wasn't unloved or unknown. You can let it go. You need your rest for your own child now." Kenny looked her in the eyes, then looked away with embarrassment.

"What is it?"

"You look tired, much more stressed than yesterday. There are dark circles under your eyes, and the pink glow is gone from your cheeks."

"Actually, I slept much better last night. I'm just not wearing any makeup, that's all," Lizzie refuted defensively.

"Please don't take any offense. I feel sort of responsible for you, and I know the Knoxes will have my hide if they find out I'm a willing participant helping you leave this house."

"You haven't shared that with them, have you?"

"No. I wouldn't do that unless I thought you were in danger. Lizzie, I don't want you going back out there at night alone again. I'll go with you."

"But Belle may not come out with you there."

"Take it or leave it. Either you let me go with you, or I have to tell Maggie and Leland. I'll help you all I can, but it's simply too dangerous for you to wander around alone in the middle of the night."

Lizzie pursed her lips firmly and folded her arms dramatically across her torso, but she couldn't help but giggle. Kenny was indeed right: She was taking too big of an unnecessary risk, and she had more than herself to think about.

"Got anything to make a sandwich in there?" he asked, pointing to the refrigerator.

"You bet. Sit down at the table, and I'll bring the fixings over. You can tell me about Annelle Buer."

Chapter 79

Almost twenty-four hours after starting the antibiotics, Grant was feeling well enough to shower, dress, and come down to breakfast. He praised Flossie for her kindness in taking care of him during his illness but told her he would be heading back to the office the following day.

"Are you sure you've had adequate rest, Doctor?" she asked kindly. "Your office manager assured me that everything was rescheduled for a couple of weeks from now."

"Yes, all the surgeries are rescheduled, but I still need to catch up on paperwork and spend a few days at the Research Facility. Baby steps." He laughed. "I'm not a hundred percent, but I'm better. Just needed a little R&R."

"I understand," Flossie agreed with an encouraging smile. "I have a nice breakfast for you, so let me bring it out. A good meal and adequate rest makes everything better, but you're a doctor. You already know that."

Grant was reading the paper when she returned with his steaming plate and a tall glass of juice. Flossie was quite pleased when he devoured it all, and she asked more than once to refill his glass.

"No thanks," he answered. "I'll just take a bottle of water and two Tylenol. I kind of feel a headache coming on."

She fetched the things he asked for and watched as he slowly made his way up the stairs. A tender smile crossed her face. "Lizzie will come back in this house over my dead body," she whispered to herself.

After a ten-minute conversation with Jean-Luc, Grant decided to spend a few hours at his office in the Research Facility. His headache wasn't easing, and he didn't feel up to filling out the mounds of paperwork that went along with Medicare and other insurance carriers. Even though Clara handled the brunt of it, he still had to review and sign each and every form. Grant drank the rest of the water and called down to Cornell at the gate.

"Cornell Sayer. How may I help you?"

"Cornell, this is Dr. Chatsworth. Would you mind driving me over to the Research Facility on Piedmont? I'm not feeling my best, but I need to take care of a few things over there."

"Sure, no problem," Cornell answered quickly. "Is it all right to leave the front gate unmanned, or should I find someone else to come down?"

"No, it should be fine. Everyone has to enter a code to open the gate anyway. Have the gardener pick you up in his cart and bring you up to the estate. You can drive my car."

Grant was standing at the door when Santiago dropped Cornell off. The two men walked around to the garage, and Cornell cranked the car.

"You look a little under the weather, if you don't mind me saying so," Cornell said.

"Just a damned sore throat and fever," Grant barked. "I can't remember the last time I was sick. It never happens at an opportune time, ya know?"

Cornell nodded in agreement.

"How's school going for you?"

"Pretty good. The pressure gets to me from time to time, but I suppose it'll be worth it in the end. Thanks again for working around my class schedule. The money really helps."

Grant grunted and leaned his head back on the headrest. "Damn headache."

"Are you sure you want to go, Sir?" Cornell asked.

"It's going to hurt whether I'm at home or at the office," Grant snapped. "May as well try to be productive."

Cornell remained silent for the rest of the ride, leaving Dr. Chatsworth alone with his headache, sore throat, and thoughts.

Cornell exited the car when they arrived and opened the door for the sick doctor. "When should I be back to pick you up?" he asked.

"No need. I'll have someone else bring me home. Thanks for the ride."

Jean-Luc and Zahir were waiting in the lobby for him when he walked through the doors. It was difficult for them to hide their surprise. The young, handsome doctor looked like hell. His face was red from fever, and his eyes were squinting against the grinding pain of the relentless headache.

"I thought you said you're feeling better," Zahir said, leading Grant to a nearby sofa. "You don't look so good."

He allowed himself to be led and sat down hard on the couch and leaned back. "Actually, I was feeling much better when I woke up this morning. I felt sure it was strep throat, and antibiotics usually start to work their magic within twenty-four hours. I got up, showered, and ate, and then this damned headache started."

Jean-Luc returned with a thermometer and took his temperature. "You're at 100.5, still pretty high. You should be home in the bed. What are you doing here?"

"I'm probably still contagious, so I didn't want to see any patients today. I thought I could do some paperwork here."

"There's not much for you to do now, especially since you're ill. Do you want to go up to your office and discuss our latest findings?"

"Yeah, I'll do that," Grant said, standing, then sitting back down almost immediately. "My heartbeat feels a little rapid," he said.

"Let me get my stethoscope," Zahir said. "I'll be right back." He returned with his medical bag and listened to Grant's heart. "Sounds okay to me," he suggested. "Let me take a look at your throat." He pressed the flat stick of wood on Grant's tongue before turning on the penlight to take a look. "That's pretty nasty. I'd say swabbing your throat for a strep culture would be a waste of time. Why don't you let me give you an antibiotics shot? It'll work a little quicker."

"No. It's only a sign that I'm worn out and need the rest. Can one of you give me a lift back home?"

"We were just finishing up the disassembly of the primate cages. Can I get the receptionist to take you?"

"Damn. I thought we laid her off."

"We can't very well answer our own phones. That'd be much too unprofessional."

Grant wanted to go on a tangent but was just too sick. "Where the hell is she?"

"Upstairs, taking inventory of the cleaning supplies. I'll get her right away."

Grant made an effort to roll his eyes in disgust but agreed to the ride home. He couldn't remember when he had felt so bad.

The ditzy receptionist was thrilled to get to chauffeur her handsome boss back to his estate and practically threw herself at him.

He got in her yellow Volkswagen Beetle and closed his eyes, to avoid having to make any conversation. In spite of that, she talked openly the whole way, giggling and patting his leg until they reached the gate.

****

Zahir and Jean-Luc walked silently back to the primate enclosures. The primates had been humanely euthanized, not because either doctor wanted to see them die but because they feared who else may be injured by their bites if they were released in the wild. Not only that, but they had to follow Grant's orders, or they feared being euthanized themselves, with much less compassion.

Jean-Luc stood in front of the industrial refrigerator that was bound by a thick chain and large padlock. He and Zahir both knew what was inside, but neither spoke of it as if they feared they might somehow be overheard.

"He was weak," Jean-Luc finally said. "I wish he would have taken the antibiotic shot. We could have been rid of him and back to our own countries within the week."

"He'll be much better in a day or so with the amoxicillin. He's much stronger than us. How will we overpower him?"

"We may not have to," Zahir said snidely. "His heartbeat was indeed rapid. It may be more than a sore throat."

"But you said—"

"I know what I said," Zahir snapped. "Let's just see what happens before we open that cooler too quickly. Perhaps there is someone out there who wishes to take him out more than we do. I can't imagine such a man has many real friends."

Jean-Luc tugged on the padlock to ensure it couldn't be opened without a key. It would be a shame for the rhesus monkey blood samples, laced with the Herpes B virus, to be stolen before the doctor could get a taste of his own medicine.

Chapter 80

Lizzie had to be little more than an interested historian to speak with Annelle Buer. Her sweet voice was more than enough to make Lizzie feel as if she was conversing with an old friend. She sounded just like Kenny had described her, a petite woman with beautiful features, a widow who loved her job enough to stay long after she could have retired. *Just like Clara,* Lizzie thought.

"I just love doing research, especially on old cemeteries," Lizzie began. "Could I ask you a few questions?"

"Certainly, dear. I'll do what I can, but we also have a wonderful Genealogy Society I'd be happy to refer you to."

"That would be nice, but I'm looking for the birth parents of a child named Belle. I know she was buried somewhere in Mississippi, but I'd like to know more about her family."

"Is Bell the last name?"

"I don't believe so. Her name is spelled with an –e at the end."

"Do you have the dates of birth and death?"

"I don't have that either. I know this is a strange request, but for some reason, I am very interested to find out who she was."

"I don't find anything odd about that at all. Old Biloxi Cemetery is very important to all of us. As you know, Hurricane Katrina gave Biloxi quite a hit, including the cemetery. We have worked for years to repair the damage, but it will take many more to complete our efforts. There were tombstones and even caskets littering the streets. It's possible she could have been in a family plot and was redirected to another area. However, that's pretty unlikely. Much work was done at that time by many different agencies to ensure that everyone was put back in their proper resting places. I can't say I recall a Belle in any of our baby lands."

"Baby lands? I remember visiting one of those with my grandmother. I didn't know they had those here."

"We have eleven in this particular cemetery, and I'm pretty familiar with them. I don't recall a child named Belle though we do have some unmarked graves. We have an amazing caretaker who goes above and beyond his duties. I could ask him if he's aware of an infant with that name."

Lizzie had a sinking feeling. She didn't want them to go to any great trouble looking for a child she knew wasn't buried there. "I'm not even sure if she is buried in that cemetery. I just thought if she was, I might find her family," she said, aware that she was rambling and making little sense.

"No problem at all."

"I have a few questions about birth certificates. How did the state register infants who were born at home back in the 1800s?"

"Honey, all children were born at home in the 1800s. No fancy maternity wards for those young mothers! If a mother was fortunate, the doctor made it to the house in time to deliver. Otherwise, they only had midwives or merely other females who had experienced childbirth themselves. I'm not sure any births were registered until the early 1900s."

"Forgive my ignorance, but how did one ever know their exact date of birth?"

"They simply documented it in the family Bible. Unfortunately, many of them have been damaged by time, inclement weather, or simply because families no longer treasured their worth and tossed them out."

The shock of such valuable history being tossed aside broke Lizzie's heart, even though the thought never would have crossed her mind a month ago. "I've taken enough of your time today, Ms. Buer. Thank you so much."

"Not a problem. I enjoyed our conversation. Please call anytime. Would you like the number and contact at the Genealogical Society?"

"That would be very nice."

As soon as Lizzie hung up with Ms. Buer, she quickly dialed the other number, before she gave herself a chance to chicken out. "May I speak to Jaynie Shannon please?"

"Speaking. How may I help you?"

"I'm just doing a little research, nothing specific really. I'm trying to find out about a child's family and her death as well. I don't have a last name or dates of death or birth. I'm sure it's a hopeless case, but I feel compelled to continue looking anyway."

"That's the enjoyment of studying the past. Sometimes we come up empty, but other times, we learn more than we ever hoped."

"I guess my question is… Can a child be buried without anything being recorded? The tombstone appears to be consistent with those from the early to mid 1800s, but there's no surrounding family plot and no record on the cemetery website."

"Sadly, during that time period, it happened often. However, many of the deceased were transported by horse and buggy to the cemetery, the humble beginnings of the funeral home business. They were often separated by denominations. Here in Biloxi, it was either Protestant or Catholic. That was really when records began being kept in earnest."

"Hmm, I see," Lizzie said, deep in thought.

"Of course, in the late 1800s and early 1900s, more records were kept of marriages, births, and deaths. We have several ledgers, microfilms, and card catalogs here in the office if you'd like to visit. I must warn you that some are not in pristine shape, due to time and exposure to the elements. I'm sure you understand."

"Yes, thank you very much," Lizzie said before ending the call. She sat at the computer and glanced over her notes before the computer flashed on and off again and finally rested on an 1840 census page.

Chapter 81

Kenny called Lizzie at 9:00 p.m. and asked if he could come over. Lizzie was sitting on the sofa with a large bowl of popcorn and two bottled waters when he arrived twenty minutes later.

"Did you talk to Ms. Buer today?"

"Yes. She's very pleasant. I was afraid I'd feel uncomfortable, but she's so nice."

"So?" Kenny said, pulling a pair of gloves out of his jacket pocket. "Are we going out in the graveyard tonight?"

"It's not a freak show, Kenny. Belle might never show herself again, especially with you along."

"Just tell me. What did her wings look like?"

"Wings? Why would she have wings?"

"All angels have wings."

"Oh, for heaven's sake. She's not an angel. Do you honestly think people become angels when they die?"

Kenny gave Lizzie a blank stare, and his cheeks reddened with embarrassment. "I've just always assumed they do, especially children."

"That's a common misconception," Lizzie said kindly, "but angels were in existence prior to creation."

"Hmm. I guess I shoulda gone to Sunday school more often."

Lizzie smiled before continuing, "Angels serve as God's messengers, intermediaries between human kind and the divine, if you will."

"You really paid attention in church, didn't you?"

"No. I just did some research online," Lizzie said with a sneaky grin.

"You little stinker," Kenny said, "and here you are making me feel foolish for thinking all dead people grow wings!"

"I did remember that angels were created before Earth, but I needed a little refresher course."

"Can I please see this grave?"

Lizzie let out a sigh and got up to get her coat and a blanket.

"What's with the blanket?" Kenny asked. "We aren't spending the night out there, are we? I didn't bring my jammies."

"It's just chilly, and I can't stand long without feeling uncomfortable. Kenny, promise me you'll never tell anyone about this. It's not a joke to me. I really believe this little girl is trying to tell me something."

"Okay, okay. Stop worrying. Let's go. The suspense is killing me."

The two exited through the back of the house and followed the same path Lizzie had each time she had gone to Belle's grave. The night didn't grant them a full moon, but it was larger than it had been the night before, and Lizzie was grateful for the light it gave. It was much cooler than it had been, and she watched the billowing air coming from Kenny's anxious breaths.

Lizzie spread the blanket on the ground in front of Belle's tombstone and lowered herself to the ground.

Kenny waved a dismissal when she offered him a seat beside her. "No thanks. I don't plan to stay very long. I don't really feel very safe out here," he said, darting his eyes around in the dark. "I mean, anyone could be hiding behind these old trees or tombstones. It's just dangerous, Lizzie. If she doesn't make contact quick, let's go back."

"You can't be serious. Just sit down with me for a few minutes," Lizzie insisted, making a circular swoop with her flashlight. "We would hear someone rustling the leaves if we were followed. There's no one here but us."

He leaned against a tree in lieu of sitting on the quilt and listened as Lizzie spoke.

"I'm sorry I didn't bring any jonquils, little girl, but the ones from last night still look pretty. I'm sure the cold weather is keeping them from wilting. I hope you like yellow."

Lizzie remained silent for several minutes while Kenny shifted his weight from one foot to the other.

Finally, she continued, "This is my friend Kenny. He's a little worried about me, so he insisted on coming along. I hope you don't mind. He knows I want to help you. I'm not sure how I'm going to do it yet or even what you need me to help you with, but I'm not giving up. Kenny has a friend at Biloxi City Cemetery. I called her to get help, but I don't know what I should ask for. You want me to find out something about that place, don't you?"

Again, Lizzie and Kenny sat and stood in silence, but nothing happened.

Kenny opened his mouth to utter a complaint, but Lizzie cut him off.

"Why were you weeping, Belle? What's making you so sad? The ravens showed up to keep me here, didn't they?"

Again, nothing happened.

After several seconds passed, though, the fine mist formed again, only this time in a small, round form, about six inches in diameter. It floated above the broken lamb, then moved slowly toward Lizzie. She felt a deep, piercing chill as it moved past her and dissipated.

"Holy smokes!" Kenny gasped, grabbed Lizzie's arm, and pulled her quickly to her feet. "Let's get the hell outta here!"

"Wait!" Lizzie insisted, but Kenny had already grabbed the blanket and tucked it under his arm and was leading her forcefully by the hand back to the house. Neither spoke until they were inside.

Kenny was visibly shaken as he paced back and forth from the living room to the kitchen.

"Would you please just sit down?" Lizzie asked. "We need to talk."

"You're playing with fire, Lizzie. Stay out of that cemetery. I mean it. I'll tell Leland if I have to."

"You most certainly will not!" Lizzie said confidently. "You're freaked out right now, but you know she's trying to tell me something. Once you calm down, you'll understand it all. There's a bottle of wine in there. Open it and have a glass."

Kenny rummaged through the kitchen drawers until he found a corkscrew, then poured himself a full glass of Merlot. He sat down on one of the armchairs and drank deeply from it. He set the empty glass down on the coffee table and allowed the warm liquid to give its calming effect.

Lizzie gave him all the time he needed for everything to sink in and remained silent until he was ready to talk.

"I never thought I'd see anything like that," he said, finally opening up. "I have to admit that I just thought you felt sorry for the poor child dying so young. I knew it was taking your mind off whatever you're dealing with, so I left well enough alone. I figured it was harmless enough, so I never told the Knoxes."

"I know it's crazy, but don't you see it now? She wants me to know something. We have to figure out what it is."

"And how are we gonna do that?"

"So I take it you're in? As in helping me figure this all out?"

"Let's just take it day by day for now. What's your take on all this? What do you suppose this kid wants you to know?"

"I'm not sure yet," Lizzie said, "but my first question is why she's buried out there alone."

"She must have preceded her family in death. There wasn't anyone else to bury her beside."

"Could be, but in that case, she would have been buried with other babies in the same situation, unless that was a family plot and they planned to bury other family members there later."

"Possibly, but no one else is buried there."

"The family could have moved away. There's any number of reasons, but the biggest red flag is that there's no date of birth or death and no record of her ever being buried there."

"It was back in the 1800s," Kenny reasoned. "Many times, people didn't have money for burials. Maybe someone just buried her there under the cover of darkness."

"But she has a monument, and they went to the trouble of having a baby lamb carved in it, along with her name. If they engraved that why not the death and birthdates as well?"

"Who knows, Lizzie? It was so many years ago. You might not be able to find anything out. Some things even predate Google, you know."

"She's trying to *tell* me," Lizzie said stubbornly.

"So she can talk now too? You're some kind of ghost whisperer now?"

"No! I can't actually hear her. She's just been…giving me clues."

"Such as?" Kenny asked sarcastically.

"You just saw her spirit in the cemetery, Kenny. Don't pretend this isn't happening. The computer has been showing random websites. It flashed on an 1840 census, but I couldn't make anything of it. C'mon."

She coaxed Kenny back to the office and turned on the computer, then pulled up the 1840 census report for Biloxi, Mississippi. Nothing seemed to tie Baby Belle to any of it until a row of random census pages scrolled quickly by and stopped only briefly. For a fleeting second, they read a page full of women's names. Lizzie inhaled loudly as she pointed at the word following each woman's name. "Lunacy?" she said.

Chapter 82

Grant struggled into bed and refused any food or drink Flossie offered to him. "I just need rest, Flossie," he said abruptly. "Please leave me alone."

She did as he had asked and shut the bedroom door quietly. When she heard the doorbell, she was relieved to hear Rufus hurrying to answer it. She was in no mood to deal with Antoine that flamboyant party planner who insisted on insulting her all the time. Unfortunately, Rufus called for her before she could make her way to the kitchen.

"Miss Flossie," he yelled loudly, "Mr. Antoine is here."

It made Flossie furious for anyone to yell from one part of the house to the other, but for the life of her, she couldn't get the staff to understand how unprofessional it was. She hurried to the front door. It was apparent from both of their facial expressions that there was no love lost between them. Antoine considered her to be little more than hired help who put herself up on an undeserved pedestal, and she considered him a flaming homosexual who put all his work off on others. Either way, they had to deal with one another.

"What can I do for you?" Flossie asked blandly.

"I need to see Lizzie," he answered, his eyes piercing hers. "It's time to plan the Chatsworth Christmas extravaganza, and I promised her first pick on the December date." Antoine wasn't sure, but he thought he saw a brief streak of panic cross Flossie's face.

"You won't be able to do that today," she answered and offered nothing more.

"Excuse me?" Antoine said. He opened his eyes widely and threw his hands up in an overt display of exasperation. "Clearly, there's been a terribly misguided mistake."

"Misguided mistake?" Flossie scoffed. "What the hell does that mean?"

"We don't have it like that, Flossie," Antoine said directly.

"Like what?" she demanded.

"I'm a professional, one who is very much in demand, might I add. I will not tolerate cursing."

"Oh, good grief," Flossie continued. "Lizzie is sick and cannot see visitors right now. In fact, Dr. Chatsworth is sick as well. Strep throat, last I heard. I'll give her a message and have her call you."

Antoine loudly slapped the leather briefcase hanging from his shoulder. "If I don't hear from them soon, they may not get the date they desire. It will be to your benefit to pass that message along."

"We are done here," Flossie said, turning to Rufus, who was stacking wood in the fireplace. "Rufus, see this gentleman out, please."

Antoine got in his gold Benz and left the estate in a *huff*. *There's something about that woman that goes beyond my dislike for her,* he thought. *She's dangerous.*

****

Grant was able to make it to the dining room for lunch and ate much heartier than he expected. His fever was down, and except for a raw throat, he felt much better.

Flossie noticed the full glass of sweet tea when she returned with dessert. "Don't you want your tea, Doctor?"

"I don't have a taste for it," he answered. "Can you just give me a bottled water? I'll take it to the den with me. I think I'll watch a movie. It's been a while."

"How about some ice cream? It might soothe your throat."

"Maybe later," Grant answered. He flipped through several movies on his DVR, but none particularly interested him. His mind kept going back to Lizzie, and he still wondered how she'd managed to escape his well-guarded estate.

Even though he felt much better, he was still somewhat weak, but he grabbed a coat from a hall closet and went outside. For the first time since he had purchased the estate, he walked the grounds. Indeed, the large yard was beautiful. The winter flowers were in full bloom, and the grass could rival any country club golf course. When he rounded the west side of the house, he heard the Hispanic landscaper calling for Lonnie.

"On the way!" Lonnie called as he made his way into the garage.

Grant followed, stopping briefly to check the quality of the recently installed pool cover. He entered the garage and watched both men as they rambled through cans and plastic containers on the shelves. "Afternoon, fellas," Grant said, startling them both. "How's everything out here?"

They both stared at him in silence until he spoke again.

"Everything okay?"

"Oh yes, Sir, doctor," Lonnie spoke up. "Just surprised to see you."

"Yeah, I guess I don't get out here very often," Grant said, trying to smile.

"Santiago is trying to find the antifreeze. It's that time of year, ya know."

Santiago patted the hood of the old truck he used to transport the garbage and lawn debris from the estate. "I no understand," he said. "Always have antifreeze ready for cold weather."

"I'm sure it's here somewhere," Grant said, beginning to feel weak again. "How does this old thing make it?" he asked Santiago. "Looks like it might be time to upgrade."

"Upgrade? I no understand."

"Get a newer one," Lonnie explained.

"Oh, no, Sir! This one just fine. Just need antifreeze. It'll be good as new one."

"Here it is," Lonnie said as he reached down on the concrete garage floor and retrieved the jug of green liquid. "Problem solved."

"I no put it there," Santiago insisted and shrugged. "I never put things on floor, always in their place."

Damn. Does he really consider that a problem? Guess I should have been a gardener, Grant thought snidely. "I'm heading back to the house," he said. "You fellas have a nice day."

Santiago looked at Lonnie with suspicion. "I always leave antifreeze on shelf, never on floor."

"I believe you, buddy," Lonnie said. "Maybe somebody else needed it for something. Don't sweat it."

****

Grant made it back to the house and entered the sunroom that had brought such solace to Lizzie. He sat down abruptly on the chaise and closed his eyes. He felt his heart racing, and when he opened his eyes again, his vision was blurred. "Flossie!" he yelled, as loudly as possible.

She was at his side within moments. "Yes, Doctor? Is everything okay?"

"I'm not feeling well. Can you get me a Tylenol and some tea?"

"I'll be right back," she answered, then turned to rush to the kitchen.

It was then that Grant grunted. His body stiffened, and his eyes rolled back in his head. In all, the full-blown grand mal seizure lasted less than a minute, but for him, it felt like an eternity.

"Hmm. That happened quicker than I thought it would," Flossie said softly as she smiled sweetly. She rubbed her hand across the doctor's face, gently placing a soft afghan over him, and headed back to the kitchen to prepare his dinner.

Chapter 83

Kenny looked at the computer and shook his head. "Lunacy is right. This whole thing is insane." Glancing at his watch, he realized he had stayed much longer than he had intended. "Good Lord. I've gotta get out of here. Some of us have to work. Try to get some sleep, Lizzie."

"I will," Lizzie answered.

"Do I need to pick up anything for you tomorrow?"

"No, I'm fine. I'll talk with you soon."

Lizzie let Kenny out, and although she knew she should get some rest, the computer was too tempting. She retrieved the census pages again, without any help from Belle this time. Instead, she just followed the random list of families. She did see several women listed with their families, under "Lunacy." *What does that mean?* she wondered as her fingers danced across the keyboard, in search of more answers.

Hours later, Lizzie was barely able to keep her eyes open, but she was appalled by the information she had found. During the years she researched, women could be committed quite easily to asylums for such incredulous reasons as reading novels, using snuff, and not obeying their husbands. In fact, many men placed their wives there just to get rid of them. The conditions were horrific. Little was known about mental illness at the time, and the asylums did little more than house patients in overpopulated, cold, understaffed, prison-like environments. In fact, most mental hospitals were located adjacent to prisons, and the food and treatment were much the same. The deplorable conditions often caused those who were initially sane go mad and delusional, and the uncontrolled temperatures and subpar food, more often than not, led to sickness, disease, and early mortality.

"Who was put in the hospital, little girl?" Lizzie asked aloud. "You've got to give me something. I'm so tired."

Although she wanted to learn more, Lizzie turned off the computer and made her way to bed. It had been a long day, and she needed some rest. She fell asleep as soon as her head hit the pillow and didn't wake again until the cell phone rang on the nightstand beside her.

"Hello?" she said.

"Morning, sunshine," Maggie chirped. "You've got an appointment at noon today, during Dr. Redding's lunch break."

Lizzie sat up in the bed. "You mean I'm actually allowed out during daylight? I'm beginning to feel like a vampire."

"Yes, Ma'am, and I have even better news. Leland has a private eye who just so happens to owe on his retainer fee. He's willing to follow us while I take you out to lunch."

"You can't be serious!" Lizzie cooed. "How amazing is that? What time is it?"

"It's 10:30, sleepyhead. I'll pick you up in an hour. Wear the baseball cap Kenny brought, along with the large sunglasses. We can't just get crazy."

"Will do," Lizzie said, as she threw the covers back and got out of bed to shower. "See you in an hour."

She was standing at the door like a child waiting for Santa to arrive when Maggie pulled into the drive. Lizzie walked nonchalantly to the car, then squealed with delight as she grabbed his sister's hand.

"Don't get too excited, Lizzie," Maggie said sternly. "We've got to be careful."

"Where's the P.I.?"

"He's at the end of the street, in a dark blue sedan. He's very inconspicuous, but we can't just get overly confident. Dr. Redding said this will just be a quick prenatal visit."

Within ten minutes, they were pulling up to the rear of his building, and the two women walked inside, where he was waiting on them.

"First things first," the doctor said, pointing to the scales. "I can tell from the size of that tummy that you've gained a few pounds. In this case that's a good thing."

Lizzie had indeed gained weight, and everything seemed to be progressing positively.

"I'm quite pleased with your progress, Lizzie," the doctor said. "I won't need to see you for another month unless you have any problems."

"Thank you," she answered. Lizzie dressed quickly after the doctor left, and, hand in hand, she and Maggie hurried to the car.

"Where are we eating lunch?" Lizzie asked.

"There's a great little place out on the bayou. It's nothing fancy. In fact, it's barely still standing, but the seafood is fresh, and the crowd is sparse."

"Sounds perfect," Lizzie said, taking in her sister's pretty profile as she drove.

"Penny for your thoughts," Maggie said.

"I'm just so happy to be here, to be here with you. It's hard to believe I let us drift apart like I did. I've missed you and didn't even realize how much until I saw you."

Maggie's eyes filled with tears, but they remained there and didn't overflow and run down her face. "What are we going to do? As the holidays get closer, Grant is bound to come for you. Once he realizes you're pregnant, he'll drag you back to Georgia."

Lizzie looked down at her hands that were folded in her lap. "I don't know. He'll come for me, and I'm sure he won't wait until the last minute. I hate to do it, but I'm going to have to call Clara, his office manager. I've tried to keep her out of it, but I need to know what his demeanor is like if he's said anything. I'll call in a week or so. Right now, I just want to enjoy some fresh seafood with my sister."

Chapter 84

Justin had somehow managed to keep Christi in their new apartment for two days with the promise of returning to her old place after a couple of days of rest. It had been difficult to explain Albert's death to her without giving additional information, but she needed to recall things for herself, at her own pace. Christi seemed to be right on the precipice of a breakthrough, but each time a piece of memory formed in her mind, it was gone as quickly as it came.

They had just finished their breakfast when Detective Pitts knocked on the door. "Are you two ready?" he asked.

Christi was still moving slowly, but she got up from the table with more than her usual vigor. "Yes, I'm ready," she answered. "I wanna go back to my apartment."

"You do realize that it's only to aid your memory of anything that may have occurred there, right? You can't stay."

"I don't understand why," she said defiantly.

"Christi, we've talked about this," Justin said. "It's too dangerous. The good side is that you'll be able to get most of your things today."

"And bring them back to this dump?" she retorted.

Justin looked defeated but continued anyway. "It may be a dump, but you're going to be here for a while. You might as well get used to it."

"What's a while, Detective?" she asked, turning her rage on Pitts.

"Let's just go to your apartment and see what you can remember. One step at a time, Christi. You don't wanna end up back in the hospital, do you?"

She walked to the large unmarked car, pouting like a child. The drive was an awkward one filled with silence.

Justin allowed Christi and Detective Pitts to walk ahead of him as he hung back. His head was swimming, and the last thing he needed was for the investigator to see his anxiety attack and turn his suspicions on him.

Christi paused at the mailboxes and touched one of them. "Something happened here," she said quietly. "I just can't remember what."

"Don't push yourself," Pitts said. He held her elbow and led her up to her apartment. Justin steadied her as Pitts turned the key.

The crime scene tape was gone, and it appeared that the investigators had tried their best to put things back in their place. It didn't look ransacked anymore, but it was obvious something had gone on in the apartment.

Christi's hand flew up to her mouth when she saw the ripped couch cushions. "What happened? Why would someone do this?"

Pitts pulled a chair from under the kitchen table and eased her down on it. "Okay, Christi. You remember this apartment, don't you?"

"Of course, I do! Do you think I'm brain-dead? This is my apartment. I live here with Albert Tinsley, and I'm a graduate student at Georgia State. Correction. I *lived* here with Albert."

"Okay, great," Pitts said. "Now, do you remember any conversations with Albert? Any conversations pertaining to his job?"

Christi closed her eyes and sighed heavily. "Let me think. Yes, he was very unhappy with his job. He told me that a lot. Wait! I remember he didn't come home for a few days. I was pissed at first, then really worried. He always called when he wasn't coming home, always. We were just roommates, nothing romantic, but he didn't want me to worry, so he made it a point to check in."

"You're doing great, Christi. Do you remember what he didn't like about his job? Did he have a problem with a particular coworker? A problem with his pay?"

"I remember he wanted to quit but couldn't afford to. He just recently moved here and was kind of stuck." Christi rubbed her forehead again and asked Justin to get her an aspirin from the kitchen cabinet. She swallowed two of the tablets and drank heavily from a bottled water. "Something just wasn't right where he worked. He was suspicious, but I'm not sure of what or who."

"Was he afraid?"

"No, more like pissed. He kept trying to get people to listen to him, but no one would."

"What did Albert do at his job?"

"He worked in a lab. I never knew much about it. We never discussed our lives much because we were both so busy. It wasn't until recently that he even starting speaking about his job. I just know he regretted ever taking it in the first place."

"Okay. So, he wasn't afraid. We've established that. Did he have any friends he hung around with? A girlfriend?"

"There were a few guys he drank beers with from time to time, mostly at sports bars when there was a ball game."

"Were they friends from work?"

"No. He didn't like mixing business and pleasure. Business was business with Albert. I still can't believe he's dead. You never told me what happened to him," she said.

"Christi, that's not important right now," Justin said quietly. "You don't need to get upset."

"Not important? The hell it's not! I'm not a child, Justin. What happened to him? He was my friend."

"He was murdered," Detective Pitts said flatly. "I'm so sorry, but you need to know the truth. Someone killed him, and his body was retrieved from the Chattahoochee River."

"But why? Who would do such a thing? Albert wouldn't hurt a fly." Christi had held it together as long as she could and burst into tears that quickly turned into heaving sobs.

"That's enough," Justin said. "Take us back. She needs her rest."

"I agree," Pitts concluded. "We'll try this again tomorrow. We'll start fresh in the morning. Would you like to get a few things, Christi?"

She insisted on going into her bedroom alone and came back out with a floral duffel bag and makeup case. "I'm ready to go now."

Detective Pitts locked the apartment while Justin helped his sister down the stairs.

When they passed the mailboxes, she abruptly stopped again. "He was following me," she said, apprehensively at first, then gaining more confidence. "He was following me, and I was frightened, but some friends called for me. Yes!

They invited me out for pizza, and when I responded, the guy was gone, just like that," she said, snapping her fingers. "Wait! There were these two old ladies. We met at Cracker Barrel. They were afraid."

Chapter 85

Grant had spent three weeks going from feeling better to feeling worse. He had made it into the office a couple of times to see patients but finally decided to take the rest of November off, along with half of December. He just wasn't well. "Burning the candle at both ends has finally caught up with me," he told Clara one afternoon in the office. "I just need some rest."

Clara wasn't so sure; the handsome doctor had become a shell of himself, and it had happened so quickly. "Perhaps you should get a physical," she suggested.

"That's ridiculous," he said with a grunt. "I'm a doctor, and I know I'm just exhausted."

Clara held her breath, for fear of what he'd say, then continued anyway. "I've noticed some tremors, Dr. Chatsworth, and you've complained of blurred vision and headaches. It may be something more. At least let me take your blood pressure."

"As I said, that's ridiculous."

"Humor me," she said defiantly.

"Fine, but hurry up. I'm ready to go home and enjoy the remainder of the month on hiatus."

She was back within seconds with the blood pressure cuff and had it wrapped around his bicep before he could change his mind. Clara listened intently, then removed the cuff from his arm. "It's alarmingly high."

"Hell yes, it's high. Consider all the pressure I'm under," Grant all but screamed. "It's a damn miracle I haven't just keeled over. I just need some rest and for everybody to get the hell off my back!"

Clara kept silent and walked away. She listened as he rustled through papers in his office, grabbed his car keys, and stomped out of the office. *Something is wrong with him, and it's not stress or exhaustion,* she thought.

Grant stopped to get gas and grabbed a Gatorade and pack of crackers. He decided to stop by the Research Facility before going home. He had no intention to go back out anytime soon, so he wanted to take care of his errands all at once.

The building was open, but there wasn't anyone in sight, so he called Zahir from his cell in the lobby. "Where the hell is everybody?" Grant demanded.

"I'll be right down, Sir," Zahir said. When he exited the elevator and saw Dr. Grant Chatsworth, his mouth fell open. The doctor had lost at least twenty pounds since he had last seen him, and he looked like death warmed over. "I didn't know you were stopping by today," Zahir said, trying to hide his shock at his boss's appearance. "The receptionist is at lunch. Are you going up to your office?"

"Yes. I figured I'd stop by for a couple of hours. I've been so tired lately. I'm going to take a couple of weeks off, try to build my strength back up, ya know?"

"Indeed I do," Zahir said, punching the button to the elevator. "Jean-Luc is upstairs too. Perhaps we can discuss what the next couple of months will hold."

"Very well," Grant said.

The two walked slowly to Grant's office, and he plopped down behind his desk. "Would you grab me a water please?"

"Yes...and I'll get Jean-Luc while I'm out." Zahir returned with the water and his coworker in short order.

Jean-Luc didn't fare as well in hiding his surprise at Grant's appearance. "Oh, my God," he said. "You are very ill, Doctor. What is wrong?"

"I'm just fucking tired, that's all. I've been pulled in twenty different directions for over two years now. I'm worn out!"

"No, Sir," Jean-Luc insisted. "You are sick. Something is wrong."

"I'm taking a break for a few weeks. I just want to wrap a few things up here, and I'm going home to rest. Let me see the latest reports."

"It's right there, Sir," Zahir said, pointing to a folder on Grant's desk.

He picked it up and immediately threw it back on the desk. "I can't read that. Who wrote that chicken scratch?"

Both doctors looked at one another, then back at Grant.

"No one, Sir," Zahir said. "It was printed from the computer."

Grant's eyes rolled back, and he slumped forward onto his desk.

****

When Grant woke up, he was on a gurney at Emory Hospital in Midtown. Needless to say, he was not a happy man. Zahir and Jean-Luc were both seated on either side of his bed in his room, which was cordoned off with curtains.

"What the hell?"

"Doctor, it was in your best interest for us to bring you here. You passed out, and your blood pressure was very high, stroke level, in fact."

Grant sat up and pulled the IV from his hand. "I demand that you take me home."

"Wait just a minute, Doctor," a young, dark-haired woman said. "I am Dr. Smoltz. We have been able to bring your blood pressure down to an acceptable level, but I understand, from your friends here, that you've experienced dramatic weight loss and blurred vision and passed out on them."

"Use the term 'friends' lightly please," Grant said flatly. "I'm just an overworked doctor. I'm sure you can relate to that."

"I'd like to run a few tests. Besides the exhaustion, have you had any other symptoms?"

"Just a chronic headache, which is coming back rapidly. I had strep throat a couple of weeks ago. Dr. Chavan here gave me some antibiotics. Since I recovered from that, I've had headaches, some nausea, and, according to my office manager, a few noticeable tremors."

"When was your last physical?"

Grant looked at her as if he was ready to explode. "I'm a doctor. I know my body."

"Really?" the attractive young doctor said sarcastically. "You can't be serious."

"Zahir, get me out of here."

"Listen to her," Zahir retorted. "You are sitting here with three doctors who all agree that you should undergo some tests."

"Very well," Grant conceded. "What do you suggest?"

"I'd like to do some blood cultures and a CT scan. With the persistent headaches, tremors, and nausea, I want to rule out meningitis."

"Jesus Christ," Grant said.

"It may be true that you are simply overworked, Doctor, but it's best to rule out all possibilities."

"Fine," Grant said rudely. "I'll stay overnight, but after that, I'm going home."

****

Four days later, Grant was still in the hospital. His vitals were much better, his appetite was back, considering the food choices, and he felt stronger.

"Good morning, Doctor," Zahir said as he opened the door to the hospital room. "You look great. Perhaps you were right. You just needed some rest."

"I hope you're here to take me home," Grant said. "I hate hospitals."

When they pulled up to the estate, Rufus was waiting for them at the front door. "Great to see you home, Sir," he said with a wide grin. "We were very worried about you."

"Everyone needs to stop worrying. There's not a damn thing wrong with me."

Flossie almost tripped over herself getting to Grant. "I have one of your favorite meals waiting for you in the dining room," she said. "It won't take long for me to put a few pounds on you."

Zahir detested how the housekeeper overlooked him as though he wasn't even present. Something about her had never set right with him. She was too overbearing, and it wasn't like Dr. Chatsworth to allow it. "How is Ms. Elizabeth?" he asked Flossie.

She refused to make eye contact with him and merely dismissed him with a wave of her hand. "She's fine. Upstairs reading, I suppose."

It's strange that Elizabeth didn't bother to visit her husband in the hospital, Zahir thought to himself. The whole scenario at the house gave him a bad vibe. He wasn't sure what it was, but something was eerily peculiar. "I'd like to speak to her," Zahir said innocently. "It has been quite some time since I've seen her. I'm sure she's been worried about her husband."

"I need to tend to the doctor right now," Flossie replied quickly. "I'll pass your concern along to Ms. Lizzie. Now," she said, grabbing Grant's arm, "let's go eat a warm meal."

"You always cook too much, Flossie. Zahir, join me for lunch. Flossie is a wonderful cook."

The look of shock that flashed across Flossie's face did not go unnoticed by the Indian doctor.

"Not today, Sir," Flossie said. "There is only enough for you, and you need your rest. Good day, Doctor," she said, clearly dismissing Zahir. "Rufus, will you see our guest out?"

Our guest? Zahir thought. *Something is going on here.* The absence of Elizabeth was enough to set him on edge, but there was also the fact that the doctor had become so ill while he was at home and only improved in the hospital. He needed to get back to the Research Facility to talk to Jean-Luc. *Something in the milk isn't clean as the Americans would say.*

Chapter 86

Lizzie's day with Maggie was absolutely delightful for both sisters. The thought of having a new life without fear or uneasiness was more than she would have ever dreamt a few months earlier. She stood at the back window and observed the heron as it stood watch over the bayou. The bird was truly a beautiful sight, and she was glad it had returned.

She decided she would not visit the cemetery or turn on the computer that night. Instead, she would watch something lighthearted on television and read until she fell asleep. *Tonight, I will dream of my own daughter who is growing inside me,* she thought with a smile.

Lizzie found herself laughing out loud to one of the latest game shows, and it felt good. She felt alive again. She ran a warm bubble bath and stayed in it until the water turned cool. Skipping pajamas altogether, she slipped on the extra-thick chenille robe and climbed into bed with a romance novel.

Twenty pages in, she fell asleep but was soon awakened by the paperback hitting the hardwood floor. She reached down, picked it up, and placed it on the nightstand, then flipped the lamp off. Lizzie pulled the fluffy robe around herself and sank deep into the soft, comfy bed. She was just drifting back to sleep when she heard what sounded like something falling down the stairs. Everything she needed was on the first floor, so she had only been upstairs once to see the guest rooms and extra bath. She couldn't imagine what could have fallen.

Lizzie sat up in bed, felt around with her bare feet until she found her slippers, and stood to see what was going on. She turned on the overhead light in the bedroom, followed by the hall light. She switched on the dim lights in the sconces when she reached the foyer.

That's funny, she thought. *There's nothing at the bottom of the stairs. Perhaps a picture fell off the wall.* She looked up the darkened staircase, then grabbed the railing so as not to fall from the shock of it. At first, it was almost like a shadow dancing across the top of the stairs, back and forth across the hallway, but it could still be seen between the bannisters. "I'm dreaming," she said aloud. "It's all a dream."

Then the loud noises started almost like a squall from a storm raging in the gulf. The wind ruffled her hair as if she was outside in a summer rainstorm. Lizzie held on tight to the railing to keep herself from falling, but her eyes never left the shadowy image. It swayed back and forth like a vaporous sheet until the noise started to soften and the mist began to take form. It was a young boy, probably around twelve years of age, judging by his clothing and stature. He wore knickers that cuffed just below the knees, along with a tunic in the popular style of the early to mid 1800s. His hair was cut but not closely cropped. He wore some type of hat that resembled something a Navy man might wear. He, too, was a fine mist, but she could make out his features and his clothes. Lizzie could also make out that he was not happy to see her there. He raised his hands in her direction, and the deafening sounds started again. Her ears were ringing, but she could hear the distorted taunts coming from all around her: "Get out! Get out!"

As quickly as the whole event had started, it ended. Every light in the house was on, and silence ensued. Lizzie thought of sitting on the steps but decided she could make it to the couch. Her hands were shaking quite forcefully, so she folded them tightly and placed them in her lap. "Warm milk will do the trick. I'll just heat some up and go to bed," she said aloud. She waited a few seconds to ensure she was stable before making her way into the kitchen. The steaming milk felt good going down, and it quickly settled her nerves. Lizzie rinsed her cup, put it in the dishwasher, and turned to go back to bed but not before seeing the large flock of ravens balancing on the back deck railings.

It was the early morning sun that woke Lizzie from her uneasy rest, not a young boy's ghost or threatening, jeering words. She brushed her hair and pulled it into a ponytail before toasting a bagel and taking it with her to the computer. Even after the events from the night before, she wouldn't be deterred.

Lizzie read more disturbing material about asylums until she had had her fill. It was difficult to even imagine people being pushed away to such horrible places. *Who was there?* she wondered. *Was it the young boy at the top of the staircase? Was it poor Baby Belle?*

"That's enough for today," Lizzie announced as she shut down the computer. She finished her juice just as the stubborn computer powered off, then flickered back on. "So you've got something to tell me, little one," she said. "I hope it's something I can work with."

"Birchwood Forest Lunatic Asylum...Birchwood Forest Lunatic Asylum..."

The odd message must have run across the screen hundreds of times. Lizzie grabbed a pen and wrote it down, fearing she might somehow forget the name. When she touched the mouse, the repetitive name stopped and allowed her to utilize the search engine. She typed in the institute name and waited for the results. The outside of the dilapidated, deserted building looked like a cross between a haunted castle and a penitentiary. According to the article, it had been built in the early 1800s and was utilized until approximately 1895, when it was simply vacated and left to its own demise. The pictures were quite unsettling, ranging from lobotomy rooms to morgues, cells, and unmarked graves. Apparently, the place was still standing, but it was certainly not occupied. Lizzie put the address into MapQuest and found that it was merely three hours away. It was simple: She had to go to Birchwood Forest Lunatic Asylum. There had to be a clue there, something to tie the whole troubling story together. Without a second thought, she picked up her cell phone and dialed Kenny.

"Hello?"

"Wear black clothes, bring flashlights and extra batteries, and pick me up at 10 o'clock tonight. Don't be late."

"Have you lost it?" he whispered, much louder than he intended. "Where would we go dressed in black at 10 o'clock?"

"Birchwood Forest, Louisiana."

"Dare I ask what we are going to find in Birchwood Forest?"

"An abandoned lunatic asylum. Don't be late," Lizzie said, then disconnected the call.

Chapter 87

Justin had somehow been able to stop Christi's revelations at the mailboxes and get her into Detective Pitts's car. She was hyperventilating and sweating, and Justin cursed at Pitts for pushing her too far.

"We're very close, Justin," the detective said, much kinder than he intended. "We're right on the cusp of discovering who might be after her. Don't you want to know what's going on?"

"Not at the risk of my sister having a nervous breakdown," Justin said as he got in the back seat and sat next to Christi. "Let's go back home."

"That's not home, Justin," Christi said, her voice sounding much calmer. "It's a rat hole."

"How about some lunch, my treat?" Pitts suggested. "I do feel bad about pushing you so hard. Let me make it up to you."

"I'd like that," Christi said cheerfully. "It's wonderful to be out of that hospital."

"We'll grab something on the way back to your place, Justin. That'll give Christi more time to rest."

A couple of blocks later, Pitts pulled into a popular pizza chain. "One of the best in the city."

Pitts said it innocently, but Justin knew exactly what he was doing. Clearly, he was trying to trigger Christi's memory from the day she went out for pizza with her friends, the day Gunnar had frightened her at the communal mail slots. He held his breath as they got out of the car and found a booth near the back of the busy restaurant.

"What can I get you to drink?" asked a young girl covered in piercings and tattoos.

"I'll take a Bud Light," Justin spouted, "followed by another one after that."

"You can't drink, Justin," Christi said. "What are you thinking?"

"I'm thinking this nice detective has offered to treat, and I'd like a beer…or two."

"But you're not old enough."

"I celebrated my twenty-first birthday two weeks ago, in your hospital room. Kinda wanted to wait for you to celebrate with me."

Christi opened her mouth to speak, but nothing came out. Tears streamed down her face as she reached for her brother's hand. "I'm so sorry, Justin. I-I forgot. For the first time ever, I forgot your birthday."

"No problem," Justin said. "You had a good excuse."

They were interrupted by the waitress clearing her throat. "Not that I want to interrupt a sentimental moment, but I'll need to see your ID."

Justin pulled it from his wallet and handed it to her.

She studied it carefully. "Okay. One Bud Light. What else?"

"I'll have water," Christi said, and Pitts agreed to have the same.

They ordered the house special pie and waited for it to be baked perfectly in the brick oven.

"Do you feel like talking anymore, or are you through for the day?"

"Maybe a little more," Christi answered, against Justin's pleading.

"You said someone was following you, a male, and you saw him at the mailboxes."

Christi frowned briefly and looked up at the tin ceiling. "Yes, a man. I'm not certain he was following me, but it was a gut feeling—you know, that feeling a woman gets when something just isn't right. He asked me something. I can't remember exactly what, but it was a generic question, something about how much rent the complex charges or something like that."

"Then what happened?"

"Several of my friends from Georgia State hollered to ask if I wanted to go out for pizza. I had finished classes for the day, and, frankly, the guy was really creeping me out, so I was anxious to go with them. Yeah, I remember being really grateful they showed up."

"Okay, try very hard with this one. Do you remember anything about his appearance, anything that might stand out?"

The waitress showed up with their drinks, and Christie toyed with paper on her straw until Detective Pitts thought he might scream.

"He was very... I don't mean to sound cruel, but he looked odd, almost like a giant. It was like he was trying to disguise some kind of weird accent. Either that, or he had some sort of speech impediment."

Pitts could feel his heart beating out of his chest, and Justin drank heavily from the frosted beer mug. "Anything else? Anything at all?" Pitts pressed.

"Yes. His eyes were an unusual color, gray, almost like a wolf's or something."

"House special," the waitress said as she placed the steaming pizza on the table and passed out silverware wrapped in paper napkins. "I'll grab another Bud Light for the birthday boy."

"I may have some photos for you to look through," Pitts said as he bit into a piece of pizza, "but for now, let's just enjoy the food."

The three were quiet as they ate their pizza, and Justin allowed the beer to calm his nerves. Even if Christi could identify Gunnar, he was dead, and no one would ever know who killed him.

Christi was chewing on her second piece when she abruptly wiped the napkin across her mouth. "I remember! Oh, my God! I remember now. I was worried about Albert. He hadn't called, so I called his job to check on him." She started fanning herself with the menu.

"Did someone tell you what happened to him?"

"I was eating pizza with my friends when my cell phone rang. It was a woman who worked in a different office from Albert, but she told me I might be in danger. She told me to spend the night with a friend and meet her and her friend the next day at Cracker Barrel."

"Did you meet them?" Pitts asked, hoping that all the pieces were about to fall into place.

"Yes, I sure did. Those two old ladies!"

Chapter 88

Lizzie dressed in her darkest clothes and packed several bottles of water, her only small flashlight, a hammer she had found in the garage, and a couple of granola bars in an overnight bag. She had no idea what she was getting into, but she was sure the apparitions would never stop until she found out the truth about Baby Belle. "Maybe this was all meant to be, little girl," Lizzie said. "You needed someone to come along who had time to help you find peace, and I needed someone to help take my mind off my troubles. We're kindred spirits."

Kenny pulled into the driveway, and Lizzie grabbed her bag and left out the back door. When she jumped into the passenger seat, Kenny almost had a heart attack. "Oh, dear Lord," he said faintly. "Are you seriously trying to kill me?"

Lizzie had to laugh. Kenny looked ridiculous in his black sweat pants, black dress shirt, and black stocking cap. "If we get pulled over, the police will think we're a couple of burglars," Lizzie said.

"And I wouldn't blame them," Kenny said nervously.

"I like the dress shirt."

"It's the only black shirt I have, and this was all sort of spur of the moment. I don't have a wide array of armed robbery attire."

That drew a snicker from Lizzie.

"I'm not trying to be funny. It's one thing walking around a cemetery in the middle of the night, but driving three hours to walk through an abandoned asylum is quite another. This is like a horror movie, a bad one at that. Why can't we just do this stuff in the daylight?"

"Because I'm hiding out, remember?"

"Well, you're not doing a very good job of it. And another thing. If this child can give you all these hints, why the hell doesn't she just tell you the whole story? Are all these field trips really necessary?"

"Oh, you love it," Lizzie teased. "Admit it. You do."

Kenny offered little more than a huff.

"To be honest, I've questioned the same thing myself," Lizzie said. "I don't know anything about spirits or ghosts or whatever it is we're following, but I do know Belle won't rest in peace until her story is told."

"Then she should just tell us. Why doesn't she just write it across the computer?"

"Because then we'd be the only ones to know. There must be some type of evidence out there that we have to retrieve to prove her story."

"Good grief. I guess we're in it up to our eyeballs now."

The three-hour drive went by quickly, and the two made easy conversation. Kenny was the innocence of youth, bright, energetic, and full of promise. Lizzie remembered herself like that, and she envied him; for her, that all seemed like so many years ago.

"Look, Kenny. It's a full moon. That'll bring us some good light."

Kenny listened to the GPS which reported that they were less than ten minutes from their destination. "I have to admit, I'm more than a little nervous. This time, we really will be trespassing, you know."

Excitement filled Lizzie's belly as they navigated through the back roads to the old institution that had been witness to such horror.

"Oh, my God!" Kenny exclaimed nervously. "Look at that place. It's huge."

It took them a few minutes to allow the daunting sight to sink in. It was far back in the woods, and the mere expanse of it was breathtaking. The main building spread across several acres, and various other buildings dotted the landscape. It was surrounded by weathered chain-link fencing, most likely put there decades later to keep lurid trespassers from making their way inside.

Kenny opened his trunk and pulled out a pair of bolt cutters. "I figured we might need these," he said.

"You were thinking ahead. See? You *are* intrigued by this whole story."

He didn't answer and just pulled out a dark duffel bag and threw it over his shoulder. "You need to be very careful, Lizzie. The last thing you need is a nasty scratch from any of this rusty stuff."

"Do you think the car will be okay?" she asked.

"I don't see anyone in sight, and I can't imagine anyone else coming up that rutted dirt road without us hearing them or seeing their headlights. Looks like we're the only crazies out here, breaking into the looney bin."

They made their way to the main gate that had been quite elaborate at some point. The years hadn't been kind to it, though, and it hung desperately on tired, weakened hinges.

"I'm afraid to open it," Kenny said. "It's very heavy, and we don't need it falling on us. Our best bet is to cut an opening in this fencing and go through over there."

It didn't take long before they were through and on the official property of Birchwood Forest Lunatic Asylum where trespassers were not allowed and could be prosecuted under penalty of law.

Kenny had two large Maglites, and he handed one to Lizzie. "Keep yours facing the ground. We don't need you falling. Where to first?"

"I think we need to find the administrative offices. We need to look for any records of who was placed here. I'm not sure who it is we're looking for. It may possibly be Baby Belle."

"I'd think the offices would be in the main building. It looks like the others were utilized as dorms or some form of housing. Let's check here first," he said, pointing to the oversized double-doors that had welcomed visitors two centuries ago.

Lizzie and Kenny looked uneasily at each other as the doors gave way with one push and opened wide for them to enter. In its day, Lizzie was certain the entrance hall that met visitors had been grand and inviting since the administration would have wanted families to believe a patient's stay would be wonderful and pleasant. Now it wore the wrinkles of age. From the halls of previous grandeur hung sheets of paint that were separating from the plaster. Any of the finer furniture had long since been taken to some other thriving hospital, and what lingered was simply dust and fallen debris. A few broken chairs and what appeared to have been a desk was all that remained in the main reception area.

With Lizzie shining her flashlight toward the ground, Kenny shined his down the corridors. The only noises were the shuffle of their feet as they brushed away any rubble in their path. They passed several rooms. Some appeared to be offices, and others seemed to be waiting areas, but none housed any type of records or storage.

"It looks like we're gonna have to look at some of the other buildings," Kenny said regretfully. "I was sure we'd find any medical records left behind in this building. It's clearly the admission office."

The main structure was large, built from granite and other ornate stonework. Lizzie was sure it had been something to see in its day.

The two made their way out of the building and headed around to the east side of the campus. Obviously, the other buildings hadn't been constructed with as much care. Their exteriors were a combination of brickwork and what would modernly be considered rail fencing. There were only a few still standing as most had caved in from years of neglect and abandonment.

"It's too unsound for you, Lizzie," Kenny insisted. "We can't risk you falling."

They walked around the grounds for a few more minutes until Lizzie saw a loftier structure that seemed somewhat sturdy. "Let's go in," she insisted. "Maybe there's something in there."

Kenny decided against challenging her and followed her to the entrance. "I can't believe these doors aren't secured," he said.

"Well, this one is just hanging on by a thread. I'm thinking they don't get a lot of visitors out here anymore."

"No comment," Kenny said as he followed her inside.

"Oh, Jesus, this is creepy," Lizzie said, looking at the rusted twin beds that lined the walls, along with what was left of stained padding that must have acted as some form of mattresses. "Let's keep going," she said to Kenny, grabbing his hand.

Unlike the large vestibules in the administrative building, these hallways were narrow and led them on a cavernous journey through a maze of passages. Lizzie grabbed Kenny's elbow as they glanced in several rooms. Although most of what was left behind was damaged, there was enough remaining for them to be aware of what they were observing. Two large morgues still contained metal drawers for the deceased as well as some form of concrete autopsy or embalming tables. Several rooms contained gurneys, while others had heavy wooden chairs, much like electric chairs, with some type of leather headgear attached. It sent shivers up Lizzie's spine.

"Okay, we've seen enough," Kenny said. "We still have a three-hour drive home."

"Just a few more minutes," Lizzie pleaded. "There's gotta be something here, something we're missing."

The hall merged into a large, two-story room that appeared to have been a common area for the patients.

"Nothing here but some old, dusty furniture," Kenny said. "Let's find our way back out of here."

"Let's go upstairs. Maybe that was where the patient records were kept."

"No way. They're probably rotted by now anyway, and it's too dangerous."

"Please, Kenny? We've come this far."

"You're a real pain in the ass," he answered angrily. "It's not that I'd mind you falling through the stairs at this point, but I don't want my ass kicked by my boss!"

Lizzie wanted to giggle but bit her lip instead.

"Nobody seems to be around, so I'll go take a quick look," he said. "You stay right here and keep the light shining on me."

"Okay, but don't get out of sight."

"You think you need to tell me that?" Kenny asked sarcastically.

Lizzie watched as he held on to the railing and made his way up the curved stairwell. It squeaked and moaned but appeared to be holding him up.

He reached the top step and held the bannister, then looked down the hallway. "More open space. It looks like a lot of the same beds we saw downstairs. It's some type of dormitory. Do you want me to take a closer look?"

As Lizzie was contemplating his question, she heard crying. It sounded like a child at first, but then it became clear that it was undoubtedly an adult's anguished cry.

"Lizzie," Kenny said anxiously, "look! Look at the bottom of the stairs."

It wasn't a mist like she was used to seeing in the cemetery. This time, it was a three-dimensional white fog, thick enough that

362

she couldn't see through it. The fog manifested momentarily into a young woman, sitting on the ground, her upper body leaning forward and touching the floor as she wailed from grief. It was not the type of cry one would hear from physical pain; it was the cry of a broken heart.

Lizzie stood frozen, chills running through her body, the hair on the back of her neck standing on end. She turned to run, then realized Kenny was at the top of the stairs. She turned the flashlight back up to him, and there he was, standing just behind Kenny. It was the same young boy she had seen on the stairs back at the house in Ocean Springs. "Kenny!" Lizzie screamed. "Look behind you! Run down the stairs."

Just as Kenny turned to see what she was warning him about, the young boy pushed him, catching him off guard and sending him tumbling down the aged staircase.

Just as Kenny hit the floor at the bottom of the stairs, the building turned eerily silent. There was not a sound, no more wails of grief, no young boy moving at the top of the stairs, and no signs of life coming from Kenny Deveaux.

Chapter 89

Three days later, Detective Pitts was at Dr. Chatsworth's office. There was a "Closed for the Holidays" sign on the front door, but he could see lights on and the young receptionist in the front office. He held up his badge and knocked.

Harper smiled broadly and unlocked the door. "Good morning. How can I help you?"

"Is the doc in?"

"No. He won't be back until just before Christmas. He's been sick."

"What about the older nurse who was here the last time I stopped by?"

"Ms. Clara?"

"I suppose."

"She's in the back, working on some files. Would you like to speak with her?"

"Sure would."

"Come on back," Harper said, oblivious to anything out of the ordinary. "Clara," she said, interrupting Clara's filing, "this detective is here to see you."

The older nurse turned around and almost lost her footing.

Pitts reached for her shoulder. "Easy now. We don't want you taking a tumble."

"Sorry. You just startled me. Harper and I are the only ones in the office these days."

"So I hear. Miss Harper, would you mind giving us a few minutes?"

"No problem," she answered, then made her way back to the front.

"What can I do for you, Detective? Dr. Chatsworth isn't here."

"I've been speaking to Christi Cates the past few days. Her memory is coming back."

He watched as Clara swallowed hard and perspiration formed on her forehead. "Christi Cates? Is she one of our patients?"

"No, she isn't, Ms. Samples."

"Her name doesn't ring a bell. Perhaps you can speak to the doctor when he gets back."

"Cracker Barrel? A big Russian named Gunnar? A young man named Albert Tinsley? Any of *that* ring a bell?"

"Oh dear," Clara said, reaching for a chair. "I knew I should've stayed out of it."

"Why don't you tell me what you know?" Pitts said. "You can only help me."

"None of what I know is factual. It's merely circumstantial, and an old lady like me had no business sticking her nose in it. I'm afraid to tell you," Clara said nervously. "I don't want to end up like Albert."

"I'm not gonna let anything happen to you, Ma'am," Pitts assured her.

"I've been suspicious of the doctor for a while now, I guess since he opened that Research Facility. He was never one to hold conversations with the nurses or staff, but he became increasingly secretive and angry after that. He started doing things out of character, like getting a phone call from one of the doctor's at the Facility and up and leaving his patients here. I overheard some angry, threatening calls a few times, but I'm not sure who he was talking to. Call it a gut feeling, but something isn't right over there."

"How do you know Christi Cates?"

"I don't. The doctor left early one day, but I was still doing paperwork. I let the answering machine catch the call, and when I listened to it, I realized she was a friend of one the Facility employees. She said he'd gone missing. Then I remembered a conversation I overheard the doctor having on the phone. He said, 'You take care of it, or I will.'"

"Do you think he had someone kill Albert Tinsley?"

"Oh, for heaven's sake, I don't know. I let my imagination run away from me. I called her back to warn her and even met her for lunch at Cracker Barrel. I think she was angry at me for not having more information but frightened of me as well. I figured she considered me some sort of nut because I never heard from her again."

Detective Pitts closed his notepad and looked at over at Clara. "So just what do you think is going on over at the doctor's research joint?"

"I have no idea. Supposedly, he's coming up with some miracle drug that will ease the suffering of millions of heart patients around the world."

"Do you think he's doing anything…dishonest? Criminal?"

"I feel like I should say yes, but I'm just not sure."

"Do you like him?"

"He's one of the best cardiologists in the country."

"Yes, I know, but do you like the man? Personally, I mean."

"Hell no," Clara said as her hand flew up to her mouth. "I'm sorry."

"I feel the same way. Now, don't you worry about anything, Ms. Clara. I'll catch him at his own game if it's the last thing I do."

"Thank you so much, Detective. Is there anything else I can do?"

"Not for now, Ma'am. You've been a lot of help. I'll let myself out."

Clara waited for five minutes to pass before she phoned Justin in a panic. "He was just here. Thank God, you stopped Christi from saying too much, and thank you for warning me about it all. If you hadn't, I surely would have admitted to everything."

Chapter 90

"You've been a very bad boy, Doctor," Flossie said quietly as she stripped him down and gave him a sponge bath. "You're much too sick to go out. That's why those evil doctor friends of yours had you admitted to the hospital. Anyone as sick as you should be at home. They think you're crazy, but I know better."

Flossie was a blurry image in front of Grant, and her words sounded garbled to him. "I have a headache," he stuttered.

"Yes, I'm sure you do. You had another one of those dreadful seizures, and you urinated on yourself, but that's okay. Yes, Sir, Miss Flossie is here for you. Just rest now, and I'll get some of my sweet tea that you love so much." In short order, she returned with a tall glass and a straw.

Grant sipped from it and turned his head. "I wanna get up and get dressed. I need to—"

"Nonsense," Flossie said bluntly. "You stay right where you are. You don't want to get dressed, then have someone see you peed on yourself, do you?"

She thrust the straw toward his mouth again, but he pushed it away and laid his head back on the pillow. "Let me rest," he whispered. "Just let me rest."

Flossie took the laundry and shut his bedroom door, then instructed Rufus not to bother him.

Grant wasn't sure how long he had slept, but his mind was somewhat clearer. He managed to get himself to the bathroom, but when he caught sight of his reflection in the mirror, he almost fainted. He could only open his eyes to small slits, but he noticed that his lips were blue, and his hands were trembling. He felt his way down the vanity to the toilet where he vomited violently. *Poisoned! I'm being poisoned,* he thought. *The antifreeze, the stuff the gardener couldn't find. He swore he always returns it to its proper place, but...*

Flossie found him bent over the toilet and wiped his forehead with a wet cloth. "Now get back to bed. I'll take care of you. You're very ill, but I'll handle everything."

Grant allowed her to lead him to bed; he was much too weak to fight her anyway. He would just play along until he could get to his phone. When she offered him more tea, he feigned gagging, and she let it go. Flossie only left his side when she thought he was in a deep sleep.

Grant sat up in bed and looked for the bedside phone. As he expected, it had been disconnected and removed, quite like he had done to Lizzie. He wasn't sure if he had enough energy to make it to his office, so he looked for his secret cell phone, the one he used only to call Rayne. When he found it, he dialed Zahir's number.

"Dr. Chavan. How can I help you?"

"Help!" Grant whispered just as the phone started to beep and the low battery icon flashed across the screen.

"Dr. Chatsworth? Is that you?"

"Poisoned...antifreeze...ethylene glycol... Help me! I—" When the phone battery finally died, Grant was left to wonder if Zahir had indeed heard his plea, most likely his last chance to call for help.

"What was that about?" Jean-Luc asked as he looked across his desk.

"It was Chatsworth, or at least I think it was," Zahir answered with a look of confusion.

"What do you mean, you think it was?"

"His voice was distorted, and it wasn't his cell number. He asked for help, said something about ethylene glycol poisoning."

"That makes perfect sense," Jean-Luc said. "It has to be poisoning. What else could explain his sudden illness, with all those symptoms?"

"We've got to get to his house. It's that housekeeper. I've never trusted her."

"Just last week, you were ready to kill him yourself with monkey blood. Why the sudden change of heart?" Jean-Luc asked suspiciously.

"Are you ready to flush these past two years down the drain and go back to France empty-handed? I, for one, want my part of the cash before Chatsworth disappears with it."

Jean-Luc grabbed his keys off the desk. "I'll drive," he said, running for the parking lot.

368

They reached the front gate, only to be questioned by Cornell Sayer. "Sorry, fellas," he said, "but I've got strict instructions that Dr. Chatsworth is not to be disturbed. He's been ill."

"We know that, you idiot!" Zahir yelled. "I drove him home from the hospital. I knew something was wrong, but I brought him home anyway. I just got a suspicious call from him. He believes he's being poisoned, and he asked me to come."

Cornell looked at both doctors with suspicion. "Why wouldn't he call the police or me?"

"The cell phone had a low battery and went dead. I suppose he felt we'd believe him because we were at the hospital with him. It's that abhorrent housekeeper, Flossie. I shouldn't have to tell you that time is of the essence," Zahir hissed.

"Again, why didn't you call the police?"

"Because she'll tell them anything! They'd need a warrant or a call from the estate to do a welfare check. Help us, or you'll have his blood on your hands too," Jean-Luc demanded.

"Very well," Cornell said. "I'll open the gate, but that's all I can do."

Jean-Luc skidded through the opening and around the drive, then stopped abruptly at the house. Rufus was just opening the door as both men rushed him.

"Where is the doctor?" Zahir demanded.

"He's not to be disturbed," Rufus said.

In a flash, Flossie dashed to the door. "Get out of here, or I'll call the police!" she screamed. "Leave the doctor be. He's ill. Rufus, do not let them enter. It could mean our jobs! Dr. Chatsworth said no visitors. You like working here, don't you, Rufus? Do you want to have to clean toilets after those wretched rock concerts again?"

"Rufus," Jean-Luc said calmly, trying to be the voice of reason, "don't listen to her. It's a trick."

The sound of a siren and the flash of a blue light distracted them all as they turned to see Detective Pitts getting out of his car. "What's going on here?" he demanded.

"Dr. Chatsworth called me and said he's being poisoned," Zahir blurted. "I recently brought him home from the hospital, and he's been alarmingly ill. I demand we go inside and check on him."

"He's fine, just under the weather," Flossie said. "This man is lying. He simply wants in the house for some other reason, possibly to steal some of my boss's valuable artwork."

"What?!" Zahir screamed. "This woman is poisoning that man! I work for him at the Cardiac Care Research Facility. He could perish at any moment. He needs to be in a hospital."

"Step aside, Ma'am," Pitts said. "We need to see the doctor."

"Where is your warrant?" she said haughtily.

Rufus pushed Flossie to the side to make space for the men to enter. "Follow me. The doctor is upstairs in his bedroom," Rufus said.

Chapter 91

It wasn't the ghost of a young woman wailing with grief. This time, it was Lizzie, holding Kenny's shoulders and head in her lap as she sobbed. "God, please forgive me! I'm so sorry, Kenny. What I thinking?" she screamed as the tears flowed down her face.

Kenny's body slowly moved, and his eyes opened to meet Lizzie's. "Damn, that hurt."

"Oh, thank God!" Lizzie said as she kissed his forehead and cheeks. "I was so frightened."

"I have to tell you something," Kenny whispered. "I'm gay."

"And I'm married and pregnant. Let's get the hell outta here. Can you walk?"

"Gimme a minute. It knocked the breath out of me, and I have a feeling I've broken every bone in my body," Kenny said as he reached for the bottom step and helped himself up. "I've got to stop hanging out with you."

"Hurry!" Lizzie said, just as the noises started again. The gales of wind thrust them forward as screams came from what sounded like hundreds of tortured souls.

Kenny's flashlight wouldn't work, so he grabbed Lizzie's hand and took her flashlight to lead them. "I can't remember the way out," he said. "These hallways are all alike."

This time, the appearance of dozens of ravens didn't frighten Lizzie. Instead, the birds gave her a sense of relief. On the contrary, their squawks brought forth spews of profanity from Kenny as he swatted at them with the flashlight.

"Don't hurt them!" Lizzie yelled over the noise. "I think they're here to lead us out. Follow them."

The maze of hallways didn't seem to be the same as when they'd entered, but Lizzie pushed Kenny forward in the direction of the birds, only to reach a dead end, with metal double-doors held together with a chain and lock.

The noises seemed to be getting closer, and it became too loud for Lizzie and Kenny to communicate. Lizzie pressed on the doors with all her might. Kenny had left his bag somewhere on the staircase, and they had no tools to cut the lock.

"We can't break the lock," Kenny screamed. "There's no way."

"It has to be where the records are!" Lizzie yelled back. "Try hitting it with the flashlight."

Kenny aimed the back end of the Maglite, but just as he was about to strike the lock, it released by itself, and the chain fell from the doors. There wasn't time for shock; the two just had to make their way into the room filled with boxes of papers, some scattered and others filed in random order.

"Now what?" Lizzie yelled. She knew they needed to get out as there were evil spirits there who wanted them to leave and didn't wish to be disturbed.

Kenny looked around in desperation. "We've got to go, Lizzie. It's just too dangerous."

It was then that the grieving woman returned. This time, the apparition was sitting in the far corner of the room, next to a stack of papers held together in some form of a notebook. She wasn't wailing this time but she was wiping tears from her face, just as Baby Belle had done in the cemetery.

Lizzie ran to her and grabbed the notebook. She felt an embrace; it wasn't physical but was more like being surrounded by cold air. "I promise I'll do what I can," she said. She ran back to Kenny, and they followed the swarm of ravens out of Birchwood Forest Lunatic Asylum.

Chapter 92

Grant lay in the hospital bed, looking much better than he had when he was rescued from his own home. His vision had returned to normal, and his head was clear. He was conversing with Jean-Luc and Zahir when Dr. Smoltz came in, followed by Detective Pitts.

"Well, it appears not to have been the antifreeze after all," the doctor said. "There weren't any oxalate crystals in your urine, and you would have died already had you been given ethylene glycol."

"I don't understand," Grant said. "I know she was trying to poison me. I realize my memory is vague, but she was trying to kill me," he insisted.

"That's where you're wrong," Detective Pitts said. "She wasn't trying to kill you at all. She just wanted to keep you sick enough that you would have to rely entirely on her to take care of you."

"What?! That's absurd. Why would she do that?"

"Simple. She's in love with you."

"I don't believe it."

"Well, I have a five-page signed confession down at the precinct where she's being held on a $200,000 bond. Apparently, when your wife left you, she decided she wanted you all to herself. When you told Flossie you were going to pick your wife up before the Christmas holidays, she decided she'd keep you just sick enough to be bedbound at home."

Grant turned to the doctor. "Is he serious?"

"Indeed he is," she answered. "She admitted to putting just enough Visine in your tea to make you ill but not kill you. We found tetrahydrozoline in your system."

Grant was speechless. "I hope she rots in there," he seethed. "Has anyone put up a bond?"

"No, Sir," Pitts answered. "It's a big one, and I don't think anyone is willing to come forward to pay it. It was your butler, Rufus, who ultimately saved your life."

"And to think he was the one I never really trusted."

"Yeah, well, the butlers often get the brunt end of suspicion."

"When do I get out of here?"

"I'm dismissing you today," the doctor said. "Good luck to you."

"I'm afraid I'm not finished with you just yet, Doctor," Pitts said. "It appears your Russian employee is the one who tried to kill Albert Tinsley's roommate."

"What are you talking about?" Grant asked, looking over at Zahir and feigning disbelief. "Were you aware of this?"

"No, Sir, I was not," Zahir said. "This is the first I've heard of it."

"Well, take a few days to recuperate, and I'll stop by. I know where you live."

"No shit," Grant muttered.

Chapter 93

By the time Kenny pulled into Lizzie's driveway, the sun was coming up. "Guess I'll call in sick today," he said. "I'm too frazzled to sleep, and I'm still trying to comprehend all that happened to us back there."

"Come in. I'll fix us both a cup of hot coffee."

"None for me," he said. "I can't risk being caught here. I'm going home. You're too much excitement for me. Still, call me later and let me know what you find in those records."

"Will do," Lizzie said as she hurried out of the car and into the house. She went straight to the bathroom and took off her filthy clothes while she ran a steaming bath. She was eager to get cleaned up, have some coffee, and hopefully muster up enough stamina to go through the records.

Unfortunately, the warm water zapped what little strength she had left, so she dried off and crawled in the bed in the nude. She slept for several hours, and it was 2:00 in the afternoon by the time she dressed, ate, and sat down at the kitchen table with the wooden notebook held together by brown string.

The notes were all in some type of fancy calligraphy, difficult to decipher. Lizzie was unsure if they were written by a psychiatrist, a medical doctor, or simply a nurse, but they were taken over a period of three years.

She took several breaks to rest her eyes and let the full scope of what had happened sink in. It was such a tragedy, one that never should have happened.

It started as a beautiful love story between a mother and her beautiful daughter, Belle, affectionately known to everyone as Baby Belle because she was the only daughter and the younger of two children. Belle was the apple of her mother's eye, and her sweet disposition brought much warmth and attention by all who knew her. As the years went by, according to her mother Brenna, her brother's hostility and jealousy grew. One afternoon, Brenna found her daughter at the bottom of the staircase in their home, dead from a broken neck. As Brenna held her deceased daughter in her arms, her brother stood at the top of the stairs, smirking and laughing.

The grief was simply too much for Brenna to bear, and when her husband arrived home from work, he found her still at the foot of the stairs, rocking their cold, dead child. Afraid of losing his only son and the mark it would make on the family name should the secret get out, he swore Brenna and the son to secrecy and buried poor Baby Belle, under the blanket of darkness, in a cemetery in another town.

Brenna was never the same. She wept incessantly and never got out of bed. Fearing the truth would get out, her husband had her committed to Birchwood Forest Lunatic Asylum and told friends and churchgoers that he had sent their daughter to live with family in the northeast because his wife had been committed to a lunatic asylum.

The young mother's tale remained, and she pled with the staff to verify her story, but every time they contacted her husband, he insisted that she was crazy, that she was unable to conceive another child after the birth of their son, and that Baby Belle was just a figment of her imagination.

After days, weeks, months, and years of grieving and being told she was delusional, Brenna died in her sleep from malnutrition and influenza. Her husband instructed a funeral home to bring her body back to Biloxi via horse and buggy and buried her in a grave toward the back of the cemetery. According to cemetery records, neither the husband nor the son were ever buried alongside her.

They probably got the hell outta Dodge and never looked back, Lizzie thought.

She laid the notebook down and walked to the window that overlooked the bayou. "All you really wanted was to be buried beside your mother, didn't you, Baby Belle? You were aware of her grief and her love for you, and you wanted her to rest in peace."

Chapter 94

Grant was back on his feet within a few days and concerned mostly with hiding any evidence of wrongdoing with the drug scam. Jean-Luc and Zahir were working on it at the Research Facility while he went through any incriminating records at his estate. Most of it was well hidden, but when he couldn't find his personal record book with names, dates, and monetary transactions, he literally flipped out.

Even though it was encrypted with coded messages, he knew it would easily be deciphered if it ever fell into the wrong hands. *Who was in my office?* he wanted to know. If Flossie had gotten it, she wouldn't have known what it was and would likely have already blackmailed him into paying her bail. He thought of the staff and crossed them all off his list. Ultimately, anyone who had such information surely would have already used it against him, striking while the iron was hot, so to speak. Grant slammed his hand on the desk and pulled out drawers from the filing cabinets and slung them across the room. Somebody had clearly taken it, but he had no idea why. *What are they planning, and why haven't they contacted me?*

Suddenly, it hit him like a ton of bricks. "You little bitch!" he said aloud. "I knew it!" He was seething with such anger that he had to sit down. *It had to be Lizzie,* he thought. *That's why she isn't afraid of me and why she hasn't hurried home. She has a little insurance policy. I have to get to her before she turns it over to the authorities. She hasn't yet, or they'd be knocking on my door. Once I get that back in my hands, I'm out of here, out of this country and on to my next life. Let Zahir and Jean-Luc take the fall, and let that damned detective investigate till he falls in the damn grave himself. He'll never find me, and even if he does, he won't be able to extradite me back for prosecution.*

Grant packed a small bag with a couple of guns, his passport, the jewelry from the safe, and all the cash he had on hand. He didn't bother to lock the estate as he had no intention of ever returning and really didn't care what happened to the place. It was every man for himself, now, and he figured he could make it almost all the way to Biloxi on one tank of gas.

The address of Maggie and Leland Knox was easy enough to find. He programmed it into his GPS and started his five-hour drive from Atlanta. It was late afternoon and would be dark by the time he got there, but he would find Lizzie if it was the last thing he ever did.

Grant stopped about halfway and filled up with gas, just so he didn't have to risk being seen in Biloxi. He didn't bother to grab anything to eat; his adrenaline was pumping so fast that hunger didn't even affect him.

It was after 9:00 p.m. Biloxi time when he turned his headlights off and drove down Maggie's street. He pulled the car over, got out, and walked around the house. The lights were on, and two rambunctious boys were vetoing bedtime. Leland was at the kitchen table on a laptop, and Maggie was pleading with the children, begging them to go to their rooms. There was no sign of Lizzie. He walked around to the back and peeked in the guesthouse, but there weren't any lights on, and he saw no signs of life there.

Grant saw headlights coming, so he ducked around the corner of the house and watched as a Honda pulled into the drive.

Maggie came to the door and opened the screen. "Hey, Kenny. Sorry, you missed work. Leland said you weren't feeling well."

"Yeah, I had a bad headache, but I'm better now. You said you have a few things you need me to take to Lizzie?"

Oh, this is just too good to be true, Grant thought as he eased his way to his car. He quickly slid into the seat and waited for the young man to lead him straight to Lizzie.

Kenny was standing at Lizzie's front door when Grant grabbed him from behind. Lizzie opened the door just as Grant pushed Kenny to the side and reached for her. She slammed the door and locked it, then she ran to the back door and out of the house.

The cool night air in Ocean Springs, Mississippi bit at Lizzie Chatsworth's ears as she made her way through the headstones of the old cemetery. What would have seemed an eerie place for some had become a place of comfort for her. The heavy fog seemed to illuminate the moss that draped down from the large, overbearing oaks, helping her to stay ahead of him as he hunted her.

Run toward the bayou. You can do it, Lizzie.

Why? Why are you telling me to run toward the water, a dead end? Surely, he'll catch up with me there and—

It's the only way. Follow my voice. He's getting closer!

Lizzie grabbed her stomach, bending over, in an attempt to catch her breath. All along, she had known this day would come; it had only been a matter of time. A great deal was at stake for him, and she was a threat—or at least that was how he would see it.

"Lizzie! You can't run forever. I'll find you."

She dared not answer, for that would simply lead him closer. The wet grass silenced her footfalls as she made her way toward the marsh.

"You can't just walk away! I gave you everything. Why wasn't it enough?"

She wanted to scream at him, to explain that there was more to life than money, but she knew he'd never understand. The baby was unhappy with her, violently kicking the inside of her belly. "Hang in there, little one. We're gonna be okay," she whispered.

The bayou, Lizzie. Concentrate. You're almost there.

But what am I supposed to do when I get there? He'll catch me, and it'll all be over.

Just follow my voice. Don't give up now.

Weaving in and out of the tombstones she had come to know so well, Lizzie could see the water coming into view. She ran down the old dock, hoping to reach the boathouse, but the baby had other plans for her.

"Oh, God!" she screamed as a painful contraction radiated through her body. "Help!" she shouted. "Someone help!"

"It is too late for that," he said calmly, his figure becoming visible. "You are the last of my unfinished business, the final loose end to tie up before I can begin my new life."

"Who is she? Who's in this with you?" she demanded.

"You don't need to know that, Lizzie. You have learned far too much already. It's over now."

Lie down, Lizzie. Just lie on the dock.

"Why?" she wanted to ask but instead allowed her legs to bend into a squat. She then fell and lay back, shut her eyes tight, and wrapped her arms around her stomach and unborn child. *I never*

thought it would end like this, she thought as the sound of the gunshot reverberated through her ears.

****

Lizzie lay still as pain still seared across her belly. She couldn't believe she was actually alive. *Where is Grant?* she wondered in great horror. *Oh, my God! Is he right over me?*

"Lizzie? Lizzie, are you okay?"

It was a familiar voice, but Lizzie couldn't pinpoint it in such a state of shock.

"Lizzie, answer me, honey. It's Devan. Grant is dead. Just stay where you are."

Devan? What would Devan be doing here and not in the Caymans?

It sounded like the footsteps of an army as several agents dressed in black surrounded Lizzie.

She tried to sit up. "The baby! I'm going into labor."

"It's much too early for that," Devan said. "Grab her, guys. We've got to get her to a hospital right away."

Chapter 95

Lizzie awoke in the hospital the next morning, to a roomful of people. Dr. Redding was there to confirm that the baby was all right and assured her they'd been able to stop the early labor. Maggie was smiling but looked like she hadn't slept at all the night before. Then there was Devan, the woman who had befriended Lizzie when she had needed it the most.

Lizzie reached for her hand. "What is going on? What are you doing here?"

"It's a long story, one I'll tell someday over a lunch of fried snapper and conch fritters," she said with a gentle smile. "For now, all you need to know is that you are safe. Grant is dead."

"But how did you know he was coming?"

"Easy," she said, then pointed to Cornell Sayer, who was standing in the corner. "Cornell and I are both FBI agents. We've been looking into Dr. Chatsworth's illegal wrangling for the past couple of years."

"You?" Lizzie said as she looked over at Cornell. "You saw me when I was escaping with Santiago, but you let me leave anyway. Is Santiago with the FBI too?"

"No," Cornell said. "Santiago is just a very kind man. We had surveillance on you two and figured he'd be the one to help get you out of there. We never suspected you were in immediate danger because Mr. Chatsworth needed you as a front for his perfect life."

"But Devan? The house in the Caymans—"

"All a front, but wasn't that a great house?"

"But you knew so many people."

"The Caymans are a hotspot for criminals, for various reasons," she said with a laugh. "Lucky for me, I can think of worse places for an assignment."

"What about Kenny? Is he okay?"

"Right here, all in one piece, present and accounted for," he said, stepping forward.

"Are you with the Feds?"

"Ha! You've gotta be kidding.

Being friends with you is all the excitement I can handle!"

As everyone around her smiled and laughed, Lizzie drifted off into a much-needed rest, the best rest she'd had in a long, long time.

Epilogue

Lizzie stood in Old Biloxi Cemetery on a beautiful, sunny day, holding her healthy daughter, Isabelle Hope. She was surrounded by Kenny, Maggie, Leland, and her friend Devan as the priest eulogized the lives of Brenna and Baby Belle. It was a simple and sweet service. Belle's remains had been placed in a new pink casket that was lowered into the ground beside her mother. Never again did Lizzie see apparitions or misty figures, and she didn't expect to. Finally, the young mother and daughter were at peace, so they had no reason to visit her again.

The group went back to Lizzie's new home, the guesthouse behind Maggie's.

"Your place is perfect," Devan said, "but it was missing something."

"What?" Lizzie asked.

"Look over your fireplace. I took the liberty of hanging it there, but you can move it if you want to."

Lizzie felt the tears flow as she saw the painting of the old woman throwing the kernels of corn to the chickens. "It's the one I loved at the museum!"

"Yes," Devan said. "I saved it for you. I knew you loved it, but somehow, I didn't think Grant would've approved."

"It's the most wonderful gift ever," Lizzie exclaimed.

****

"Okay, that will take care of the transfer of all your offshore accounts. Your funds will be secure here in Andorra," the banker said without even raising an eyebrow at the large sum of money that had just landed at his bank. "I hope you enjoy your new home and find our people welcoming, Mr. Rayne," he said.

"Thank you. I already do," Mr. Antoine Rayne, the former party planner, said with a dazzling smile. His smile faded briefly as he exited the bank. *I'm sorry about all your heartache, Lizzie,* he thought. *I've always wished you well.*

****

"Okay, that'll be $2,500, first and last month's rent and your security deposit," the older man said. "I don't understand why you ladies feel safe in this seedy part of the city. It's riddled with crime."

"That makes it perfect for business," the sign man said as he put the finishing touches on the front window: "Clara and Iris, Private Investigators."

Sneak Peek

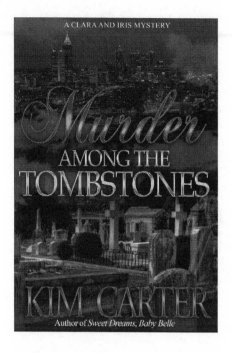

Sneak Peek at Murder Among The Tombstones.

A Clara and Iris Mystery

When Atlanta homicide detectives are called in to investigate the murder of a nineteen-year-old girl found dumped in historic Oakland Cemetery, they immediately begin working the case. But with no leads to follow, and their case log growing larger by the day, the murder quickly grows cold.

Desperate to keep the investigation of her deceased sister going, Ginger Baines hires two novice sleuths to solve the case. Widowed, well into their seventies, and new to the world of private investigating, Clara Samples and Iris Hadley aren't your average private eyes.

When a second body is found in a neighboring cemetery, the plot thickens. With two bodies wrapped, almost lovingly, in a soft blanket before being discarded in a cemetery, could a serial killer be on the loose?

Joined by their young apprentice Quita, Clara and Iris are determined to stop at nothing to find the killer before they can strike again. But, will their bodies be the next ones discovered among the tombstones?

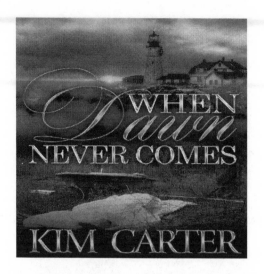

Sneak Peek at When Dawn Never Comes

Jordan Maxwell, a twenty-seven-year-old freelance journalist, ventures to New York City to make a name for herself. With both of her parents dead, she struggles to get by living in one of the worst neighborhoods in the city. In a twist of fate, Jordan finds herself the sole heir to her great-uncle's estate in Solomon Cove, Maine.

Packing her bags, she heads to Maine where she soon realizes that her rags to riches journey entails much more than she bargained for.

Crime was unheard of in the small fishing village of Solomon Cove, a town where everyone knows everyone. It was the last place anyone expected crime, especially murder. However, the tides turn for this quaint town when the body of a young girl comes crashing in with the waves.

As the victims continue to mount, Jordan starts to believe the murders are connected to her and the family she never knew. Digging deeper into the past, Jordan must protect herself before she becomes the serial killer's next target.

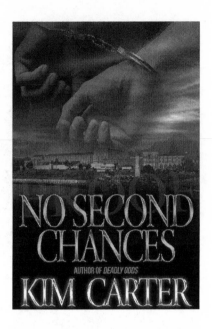

Sneak Peek at No Second Chances

Falling from a life of wealth and substance, to inside one of America's most notorious prisons, prominent orthopedic surgeon Phil Sawyer is incarcerated for the voluntary manslaughter of his wife. While confined, he finds himself on the trail of a serial killer that infiltrates the walls of San Quentin. After finding himself in the infirmary for getting involved in an incident that didn't concern him, Phil struggles with the decision to stick his neck out. But he can't ignore the rise in suspicious deaths among the African American inmates. With the aid of an empathetic nurse and help from the outside, he tries to identify the unexplained cause of their cardiac arrests. He finds himself out on early release and heads to Solomon Cove, a peaceful town in Maine. But, could the tranquil town all be a façade, or has the serial killer made their way across the country to seek revenge?

From wealthy Los Angeles, to the justice in San Quentin, and the serene landscapes of Maine, you will applaud the friendships and hear the cry as you ride the roller coaster of emotions this story will bring.

Sneak Peek at Deadly Odds

Two worlds collide in this edge of your seat thriller.

Georgia bounty hunter Nathaniel Collier finds himself in perilous danger as he hunts down the notorious Mad Dog Consuelos.

As Nathaniel draws near, Consuelos strikes again leaving behind a bloody path of violence. Collier, along with Gracie, Mad Dog's daughter, take the brunt of the assault, leaving them struggling to survive for weeks in the hospital.

Meanwhile, Atlanta PD officer Reid Langley decides to leave the violent city behind and take a cushy job as Sheriff in the small town of Hayden, Wyoming. All appears to go as uneventful as planned until a serial killer shows up to wreak havoc on the safe haven Reid is determined to protect. Just when he thinks he has all that he can handle, Reid finds himself harboring his old friend, a nurse, and an innocent young girl.

The battle is on as this group of characters embark on a race against time to locate a serial killer and to track down the elusive Consuelos before he can take his revenge.

Sneak Peek of And The Forecast Called For Rain.

Detective Jose Ramirez and the Sierra Hills Police Department are scrambling for leads on a killer who has already struck five times, each time leaving his signature trademark: large butcher knives piercing the abdomens of his young female victims.

Profiling the killer is proving to be difficult, and Detective Ramirez knows that it's only a matter of time before their perpetrator strikes again.

As if Ramirez isn't frustrated enough, to his dismay, he is assigned a partner. Officer Daniel Chatham, a handsome, young man, fresh out of grad school, has pulled some strings to join the division and becomes Ramirez's, right-hand man. The lead detective's anger slowly begins to dissipate as he discovers the book smart kid can be quite the asset.

With Ramirez's experience, Chatham's sharp mind and quick thinking, and the insight of Erin Sommers, a beautiful, young journalist, the three make a powerful team gaining on their criminal.

It's raining... it's pouring, and a killer is on the loose in the rainy Sierra Hills of Washington State. No one is who they seem, and the plot thickens with every turn. You'll never guess the ending of this enigmatic tale.

Biloxi Main Street is an independent organization entrusted with the responsibility to preserve, promote, and protect the historical character of old Biloxi. They have been instrumental in raising funds, repairing, and maintaining The Old Biloxi Cemetery. Their great works and passion for the city are immeasurable. Please consider making a donation, in memory of Baby Belle, to continue their works in restoring the many aging gravesites still in need of renovation. Checks can be made to:

Biloxi Main Street
P.O. Box 253
Biloxi, MS 39533

About the Author

Kim Carter is an author and prolific writer of contemporary mystery, suspense, and thrillers. She has won the "2017 Readers Choice Award" and has an array of titles relaunching soon for; "When Dawn Never Comes," "Deadly Odds," and "No Second Chances." Her novel series titled; "The Clara and Iris Mystery" comes "Sweet Dreams, Baby Belle" has rereleased as book one of the series June 2017, and now book two is available titled, "Murder Among The TOMBSTONES" on Amazon and published by Raven South of Atlanta, Georgia.

Kim has been writing mysteries for some time and has a large reader fan base and she enjoys interacting and engaging with them all. One of her favorite things about writing is the traveling and research required to bring her novels to life. Her research has taken her to places such as morgues, death row, and midnight cemetery visits.

Kim and her husband have raised three successful grown children and have a vested interest in and love retired greyhounds. They enjoy attending the many events held annually for them, as well as educating others about their need for great homes and what great pets greyhounds make after they retire from racing.

She is a college graduate of Saint Leo University, has a Bachelor Degree of Arts in Sociology, and now has become a career writer and author. She lives in Atlanta, Georgia. Between reading and traveling with her beautiful family, she will continue to write mysteries for some time to come for her avid readers.

Get In Touch With Kim Carter:

About.Me: https://about.me/kimcarter.mysteryauthor

Amazon Author Page: https://www.amazon.com/Kim-Carter/e/B019QSNFI0/

GoodReads:https://www.goodreads.com/author/show/4075351.Kim_Carter

FB: https://www.facebook.com/AuthoressKimCarter/

Twitter: https://twitter.com/KimCarterAuthor

Google+ https://plus.google.com/105425029849895301377

For speaking engagements, interviews, book copies, please get in touch with Raven South Publishing.

96471824R00242

Made in the USA
Lexington, KY
21 August 2018